Piecing It All Together

Books by Leslie Gould

THE COURTSHIPS OF LANCASTER COUNTY

Courting Cate

Adoring Addie

Minding Molly

Becoming Bea

NEIGHBORS OF LANCASTER COUNTY

Amish Promises

Amish Sweethearts

Amish Weddings

THE SISTERS OF LANCASTER COUNTY

A Plain Leaving

A Simple Singing

A Faithful Gathering

An Amish Family Christmas:
An AMISH CHRISTMAS KITCHEN *novella*

PLAIN PATTERNS

Piecing It All Together

Piecing It All Together

Plain Patterns • 1

Leslie Gould

BethanyHouse
a division of Baker Publishing Group
Minneapolis, Minnesota

Published by Bethany House Publishers
11400 Hampshire Avenue South
Bloomington, Minnesota 55438
www.bethanyhouse.com

Bethany House Publishers is a division of
Baker Publishing Group, Grand Rapids, Michigan

Printed in the United States of America

Library of Congress Cataloging-in-Publication Data
Names: Gould, Leslie, author.
Title: Piecing it all together / Leslie Gould.
Description: Minneapolis, Minnesota : Bethany House Publishers, [2020] | Series: Plain patterns ; 1
Identifiers: LCCN 2019056913 | ISBN 9780764235221 (trade paperback) | ISBN 9780764236365 (cloth) | ISBN 9781493425167 (ebook)
Subjects: GSAFD: Christian fiction. | Mystery fiction.
Classification: LCC PS3607.O89 P54 2020 | DDC 813/.6—dc23
LC record available at https://lccn.loc.gov/2019056913

This is a work of fiction. Names, characters, incidents, and dialogues are products of the author's imagination and are not to be construed as real. Any resemblance to actual events or persons, living or dead, is entirely coincidental.

Cover design by Dan Thornberg, Design Source Creative Services

Author represented by Natasha Kern Literary Agency

20 21 22 23 24 25 26 7 6 5 4 3 2 1

For Sallie Houston Fisher, my beloved aunt
who has kept our family stories alive
for generations still to come.

Religion that God our Father accepts as pure and faultless is this: to look after orphans and widows in their distress and to keep oneself from being polluted by the world.

James 1:27 NIV

PROLOGUE

Jane Berger

December 23, 2016
Nappanee, Indiana

The clock in the quilt shop chimed six times as Jane Berger's hands rested on her manual typewriter. She still had bolts of fabric and books of patterns to put away, plus a tray of coffee cups to wash.

Outside, the snow fell as if God were sifting sugar over the Indiana landscape. She needed to get home and start a fire in her wood stove, but first she had to finish her monthly column for the *Nappanee News.*

She glanced at her notes on the origins of the town. The first settlers to the region were the Miami Nation, but they were forced out by the Iroquois in the 1700s. Soon after, the Potawatomi Nation settled in the area. By the time the first of the Amish and Mennonites arrived in the early 1840s, the Potawatomi had been gone for a few years, sent to Kansas on the "Trail of Death."

Jane shivered. She didn't want to touch on that particular story, not now. What happened to the Native Americans was so shameful that she found it heartbreaking to even think about, although she vividly remembered stories from her childhood that examined the topic in depth. Someday she would need to pass down the story about a particular Potawatomi woman to just the right person.

But she wouldn't think about that now. She'd concentrate on the story for Arleta, a woman who came to Jane's quilting circle from time to time.

Arleta had moved back to the area a year ago after marrying a local bachelor. The woman had been a widow and had two children in their teens, who'd grown up in nearby Newbury Township. Arleta's previous years spent in the Nappanee area hadn't been happy ones, and although she was trying to stay faithful, she feared the same unhappiness now, for herself and her children.

"The past is never dead" was something Jane had heard from time to time. *Jah*, the past was always with us. She firmly believed that. But she also believed that nothing ever stayed the same. Sometimes life changed for the better. Sometimes for the worse.

The town of Nappanee wasn't platted and named until December 1874, when the railroad arrived. By then, Jane's ancestors had been farming on their land, where she currently sat, for over thirty years. She was a fifth-generation descendant of those original Amish settlers.

The word *Indiana* meant "land of the Indians" and the word *Napanee* seemed to be a Native American word too, although the meaning wasn't clear. The spelling was later changed to *Nappanee*.

She'd attended an Englisch elementary school as a child,

and she remembered learning that Nappanee was the only city name in the United States with four letters of the alphabet that were all repeated twice. She'd always loved saying the word—*Nappanee*—because of the way it rolled off her tongue.

Jane continued writing, explaining how the land Nappanee now sat on had once been a marsh. She wrote that when the railroad came through, a group of people had a vision for a town, and they built it, structure by structure. The townspeople had cared about education, industry, and shipping crops to a wider market. Good had come, for all of them, from change.

She prayed for the same sort of change to come to Arleta's life. She prayed that the women in the quilting circle would be a blessing to Arleta and her family too.

Jane prayed extra hard, knowing the woman was married to Vernon Wenger. He was a harsh man with a quick temper. She prayed for Arleta's teenaged children too. Both were on their *Rumschpringe*. Running around was a tricky predicament with Vernon as a stepfather.

Jane left her prayers with God and cleared her mind from her present-day thoughts. Then she continued to write as quickly as she could, the keys clicking, one after the other, creating words, sentences, and paragraphs. Sometimes Jane wrote about a place, such as the town of Nappanee. Other times she wrote about a person—a pioneer or another resident of the area from a different time who had made a difference in the community. There was nothing Jane enjoyed more than writing, than piecing the past together. Although quilting was a close second.

Once again, Jane became so caught up in the past that it was as if she was living there. She waited at Locke Station, thankful her family could now ship out their onions, potatoes, and mint to a larger market. She stepped onto the platform and looked down the new train tracks, anticipating all the changes the railroad would bring. Change might not be a typical topic for an Amish woman, but Jane ended the column with that image of change coming to Nappanee anyway.

The clock struck the half hour, and she rolled the second sheet of paper out of the typewriter, stacked the two together, and then slipped them into a manila envelope. She addressed it from memory, put on the correct number of stamps, and left it on the desk as she took off her reading glasses and let them dangle from the string around her neck. Then, she put away the bolts of fabric—mostly solid colors. Maroon and sapphire blue. Black and forest green, though there were a few modest floral prints.

Besides offering her stories for the entire community, she was especially blessed that so many of her customers appreciated her historical knowledge. Not only did it allow her to share her stories verbally, but it also encouraged customers to come to her with ideas for new stories, ones she hadn't heard of before but was happy to research.

She washed the mugs at the sink at the back of the shop, looking out the window into the darkness as she did. At least she didn't have far to travel to reach her little home. It was just across the lane.

After she slipped on her warm coat, pulled on her gloves, and secured her bonnet, she picked up the envelope off the desk. As she stepped out into the blast of the icy wind and swirling snow, she held on tightly to the envelope until she reached the mailbox. With another prayer for Arleta and her family, Jane slid the envelope inside the box and raised the flag.

Another story in the mail, ready for her readers.

She'd lived on her family farm her entire life, all sixty-three years. For the last thirty, she'd lived in the *Dawdi Haus* on the other side of the lane. Her brother had built the large quilt shop four years ago. Before that, she'd run the business from the front room of her house.

She was grateful for the life she had: the column for the paper, the quilt shop, the women who shopped there. Jah, God was good.

As Jane reached her front porch, she turned toward the shop and wondered about the next column she'd write. She prayed silently for a story and then for the next woman the Lord would send her way. One who needed the sort of perspective only a historical tale could provide, who needed to seek the Lord's will in her life.

Make me an instrument of your truth, Jane prayed. It was a desire that stayed consistent, past or present.

Perhaps there were some things that stayed the same, after all.

CHAPTER 1

Savannah Mast

December 23, 2016
Oakland, California

The countdown was on. In one week, Ryan and I would be at our wedding rehearsal at Grace Cathedral, getting ready for our New Year's Eve wedding the next day. Dreams did come true. I'd soon be Savannah Woodward instead of Savannah Mast.

I pushed away from my desk and stepped to my office window, gazing out toward the Bay Bridge. It wasn't that I had a view, just a glimpse of the ribbon of asphalt lanes suspended over the water. Just enough to encourage me to leave and head to San Francisco for the rest of the afternoon. It was the day before Christmas Eve, and my boss, Mr. William Hayes, had already left an hour ago.

I worked as a manager for a nonprofit health company, mostly guiding my team in their attempts to control costs, while Ryan worked across the Bay at the medical center as an administrator in the information systems department. He was on track, according to some, to become a vice president of the organization.

After stuffing my wedding to-do list in my bag, I sent Ryan a text. *On my way!* Then I slipped into my raincoat and straightened it over my skirt and blouse. As the heels of my boots clicked down the hallway, my phone pinged.

Wait, Ryan had replied.

What did he mean? Surely, he wasn't having a last-minute meeting.

Why? I texted back.

Something's come up. . . .

The ellipses gave me an ominous feeling. *Is everything all right?* I typed.

I waited in the hallway for him to reply. I was getting worried. Finally, I texted, *Ryan?*

When he still didn't reply, I took the elevator down to the street level, pulled up my hood against the December drizzle, and walked the six blocks to my apartment. I hoped Ryan would text back soon. Perhaps a system server was down, or the electronic charting software had crashed. Or the pharmacies had gone offline.

I sidestepped a thirtysomething woman wearing a rain poncho and a beanie, panhandling on the corner, and then dodged two men wearing designer suits who were deep in conversation.

Oakland was home to all kinds. I'd enjoyed my time in the city on the east side of the Bay but looked forward to living across the water. My father had been horrified—even more so than when I enrolled at UCLA—when I moved to Oakland. He still remembered how it had been in the late eighties, when he first moved to Northern California from Indiana. He remembered the crime, the drug trafficking, the robberies, the killings.

It wasn't that there wasn't still crime in Oakland—there was in any big city—but it wasn't as bad as it had been. Like many other places on the West Coast, it was being gentrified, which meant housing costs had skyrocketed. Hardly anyone could afford rent in the area anymore, a horrible affront to those who used to call Oakland home.

I reached my building, a brick three-story complex, and walked up the staircase to the second floor. After digging my keys from my bag, I unlocked the door as I checked my phone again. Still no text from Ryan.

I turned on the lights, pulled the blinds against the darkness falling outside, took off my raincoat, and placed my bag on a chair. I unzipped my boots, feeling a little lost with the recent change of plans. Should I put on my sweats? Or stay in my skirt?

I pulled off my boots and stepped into my fuzzy slippers. Then I checked my phone again. It was now 4:50. It had been thirty minutes since Ryan texted me last. Even with an emergency, it wasn't like him to not respond.

Something's come up. . . . What did he mean by that?

I held my phone in the palm of my hand, weighing my options. I sent him another text. *Can you talk?*

He didn't answer that one either, so ten minutes later, after I changed into my sweats and a long-sleeved T-shirt, I called him. He didn't answer, so I left a voicemail, trying to sound as upbeat as possible. "Hey, I hope everything's okay. Call me ASAP."

I dropped my phone on the couch and sat down to watch HGTV, barely concentrating on the *Love It or List It* episode. Every few minutes, I checked my phone. No text. No call. No nothing. An hour later, I called Ryan again.

Just as I expected it to go into voicemail, someone picked up. "Hello?" It was a woman's voice.

"Hello," I managed to say. "I need to talk to Ryan."

"With whom am I speaking?" she asked.

I stuttered out, "Sa-van-nah. And with whom am I speaking?"

She laughed. "Guess."

I stifled a gasp. It was Amber. His ex. Why was she in town?

And she obviously knew it was me. My picture would have come up on the screen when she answered the call.

She called out, "Ryan. Phone!"

After a long pause, she said, "Sorry, he can't talk right now. He'll call you back."

My heart raced as the call disconnected. What was going on?

UNABLE TO EAT or sleep, I stared at the TV for the next six hours, along with bombing Ryan with texts and phone calls. There hadn't been an emergency. He was with Amber, the woman who'd dumped him three years prior. I'd met her once when she crashed a work party of Ryan's a year ago. She had a memorable face and body—beautiful and svelte. And an unforgettable deep and sexy voice.

People seemed to either love her or hate her, and whenever her name came up, everyone went silent. She was older than Ryan by five years. I'd had more than one person tell me, quietly, that she was the reason he'd become an administrator by the time he was twenty-eight. Why he was on track to become a VP by the time he was forty.

She'd pursued him relentlessly, then dumped him and left for Washington, DC, where she took a job at a health policy think tank.

Why had she returned? Why had he agreed to see her?

Ryan had been so honest and vulnerable when he'd told me

about how she'd broken his heart. Life had broken my heart too, which made me sympathetic toward him. And made me feel, all the more, as if I could trust him. He wouldn't break my heart the way Amber had broken his—I was sure of it.

Or at least I had been.

Eventually, I forced myself to stop texting and leaving voicemails, knowing I sounded as desperate as I felt. I needed to give him the benefit of the doubt. Maybe Amber had come back for the holidays and decided to take the opportunity to apologize to Ryan for how she'd treated him. And maybe he thought seeing her would be freeing before he and I married. Perhaps there was some other reason. Surely he would call any minute and explain what had happened—even thank me for being understanding.

At some point, I fell asleep on the couch, under the baby blue afghan Mammi Mast had crocheted for me years ago. I awoke just after five in the morning and checked my phone, expecting to see a text from Ryan sent hours before. There was nothing.

A garbage truck rumbled by on the street below. I'd planned to move most of my things to Ryan's condo in South Beach today and then the rest into storage when my lease was up, right after we returned from our honeymoon. Should I still plan on doing that?

Unable to fall back asleep, I grabbed my warmest coat, stuffed my phone into my pocket, slipped into my sheepskin boots, and headed out for a cup of coffee. The sky was dark, without a single star shining, but the glow from the coffee shop was like a lighthouse on the edge of the sea. I'd planned to grab a cup and head back to my apartment, but instead I slumped into a chair and checked my phone again.

It wasn't as if Ryan would call or text me now. He wasn't a morning person, especially not on a Saturday. Perhaps it was my dad's work ethic, an essential part of who he was from being raised on an Amish farm, but I grew up thinking that sleeping in was for sloths.

That wasn't the only difference between Ryan and me. I jumped in to help whenever we were guests in someone's home, while he was fine being waited on. I could clean up a mess in minutes, while he'd simply stare at it. I was frugal; he was a spender. He had to eat at all of the latest restaurants in town. I was fine cooking at home. In fact, I could do more than cook—I could preserve food, sew, and live on a budget. Both my Mammi Mast and my mom had taught me well. Mom had been a hippie midwife, which, surprisingly, ended up having a lot in common with an Amish grandmother.

Ryan found my domestic skills "sweet" and "comforting," which made me feel as if I was the opposite of Amber's sophistication. Now I feared that's what he valued more.

I checked my phone again. Nothing.

If it wasn't so early in the morning, I might have called or texted his mom. Not to bring her into our drama, but to make sure everything was fine with Ryan. Both of his parents had been kind to me, but I'd especially bonded with his mother, Nita, even though I'd only spent a handful of time with her—the previous Christmas, when Ryan asked me to marry him, and then in the summer when she came up to San Francisco to help with wedding planning. She seemed especially sympathetic to the fact that my mother had died when I was a teenager.

But what would I say to Nita now? Ask if she knew what Ryan was up to? He got along with his parents, but they weren't particularly close. If I did contact his mom, it would probably come across as if I were tattling on him.

I tried to calm my jagged nerves with a sip of coffee, but my heart only raced faster. Caffeine probably wasn't the best idea. My thoughts began to fly as fast as my pulse. Perhaps Ryan had been hurt. Maybe he was in an ER somewhere. Maybe Amber had done something to him out of spite, even though she'd broken up with him.

I felt utterly helpless sitting in the coffee shop at 5:30, all alone. What would my mother tell me to do if she were alive?

Move!

I reached my hand into my pocket and felt my key ring. I had a key to Ryan's condo. Why hadn't I marched over there and thrown open the door the night before?

I'd do it now.

I'd sold my car the week before, so I ordered a ride-share. Thankfully, my driver wasn't the chatty type and didn't ask any questions. I kept my eyes on the water as we crossed the Bay. For someone who grew up in the hinterland of Northern California and spent summers in Indiana, the Bay enchanted me. I never tired of watching the water.

Once we reached San Francisco, the driver quickly maneuvered along the narrow streets and then double-parked in front of Ryan's condo. I thanked him and jumped out quickly, glancing at Ryan's bedroom window. The light was off.

Fearing I'd lose my nerve, I marched up the front steps and unlocked his door. The alarm was off, which didn't mean anything. He often forgot to set it.

As I turned on the lights, I noted that nothing seemed out of order. I flipped on the switch near the staircase, imagining him seeing the light and stumbling from bed, ready to apologize. And then he'd give me a convincing explanation for his behavior over the last fourteen hours.

I reached the top stair. The door to his room was open.

No one was home.

I checked his closet and then his bathroom. No clothes seemed to be missing. Neither was his toothbrush.

The helplessness I'd felt before grew more intense. Where could he be? Most likely with Amber. But I'd check his office just in case. Maybe a system *was* down.

I called for another ride and took it to the medical center. However, not surprising, the administration building was locked. I called his number again, vowing it would be my last time. At least for a few hours.

Surprisingly, he answered with a weary, "Hello."

I could barely contain how crazy I felt. "What's going on?" I tried to keep my voice from wavering. "Where are you?"

"I should have called last night. Sorry."

I didn't reply, afraid of what might spew from my mouth.

"Listen," he said. "We need to call off the wedding. I'll pay for anything we can't get refunds on, of course."

"What . . . what's going on?" I asked again, even though it was obvious. He was dumping me a week before our wedding. Why did my voice sound sympathetic when inside I felt like I was going to implode?

When he didn't answer, I lowered my voice even more, whispering, "What happened?"

"I've had a . . . complication."

"Amber?" I was juggling pain, rage, and despair, trying not to reveal any of them.

"Look, I'm sorry I didn't explain things last night. I haven't slept because I've been thinking about you. But I can't go through with the wedding. Not right now."

My nostrils flared as I spoke. "Where are you?"

"At home."

I clenched my fist, my nails digging into my palm. Now, besides being deceptive, he was outright lying to me too. "I was just at your place. You weren't there."

"I *was*," he said, without hesitating. I was taken aback by how easy deceit seemed to come to him. “I left about an hour ago.”

“Where are you?” I asked again.

His voice grew deeper. “At a hotel. Downtown.”

“Are you alone?”

“I think you already know the answer to that.”

“Can we meet? And talk?”

“That’s not a good idea. Look—” his voice faltered for half a second, but then he continued. “I’ll contact my guests. You contact yours. You cancel the vendors. I’ll cancel the honeymoon. It won’t take long to clear up this mess.”

Mess? Was that how he thought of me now?

“I wish you the best, Savannah. I do. And I’m sorry, but in the long run, this is what’s best for both of us.”

He made it sound like a middle-school breakup. “So that’s it?”

“Pretty much.”

I heard a rumble of laughter in the background on his side of the phone.

“I’ve got to go,” he said. “Bye.”

The call ended before I could say another word.

I SPENT CHRISTMAS sobbing and ignoring phone calls from my father.

The next day, it took me a couple of hours to work up the nerve to do what I needed to do. After two cups of coffee and another good cry, I began calling the vendors, asking them to put all the costs on Ryan’s credit card, which they also had on file, instead of mine. Originally, he and I had decided to put the wedding charges on my card for the air miles, for future trips.

Once the final bills for the wedding all came in, we would then split the costs and pay off my card.

Everyone was sympathetic. The florist said, "This happens more often than you'd think." But I doubted that many grooms called it off just a week before the wedding, not like Ryan had.

Next, battling my embarrassment and shame, I called my father on his landline because he still didn't have a cell. I hoped he was home. It would be like him to work the day after Christmas.

My stepmother, Joy, answered. I could hear their little girl in the background. My father had been forty when my mother died. Two years later, he married Joy, who is just ten years older than me. A year after that, they had a baby. I was twenty-one when Karlie was born; she'd just turned six a week ago.

My feelings toward my father and his new family were complicated. To anyone but us, it would appear we were estranged. But we weren't, not technically. True, we hardly saw each other, but without a doubt, I loved my dad. I loved Joy and Karlie too.

But it was a painful love. Too much of a reminder of what I used to have—and what I'd lost. And a reminder of how quickly Mom and I had been replaced.

"Savannah," Joy cooed. "How are you? Making the most of your last week as a single gal?"

"I need to talk to Dad," I said.

Her voice grew concerned. "Everything all right?"

Afraid my voice might give out, I managed to say, "Not really."

She paused. I prayed she wouldn't ask me anything more.

"I'll get your father," she said. "You just caught him. He was ready to leave to check on the calves." He worked for one of those big operations where the cows calved year round.

"Savannah." Dad's voice was as deep and soothing as ever. "You okay?"

I took a deep breath. Best to be matter-of-fact and to the point, just as I'd been with the vendors. Best to leave my emotions out of it. "Ryan called off the wedding. You don't have to come to the city after all."

"Baby," he said. "I'm so sorry."

I burst into tears. So much for leaving my emotions out of it. The last time I'd felt so lost and alone was when Mom died. Well, when Dad remarried too.

"Do you need me? I'll drive down right now."

"No." I may have said it more forcefully than I needed to. "I'll be fine. I just wanted you to know so you and Joy could change your plans." Since they were going to stay in my apartment, they didn't have to cancel a hotel reservation, but I knew they'd both taken time off work.

"We can still come down," he said.

"No, please don't," I answered.

"Savannah . . ."

"I need time alone. To process everything."

I expected him to say more. That he wasn't surprised. That he'd never trusted Ryan. That he hoped I'd find someone more down-to-earth. That it was better it happened now instead of after we married.

But he didn't say any of those things. Instead he said, "I'm so sorry, baby. I really am."

"Thanks. I'll call in a few days."

"All right," he said. "Talk to you then."

After I hung up, I started texting guests I had numbers for and tracking down contact information for the rest. It was a long, tedious process, something I knew Mom would have helped me with if she were alive. Although, it registered—again—that I wouldn't have ever met Ryan if Mom had lived.

A call came through during the middle of it all, but I didn't answer. When I listened to the voicemail, it was Joy, saying how concerned she was for me, and then asking all of the questions Dad hadn't thought to ask. Did I need money? Did I have anyone to talk to? She asked if I had a friend staying with me or anyone to help notify the guests, that sort of thing. She ended her message with an invitation: Did I want to come up to their place for a few days to get away from it all?

I fought back tears as I listened to her kind words, but I wouldn't call her back. She had a cell phone, so I sent her a text assuring her I was all right and that I didn't need financial help. Any extra money they had was in their savings, which they hoped to use for an acreage of their own.

I finally made it through my list, trying to imagine Ryan doing the same. Maybe Amber was helping him. The thought sent another wave of nausea through me. I poured myself another cup of coffee and headed into my bedroom. My dress, wrapped in plastic, hung on the outside of my closet door. I had the urge to hurl my full cup at it, but I didn't have the energy to clean up the mess.

What to do now? I'd sent my boss a text saying the wedding was off. But there was no way I was going into the office. Maybe I'd spend the week searching for other jobs as far away from the Bay Area as possible. New York. Philadelphia. Boston. Miami. Atlanta.

But definitely not Washington, DC.

My phone dinged again as I stared at my dress. It had been buzzing all afternoon with return texts.

I'm so sorry!

Better now than later!

What happened??!!!

I'd checked the phone each time it dinged, half hoping it was Ryan saying it had all been a big mistake. That he'd had a bad week at work. That he'd had a reaction to a medication. That Amber had temporarily hypnotized him.

But when a text came through from Nita, I knew it was all over. *I just got off the phone with Ryan. Savannah, I'm so sorry. I can only guess how this must be for you. It seems so out of character for him. I'm not sure if it would help you to speak with me. If it would, please call. I'd like to do whatever I can to help you through this.*

I knew I couldn't call her without sobbing. She was a sweetheart who led a Bible study for new moms and still volunteered at the elementary school Ryan had attended.

I texted her back, thanking her for her kind message and assuring her I'd call sometime in the future. She responded with a broken heart emoji, and then that was all. But she'd reached out, and I appreciated that. I also appreciated that Ryan had been honest with her that it was his idea to call off the wedding.

A few minutes later, my phone dinged again. My boss. Mr. William Hayes. *Sorry to hear that. I need you in the office tomorrow. It's urgent.*

I stared at the text. How could I answer? I finally settled on, *Sorry, I'm in no shape to come in.*

His reply arrived immediately. *Well, get in shape or lose your job.*

Pardon?

No excuses, he texted back. *This is an emergency.*

My vacation was approved, I texted back.

I just officially unapproved it. We're in the middle of a fiscal emergency. Be in the office tomorrow.

I began to pace but lost my balance and grabbed the back of the couch to steady myself. I wouldn't text him back. I couldn't go to work tomorrow. I couldn't stay in the Bay Area at all. I had to leave.

But I couldn't go to Dad's. Seeing his happy life with Joy and Karlie wasn't what I wanted.

Where could I go?

My eyes fell to the blue afghan inches from my hand. How many times had Mammi Mast told me I was always welcome, no matter what? She still told me that in her letters and phone calls, without fail. Nappanee, Indiana, might be the end of the world to some people, but to me, it always felt like home.

Or, at the least, it would be the perfect place to escape until I could find a new job as far away from San Francisco—and Ryan Woodward—as possible.

CHAPTER 2

I flew out of San Francisco International Airport four days later with a one-way ticket to South Bend, Indiana, and one bag. I'd put everything else into storage in Oakland, including my engagement ring. I'd wanted to throw it into the Bay but talked myself out of it, deciding if I still felt the urge when I returned, I'd do it then. I'd have to come back to sort through everything, but for now, it was all out of sight and out of mind. The apartment was empty and cleaned. All I needed to do was mail my keys to the property company when my lease was up at the end of January.

I landed in Chicago at 6:15 p.m., with an hour layover before I needed to catch my puddle jumper to South Bend, but the flight wasn't on the electronic reader board. When I checked at the desk, I found out it had been canceled for weather-related reasons. That sounded ominous. When I'd told Mammi I was coming to visit her, she'd said to hurry and to bring my warmest coat, scarf, gloves, and boots. I checked my weather app for Nappanee. Twenty-three degrees with snowflakes.

The next flight wasn't for another twelve hours. I left a message on Mammi's machine, housed in the shed at the end of her lane. I hated the thought of her walking to check the messages once she realized I was late. It would be dark, cold, and snowy. I called her brother, Seth, who lived a mile away from her. He was Mennonite and had a phone in his kitchen.

He answered on the second ring. When I explained the situation, he asked, "Want me to come get you?"

"Definitely not, Uncle Seth," I answered. He drove a 1975 Chevy pickup. I didn't like the thought of him driving it into town, let alone to Chicago, more than one hundred miles away.

"I can pick you up at the airport tomorrow," he said.

"I'm going to rent a car in South Bend," I answered.

He didn't argue with me. Instead he said, "Make sure and get one with four-wheel drive. Another storm is blowing in tonight."

"All right." I dreaded driving in the snow, which was why I wasn't trying to rent a car in Chicago. The shorter the distance I had to go, the better. "I'll call you if the flight is delayed again. Otherwise, would you tell Mammi I'll arrive tomorrow? It'll probably be in the afternoon."

"Jah," Uncle Seth replied. "I'll drive over right now and let her know."

"*Denki*," I said. Uncle Seth might be Mennonite, but he still spoke Pennsylvania Dutch, a language I learned during the summer months I spent with Mammi Mast while I was growing up. I still spoke Pennsylvania Dutch with Mammi over the phone because I wanted to retain as much of it as possible.

I got something to eat and then settled down in a corner of the airport to watch movies on my laptop, to do all I could to pass the time and *not* think about Ryan. Of course, I wasn't successful.

After dozing on and off throughout the night, I woke to find out that the next flight to South Bend had been canceled too.

"You can take the bus," the airline representative told me. "The terminal is across the street."

I had to go to the bowels of the airport to request my bag, then wrestle it out of the airport and to the bus terminal. It looked like there was a bus that could take me directly to Nappanee.

I changed my mind about Uncle Seth driving into town—he probably did it all the time, anyway—and gave him a call, asking if he could pick me up at the grocery store that doubled as a bus station at eight that evening.

He quickly agreed. "I'll let your grandmother know," he said. "She was worried about you flying in a blizzard. She'll feel better about you being on the bus."

After waiting most of the day, charging my phone as I did, I finally boarded the bus just before four. I dozed with my head against the cold glass window, waking up every now and then to a flat, wintery world with more snow coming down. The landscape couldn't be more different from the mountains of Northern California. The woods in Indiana, which were really just patches of trees at the back of fields, were nothing like the forests I was used to.

The plows seemed to be staying ahead of the bus, until we reached Elkhart County. By then, the snow was coming down in buckets, and the bus slowed significantly. I shivered at the thought of Uncle Seth waiting in his old pickup for me. He was in good shape, but I still hated he was out in the cold. All for me.

Finally, the bus reached the outskirts of Nappanee just as my phone rang. It was the florist. I answered it with the cheeriest hello I could muster. "Hey, sorry to bother you," she said. "But Ryan's card was declined."

I groaned.

"What do you want me to do?"

"Can you call Ryan?" I said. "You should have his number."

"I can do that," she said. "But if I can't get a hold of him, I'll have to run the other card on file, which is yours."

"Could you hold off on that?" I asked. "I'm sure he'll take care of it."

"I'll give him a call and see what he says," she answered.

I hung up with a sick feeling. Hopefully it was just a glitch. Ryan *had* to take care of it like he said he would. I would need the money I'd put away to relocate, not pay for the wedding he canceled.

The driver swung the bus into the parking lot of the grocery store. Just as I expected, Uncle Seth sat in his pickup. He left the engine running as he climbed out. He wore a heavy coat, a stocking cap over his white hair, thick gloves, and work boots.

I stepped off the bus and retrieved my bag from the driver. Uncle Seth took it from me, despite my protests, and swung it into the bed of the truck as if it were weightless. I was too tired to talk much, but I managed to ask about his family.

His seven children, forty-plus grandchildren, and eighteen great-grandchildren were all doing fine, apparently. Delores, his oldest daughter, was still working as a midwife. Years ago, she and I used to talk business.

"She has her office on my property now," he said. "It got to be too much for her to make all those home visits, and my place is in a good, central location."

He paused. "Of course, I miss Edna every day."

I reached over and patted his arm. His wife had passed away three years ago. I'd sent a card, and Uncle Seth had written a kind note in return. The two had been married for fifty-four years.

As Uncle Seth turned into Mammi's driveway, the lights from

the pickup illuminated the two-story farmhouse and then the white barn. My heart swelled with the feeling of home.

Mammi, bundled in a thick sweater, greeted us at the back door. As Uncle Seth headed up to my room with my bag, Mammi put her hands on both of my shoulders and locked her eyes on mine. "I'm so glad you're here," she said.

Overcome with emotion, I simply nodded.

"Are you hungry?"

I shook my head.

"Exhausted?"

I nodded again.

"Go on up to bed," she said. "Everything is ready for you."

"Denki," I said. "We'll talk in the morning." I exhaled, relaxing a little for the first time in almost a week.

The farmhouse smelled just the way it had when I was a girl, like coffee and cinnamon. Wood and lavender. Love and comfort.

Uncle Seth came down the staircase, and after thanking him profusely, I went up, crawling into my childhood bed with my coat still on. Even with that, it was cold. In my tired stupor, I remembered that the bedrooms in Amish homes had no source of heat. I also remembered that I'd only ever visited Indiana in the summer.

I shivered until I finally warmed enough to fall asleep.

Perhaps I dreamed about my childhood, because when I awoke—on what should have been my wedding day—my thoughts weren't on Ryan. They were on my parents.

My father, James Jonathan Mast Jr., left the Amish as an eighteen-year-old. He loved the land, farming, and his family.

But he couldn't, as much as he tried to force himself, join the church. It wasn't that he didn't believe in God. It was the many rules that he couldn't accept.

One warm spring night in 1989, he left a note to his parents in the middle of the big oak table, the edge of the paper tucked under the sugar bowl. He aimed west and finally, as the sun rose, hitched a ride. Once a week he'd send a postcard to his parents, trying to save them as much worry as possible.

First, he worked on a dairy farm in Illinois and then, in the fall, headed west again. He found a job operating a ski lift in Colorado. The next spring, just after he turned nineteen, he headed to Northern California. He took a job working on a cattle ranch outside of Grass Valley, a town of twelve thousand people, located between Sacramento and Donner's Pass.

My mother worked in the area on an organic vegetable farm with some of her girlfriends. She and Dad met at a farmers' market that August, and they both swore it was love at first sight. She was all of nineteen and, of course, more worldly-wise than Dad. But right up until the end of her days, she'd had a sort of childlike innocence to her. Somehow my mother managed to always live in the moment, finding joy in even the mundane.

"Savannah." Mammi's low voice was followed by a quiet knock on my door. "Breakfast is ready."

Although awake, I finally opened my eyes to the gray morning light coming through the east-facing windows.

"Be down in a minute," I said.

"The kitchen is warm . . ." Mammi's voice trailed off.

The room, my room, had been my father's. It was furnished as simply as every bedroom in the house, with a bed, a bureau, and pegs on the wall to hang clothing.

The first time Dad put me on a plane for Indiana, I was six. Mom's parents had divorced when she was little, and she never had much of a relationship with her father, who'd moved to Houston. And, according to her, her mother wasn't the "grandma type."

All I had were Dad's stories, but I was pretty sure Mammi Mast *was* the grandma type. She cooked and baked and gardened and quilted. And at the time, because my grandfather had died the year before, she also managed the farm, leasing out most of the land and hiring a farmhand to do the rest.

Mom had had fifteen babies to deliver that summer, and Dad was working fourteen-hour days on the ranch. I often accompanied both of them to work, and I could have easily done that all through the summer. But instead I asked to go see my Mammi in Indiana. So Dad left a message for his mother, and she called back and said, "I'd like to have Savannah visit."

Looking back, it seems awfully trusting of Mom to let me go stay with a woman she'd never met. She must have trusted that Dad wouldn't send me if I wouldn't be safe. He was overprotective, to say the least, but he never had qualms about my visiting Mammi.

There may have been another reason too. All in all, we were a happy little family, but I sensed tension between my parents from time to time. Now, as an adult, I guessed Dad probably didn't talk much about his feelings and that Mom, who was the most emotionally honest person I've ever met, was probably frustrated with him. And perhaps hurt. Looking back, I hope it was good for them to have those weeks without me during the summer. I doubted that Dad opened up more, but at least they didn't have to juggle me along with their jobs. At least they had a little bit of time for just the two of them.

That first summer, Uncle Seth picked me up at the tiny South Bend airport and dropped me off at the Mast family farm. That began an annual tradition, which continued every summer until

I was fifteen. After that, I started officially working as Mom's assistant and began an apprenticeship, sure I wanted to follow her into midwifery.

I think my trips to Indiana did Mammi almost as much good as they did me. Most Amish widows remarried soon after a spouse passed away, but Mammi didn't seem to have any interest in that. I know managing the farm, keeping the house in good repair, helping those in need, and quilting took up most of her time, but she said her favorite weeks of the year were when I was with her.

Still in my coat, I finally crawled out of bed and slipped into my boots. Then I shuffled down the hall to the bathroom, which was just as cold as my bedroom, and then downstairs to the kitchen. Mammi was right. It was, by far, the warmest place in the house.

She looked so small in her layers of clothes and bulky sweater. "There's coffee," she said. "And biscuits and gravy."

My mouth watered. I hadn't had biscuits and gravy in years.

She had the table all set, and while I poured myself a cup of coffee, she placed the biscuits in a basket and the skillet of gravy on a trivet. In the middle of the table was the same sugar bowl my father had used to secure his farewell note.

Mammi led us in a silent prayer, and then we ate. Suddenly, after hardly eating all week, I was famished. Mammi ate a half biscuit with gravy, while I ate three. When I was finally full, she led us in a closing silent prayer.

As we cleared the table, I asked what she had planned for the day. "I was going to quilt at Jane's shop," she said. "But I think I'll stay home."

"Because of me?" I didn't want her to change her plans.

She smiled. "Well, I'd stay if you needed me to. But the truth is I don't want to take the horse and buggy out. With this storm, it's a good day to stay home."

"Could Seth take you?"

"It's not necessary." She gestured toward the living room. "I have a quilt to work on here."

That wasn't surprising. She always had a quilt she was working on.

"And I can go Monday for the quilting circle. Would you go with me then?"

"Sure." She'd taught me how to quilt when I was a girl, but I hadn't done it in years.

The day seemed to stretch ahead of me, as endless as the snowy landscape. I should have been getting my hair done for the wedding. We would have been leaving for Saint Lucia tomorrow. Instead, I was trapped in a cold farmhouse with a dying phone and no car.

But at least I was with Mammi.

I TOOK TWO naps, one before dinner, as Mammi called it, even though it was the noon meal, and then another one after. I felt restless. I needed to charge my phone and go to a coffee shop where I could get internet on my laptop. I needed to call Dad and let him know where I was. I needed to make sure Ryan really was paying for the wedding he'd canceled.

Later, as dusk fell, my mood grew even darker as I looked out the bedroom window into the dreary afternoon. Had I thought I'd come to Mammi's at the end of December and it would be sunny and bright, like it was in the summer?

I needed to come up with a plan to get on with my life.

I checked my phone by the fading light. No missed calls. No voicemails. No texts. Had everyone forgotten me on what should have been my wedding day? I clomped down the stairs and then wandered into the living room, where Mammi was quilting and humming quietly to herself.

"Are you hungry?" she asked.

"A little." Actually, I was starving again.

"I have ham and corn bread. And canned green beans and applesauce."

"That sounds lovely," I answered, thinking of the cucumber salad with lemon vinaigrette, the grilled salmon, the sliced flat iron steak, and the garlic mashed potatoes we'd chosen for our wedding dinner.

Where was Ryan now? Most likely with Amber.

"Savannah, are you all right?"

I focused on my grandmother. "Mostly," I answered.

"I'm sorry for your *hatz* ache."

"Denki," I replied.

After supper, before we cleared the table, Mammi read from the Bible, reading Matthew chapter 18 by the light of the propane lamp hanging above the table. I barely listened as she read Jesus' words about becoming like a little child to enter the kingdom of heaven.

Mom and Dad had gone to a little community church with a congregation of around a hundred, taking me with them. I also attended Sunday school and a Wednesday night kids' club, where we memorized Bible verses. I'd already had a faith tradition when I first started visiting Mammi, but her lifestyle was so simple and her faith so visible that it really impacted me.

But after my mother died, I resented God. Why had He allowed it? Dad seemed so lost and hurt that I didn't feel as if I could talk through it with him. And when I talked with Mammi on the phone, I never admitted my spiritual despair.

Distantly, I heard Mammi read Matthew 18:20. "For where

two or three are gathered together in my name, there am I in the midst of them."

In my pain and grief, I had found myself praying less and less. I also stopped seeking out the fellowship of other believers. But when Ryan and I started dating, he was the one who led me back to church. He'd gone with his mother as a child, and although he'd quit going during college, he'd missed it. So we found a community church to attend.

Ryan's spiritual seeking was one of the things that had truly endeared him to me. We didn't have time to get involved much more than Sunday mornings, but we figured we'd do that after we were married.

When Mammi reached the end of the chapter, she closed her Bible and then, without saying anything more, began collecting the plates. I stood up to help, eager for some activity to warm me.

Later, once I was back upstairs, I plugged my nearly dead phone into thc portable battery pack I'd brought along. Then, as I lay in bed staring at the pitch-black ceiling, I tried to pray. Really I did.

Dear God . . .

But then nothing more came.

Just as I was finally starting to drift off to sleep, my phone startled me awake. In my half-awake state, I was sure it was Ryan.

It wasn't. It was an Indiana number.

I woke up enough to accept the call and croak, "Hello?"

"Sorry to call so late. It's Delores." My Uncle Seth's daughter. "I have the flu. High fever, aches, and chills. Sore throat and cough. The whole deal."

"I'm sorry to hear that. . . ." Why was she calling me?

"I have a mother in labor. I can't find another midwife to cover for me. Would you do it?"

I was wide awake now. "I'm not qualified."

"It's her third *Boppli*. I don't foresee any problems."

"I don't have any equipment," I said. "Or a vehicle." Surely she wouldn't expect me to take Mammi's buggy.

"I know," she said. "I have an extra set of gear in my shop. Dad will bring it to you. And you can drive his pickup."

When I didn't answer, she said, "I'm guessing that going out in a snowstorm to a birth is the last thing you want to do. . . ."

I didn't say anything. She was right about that.

"This woman just needs someone with her, another woman. She'll do fine."

"How about a neighbor? Or relative?"

"She recently came back to Nappanee after being away for years. She's a widow who remarried a year ago. Her name is Arleta. She has two older children, but she doesn't have any relatives in the area. I did leave messages for a couple of her neighbors, but no one's called me back."

I doubted any Amish were checking their messages on a night like tonight.

"Can't your dad drive me there?"

"He could except he's not feeling very well either. I told him to wear a mask when he picks you up. You'll need to drop him off at his place and then keep going."

"He'll be there in a few—" She broke off in a deep cough.

When she stopped, I said, "I haven't been to a birth in nine years."

"You used to assist your mother. And you'd started an apprenticeship."

"But I never delivered a baby on my own."

"Your being there will only make things easier for Arleta. There's no way it will make it worse."

I swung my legs over to the side of the bed. "What about liability issues?"

"You will simply be helping a woman in need. No one's going to sue."

I wasn't so sure. "Why don't you send her to the hospital?"

"I tried," Delores answered. "Her husband was the one who called me, and he refused. Believe me, I've tried every other option possible."

A horn honked outside.

"What if something goes wrong?" I asked.

"Well, if you have a question, call me. If it's an emergency, call 9-1-1."

"All right," I finally said. "I'll go. What's the address?"

"Dad has it," she answered. "Plus special driving directions."

I stood and grabbed my car charger from the front pocket of my suitcase. "And you're sure Uncle Seth has everything I need?"

"Jah, positive."

I shuddered. God help me. I could be making the biggest mistake of my life, but the thought of a woman laboring by herself in a snowstorm was more than I could bear.

CHAPTER 3

The snow fell fast as I steered Uncle Seth's pickup along the country road. I had my phone plugged in to the cigarette lighter—luckily I'd been able to find my old-school adaptor—and my GPS was set for Arleta's house.

Plus I had Uncle Seth's special instructions. *"If your GPS tells you to turn left at the county road, keep going until you come to the next lane. Vernon always keeps that lane plowed."* He'd told me that between coughs, behind the mask that he must have retrieved from Delores's office, as I took him back to his house. He also told me to make sure not to flood the engine of the pickup when I restarted it the next morning.

Not all babies came in the middle of the night during a snowstorm. I'd assisted Mom plenty of times when babies came during the day, in the summer, or the fall, or the spring. But of course, even in Northern California, they came in the middle of the night during a snowstorm.

That was one of the things I'd liked best about the Bay Area. No snow.

Perhaps I should start my job search in Florida. That was far away from the Bay Area. And blizzards.

The pickup lurched forward and jerked three times. It hadn't done that yesterday when Uncle Seth was driving. I pressed harder on the accelerator. The engine caught. Relieved, I grasped the steering wheel tighter and started up an incline. It couldn't be called a hill.

The sputtering started again. I checked the gas gauge, horrified for a moment. But it was fine, showing the tank was nearly half full.

The GPS on my phone instructed me to turn right. As I did, the sputtering grew worse. I managed to steer the pickup toward the side of the road before it lurched again and then stopped as the engine died altogether.

After turning the key on and off, I pressed my head against the cold steering wheel. I must have been delusional when I told Delores I'd drive on a wintery road to deliver Arleta's baby. Maybe grandiose. At this rate, Arleta would deliver on her own.

"Come on, come on," I said into the dark night, trying the key one more time. "Please," I added, as if using good manners might make the difference.

What if I didn't make it to the birth? Arleta's house was still three miles away. I couldn't walk, not in this weather.

I grabbed my phone, wondering if the ride-sharing app I used in Oakland would have any drivers out here. I entered Arleta's address, dropped the pin for my location, and then scanned the available vehicles. There was only one, all the way back in Nappanee, five miles away.

Hopefully the driver wasn't asleep.

I checked the weather app. Thirteen degrees. I'd never been in such cold conditions, not even when I used to go cross-country skiing with Mom and Dad in the Sierras. I opened the pickup door, trying to imagine walking three miles in the cold as a gust of icy wind blasted through me.

Good God. Was that a prayer? I quickly pulled the door shut. It wasn't a curse, so I went with the prayer. "Please," I said out loud again.

My phone dinged.

Thank God. The driver was on the way. *Kenny M*. He was driving a Toyota Camry with an Indiana license plate. I hoped he had chains. And that I'd actually make it to the birth before the baby arrived.

FIFTEEN MINUTES LATER, I clapped my hands together in the frigid cab. When I used to visit in the summer, I loved the thunderstorms, the fireflies, the calves, and kittens. The propane lamp Mammi lit in the early mornings and then again at dusk. The breeze that came through my open window, cooling my room.

Never once had I come here for Christmas. Or anytime in the winter, for that matter.

"That's why I left," Dad had said wryly. *"Well, that and about a thousand other reasons."* The truth was, he avoided Indiana. He phoned home once a month, but he'd never returned. Not even for his father's funeral.

I checked my app again. It said the driver was close, so I looked in the rearview mirror.

Headlights approached. Slipping my phone into the pocket of my coat, I grabbed Delores's midwifery bags, popped open the pickup door, and jumped down. Then I slammed the door and locked it, tucking the key into my pocket. But when I turned toward the car behind me, it wasn't a Camry.

It was an older model Jeep Cherokee. In fact, I was sure it was too old to qualify as a ride-sharing vehicle.

And I didn't see a sign on it either.

The driver rolled the window down a crack. A man, who I thought was on the youngish side—although it was hard to tell, wore a black stocking cap, a black scarf, and a black parka. And black gloves. "Savannah?"

I nodded. "Are you Kenny M.?"

"I know I'm not in the Camry that's listed on the app," he said quickly. "I thought this would get around in the blizzard a little better."

Well, he knew my name and the vehicle the app told me he'd be driving. And he was making sure I knew that he did. It was either this or possibly wait a long time for a tow. And miss the birth.

I yanked on the back door of the Jeep. It didn't budge.

He opened his door and jumped down. "Hold on." He yanked on it, but nothing happened. "Frozen," he muttered.

He walked around to the other back door. Thankfully, it opened. Tromping around to the other side, I tossed my bags on the seat and then climbed in. Kenny slammed the door after me as I searched for the seat belt.

I finally found it, just as the Jeep lurched forward and into a skid.

After a slide toward the opposite side of the road and then back, barely missing the pickup, Kenny gained control, and I let out an audible sigh of relief. Surely he could get me three miles up the road.

When his GPS told him to turn left, I told him what Uncle Seth said.

He kept going, turning onto the lane.

It appeared Vernon had plowed the lane, but not for a few hours. The Jeep slid again, but Kenny managed to pull out of it a second time.

He was quiet, but I wasn't saying anything either.

The snow had drifted and the going became even slower.

I remembered that Delores had said this new baby was the husband's first. I wondered how old Arleta's other children were.

Kenny slowed even more. "What brings you out this way?"

I answered, "There's a woman in labor."

"Oh. Are you a midwife?"

"No," I squeaked. "But I'm going to help."

We passed the phone shack where Vernon probably called Delores. The Jeep came to a slow stop in front of the barn.

I pointed out the window, to what looked like a shadow in the dark. "The house is that way."

"I can't get over there." Kenny gripped the steering wheel with his black-gloved hands. "You'll have to walk from here."

I gripped the door handle and pushed, probably with more force than needed. But nothing happened.

Kenny met my eyes in the rearview mirror. His stocking cap had slipped down on his forehead. Had he locked the back doors on purpose?

A wave of fear washed over me. "What's going on?"

He met my eyes in the mirror. "I don't know what you're talking about."

"The door won't open."

"Oh." He fumbled for a moment and then said, "The safety locks are on." I heard a click. Maybe he had children.

I swung the door open and jumped down into the snow, tempted to march to the house without saying anything more. But then, realizing I was going to need a ride back to the pickup, I thanked him. "Will you be driving tomorrow, say midmorning or so? Maybe around noon?"

"Depends on the storm." He met my eyes again. "You can

call me directly, if you want." He rattled off his number, and I quickly entered it into my contacts under *Kenny M.*

I called out, "Thanks!" and then slammed the door. I was pretty sure he yelled, "Good luck."

With the birth? Or getting a ride? I wasn't sure.

As I trudged through the snow, the back door opened, showing a crack of light. "Tell the driver to wait," someone yelled.

I was halfway to the house. I wasn't going back to the Jeep, even though it was still parked by the barn.

"Wait!" A young woman slammed the door and came running down the back steps, zipping her coat as she did. She wore a black bonnet and snow boots and appeared to be in her late teens. It obviously wasn't Arleta.

"I have to find my brother," she said as she rushed past, just loud enough so I could hear.

The back door opened again. A huge man with a wild beard and hair filled the frame. "Get back in here!" he bellowed. I assumed he was Vernon.

The girl continued running.

"Miriam! Now!" Vernon yelled.

A woman wearing a flannel nightgown stepped behind him. She poked her head to the side, just enough so I could see her round face. Her dark hair, with a single streak of gray, was uncovered. "Delores, is that you?"

"No," I answered. "I'm her cousin, Savannah Mast. Delores really does have the flu."

She sighed. "Well, come along."

I had made it to the steps and started up them as the man came lumbering past me, wearing boots but no jacket. I looked over my shoulder as I reached the door. The dome light of the Jeep was on, and Miriam was climbing into the front seat.

Kenny took off with as much speed as he could in the snow. Didn't he see Vernon stomping toward him?

I turned back to the door, eager to get into the house before Vernon came storming back.

I TOOK A deep breath and held it as I stood alone in the dim lamplight of Arleta's kitchen. Things had definitely gotten off to a bad start. I needed to regroup. That's what Mom would have done.

A baby was going to be born.

Once I exhaled, I called out, "Arleta?" She had completely disappeared.

After a long pause, a quavering voice came from down the hall. "Back here."

I left my coat on. The house was cold, even worse than Mammi's. I headed down the hall, stopping at the only open door. Arleta held on to a bedpost, panting. The cold might be all right for the time being, but it wouldn't do for the baby, or for Arleta, once the delivery was over.

I stepped to the woman's side and waited quietly. By the time the contraction had passed, Vernon was thundering down the hallway, yelling in Pennsylvania Dutch, "The driver didn't stop. He just kept on going, taking Miriam with him." He turned toward me and spoke in English. "Who was in the Jeep?"

"A ride-share driver," I answered. Vernon most likely didn't realize I could understand Pennsylvania Dutch. "His name is Kenny M."

Vernon shook his head. "That wasn't Kenny." His wild blue eyes drilled into me. I recognized that look. It's how I felt the morning I'd gone searching for Ryan.

Vernon took a step toward me. "I'd recognize Kenny Miller—he's come out here before, looking for Joshua. I didn't recognize that man."

I winced, feeling responsible that Miriam had escaped with my driver. *Miller.* The surname was familiar from childhood. I'd known a Tommy Miller. He used to live adjacent to Mammi's farm, but his family had sold their land years ago. Of course, Kenny Miller might or might not be related to Tommy. Miller was a common Amish surname.

Vernon turned toward Arleta. "I'm going after her."

"No." I turned toward him. "You need to stay here in case we need someone to go to the phone shack to call for help."

"Joshua can do that."

I raised my eyebrows. "Joshua?" I'd thought Delores said Arleta had two older children, but she must have had three: Miriam, the brother whom Miriam left to find, and Joshua.

"He's asleep. In the room next door."

"Let Vernon go." Arleta didn't look at her husband. "Joshua will wake up if needed."

"All right." I had no idea how to read the dynamics between the two of them, but I would follow Arleta's lead. If she was fine having Vernon out of the house during the birth, then I was too.

"I need the driver's number," Vernon said. "The one who dropped you off. I'll call him from the shed."

"Do you have something to write it down on?" I took my phone from my pocket.

He shook his head. "I'll remember it."

I read the number from my contacts and then said, "I'll call him." I pressed the button to connect, but it rang and rang. Finally, his voicemail picked up, and I left a quick message that Miriam's parents needed to know where she was going.

Once I ended the call, Vernon said, "I know a driver who'll

pick me up. I'll call him from the phone shack." Then he nodded, as if he might be thanking me, and left the room without telling Arleta good-bye. She was already in the middle of another contraction. Perhaps he didn't realize the baby could be born before he returned. Or maybe he didn't care.

"We need to get you into the living room," I said. "It's too cold in here."

"But everything is set up." She gestured toward the bureau where an old shower curtain, towels, a few cloth diapers, rubber pants, and some blankets were stacked.

"Where's the birthing kit?" I asked. Expectant mothers purchased a kit by mail order that contained underpads, a plastic-lined sheet, sponges, and all the other items needed for a sanitary birth.

"I put one together as best I could."

"Why didn't you buy one?"

"Vernon didn't think it was necessary—" Another contraction gripped Arleta, and this time she gasped.

I stepped to the bureau, wishing Delores had sent a kit along with her midwifery bag. It appeared the shower curtain had been scrubbed, but it certainly wasn't sterile. At least there were clean towels and washcloths, but there were no gloves, no syringe, no cord clamp, and no iodine. I guessed Delores had gloves and clamps in the bag, and hopefully a syringe, but I'd have to do my best as far as the rest.

Gathering up the supplies on the bureau, I slipped them under my arm and grabbed my bags with one hand. I put my other hand on the small of Arleta's back. "Let's get to the living room before another contraction hits."

The woman hesitated but then shuffled along.

Once we reached the sparsely furnished living room, the first thing I did was stoke the fire. Next, I checked Arleta, who seemed to be a textbook multigravida. She was already at eight centimeters. She'd be transitioning shortly, which meant the baby could be born soon.

The woman's blood pressure and pulse were normal. I recorded both and then timed the next two contractions, all the while pushing memories of assisting Mom on births out of my mind. The contractions lasted around sixty seconds and were two minutes apart. It wouldn't be long now.

I spread the shower curtain over the sofa, draping it down to the floor and double-checked my watch. It was now 12:26 a.m., New Year's Day. A new life for the new year.

Arleta breathed through another contraction and then began pacing.

"How old is Miriam?" I asked.

Arleta shook her head and continued to walk. Obviously she didn't want to talk about her daughter. It had been foolish of me to ask. I looked outside at the snow swirling past the window.

I thought about the birth ten years ago that I didn't go on. Mom had asked me to, but I was tired from the one the night before. The family lived in a cabin on Blue Canyon Road and already had five kids. Per usual, I'd probably spend all my time entertaining the children, something the older kids in the family could do as easily as I could, instead of assisting with the birth and getting more experience toward my credentials as a midwife.

Three hours later, the husband called our house phone to say Mom hadn't arrived. It was only a forty-five minute drive. Dad called the county sheriff and then pulled on his boots. Overcome with guilt, I'd grabbed my coat. Mom had a four-wheel-drive Subaru. She knew the roads as well as anyone. But there was a full-blown blizzard raging outside, something I hadn't realized when I declined to go with her.

I shook my head and looked away from the window. Too often, grief snuck up on me, even though the accident had been nearly a decade ago, and shut me down. I couldn't risk it now, not when I needed to be at my best.

Arleta stopped for another contraction, leaning against a hardback chair.

I fed the fire again and then stepped into the kitchen. I could sense that Arleta was one of those women who definitely did better on her own. A kettle simmered on the back of the propane stove. "Would you like something to drink?" I called out.

"No," Arleta said, followed by a gasp.

I turned.

She stood in a puddle of water in the middle of the living room. Arleta glanced up at me, and I nodded. Her water had broken. Her contractions were bound to grow even closer together now.

One came on fast, and I started to time it, but immediately Arleta shuffled over to the sofa and kneeled. "I need to push."

I barely had a chance to pull on gloves and lift her nightgown before the baby came flying out, wide-eyed with a furrowed brow. The little girl gulped and then began to wail. I checked my watch. 1:27.

Arleta managed to crawl up on the couch, on the shower curtain. I put the baby on Arleta's chest and then covered her with receiving blankets and then both of them with the quilt.

I had never been to a birth without several people in the room. The father. The grandmother, sisters, friends, neighbors. I reminded myself that we weren't completely alone. Joshua was sleeping down the hall, but there was no reason to wake him.

God had answered my prayer. The ride-share had arrived. The birth had been as simple as possible. And I'd mostly managed to avoid painful memories of my mother last night. At least so far.

I waited until the cord stopped pulsing. Once it did, I cut it and then wrapped the baby in her own blanket and tucked her next to Arleta. Then I covered them both with another quilt and fed the fire another piece of wood. After that, I cleaned up the living room floor.

Then I checked on the mother and child. "We should get her nursing."

"Give me a minute." Arleta's eyes were closed.

Finally, the baby began rooting around, and Arleta opened the front of her nightgown.

The placenta still hadn't delivered, and I hoped the nursing would help. A couple of times I tugged on the cord, but it wouldn't budge.

Wondering if stress could have slowed the separation and expulsion of the placenta, I asked, "Are you worried about anything?"

She shook her head.

"The baby? Miriam? Your husband?"

"*Nee*," she answered. "I know God is in charge."

A half hour after the baby had delivered, I pulled out my phone, knowing they were forbidden in the house. "Sorry, but it's necessary," I said.

Arleta pulled the baby from her breast.

"Have her keep nursing," I said. "It will help your uterus contract and push out the placenta."

She did what I asked without commenting. Thankfully, the baby latched on again.

I scrolled through my recent call log, found Delores's number, and put the phone on speaker.

She answered after several rings and sounded groggy.

I gave her a quick update about the birth.

"Thank you," she said.

"But it's been a half hour and the placenta hasn't delivered." Delayed separation and expulsion of the placenta could lead to hemorrhaging. In that case, I would need to call 9-1-1. But with the storm raging, what if the EMTs couldn't get to Arleta in time?

Delores's scratchy voice cut through my worry. "That's not all that unusual for a third baby."

"When should I be concerned?"

"Well, if it goes much longer . . ." Delores coughed. "Have you tugged on the cord?"

"A little," I answered.

"Tug harder while I stay on the phone."

Arleta closed her eyes as I put on another pair of gloves and explained what I was going to do. "Push if you can," I said.

I tugged and could tell Arleta was bearing down.

"It's budging," I told Delores, positioning a basin closer with my free hand.

"Keep pulling on it."

I did, increasing the pressure. Arleta pushed again. The placenta shifted. I pulled even harder and it flew out, followed by a gush of blood. I maneuvered the placenta into the basin and grabbed a clean towel.

"It's out." I kept my voice calm, even though I felt alarmed. "There's a significant amount of blood." But then I remembered that it was normal for a woman to lose a half quart or so of blood during a vaginal delivery.

I also knew it was really hard to estimate amounts of blood.

"Check the placenta," Delores said, "to see if any pieces are missing. Then massage the uterus."

I left the phone on speaker as I cleaned up as best I could, packed a towel between Arleta's legs, and then covered her up again.

The placenta looked good. "It's intact," I said to Delores. "I don't have much battery left. I'll call back in a few minutes."

"All right," she said.

I pulled off my gloves, ended the call, washed up, and then reached under the covers and began massaging Arleta's uterus, bumping against the baby as I did. After a few minutes, I checked the towel. The bleeding had slowed.

I gave Delores another call.

"Whew!" she said and then added, "Thank you so much."

"I'll call again if I need to," I said. "Or later on this morning."

It was 2:17. Surely Vernon had found Miriam and the other boy by now.

I swaddled the baby and then helped Arleta to the bathroom and into a clean nightgown with her robe over the top. I pulled socks and then slippers over her feet. Then I wadded up the shower curtain, put down a pad, and helped her back onto the couch.

"What would you like to eat?" I asked.

"There's bread and peanut butter. And grape jelly. That would be fine." Arleta had her eyes closed again.

When I returned with the food, I took the baby and rubbed the vernix from the little one's skin. Then I weighed her. Eight pounds three ounces. She was alert and pink. Everything seemed textbook, or at least as much as I could remember, which had been a surprising amount. I'd retained a lot from training all those years ago,

I put a diaper and rubber pants on the baby and then slipped her into a T-shirt and then the sleeper. I held her close for a moment, breathing in her scent. Every baby smelled unique.

I'd forgotten the pure joy of witnessing a new life come into the world. No wonder Mom had loved her job so much.

For a moment, my breath caught in my chest, thinking of Mom and then the babies I'd hoped to have with Ryan. I forced myself to exhale.

Arleta was watching me as she finished the sandwich, but she didn't smile. Nor did she seem anxious to have the baby back.

So I continued snuggling her, fighting back tears—and not just because I should have been in the middle of my wedding night.

It was because delivering babies was what I'd left behind when I enrolled at UCLA. I'd missed it at first, but as the years went by and my life changed so drastically, I hadn't anymore. Until tonight.

Car doors slammed, jerking me back to the present.

Boots fell on the back steps and then the door swung open. A teenage boy came stomping through the house. Arleta had her eyes closed again.

Vernon followed the boy, yelling, "Joshua, there's no need to go to bed. We have to start the chores soon."

But he kept going, down the hall, his coat and boots still on.

Joshua? "Do you have another son?" I asked Arleta.

She shook her head.

It appeared there hadn't been anyone else at the house after all.

Vernon retreated to the back porch and slammed the kitchen door shut. A minute later, he appeared without his coat or boots. "He snuck out before Miriam did. It turns out she went to find him. I sent her back with that man, the one who claimed to be Kenny Miller." He turned toward me.

I shrugged. "That's what he said his name was."

"I got an even closer look at him when he gave us a ride home just now. I've never seen him before. He's not Kenny Miller."

"Did you ask him what his real name was?"

Vernon nodded. "He didn't answer me."

Weird. Perhaps Vernon was confused.

"But Miriam's not here," Arleta said.

Vernon didn't seem to hear her, and she said it a second time, louder.

I finally put it together. "Stop the driver." I pointed to the door. "Ask him where he dropped her off."

Vernon ignored me and headed down the hall, most likely to see for himself if Miriam was home.

I tucked the baby back beside Arleta and rushed to the door, stumbling onto the porch and then down the back steps. The birth had gone fine and Arleta's baby girl was perfect. But now her other daughter was missing.

The Jeep fishtailed, the taillights wavering in the dark as it turned back onto the road.

CHAPTER 4

Arleta slept on the couch, the baby in the crook of her arm, while I curled up on the end of it, wearing my coat. There was no other place to doze. Well, there were six hardback chairs at the table, but I knew I wouldn't be able to sleep sitting on one of them.

I stoked the fire every half hour or so, checking on both the baby and Arleta when I did. At 4:30 a.m., Vernon shuffled into the living room and lit the lamp that I'd extinguished an hour earlier. His suspenders hung around his hips.

He headed straight to the kitchen without turning his attention to Arleta or the baby.

Arleta stirred. "Could you make him coffee?"

"Probably not," I answered. "I haven't made coffee on a propane stove for years."

She sat up and extended the baby to me. "Would you hold her?"

I took the baby as I asked, "Can't he make his own coffee?"

"Probably not," Arleta answered.

I held the baby in one hand and scooted off the couch, feeling as if I was being petty. "Tell me how to make the coffee."

She shook her head. "I'll do it."

I gave her my arm as she twisted her legs out from under the blankets and stood.

"Do you feel all right?" I hoped her blood pressure was staying steady.

She nodded.

A pan banged in the kitchen. Arleta shuffled over the hardwood floor. I drew the baby close, wondering what they would name her.

A minute later, Vernon hustled back through the living room, yelling, "Joshua! Time to get up."

The baby startled, and I held her closer. Vernon kept on going down the hall.

A minute later, he returned, and soon after, Joshua came stumbling through the living room, oblivious to me or the baby.

I dozed on the couch with the baby in my arms, relishing the weight of her body and her sweet breaths, then woke to the smell of coffee and ham. Maybe toast. I groaned. Arleta had made breakfast too. I checked my phone, which only had five percent of its battery left. I still needed to arrange for a ride back to the pickup and call for a tow.

Vernon barked, "Let's get going." The back door banged.

I stood with the baby and headed into the kitchen.

Arleta sat alone at the table with a cup of coffee and full plate of ham, scrambled eggs, and toast in front of her. "Hungry?" she asked.

"No, thank you." I sat down across from her. What would Mom think of a new mother cooking me breakfast?

Arleta cut the ham with her fork and took a bite.

I asked, "Do you have a name picked out for the baby?"

She shook her head as she chewed.

"A top-three list?" I asked, hoping to make some sort of conversation.

She shook her head again and took a bite of the eggs. Maybe she had a name in mind but didn't want to talk about it.

"Do you have anyone to help you today? A relative or neighbor?"

"No," she answered. "Miriam was going to help."

"Where do you think she is?"

Arleta shrugged, her face expressionless.

The baby stirred, and I shifted her to my shoulder. "Are you going to call the police and report her missing?"

Arleta wrapped her hands around her mug. "Vernon will call the bishop once he's done with the chores."

"All right . . ." I wondered what the bishop would do. "Delores will come by tomorrow to check on you and the baby and fill out the birth certificate. But I'll go out now and ask Vernon to ask the bishop to send someone over to help you."

Arleta ducked her head. "That won't be necessary. I'll be fine. Tell Delores I'll call her if I need anything." That wasn't how it worked, but I didn't tell Arleta that Delores would visit no matter what. If she was still ill, she'd find another midwife to do it.

As I cradled the baby, she began to root around. I'd give Arleta a few more minutes to eat and then get her nursing again. I was thankful for the chance to meet this little one, and I'd be forever grateful that both she and her mama were all right. And it had been a thrill to witness a birth again.

But I was done masquerading as a midwife. Sadly, I was anything but.

AFTER THE BABY nursed again, Arleta folded up the quilt and blanket, stashed them back in her bedroom, and pulled a baby bassinet out of a closet and placed it close to the wood stove.

"You need to not overexert yourself." I slipped the baby onto the little mattress. "Too much activity can cause you to bleed. That's a big no-no."

"I'll be all right." She sat down on the couch.

I gathered up my things and then headed into the kitchen to do the breakfast dishes. A pot of water was just coming to a boil on the back burner. I cringed at the thought of Arleta filling it.

I put the plates in the dishpan.

"Leave those," she called out.

"It will only take me a minute." When I'd assisted Mom, I'd done dishes, along with sibling duty. She'd always had mama and baby duty. And calm-the-father duty too, when needed.

As I scrubbed the dishes, I had a view of the side yard and the pasture but also a sliver of the barn, if I leaned to the left. I caught glimpses of Vernon and Joshua in the bit of light that spilled out from the barn from time to time. They'd been feeding and milking a small herd, probably around twenty cows, and then feeding the horses and chickens.

When I finished the dishes, I dried my hands and took out my phone, figuring I should arrange my ride. I decided I'd wait until I got to the pickup to call for a tow truck, just in case it would start this time.

I called Kenny M.'s number and was sent straight to voicemail. I didn't bother to leave a message and instead got back on the ride-share app and found a car ten minutes away. I headed back into the living room. Both Arleta and the baby were sleeping. I stoked the fire and said Arleta's name quietly.

She stirred.

"I'm leaving in a couple of minutes." I held up the list I pulled from Delores's bag. "I need to go over a few things before I go."

"I remember all of this from last time," Arleta said.

"Well, it's been a while." I guessed Joshua was fifteen or sixteen. I sat down beside her and talked about getting enough fiber, using ice and taking acetaminophen for pain, and monitoring her bleeding. "Call Delores—I mean, have Vernon call her—immediately if you start to hemorrhage or if you pass a large blood clot. Wear your nursing bra at all times, let your breasts air, and apply some sort of cream—lanolin or udder ointment—on your nipples."

She nodded. "Like I said, I remember all of this."

"All right." I handed her the list. I'd tell Delores she needed to go over the entire list with Arleta, just to make sure everything was covered.

I checked my phone. The car was just minutes away. "I'm going to go ahead and leave," I said. "It was wonderful to share this experience with you and your baby."

Arleta nodded, with a hint of a smile on her face, the most I'd seen since I arrived.

I slipped my coat on, pulled on my gloves, and picked up the bags.

It was still pitch black outside, except for the light from the barn. I headed for it. The snow had stopped, but at least a foot had accumulated in the barnyard.

Perhaps Vernon sensed me because he stepped through the side door of the barn. "Are you leaving?"

"Yes," I said. "I left Arleta a list of things to do to ensure she gets good postnatal care. Please take a look at it."

"All right."

"And make sure she doesn't work too hard. She needs a woman to come in, or at least an experienced girl. Would you talk to the bishop about that?"

"Well, I expect Miriam will be home any minute."

"Hopefully so, but Arleta needs help. And perhaps the police should be notified about Miriam, in addition to the bishop."

He crossed his arms over his heavy coat. "I'll think on that."

"Call Delores if you have any questions about anything."

"I've delivered plenty of calves." He nodded his head toward his herd.

I sighed. "Some things are similar, but it's not the same. Believe me." I nearly laughed at myself. What did I know anymore?

An SUV turned into the driveway.

"*Mach's gut*," I said.

He grunted. "Good-bye to you too" in English, most likely happy to see me go.

The driver, whose name flashed on my screen as Nancy S., was a middle-aged woman. "Well, I can guess what you've been up to," she said as I put my bags in the back and then climbed up front. "New baby for this family?"

I nodded.

"Everything go all right?"

"Perfectly." Well, except that their oldest daughter had gone missing in the middle of the night, but I wouldn't tell a stranger that. I covered my mouth as I yawned.

"Yep, I bet you're tired." She pulled around and headed back to the lane. "I actually have come out this way a number of times. Two kids on their Rumschpringe, sneaking out at night."

I hesitated about asking her anything more. It wasn't my business. But I couldn't keep quiet. "Did you see the girl last night by any chance?"

She shook her head. "But I saw her the night before, and she was quite upset."

Mercifully, Uncle Seth's pickup started. I waved to Nancy and then, after I'd plugged my phone into the charger, called Delores as the sun peeked over the woods to my left.

"How are you feeling?"

"My fever broke," she said, "so I'm on the mend. Hopefully I won't be contagious by tomorrow."

I gave Dolores an update, including Miriam's disappearance, and then said, "Do you think she's in danger?"

"I know Miriam has been troubled, running with the wrong crowd and that sort of thing. Hopefully she just crashed at someone's house and will be home soon." Delores coughed deeply several times.

When she stopped, I asked, "Do you think Arleta is safe?"

"What do you mean?" Delores was growing hoarse. "Do you think she's physically at risk?"

"She doesn't have anyone coming to help her," I replied. "And Vernon seems completely disengaged—not that interested in Arleta or the baby. Honestly, Arleta didn't seem that interested in the baby either. I mean, she nursed her, but everything she did seemed robotic, as if she knew what was expected but there was no feeling to it."

"I think she has a pretty flat personality. . . ." Delores's voice trailed off. "Arleta only came to two prenatal appointments, both times by herself. And I haven't met Vernon."

"Well, see what you think when you go visit her tomorrow." I shivered. "Should I take Uncle Seth's pickup back now? Or wait until later?"

"Wait. I just spoke with him, and he's feeling worse. If you need to use it to run an errand or anything, feel free."

"All right," I said. "Let me know how Arleta is doing."

She assured me she would and then hung up. I checked to

confirm the battery on my phone was still charging and then headed back to Mammi's.

As I drove through the winter wonderland, thoughts of my mother returned. She'd had some friends from the organic farm where she'd worked who used a midwife for their children's births, so when she realized she was pregnant with me, she chose to do the same. Then she checked out every library book on pregnancy, childbirth, postnatal care, and caring for a newborn that she could find.

I was born on a hot July night in the cabin where Dad still lived, only now with Joy and Karlie. Mom's friends had gathered on the front porch in support, while Dad massaged Mom's lower back in the living room, with her midwife, Hazel, standing watch. After my mother labored for nearly thirty hours, I finally slipped from her body.

Mom said it was the holiest moment of her life. She was changed. Completely transformed by motherhood. She scooped me up and held me to her chest, not letting anyone else even see me.

"You were perfect," she would coo when she told me the story.

Two years later, she lost a baby, a stillborn little boy. She was heartbroken. After that her midwife—who was in her fifties—asked if Mom wanted to train with her, to be a partner. Hazel saw Mom had both an interest and an aptitude for the business. Mom embraced becoming a midwife, sure it was her calling. She took classes, correspondence courses, and assisted Hazel. Step by step, she grew more experienced. By the time I was old enough to go to school, Mom was going out on births alone. She decided to homeschool me so she wouldn't have to worry about after-school childcare. I went with her, whenever she was needed.

Dad continued to work on the ranch, herding, branding, and calving. Sometimes I'd go to work with him too, and I even thought, for a short time, about being a cowgirl. But that didn't last long. I knew I wanted to be a midwife like my mom. As I grew older, I still loved going to Indiana and spending time with Mammi, but I also loved returning home. Not only did I miss Mom and Dad, but I missed the newborn babies too.

I'd never be a big sister—Mom finally told me only a miracle would make me one—so I poured the love I had stored up inside of me for a sibling onto those babies. It wasn't until after Mom died that I realized she'd done the same thing. She'd poured all of her grief for the baby she'd lost and the ones she'd never have into those babies and mamas and their husbands and the children they already had.

She turned grief into love.

She did all that after she'd already poured so much into Dad and me. She never sat down. She was always on the go. At the time, I thought it was because she was such a good person, such a good mom. But now I wondered if that fast pace was a mask for her insecurities and fears. She didn't have the best example of being a wife and mother. Did she fear becoming like her own mother? Did she think that working nonstop both at home and as a midwife would protect all of us from that? I think, looking back on the tension between them from an adult perspective, that all Dad wanted was more time with her—not the unpredictable life that we ended up living. He'd been raised with the certainty of his mother's availability. With the security of community. With a schedule set around chores and seasons and farm work. He had that at his job but not at home.

It wasn't that Mom shouldn't have worked as a midwife—she was amazing at it—but maybe she shouldn't have taken on so many clients. Maybe she needed better boundaries. Not that I blamed her death on any of that.

It did snow in Grass Valley, where we lived, but not nearly as much as it did east of town, up on the pass. That night Mom didn't arrive at that cabin, Dad and I both stayed silent as he drove as fast as he could up the mountain. We saw the sheriff's lights before we saw Mom's car. It had gone over the guardrail, straight down a ravine.

As my heart raced at the memory, I slowed Uncle Seth's pickup, signaled to turn, and eased down Mammi's driveway, only to find her shoveling the walkway leading to the house. I parked and jumped down, leaving the bags in the pickup. "I'll do that!" I called.

She shaded her eyes against the rising sun. "How is Arleta?"

"Fine," I answered, taking the shovel from her. "So is the baby—a little girl."

I wouldn't tell her about Miriam disappearing. If I'd learned one thing from Mom when it came to midwifing, it was not to talk about any client's business.

"The neighbor boy who does the chores didn't have time to shovel this morning. Are you sure you don't mind doing it?" she asked.

"Of course not."

"Then I'll go start breakfast."

That sounded like a fair trade. I was starving.

I soon grew warm under my down coat. It had been years since I'd shoveled snow—since I'd moved away from Grass Valley, in fact. There was no snow to shovel in Los Angeles or San Francisco.

I kept moving—bend down, scoop, stand up, fling—until I reached the driveway. My eyes watered. It took me a minute to realize I was crying. I brushed my gloved hand against my face. Arleta was fine. The baby was fine.

The last baby, the one Mom had been on her way to deliver, wasn't fine. He was born with the cord wrapped around his neck, something Mom would have most likely been able to slip over his head, but the father didn't know what to do.

I brushed my tears away, tears for Mom and that dead baby in the cabin on Blue Pass. But also tears of relief for Arleta and her new little girl.

When I'd finished shoveling, I grabbed Delores's bags from the pickup and trudged into the house. Mammi had coffee and oatmeal ready. After she led us in a silent prayer, she asked, "How are the roads?"

"Not cleared yet," I answered as I ate. "I slid a bit in the pickup coming home. Last night too—before it broke down."

"Oh no," Mammi said. "What did you do?"

"I got a ride-share. Do you know what that is?"

She nodded. "I know you have to use a smartphone and have an app for it." She smiled. "I just use the 'dumb phone' in the shed and call for a driver."

I laughed. "Do you have church today?"

She shook her head. "It's our off Sunday." The Amish met every other Sunday for services. Often they'd visit a church in another district on their off Sundays or visit family and friends. But Mammi hadn't made any such plans.

I ended up sleeping most of the day—and all night too. When I awoke, I thought of Ryan first. Thoughts of our last phone call played in my head over and over.

The next morning, when I came down for breakfast, Mammi said, "I'd like to go to the quilting circle this afternoon, but it snowed more during the night. I don't think I can take the buggy unless the plows come through."

"I can take you in Uncle Seth's pickup," I said. "Delores said he's under the weather and to go ahead and use it if I needed to." As long as it started again.

"Denki," she said. "It begins at one. I'll call Seth and make sure he doesn't need it back today."

"Ask him how he's feeling and if he needs anything." I took another bite of oatmeal. Of course she would want to check with Seth and make sure it was all right to use the pickup. She didn't want to take advantage of anyone, not even her brother. I'd need to tell him at some point about the engine trouble, but I wouldn't bother him with it now. If it broke down on the way to the quilting circle, I could always use the ride-share app.

Or call Kenny M.—whoever he was.

CHAPTER 5

I ended up accidentally taking another nap that morning. I'd curled up on Mammi's couch, and the next thing I knew, I'd woken up with a start, cold and unsure of where I was, with that hollow feeling I'd struggled with since Mom had died.

Had I been dreaming about her? About her accident? About finding her that day?

I fished around for my cell phone. 12:15. The battery was at three percent. I'd charge it in the pickup again. Maybe I could get it up to ten.

As I stood, my phone rang. It was the florist again. I let it go to voicemail. I'd deal with it once my phone was charged.

Mammi had a bowl of chicken noodle soup ready for me when I stepped into the kitchen. "I called Seth," she said. "He wondered if we could stop by the store for cough syrup and crackers. I have soup for him too." She patted the top of a jar on the counter.

Ten minutes later, we were in the pickup, which luckily started on the second try. Once we were on the highway, I passed two Amish men on bicycles, their stocking caps pulled down over their ears, and then a buggy driven by a young woman. They all seemed to be undaunted by the twenty degree weather. Farmers were outside, breaking ice in watering troughs, spreading bales of hay, and checking on their livestock.

No more snow had fallen while I slept, and the plows had cleared the country roads. Mammi wore a wool coat, and I guessed she had long underwear on under her dress and long socks too. She wore boots and mittens, and had a scarf wound around her neck. She sat with her hands folded in her lap, leaning forward just a bit. I double-checked that her seat belt was fastened. It was.

The quilt shop was about a three-mile drive from Mammi's house, far enough that the thought of her going there in her buggy alone and in the dead of winter bothered me. It sounded as if she went several times per week.

As we approached the driveway of Plain Patterns, an Amish man on a tractor with a snowplow attached to the front of it exited the parking lot of the shop. Two large mounds of snow sat at the back of the lot.

"That's Jane's brother, Andy." Mammi pointed to a small house across the lane. "And that's where Jane lives." It was a cute cottage with window boxes and a wide porch. "Her brother built the quilt shop a few years ago. Before that, she hung a shingle in front of her house. Her living room was the store back then."

I frowned. That sounded crowded to me. "That's the farmhouse over there." Mammi pointed across the lane to a large white house back in a grove of trees. "The original house, built in the late 1830s, was up here, closer to the road."

I whistled. "It's quite the property, isn't it? With quite the history, I bet."

"Jah," Mammi said. "No doubt, Jane will tell you more about it someday."

I waited for Andy to pull out onto the lane, and then I turned into the parking lot. There were two buggies parked in front of the shop, sans horses. I guessed they'd been taken to the small stable near the side of the shop. Thankful Mammi didn't have to deal with any of that today, I parked, turned off the pickup, and then opened the door and jumped down, scurrying around to Mammi's door to help her. But by the time I arrived, she already had both of her feet firmly planted on the ground.

Just then, a black buggy pulled by a black horse approached. I was struck by the contrast of the two against the snow-white background. I couldn't think of anything as graceful and comforting as a horse pulling an Amish buggy. The beat of the hooves against the pavement had always soothed my soul. Even though it was freezing outside, I stayed still for a moment so I could hear it. The horse, head held high, trotted past, a reminder of the steadiness and predictability of Amish life.

Mammi smiled up at me. "I'm so glad you came today. You met Jane when you were little, but I'm pleased you'll get to see her again."

I didn't remember meeting her, but once we were inside and Mammi introduced us, she seemed familiar. Jane wore a navy blue dress with a white apron. I guessed she was in her mid-sixties or so. She was slim and probably five foot four. Her silvery hair was tucked under a white *Kapp*, except for the strip at the front. She wore a pair of reading glasses attached to a plain blue cord around her neck.

Her complexion was smooth and her eyes a deep brown. I could still see a hint of the girl she once was in her lively smile, as she greeted me. "Welcome, Savannah," she said. "I remember you from when you were small." She held her hand to her hip and then raised it to the top of her head, indicating I'd grown up. She grinned. "It's so good to have you join us."

I thanked her and then glanced around the shop as she and Mammi spoke. The store was filled with bolts of fabric, thread, patterns, and beautiful quilts that hung from racks. A wood stove, located in the far corner, provided heat. In the back room was a small kitchen area and a quilting frame surrounded by chairs, with a large queen-size quilt stretched over it.

I didn't recognize the pattern, but that wasn't surprising. My expertise didn't go beyond the usual log cabin or double ring patterns. Now I only looked at quilts on Pinterest instead of making them.

Turning toward Jane, I asked, "What's the pattern called?"

"Hearth and home," she said. "It's a little fancy, but I think we can get away with it."

Each block was made of six squares in the central part and three squares and four triangles in the border. It was definitely more complicated than a basic block quilt. The colors were all shades of blue, with just one patterned fabric that looked like forget-me-nots. I exhaled. They were Mom's favorite flower.

"Who's it for?" I asked.

"I don't know yet." Jane smiled at me. "But I will soon enough. The Lord always reveals who needs a quilt, a specific quilt, when the time is right."

Two Amish women, both probably in their early fifties, were already quilting, pushing tiny needles through squares of the forget-me-not fabric.

I kept my coat on and introduced myself to the two.

"Hallo, Savannah," the closest one said to me. "I'm Phyllis Raber." She was plump with a full face and a wide smile.

The other woman poked her head around Phyllis and said, "I'm Lois Shelter." She had a sharp chin and gray eyes.

I sat down next to Phyllis and pulled a needle and thread

from the solid blue fabric in front of me. I hoped I could still make tiny stitches.

I started, following the pencil marks on the quilt top. When Jane and Mammi joined us, Lois said, "I heard Arleta had her baby the night before last. A little girl."

Neither Mammi nor I said anything, but Jane did. "Did everything go all right?"

"As far as I know." Lois looked at me. "I heard an Englischer by the name of Savannah delivered the baby because Delores has the flu."

My face grew warm, even in the cold room. "Delores is my cousin." I wasn't sure what the HIPPA rules were when it came to midwifery in Amish country, but I didn't want to reveal anything.

Lois nodded, as if my reaction explained everything. Then she continued, "I also heard Miriam has gone missing."

Jane peered over the lenses of her reading glasses. "What?"

Lois glanced at me. I redirected my eyes to the quilt.

"And Tommy Miller was the last person to see her."

"Tommy?" The needle slipped out of my fingers. "Not Kenny Miller?" Immediately, I feared I'd said too much.

"No, it was Tommy *posing* as Kenny," Lois said. "And now he's suspected of kidnapping Miriam."

Jane gasped, and so did I.

Wouldn't I have recognized Tommy? He'd been my childhood friend. But maybe his coat, scarf, and hat had concealed who he was. Or maybe I wouldn't have recognized him anyway. It had been thirteen years since I'd last seen him.

"That's impossible." Mammi was just as surprised as Jane and I were. "Is there any proof?"

"I heard it from the bishop's cousin." Lois kept her eyes on the quilt top. "And it doesn't surprise me one bit. Tommy's not nearly as trustworthy as people think."

No one responded to Lois's accusations. Mammi and I continued stitching, while Jane stepped to the front of the shop to wait on a customer.

Perhaps Phyllis felt uncomfortable with the silence—or maybe she felt the need to come to Lois's defense—but she finally asked, "Savannah, did you know Tommy?"

I nodded. "When we were children, we used to help each other with our chores." We also rode horses together, fished in the pond on the other side of the woods, and raced bicycles down the road. For five years, he was like the big brother I never had. He was always kind to me and protective, in a respectful and non-intrusive way. In fact, when I first met Ryan, he reminded me of Tommy. Both were leaders who treated others with dignity and empathy. Or so I'd thought.

I'd been wrong about Ryan. Perhaps I'd been wrong about Tommy too.

When I was thirteen and Tommy was fifteen, I arrived at Mammi's farm, ready for another six weeks of being his shadow.

But Tommy had changed. His voice was deep, his chin scruffy, and he'd grown a foot taller. It soon became obvious he didn't want anything to do with me. He wasn't mean about it, but he avoided me as best he could. A couple of times I saw him in a buggy with other boys his age, and several times I saw him walking with an Amish girl, Sadie Yoder, who lived about a mile away.

I was crushed. Jah, Tommy had been my first love. But of course I never told him. I'd never told anyone.

The next summer, he was away working as a farmhand for an uncle in Michigan. And the summer after that, when I was fourteen, he was on his Rumschpringe and driving an old Thunderbird. One time I was biking down the lane and nearly ran into the fence trying to get out of his way.

That was my last summer going to Mammi's. For the next three years I assisted Mom, working my way into an apprenticeship. When I spoke with Mammi on the phone, I never asked about Tommy, and she never offered any information. I figured he'd married years ago and probably had a bowl cut, a beard, and a buggy full of kids by now.

"Savannah?" Mammi was talking to me.

"Sorry," I answered. "What did you say?"

"Was Tommy the driver who picked you up?"

"I don't think so. . . ." But, honestly, I couldn't be sure. The driver wore a scarf and a stocking cap, I hadn't seen Tommy for over a decade, and I'd never seen him as a grown man. And it was dark—really dark. Perhaps if I'd been expecting someone named Tommy, I would have recognized him. Perhaps my mind was tricked by the name Kenny.

"Don't you think if it was Tommy that he would have recognized you?" Mammi asked. "Did you tell him your name?"

"He knew it from the app," I said.

"Well, he wouldn't necessarily have admitted to knowing you," Lois said. "Not if he was pretending to be Kenny."

That was true. "Did I ever meet Kenny?" I asked Mammi.

She squinted a little, as if looking back through the years. "I don't believe so," she answered. "He moved here from Michigan after you stopped coming out for the summer."

"Kenny was a bad influence on Tommy," Lois said. "Seems like he still is—or maybe its vice versa now."

"I don't know anything about Kenny," Mammi said. "But Tommy had a good heart as a boy. I can't believe he'd kidnap Arleta's daughter."

"Did Tommy join the church?" I asked.

"No," Lois answered. "And he was gone from the area for several years. Lots of years, actually. Seven or eight."

"He worked all over," Phyllis said. "New Mexico. Arizona. Nevada—Las Vegas, even. Mostly on the move, usually with Kenny at his side, from what I understand."

I glanced over at Mammi, and she nodded. She'd never told me he was so close to California. I would have liked to have seen him.

Lois picked up the story. "Then they came back here in September. Tommy had been working construction in the fall and then started on an interior renovation project when the weather turned bad."

"What about Kenny?" I asked. "Besides being a driver?"

Lois and Phyllis exchanged glances. Finally, Lois said, "There have been a few rumors. . . ."

My stomach sank. They must be pretty bad rumors if she was mentioning them.

The two exchanged glances again, and then Phyllis whispered, "There have been rumors about selling drugs."

"Oh. . . ." Amish in the area were sensitive about that topic. Not long before I stopped spending summers in Indiana, a documentary called *Devil's Playground* came out about Plain youth in the next county over, and the Amish, even though they didn't actually see the film, heard all about it. It explored a small group of Amish Youngie on their Rumschpringe who drove cars and partied with large groups of other Amish youth, some of whom came from as far away as Montana. One boy even sold drugs. There were those in Amish communities nearby who feared the documentary would lead people to believe all Amish Youngie behaved that way.

I'd watched the documentary with Dad back home and asked him if the kids he grew up with partied like that. *"Pretty much, although I never had enough money to buy a car while I was on the farm."* He looked me in the eye. *"I never had money to buy drugs either, and even if I had, I wouldn't have."*

That was about as much as he ever said about his growing-up years, although the last summer I went to Indiana, he told me not to go to any Amish Youngie parties. *"I'll ground you when you get home if I find out you did"* was all he said. I didn't go to any parties. Then again, no one asked me to either.

"How old is Kenny?" I asked.

Lois answered, "A year younger than Tommy."

So if Tommy was twenty-nine now, then Kenny would be twenty-eight. Way too old to be on his Rumschpringe. Perhaps selling drugs had become a way of life for him.

The subject changed to Arleta. Her first husband had died three years ago of complications from diabetes, and she married Vernon a year ago, moving from Newbury Township back to the Nappanee area where she'd grown up.

"Miriam's been running around all year," Lois said, "and Joshua just started." She shook her head. "If only these kids knew how much heartache they could save themselves if they'd just join the church and quit living such foolishness."

Jane smiled kindly. "But it's only through free will that we can truly come to know the Lord," she said. "Running around serves its purpose."

It hadn't for Tommy and Kenny, though, if neither had joined the church. It surprised me that Tommy hadn't. I vividly remembered our conversations about him wanting to farm, get married, and have a bunch of kids, because the way he talked always made me sad. Because I knew I would never be the girl Tommy wanted to marry. I'd always be the Englisch girl who visited in the summer. The outsider. The one who didn't belong.

But it sounded as if Tommy didn't belong anymore either.

JANE WAS UP and down, helping customers as we quilted. After two hours, she insisted we take a break and get a snack. I was surprised at how healthy it was. Carrots and celery sticks, apple slices, hard cheese—that Jane had made—and slices of homemade whole wheat bread. There wasn't a single sweet baked good, what the Amish were famous for, on the kitchen counter.

"I'm trying to eat healthier," Jane said. "In the spring, I'll plant a garden here on the property so the quilters will have produce to take home. Not all of them have access to a garden."

"Some of your quilters aren't Amish?" I was surprised by that.

"No," Jane answered. "But even all the Amish ones don't have gardens. Some live in town now."

Mammi had told me that more and more Amish were taking jobs in manufacturing, as there wasn't enough farmland for each subsequent generation. Nappanee was known for its RV factories, which took a hit during the recession, but most had recovered and were back in full swing now.

"I'm also hoping to include some circles on preserving food," Jane said. "It'll be much like the quilting circle, but we'll be working together to promote canning, drying, and freezing food. I think those will be especially popular with some of my Englisch customers."

I nodded. Of course Mammi canned, but so did my mother. Most of my friends, however, had never learned about food preservation and thought of it as something Pinterest had invented.

Ryan thought it quaint but sweet that I knew all of those basic things. *"If the preppers are right and the apocalypse is around the corner,"* he'd say, *"we'll be fine, thanks to you."* He'd grown up in Santa Monica and liked to say his family was middle class. They weren't. They were wealthy. Not obscenely so, but enough that he was well traveled and didn't have any student loans.

Because of that, there were all sorts of things Ryan did that I didn't—until I met him. He'd rather order a ride than ask for one. He had lots of acquaintances but few friends. He would have found it amusing that I was quilting with a group of Amish women who were constrained by patterns and colors. He'd be dismayed to learn that the quilt we were working on was actually considered quite innovative, that in some districts using what was considered a fancy pattern would be entirely prohibited.

When he'd found out my grandmother was Amish, he'd said, *"But you're not that close to her, right?"* I'd assured him that I was—that I loved her very much and she was one of my favorite people in the whole world, even though I hadn't seen her for years.

For a moment I felt sorry for Ryan. I swallowed hard as I dished up carrots, celery, apple slices, cheese, and bread.

I glanced out the window. More snow was falling, and I figured we should go soon. We still needed to stop by the store for Uncle Seth. But I hated to leave. Mammi seemed the happiest that I'd seen her since I'd arrived.

I was enjoying myself too. There was comfort in being with the other women, and even though I found myself thinking about Ryan, I wasn't obsessing about him the way I did when I was alone.

Lois brought up the topic of Miriam again. "I sure hope they find that missing girl."

"I imagine with Miriam missing that Arleta needs some help," Jane said. "I'd be happy to make a casserole, although I don't know that I can run it over there."

"I could do that," I said.

"Denki." Jane smiled at me. "Will you be coming to the quilting circle on Wednesday? I could give it to you then."

I glanced at Mammi. She said, "I'd like to come that day, if it works for you."

"All right." I might as well come back for the quilting circle and to collect the casserole. Hopefully by then Miriam would be found and Tommy's name cleared.

And I'd have a few job possibilities lined up.

CHAPTER 6

Mammi waited in the pickup while I delivered the soup and items from the grocery story to Uncle Seth. He met me at the front door, wearing pajamas, a heavy robe, and slippers. His eyes were dull and red. I guessed that he had the respiratory flu.

As a conservative Mennonite, he lived a pretty austere life. No TV or computer. Modest furniture. No carpet or rugs. But he had his pickup, plus electricity, and a telephone in the house.

After I'd said hello and put the soup in the fridge, I wrote down my cell phone number on a pad of paper on the counter so he wouldn't have to look it up in his address book. My phone was up to twenty percent from charging it in the pickup.

He kept his distance from me as I said, "Your pickup stalled on my way to the birth. It's been fine since then, but any ideas why it would do that?"

"Delores gassed it up last," he said. "She probably put in the wrong kind of fuel."

I tilted my head, trying to figure out the connection.

"It's because the engine is old. It needs a richer fuel mixture, especially in the cold. Or maybe there's a leak around the carburetor or a hose." He shrugged. "Fill up the tank the rest of the way with premium, and buy an octane booster at the station and add that too."

Mammi told me once, in a joking way, that she thought Seth had left the Amish because of his love of engines and all things mechanical. Perhaps she was right.

I drove straight to the nearest gas station, where I filled up the gas tank and added the booster, and then we headed back to the farm. For supper, Mammi and I ate more chicken noodle soup. Afterward, we sat in the living room, where Mammi picked up a farming magazine to read. Not wanting to use any more of my phone battery, I picked up an old copy of *The Budget Newspaper*, which served the "Amish-Mennonite Communities Throughout the Americas," and thumbed through it. I'd read *The Budget* as a child, and I found it just as comforting now as I had back then. The columns, which made up most of the newspaper, were about visits from family members and friends, new births, the crisp weather, the full moon, and weddings. There was a familiar pattern about the columns no matter who'd written them, whether it was an Amish man from Florida or a Mennonite woman from Alaska. Some of the people mentioned in the columns were only identified by their first names, as if the entire Anabaptist population of the US would know their last names.

I read column after column, aware of what a waste of time I would have thought this was two weeks ago, but time didn't have the same value to me now. I turned the page and saw a column from Nappanee. I scanned to the bottom to see the author. *Wanda Miller.* That was Tommy's mother.

I raised my head. "Wanda writes for *The Budget*?"

"Jah, she's been doing it for years. Jane used to, but she was offered a monthly column for the local paper and started doing that instead."

"Nice." I loved what these older Amish women did. Quilting. Writing. Making soup and casseroles for their neighbors. They were an inspiration.

"Where are Tommy's parents living now?"

"His father passed away a few years ago."

I put my hand to my chest. Poor Wanda. Poor Tommy.

"Jah." Mammi looked up from her book. "He was only sixty-nine. They had moved to the Dawdi Haus on Ervin's farm—he's the oldest boy."

"What about Tommy?" I asked. "Where is he living?"

"In town." She moved her bookmark to the page she was on.

"Whom does he live with?"

"With Kenny, I think. And a little boy," Mammi answered.

"A little boy? Whose little boy?"

Mammi shrugged. "I haven't asked."

"Tommy's a dad?"

She shrugged again and glanced back down at her magazine. No doubt she didn't want to gossip. "What about a wife?"

Mammi shook her head. "Just the boy."

"What happened?"

Mammi shrugged. "He came back from Nevada with the little boy. He's just a toddler. Wanda keeps him while Tommy works."

"What happened to his wife?" I asked a second time.

Mammi answered, "I'm not certain there was a wife."

My phone started to buzz in the pocket of my sweatshirt. It was the florist again. I'd forgotten to listen to her voicemail. I ducked into the bathroom and said a quiet, "Hello."

"Savannah," she said. "Listen, Ryan hasn't returned my call. I need to go ahead and charge your card."

"Can you wait? I'll try him." I didn't want to try to collect all of the money from Ryan to pay off my card. "Just until to-morrow," I added.

"Well . . ."

My phone buzzed again. It was the photographer. "I have to go. I have another call. . . ."

"Give me an update tomorrow," the florist said. "As soon as you can."

After I thanked her, I accepted the other call. "Hey, Savan-nah, sorry to bother you . . ."

Same story. Ryan's card didn't go through for him either. What was going on?

The photographer agreed to wait a day too. When I came back to the living room, my phone battery was back down to ten percent. Mammi glanced up again. "Everything all right?"

"I think so," I answered. "Just a few wrinkles to iron out about the wedding."

She nodded as if it were all something she was familiar with and went back to her reading.

THE NEXT MORNING, as I dressed, my phone rang again, which seemed way too early for any calls from West Coast vendors. I'd left Ryan a voicemail and then sent him a text the night before, so I hoped it was him.

Of course it wasn't him. What was I thinking?

It was Delores. I groaned and then composed myself and answered the call.

"My fever's back," she said. "Could you go check on Arleta and the baby?"

"Was she all right yesterday?"

Delores coughed. "I never got out there. Listen, I wouldn't

ask but one of my backup midwives is out of town and the other has strep throat. I just need to know everything's all right."

I thought of the casserole Jane wanted to send to Arleta. I wished I had some sort of food I could take now and decided to ask Mammi if she had some extra soup she could spare.

"I'll go," I said. "What time?"

"After eight. I'll leave a message, which they probably won't get." Delores paused a moment to cough. "But they won't be surprised to see you, or at least I don't think they will be."

"What about your other clients?" I asked.

"I've rescheduled all of my appointments for next week. Thankfully, I don't have another birth until the middle of the month. This will be the last favor I ask, I promise."

Once I'd ended the call with Delores, I realized I had a voicemail from the previous night. It was from the caterer. Same story. Ryan's credit card had been declined.

I called him again. Of course he didn't answer, so I left him a testy message. "Call all of the vendors and make this right," I hissed. "You can't dump me and then expect me to cover for you." I ended the message without saying good-bye. As if he'd care.

I tried to log in to my bank through the app on my phone to check my credit card, but the app wasn't working and wouldn't reload. I'd have to do it once I had Wi-Fi at the coffee shop.

Mammi had more than a gallon jar of soup for me to take to Arleta and her family. She also had a loaf of bread and a cherry pie too. "Tell Arleta I'm praying for her," Mammi said as she handed me the box of food. "And that new baby."

I told her I would. Once I'd put the box on the floor of the pickup and the midwife bag on the passenger seat, I called Uncle Seth to see if he needed anything. He answered, his voice barely above a whisper. "I'm doing all right," he said. "I'll call this afternoon if I can think of anything."

"What about your pickup?" I asked. "Do you need it back?"

"No. You keep it for another couple of days, as long as it's running all right. Any more problems?"

I assured him there hadn't been.

The temperature had risen to twenty-eight degrees, a virtual heat wave, and the pickup started on the first try. I immediately plugged in my phone and then turned around in Mammi's snow-rutted driveway and headed for the lane and then the highway. No more snow had fallen, so the roads were fine. I arrived at Arleta's house just after eight to find a sheriff's car in their driveway. I debated whether to leave and return later or go up to the door, but I decided not to waste the trip.

I gathered my bags and the food and knocked on the door. Finally, an older Amish man I didn't recognize opened it.

"I'm Savannah Mast," I said. "I'm here to see Arleta."

He tugged on his long gray beard. "Can you come back later?"

"No." Three minutes ago I might have said yes, before I'd ventured up the back steps.

"All right, then," he said. "Come on in. But you'll have to wait your turn."

As he stepped through the door, he added, "I'm David Deiner, the bishop. A deputy is here about Miriam."

I hoped it wasn't with bad news.

Vernon, Arleta, Joshua, and the deputy all sat around the kitchen table. Everyone but the baby. And Miriam.

The deputy stood, and I extended my hand. "Savannah Mast," I said. "I'm here to check on Arleta and the baby."

He gripped my hand. "I'm Deputy Bradley Rogers, with the Elkhart County Sheriff's Office." He appeared to be in his early fifties. He was medium height and big boned. He wore his gray hair short, not quite buzzed, and his brown eyes were stern.

As he finally let go of my hand, he said speculatively, "So you're the midwife."

I wasn't sure how to respond. Would he arrest me for malpractice? I hadn't thought of that when I decided to come in now instead of coming back later. "I was helping my cousin out," I said. "She has the flu."

"You were here the night Miriam disappeared?"

"I'd just arrived."

He sat back down. "You should go ahead and do what you need to do with Arleta and the baby, and then I'll have some questions for you."

It was a statement, not a request. "All right." I turned toward Arleta. "I'll follow you." I left my coat on because I guessed she'd be most comfortable in the bedroom.

On the way through the living room, she lifted the baby from the bassinet and shuffled down the hall. I stopped in the bathroom to wash my hands and then braced myself for the cold of the bedroom, but the door was open, and it wasn't nearly as bad as it had been on Saturday night.

"How have you been feeling?" I asked as I rubbed my hands together.

"All right." Arleta put the baby, who was now awake, on the bed and sat down beside her.

"How is the nursing going?" I pulled out the scales from the bag as I spoke and then slipped on a pair of gloves.

"My milk hasn't come in."

"Right." I unwrapped the baby. "It should come in tomorrow or the next day. Is she nursing regularly? Getting the colostrum?"

Arleta nodded.

The baby had lost a few ounces, which was expected. Her reflexes were all good, and she responded to my voice. Her posture and muscle tone were appropriate. She had a bruise on the crown of her head, which wasn't unusual, especially considering how fast she flew out of the birth canal. Her lungs were clear and her respiration good.

"Have you decided on a name?" I asked.

Arleta shook her head. She had dark circles under her eyes. With Miriam missing, it must be difficult for her to think about other things.

"Any word from Miriam?"

Arleta shook her head and then sighed. I wanted to take her hand, but I didn't think she'd be comfortable with that.

I rewrapped the baby, held her close for a long moment, and soaked in her sweet essence. There was nothing in life as incredible as newborns. Mom used to say they were the closest we had to angels on earth. Newborn babies definitely had an ethereal quality, a holy presence, that perhaps only a death from old age came close to. No wonder Mom had loved being a midwife. No wonder I'd wanted to be one. Had I made a mistake not pursuing it?

FIFTEEN MINUTES LATER, I left Arleta nursing the baby in the bedroom, washed my hands in the bathroom, and then returned to the kitchen.

"Have a seat," Deputy Rogers said.

I slid into a chair next to Joshua, who appeared very uncomfortable. He shifted away from me and moved his hands from his lap to the tabletop. His fingernails were chewed to the quick.

Deputy Rogers asked me what I saw when I arrived that night. I told him about a young woman running past me and jumping into the Jeep. I looked up times on my phone—when I'd called for the ride, what time the baby was born, and when

I'd left the next morning. I added that Joshua and Vernon had arrived after the baby was born but before it was time to start the milking.

"Had you ever seen Miriam before that night?" the deputy asked.

I shook my head.

He slid two photos toward me. "Do you recognize either of these men?"

I nodded, pointing at the one of a man with a goatee. It was Tommy. "This was the driver, although I'm not sure he had a goatee. I couldn't see his chin because a scarf was wrapped around his neck and lower face."

"Have you ever seen the other man?" he asked.

I shook my head.

"Had you seen the driver before that night?"

I nodded. "Yes, but not for years, and I didn't recognize him that night because he was bundled up. And because I was expecting a Kenny M.—not Tommy Miller."

"Do you know Tommy Miller?"

"I used to," I answered. "We were childhood friends."

"How long has it been since you've seen him?" Deputy Rogers asked.

"Over a decade." I paused a moment. "Thirteen years, to be exact."

"Was Tommy wild back then, when you knew him?"

I shook my head. "Not that I knew of. He was always very kind to me."

"Well, lucky you." The deputy's eyes narrowed.

I was surprised at his comment but didn't respond.

He continued anyway. "I was well acquainted with both Tommy and Kenny when they were teenagers and in their early twenties. I was more than relieved when they headed west."

Clearly, Tommy wasn't who I thought he was. I met the deputy's gaze. "Do you expect foul play? Have you put out an Amber Alert?"

"Miriam is legally an adult," he said. "There's not a lot we can do. But I'll question Tommy Miller to see what he has to say."

"What about Kenny Miller?" I asked. "Have you questioned him?"

The deputy shook his head. "He seems to have disappeared entirely. At least Tommy's still in the area."

"She has his number," Vernon said.

The deputy raised his eyebrows.

"I saved it in my contacts in case I couldn't find a ride home from the birth. I can give it to you." He hadn't answered when I'd called him, though, so I wasn't sure if he'd answer the deputy's call, or if he even still had the phone. I opened up my contacts and rattled off the number for the deputy.

"Tommy's mother can also help you find him," the bishop said. "She lives close to here."

"Does Tommy live with her?"

The bishop shook his head. "I believe he lives in town, in an apartment."

Deputy Rogers made a note and then turned to Vernon. "I'll track him down." He turned toward Joshua. "Are you sure you don't have any more information to give me? Names of people your sister hung out with? Anything like that?"

Without looking up, he shook his head.

"Joshua," Vernon commanded. "Look at the officer and speak out loud."

Joshua did as he was told, but he had a sour expression on his blushing face. "No, I don't have any more information for you."

I doubted that was true, and by the strained expression on the deputy's face, I guessed he did too.

After he gathered up the photos and his notebook, Deputy Rogers stood and extended his hand to Vernon. "I'll leave a message on your phone by this afternoon or stop by."

Vernon shook his hand but didn't say anything.

"Take care of your wife," the deputy said as he slipped into his parka.

"Oh, Arleta's doing fine," Vernon said. "She's as hardy as they come."

I cringed. The deputy didn't, though; he simply nodded at Vernon and bid Joshua and the bishop good-bye too. He then turned to me and said, "I'll walk you out."

I said my farewells and followed the deputy to the kitchen door. Once we'd both reached the bottom of the steps, he motioned toward the pickup. "Keep going."

He stopped on the other side, presumably so no one could overhear our conversation. "What are your impressions of the family?" he asked. "Functional? Dysfunctional?"

"I don't know that I'm qualified to comment on that," I said. "I don't know them. I only witnessed them on one stressful night." I hesitated a moment and said, "And in my estimation there's not really any such thing as a fully functional family." My family appeared functional, but through the years, I realized we had our problems too. "There are only dysfunctional families, some less so than others."

He wrinkled his nose. "Fair enough. If you hear anything, let me know."

Again, it was a command. "I most likely won't see them again. And I'll be leaving Nappanee soon." At least I hoped so.

He took a card from the pocket of his coat and handed it to me. "Then call me if you hear anything. I know midwives often come across information that others don't."

I took his card, not bothering to correct him that I wasn't a midwife.

Then he took out his little book. "And could I get your number? Just in case I have a follow-up question?"

I rattled off my phone number, hoping he wouldn't call. I knew he was doing his job, but something about the man left me unsettled.

CHAPTER 7

On the way home, as I charged my phone again, a call came in from the leader of the four-string quartet we'd booked for the reception. I slammed my hand against the steering wheel. If I wasn't in Amish country, I might have cursed. I held my tongue, although I wasn't sure I could for long. Had I ever really known Ryan? How could I have been so easily deceived? He appeared kind and caring. I never would have guessed he'd treat me so poorly. Never.

When I pulled into Mammi's driveway, I gasped. A Jeep was parked where the pickup had been earlier. I pulled up behind it.

Was Tommy Miller in Mammi's kitchen?

I lugged the bag up the back steps and to the mudroom, placed it on the shelf, and hung up my coat. Next, I ventured into the kitchen. Sitting at the table were Mammi, Wanda Miller, and Tommy, who held a toddler on his lap. The little boy looked up at me and waved. He had big brown eyes, light mahogany skin, a headful of curly dark hair, and a big smile on his face.

My heart melted as I waved back.

Tommy turned his head toward me. "Hello, Savannah."

I waved at him too. "Nice to see you again."

He smiled. "Ditto."

"Did you know it was me the other night?"

He nodded.

"But you didn't say anything."

He nodded again. "You didn't either."

"Because I thought you were Kenny M. I didn't recognize you."

He stroked his goatee. "Sorry."

"Who's this?" I smiled at the little boy again.

"Mason," Tommy answered.

"Hey, Mason." I knelt down so I could be eye level with him and held up my hand for a high five. "I'm Savannah. How old are you, buddy?"

He slapped my palm and laughed, then looked at Tommy. "Dada."

Tommy smiled. "He says he's pleased to meet you, and he wants you to know that he's eighteen months."

"Sit down and have a cup of coffee," Mammi said to me. "We're all just catching up. Tommy didn't have to work today and came over to say hello." I wondered if his intention was to say hello to Mammi or to me. Or maybe both of us. I didn't ask.

I headed to the stove and grabbed the pot. "Anyone need a refill?"

"I'll take one." Tommy moved his cup away from Mason. I filled it and then filled a cup for myself and sat down next to Wanda, across from Tommy. He appeared to be a natural with the little boy. I couldn't help but wonder who the mother was—and where she was.

"So, what have you been up to?" Tommy asked me.

"Oh, you know, freelance midwifery in the middle of the night during a blizzard. That sort of thing."

He laughed.

"Why didn't you say who you really were?"

He cringed. "I feel bad about that. I happened to hear Kenny's phone buzz and glanced at it. I would have ignored it, but when I saw the name *Savannah*, I thought it might be you. My Mamm had said you were coming for a visit, and I didn't want you to be stranded on a country road. Once I saw you and realized it *was* you but that you didn't recognize me, I just decided to let it go." He sighed. "Sorry."

"Where's Kenny?" I asked.

"Why do you ask?"

"You must have had his phone for some reason."

"I did. He was . . . indisposed."

"Who had Mason that night?"

Tommy nodded toward his mother. "My mom did."

I leaned forward. "So, what's going on?"

"I don't know," he answered. "Except that you're grilling me."

"Did you know that Miriam is missing? She never came back that night."

"I dropped her off at the house." He pulled out a phone and held it up. "It was around two in the morning."

I thought back to that night. I would have been on the phone with Delores, trying to deliver the placenta. "Miriam never came in the house. And I never heard a vehicle or a car door slam or anything."

"I parked over by the barn," he said. "I couldn't get close to the house, remember?"

"Did you watch Miriam walk into the house?"

"I waited until she was on the back steps . . ." His voice trailed off.

I stood and walked to the mudroom, retrieving Deputy

Rogers's card from my coat pocket. I returned to the kitchen and handed it to Tommy. "This deputy wants to ask you a few questions."

He took the card and grimaced. Clearly he recognized the name on the card. After a long moment, he met my gaze. "I didn't have anything to do with Miriam disappearing."

I shrugged. "Tell the deputy."

Tommy, with Mason still in his arms, dug his phone out of his pocket and glanced at Mammi as if asking permission to use it.

"Go ahead," she said. "This is important." She hadn't minded me using my phone either. She'd told me sometime in the last year, more Youngie who hadn't joined the church were using their cell phones in Amish houses. It was becoming harder and harder for parents to completely enforce a "use it in the barn" or "use it outside" rule.

Tommy punched in the number. After saying hello, he said, "Savannah Mast said you want to speak with me." There was a pause. "I can meet you wherever you want." Another pause. "I'm at the Mast place right now. Dorothy Mast's farm." He gave Deputy Rogers the address and then said, "I'll wait here until you arrive."

When he ended the call, he looked at his mother. "When the deputy comes, would you take Mason to another room? I don't want him to be confused."

"Of course," Wanda said.

Mammi stood and pulled a tray of cinnamon rolls from the oven. "I just need to drizzle the icing on these," she said. "And then you can offer one to the deputy." She turned toward Tommy. "Do you want me to leave the room with your mother?"

"That might be for the best," Tommy said and then looked at me. "But would you stay?"

I nodded, although I couldn't fathom why he wanted me there. It wasn't as if I could confirm his story, or even vouch for his character. Tommy wasn't the boy I used to know.

Ten minutes later, the rolls were covered with a cream cheese icing and Mammi, Wanda, and Mason had ventured into a back room. When Deputy Rogers knocked on the front door, I opened it. He frowned and then said gruffly, "That was fast work."

I didn't reply. Instead, I asked if I could take his coat. He shook his head and motioned for me to lead the way toward the kitchen.

"Well, well, well." Deputy Rogers stopped in the archway and crossed his arms over his broad chest, made even wider by his thick parka. "So we meet again."

Tommy stood and strode toward him, his hand extended.

The deputy looked him up and down in what appeared to be a clear attempt to intimidate Tommy. He gripped his hand tightly and shook it up and down.

"I hope you won't hold my youthful foolishness against me," Tommy said.

"I will if you haven't put it behind you."

"I can assure you I have." Tommy gestured toward the table. "How about a cup of coffee?"

Deputy Rogers finally let go of Tommy's hand. "Sure."

"I'll get it." I needed something to do besides watch the alpha-male power struggle before me. I poured the deputy a cup and then dished cinnamon rolls onto three plates and distributed those too.

When we were all settled around the table, Deputy Rogers picked up his fork and held it over the cinnamon roll as if he might stab it. "What brings you back to Nappanee?" he asked Tommy.

"My mother. A job." Tommy shrugged. "The same things that draw most people back home."

Without responding to Tommy, the deputy slashed into the cinnamon roll, cut off a section, and took a bite, chewing slowly. After he swallowed, he glanced at me. "Delicious."

"Oh, I can't take any credit," I said. "My grandmother made them."

"Well, tell her thank you," he said and took another bite, washing it down with a drink of coffee. Then he turned to Tommy again. "Where's Miriam Wenger?"

"I have no idea." Tommy hadn't touched his cinnamon roll.

"When did you see her last?"

He pulled out the phone again and said, "Early on Sunday, around two in the morning, when I dropped her off at the Wenger farm."

They went over Tommy's timeline for the night, from when he picked me up to when he dropped me off and picked up Miriam. "I took Miriam to a house in Nappanee, on the corner of Main and Elm. The place was lit up, and there were lots of cars and people hanging out on the porch. Then, because I was awake, I picked up a few more riders. After I took Miriam back to the house and was headed home, I got another request. From a Joshua W."

Deputy Rogers's bushy eyebrows shot up.

"Jah, it was Joshua Wenger," Tommy clarified. "And Vernon was with him."

"Joshua has a cell phone?" the deputy asked.

"Apparently so. I picked them up at a house off Cardinal Street, took them home, and then went back to my apartment and turned off the phone."

"What's your relationship with Kenny Miller?" Deputy Rogers asked.

"He's my cousin."

"First, right?"

"Correct." Tommy held up the phone. "This is his. He's been staying with me at my apartment in town. Kenny's been driving for extra money, but he left without his phone Saturday night. When it buzzed and I saw it was a woman named Savannah, I decided to go get her."

"Why?"

Tommy glanced my way. "I thought it might be Savannah Mast because my mother said she was coming for a visit. We were childhood friends. I didn't want her stranded out in the storm."

Deputy Rogers frowned. "How did you know she was the Savannah you knew?"

"I didn't, but I figured the chances were pretty high. Savannah isn't a common name around here."

Deputy Rogers jotted something down and then asked, "Have you been in contact with Kenny?"

Tommy shook his head. "Not since around eight in the evening on New Year's Eve."

"Is he driving his Camry?"

"I assume so. It hasn't been parked at the apartment complex since then. But he doesn't have his cell phone with him, so I can't contact him to find out."

"Any idea where he might be?"

Tommy shook his head.

"Do you think he's in some sort of trouble?"

"I don't know," Tommy said. "I hope not."

"Any reason you think he might be? Has he been in trouble recently? I mean, the two of you were in trouble all the time as teenagers."

Tommy exhaled. Then he took a sip of coffee and finally answered, "Yes, he's been in trouble since then."

"For . . . ?"

"He was arrested for drug distribution in New Mexico. Evading the police in Arizona. And shoplifting in Nevada." Tommy wrapped his hands around his mug. "I think that's all."

"What about manufacturing drugs in Arizona?"

Tommy cringed. "He didn't tell me about that."

"Were you two traveling together out West?"

"Some," Tommy said. "But not all of the time."

"Can you give me names and addresses of people he hung out with here? Or whom he might have gone out with on Saturday night?"

Tommy shook his head. "Look, we moved back here in September. I got an apartment and let him stay with me. I didn't want to get involved with anything else. I figured the less I knew the better, which in retrospect wasn't the best idea. But Kenny is twenty-eight. I can't control him." He sighed again. "I've tried."

Deputy Rogers took a few more bites to finish his cinnamon roll, followed by another drink of coffee. Then he pushed back his chair. "Well, thank you, Tommy Miller. I need your cell phone number—not Kenny's."

Tommy rattled off the number.

"Make sure and hold on to Kenny's phone," the deputy said. "It might be needed later."

"Look," Tommy said. "I was going to head back to Nevada."

"You need to hold off on that until we figure out where Miriam is."

"Is this a criminal investigation?" Tommy asked. "Isn't she eighteen?"

I winced. It wasn't exactly that he sounded guilty, but still, the questions seemed a little suspect.

"We need to know she left on her own volition," Deputy Rogers said. "And that there wasn't any foul play."

Tommy nodded coolly. "I can wait a few days."

Deputy Rogers drained his mug. "I'll be in touch."

Tommy met the man's gaze and nodded but didn't smile.

Deputy Rogers stood. I did too. He said, "No need to walk me out."

I ignored him and strode after him as he walked to the front door. As we neared it, I hurried ahead and stood in front of it. "What's really going on here?"

"I can't discuss the case with you."

I crossed my arms. "How worried should I be about all of this? For Miriam's sake?"

He crossed his arms in response. "Fentanyl is being sold in the area, and there have been a few bad batches. We've been trying to figure out who the source is for a few months now, and the problem started about the time Kenny and Tommy came back to town."

"That hardly ties Tommy to Miriam's disappearance—"

He cut me off. "Call me, like you did today, if you see or hear anything suspicious."

I turned the knob and pulled the door open. He stepped through without saying good-bye. I watched him march down the steps. I knew from my work-related research into the prescription drug epidemic that Indiana, along with so many other states, had been affected by opioid abuse. Fentanyl seemed to be the next one to surface in many communities, including in Northern California, once the number of opioid prescriptions decreased. I hoped that Kenny and Tommy weren't involved, nor any Amish Youngie.

Once Deputy Rogers reached his car, I closed the door and returned to the kitchen. I wanted to think the best of Tommy, but it was proving hard to do. He was staring at his cup of coffee as I asked, “What’s the bad blood between you and the deputy?”

He shook his head. “It’s a long, tedious story. I don’t want to bore you.”

“I’d really like to hear it.”

Tommy exhaled. “Kenny and I had some bad years during our late teens. Partying. Petty vandalism.” Tommy wrapped his hands around his cup. “Deputy Rogers had every right to be after us, but he was relentless. He pulled me over thirty-four times and only once gave me a speeding ticket—for going four miles over the speed limit.” He shook his head. “To be honest, he’s part of the reason I left Nappanee. But then Rogers turned all of his attention on Kenny, who followed me a few months later.” He met my gaze. “Don’t get me wrong. We were horrible. I knew it then, and I can see it even more clearly now. But I’ve never known anyone to hold a grudge like Deputy Rogers.”

My eyes locked with Tommy’s.

“Sorry to drag you into this,” he said.

I suppressed a shudder. “Hopefully, it will all be resolved soon.” I didn’t tell him that Deputy Rogers thought he and Kenny were running drugs. Instead I said, “So, you’re headed back to Nevada?”

He nodded.

“You had that planned all along?”

He nodded again.

“Your mother knows about it?”

He frowned. “I haven’t had a chance to tell her yet. I mean, she knew I wasn’t back home for good, just for a short time.”

“What about Mason?”

“I’m taking him with me. His mother wants him back.”

THE NEXT DAY, just after noon, Mammi and I picked up Wanda at Ervin's farm. It was about five miles from Mammi's, with a huge white barn, an old farmhouse, and a large dairy herd.

Wanda was definitely bigger than Mammi or me, but there were three seat belts, and we all fit in the cab of the pickup, although it was pretty cozy.

"Where's Mason today?" I asked.

"Playing with Ervin's younger kids," Wanda answered. She didn't offer anything more, and I didn't ask about him or Tommy. I was thankful Mammi wasn't a gossiper and didn't ask any questions either. I didn't want to get any more involved with the drama than I already was.

A few snowflakes fell, but the roads were clear. When we reached the quilting shop, there were already several other women at work. Mammi introduced me around again. Phyllis and Lois were there and both greeted Wanda. The bishop's wife, Catherine Deiner, was there too.

I was surprised they didn't ask if anyone had heard anything about Miriam right away, but perhaps they didn't want to bring up Tommy in front of Wanda. Or perhaps not in front of the bishop's wife.

"I have a casserole in the fridge for you to take to Arleta," Jane said to me. "If that will still work."

"Yes, of course," I answered. "Mammi and I can drop it off when we leave."

"Denki." She smiled, her blue eyes twinkling. "And I also have a quilt for the baby." I was sure that would mean a lot to Arleta.

Lois asked Catherine about her new twin grandchildren. "They're doing well," she answered. "Nearly sleeping through the night already. They're number fourteen and fifteen for us."

Catherine appeared to be in her early fifties, definitely not more than fifty-five. It amazed me how young Amish grandmothers could be and how quickly they could amass dozens of grandchildren.

"And how is Sophie doing?" Phyllis asked.

Catherine pursed her lips together. "Just fine."

"Still in Elkhart?"

Catherine nodded. "She's working at a grocery store there."

Lois looked up from her quilting. "You must miss her."

"Oh, well . . ."

There was a long pause. I couldn't help but wonder what Sophie's story was, but obviously Catherine didn't want to talk about her. Every family had its problems.

There were two Englisch women among the quilters, an older woman named Betty and her middle-aged daughter, Jenna. The Amish women spoke a mix of Pennsylvania Dutch and English. There were a few times when I lost track of the Pennsylvania Dutch conversations, but mostly I kept up.

It was Betty who brought up the missing Amish girl. "I heard from a friend who has an Amish neighbor that she's Arleta's daughter."

Lois confirmed that she was.

"We also heard she's eighteen, so the police can't do anything," Jenna said. "Is that true?"

"She's eighteen," Phyllis said. "If she left on her own, they can't do anything. But from what I've heard, they're investigating." Mammi, Wanda, and I all kept our heads down.

"Do they have any suspects?" Betty asked.

No one responded.

Finally, Jane said, "I'm thinking of a story, one I've been saving for just the right time—and person."

"I think a story is a great idea," Wanda said.

Jane looked directly at me. "Savannah, you'll especially appreciate this one."

I left the needle in the quilt as I looked up, touched that she was thinking of me. "Why is that?"

"It's about a woman named Emma Fischer. She was a widow when she first came to the area in 1842, and she worked as a midwife."

Jane added, "Plus, she's an ancestor you and I share."

I tilted my head and looked from Mammi to Jane. "I didn't know I'm related to you."

Mammi smiled. "Jane and I are fourth cousins. Emma was my great-great-grandmother. So she would be yours too, with four greats."

"And three greats for me," Jane said. "Of course, there are a lot of us around these parts who are her descendants, that's for sure."

"I know there are some Fischers around," I said. "But it doesn't seem like there are that many." Not like the Millers, for example.

"Well, you'll have to hear the story to find out, although I won't be able to tell all of it today." Jane pursed her lips and then sighed. "Honestly, this is a hard story to tell, and I've avoided it because of a particularly tragic thread." She squared her shoulders. "But I believe it's time." She glanced around the circle with an empathetic expression on her face. "Everyone grab a cup of coffee and something to eat. Then I'll get started."

Mammi told Jane she'd wait on any customers who came in, and Jane thanked her. The women all gathered around the refreshment table and filled their plates with the same healthy fare Jane had served on Monday. I wasn't sure how she made any money.

Once everyone sat back down, pushing their chairs back a little so they didn't drop any crumbs onto the quilt, Jane placed her hands together, as if in prayer. "Now, mind you, this story doesn't start in this area. No, it started all the way back in Somerset County, Pennsylvania. I won't tell you Emma's entire story, but I will tell you that she was born in 1818, the second child and only girl in her Amish family . . ."

CHAPTER 8

Emma Fischer

October 7, 1840

A gust of wind caught a cluster of maple leaves and lifted them up in a swirl of orange and red. Emma expected her son, Hansi, to take delight in the autumn colors, but instead he stopped and lifted his arms. At three, he was too heavy for her to carry for long, especially when she was just months away from delivering her second baby. She took his hand and kept walking, but he soon began to whine.

His face was flushed, and she let go of his hand to feel his forehead, under his curly hair. It was warm.

"Walk to the top of the hill," she told him. "And then I'll carry you home."

They continued on the trail from her parents' farm, where her father had a blacksmith shop. The bucket of apples Emma had picked knocked occasionally against her leg. She planned to make a cobbler to have with their supper.

Her husband, Asher, wouldn't be home until late.

When Emma and Hansi reached the crest of the hill, he stopped and reached up for her again. She put down the bucket, hoisted him to her hip, pulling her apron to the side, and then reached down for the apples. A twinge raced across her stretched middle. She paused a moment, waiting for it to pass.

Ahead, their field of cut hay cured in the cool autumn air. It had been warm during the day, but at night, frost would appear. Beyond the field was their pasture with their cow, calf, two steers, and Emma's horse. Her Dawdi had given her the cow, named Bossie, and her own mare, Red, when she married, plus a small flock of chickens. She was grateful for her grandfather's generosity.

The hilly landscape of Somerset County had been Emma's family's home since her great-grandparents moved from Lancaster County fifty years ago for more farmland for their growing family. Now, Emma's aunts, uncles, and cousins, along with others in their Plain community, populated the area.

She breathed in deeply while surveying the autumn landscape. She couldn't imagine ever leaving. She'd been a sickly Boppli and *Kind* and was spoiled by her grandfather, according to her mother. Then she'd struggled with her nerves, something she'd been admonished about over and over. If she only trusted God more, she wouldn't give in to the fears that seemed to plague her. At least that was what her mother told her.

For the most part, Asher had been understanding of her problems—until he began thinking he wanted to sell their little farm and move. Four men from their community had traveled west in the spring and were expected home soon. Asher could hardly wait to hear what they'd found.

Some in the area had already gone to Ohio over the last decade, but land there was now more expensive, and anyone wanting to leave Somerset County for better opportunities needed to move even farther west. The travelers had planned to go through Ohio, and then on to Indiana and Illinois. Emma shivered at the thought. The name *Indiana* meant Indian Country. What dangers might lurk there? She figured Illinois would be similar, but Asher said the Native people had mostly all left, going to Kansas, to a new land.

Emma couldn't imagine any of it and didn't want to try. She certainly didn't want to experience it. She'd heard stories of raids and killings, and she wanted to stay as far away from anything like that as possible. She was safe in Pennsylvania with her little family, with her parents and brothers only a short walk away.

Her mother was a midwife, and Emma often worked as her assistant. While her mother was energetic, resourceful, and confident—as well as able to easily accept death as God's will—Emma found herself anxious and soon overwhelmed when a birth went awry. Her mother would simply say, *"The Lord's will be done,"* while Emma questioned if there was anything they could have done differently to save the baby and, once, the mother. She shivered at the thought even now, as she sweated from carrying Hansi. Mamm also stitched people up when they were injured, set broken bones, and treated people for all sorts of illnesses.

Emma's brow puckered as she thought about the differences between her and Mamm. The main one, she determined, was that Mamm was strong and easily took charge, while Emma, as much as she tried not to be, was fearful and wanted others to make decisions.

Still, she enjoyed assisting her mother with births the majority of the time. Caring for a mother and witnessing a baby come into the world brought her immense joy. There was nothing as incredible in all the world.

The trail narrowed and became rocky. Emma chose her steps carefully as she carried Hansi along the pasture. The cow bellowed, and the calf, who was in the weaning pen, called back to her. Emma would need to milk the cow once she had the cobbler baking.

Hansi rested his head on her shoulder, his curls pressed against her face, and by the time they reached their whitewashed clapboard house, he'd fallen asleep. She made her way into the big bedroom, rolled Hansi onto her bed, and covered him with a comforter.

Then, she stirred the hot coals in the cooker, stoked the fire, peeled the apples, mixed the flour, butter, cream, and sugar, assembled the cobbler in the Dutch oven, and placed it in the oven.

After she'd put the leftover sausage and cabbage from their noon meal on to heat next to the pot of bone broth, she checked on Hansi. He was still asleep. She considered waking him, because if she didn't, he might be up late into the night. Then again, perhaps he was falling ill and needed the extra rest.

Leaving him, she went out and herded Bossie into the barn and milked her. When she returned with the pail of milk, Hansi called out to her.

"Mamm!"

She put the pail on the kitchen table and rushed into the bedroom.

He sat in the middle of the room, on the floor, his face beet red and his eyes cloudy. She felt his forehead again. Before, he'd been warm, but now he was burning.

Emma took off Hansi's coat and then grabbed a cloth and the bucket of water from the kitchen. She carried him to her bed again and sat beside him, dipping the cloth in the water and running it over his forehead, pushing back his curls. She couldn't carry Hansi all the way to her parents, and she didn't want to leave him alone. If he grew worse, she'd try to ride Red while holding him.

She pulled the boy onto what little lap she had left as she pressed the cloth to the back of his neck. "Your *Dat* will be home soon," Emma said. "I'll send him for Mammi." Her mother would know what to do.

BY THE TIME Asher came through the back door, bringing a cold blast of air with him, the sun had set and darkness had fallen. His face was streaked with dirt, his sandy hair pushed back on his head, and his hazel eyes were tired.

Emma met him in the kitchen, asking him to go get her mother.

"Should we take Hansi to her?" Asher asked. "That would be faster."

Emma shook her head. "He's running a fever. I don't want him out in the cold." She lit the lantern and handed it to Asher. He headed out into the frosty cold, the lantern swinging as he strode down the porch steps.

It seemed to take forever until they returned. Emma mopped Hansi's forehead again. He complained of a sore throat, and his voice grew hoarse. After a while, he dozed in Emma's arms. Finally, Emma heard the back door bang and then Mamm came into the bedroom, followed by Asher and then Emma's younger brother, Isaac. At fourteen, he was as quiet and earnest as his Adam's apple that bobbed up and down every time he swallowed or spoke. Besides her grandfather, Emma was closest to Isaac out of all of her family members.

As Mamm stepped to the side of the bed, Asher said, "Joseph and Daniel Miller have returned. And Joseph Speicher and Nathan Smeily too. That's the word at your Dat's shop. There's to be a meeting tomorrow evening so they can tell us what they've found." Excitement had replaced his tiredness.

Emma didn't respond. She was glad the four men were safe, but moving west was the last thing she wanted to think about at the moment.

"Go get your supper," Mamm said to Asher. "And you too, Isaac, while I take a look at Hansi."

Emma appreciated her mother's intervention. Mamm sat down beside Emma and ran her fingers through Hansi's curls, massaging his head. "Mammi's here," she said. "Can you wake up for me?"

He stirred and opened his eyes.

"How are you feeling?" Mamm asked.

He touched his throat. "It hurts."

Mamm felt his forehead and then touched around his neck. "It's swollen," she said. "Has he eaten?"

Emma shook her head. "I'll get him some broth."

"And get him a cup of water."

Emma headed into the kitchen, where Isaac and Asher sat at the table, eating their meal. Asher looked up when he saw her. "Will you come to the meeting with me tomorrow?"

"Let's see how Hansi is." Lately, she felt as if she was constantly balancing Asher's dreams and desires with the reality of their everyday lives.

"Surely it's just a cold, don't you think? It seems as if the boy is sick all the time."

That wasn't true. He had colds and stomachaches from time to time, but she didn't think any more so than other children.

Emma pointed to the cobbler. "Help yourselves when you're ready."

She dished up the broth from the pot on the back of the cooker, poured water from the pitcher into a cup, and headed back to the bedroom.

Mamm hummed to Hansi, who was now completely awake.

As Emma spooned broth into his mouth, she asked her mother, "Do you plan to go to the meeting tomorrow?"

Her mother nodded. "Jah, I want to go, but your father isn't as enthusiastic."

"Do you want to go west?"

"Jah," she said. "But the duty of a *fraw* is to trust her *mann*."

When Emma didn't answer, her mother added, "The Lord leads your father, and I follow. That's my duty. Whether it means staying or going."

Emma knew it was hers too. But that didn't mean she wanted to go. And the truth was, Mamm made a lot of the decisions in the family. In fact, she could talk all she wanted about duty, but it seemed she usually got her way.

Hansi shook his head when Emma offered him another spoonful. She put the bowl on the bureau and then said, "This is our home. I have a bad feeling about leaving."

"It's because you'll be delivering soon," her mother replied. "Of course you don't want to leave. Not when you have a baby on the way."

Emma held the cup for Hansi, and he took a long drink.

"And when you have an ill little one too," Mamm added. "But I think Hansi won't be ill long. Jah, he has a sore throat and a fever, but hopefully he'll be on the mend soon." She dug in her bag, pulling out a cloth. "I'll make a poultice for him."

When she reached the door, she turned and said to Emma, "I'll stay with Hansi tomorrow evening so you can go to the meeting with Asher. Perhaps if you hear the stories of the travelers firsthand, you'll feel better about moving west."

DURING THE NIGHT, Hansi's fever broke, and he seemed to be getting better. Mamm had left another poultice, and Emma applied it early in the morning. After Asher milked the cow, Emma fixed breakfast while he talked again about the meeting. "Will you go with me?"

"Jah," Emma said. "Mamm said she would sit with Hansi."

"I've heard the land is vast and fertile." Under the light from the lamp, his eyes shone with excitement. "I'm sure they have much to tell us."

Emma's stomach roiled. When they first married, he seemed to only think about their farm and the improvements he could make. Now he seemed to be overcome with thoughts about moving west.

But he was a hard worker, and no doubt if they did go west, he would be successful. After he finished eating, Asher left to help the Millers with their hay. No doubt Joseph would be working too and filling Asher's head with more ideas, long before the meeting tonight.

She went on with her day. Weeding. Cooking. Tending to Hansi. Late in the afternoon, when he awoke from his nap, he was running a fever again. Emma placed a cool cloth on his forehead and continued fixing supper. Then she put on her newest dress, one she'd sewn a few months before.

Asher arrived before Mamm and washed up before they ate. After they'd finished their meal, he began to pace as Emma washed the dishes. "Perhaps she's at a birth," he said.

"She would have sent Isaac to tell us," Emma said. "But if you're worried about being late for the meeting, go without me." She thought he might, but just then Mamm arrived. As soon as she came through the door, she shooed them out. "Isaac will be along shortly so he can walk me home," she said. "Remember every detail of what is said so you can tell me, in case your father forgets."

The meeting was held in Joseph Miller's home, and a crowd had already gathered by the time Emma and Asher arrived. Her father and her older brother, Phillip, were sitting at the front of the living room and motioned for Emma and Asher to join them. Only a few other women were there, and Emma wished she hadn't come. But on the other hand, she was touched that Asher had wanted her there. Perhaps he valued her opinion more than she thought.

Joseph Miller, who was a preacher, strode up to the front of the room, followed by his brother, Daniel, and then Joseph Speicher and Nathan Smeily. All four men were thin and had a threadbare look about them. They needed haircuts and a month of good meals in their bellies.

Daniel did most of the talking, explaining that once they'd arrived in Pittsburgh, they took a river steamer to Cairo, Illinois. "That's where the Ohio River joins the Mississippi," he explained. "From there, we traveled upstream on the Mississippi River to Burlington, Iowa." He said that they'd scouted sites for farms and homes and then traveled northwest on foot to Iowa City, through the town of Des Moines, and on to Johnson County, for a total of a hundred miles. "The land is flatter than here but fertile. There's plenty of water and opportunities."

Iowa. Emma hadn't guessed they would go that far.

"We liked what we saw," Daniel said, "but we decided to go overland on our way home and see more of the country. We passed through Chicago, a small frontier town in Illinois, and then we crossed the southern tip of Lake Michigan by boat and reached the Saint Joseph River. Once we left the river, we traveled by foot to Goshen, Indiana, in Elkhart County."

"We saw acres and acres of open land," Nathan chimed in. "Of all the places we saw, we were the most impressed with Elkhart County."

Asher seemed as if he could hardly contain himself as he asked, "Will the four of you return with your families?"

Daniel glanced at his brother. Joseph shrugged and said, "We need to spend time in prayer before we make a decision."

Joseph Speicher and Nathan Smeily nodded in agreement. Other men raised questions about crops and water and the height of the grass. Finally, Asher asked if they saw any Native people.

"No," Daniel said. "We were told there's a tribe left in Michigan, but most traveled to Kansas a few years ago, and some on to the Indian Territory west of there."

Emma wondered, if the land was so fertile, why they had left. Perhaps they didn't want to be around the new settlers. Perhaps the Native men had chosen to go farther west, just as Asher wanted to, taking the women with them. Emma wondered if the women had been as apprehensive and hesitant as she felt now.

Mamm told her once that nothing ever stayed the same, but Emma had a hard time believing her. Life in Somerset County had been the same for her great-grandparents, grandparents, and parents. All she wanted was for it to be the same for her too.

CHAPTER 9

After the gathering broke up, Asher cornered Daniel with more questions, while Emma talked with her father. He was forty-six with a beard that was just starting to gray. "Dat," she asked, "do you think you will go?"

He shrugged. "I agree with your mother that there isn't enough land here for Phillip and Isaac to have farms of their own. We need to do something." Dat smiled down at Emma. "But it's hard for me to think about leaving my father and brothers and our community."

Emma nodded. "I feel the same way."

On the way home, under a clear sky and a nearly full moon, Asher took Emma's hand, the way he used to when they were courting. "Daniel said they'll be leaving in the spring."

"They've decided to go?" Emma stopped. "I thought they were going to pray about it first."

"Well, he said they haven't decided for sure. . . . But he said he's nearly positive his family will go. He plans to buy a covered wagon and share a freight wagon. We'll have to pack carefully, taking only what is essential. Tools. Seeds. Staples. Chickens. A few piglets. Bossie and Red. We'll need to buy a pair of oxen. The roads in Indiana are mostly widened trails, so the traveling will be slow. . . ."

"Have you decided to go for sure, then?" Emma's voice caught as she spoke.

Asher nodded. "It's what's best for us."

Emma let go of Asher's hand. The new baby would be five months old. Hansi would be nearly four but not able to walk far at a time. If her Mamm and Dat went too, and her brothers, she'd have help with the children. Tears threatened. She'd never see her grandfather again.

"What about your parents?" Emma asked. "And your brother?" Asher had a twin named Abel, whom Emma had courted—until she met Asher. "What about your family?"

"What about them?"

"Are they interested in going west?"

Asher frowned. "No. That's the last thing they would want to do."

"Won't you miss them?"

Asher sighed. "I will, but the sooner we go west, the better. The land won't last at affordable prices. It's what's best for our family."

"But it's so far away. How would we travel that far with Hansi and the new Boppli?"

"It's not that far," Asher answered. "Less than five hundred miles. Think of those heading all the way to the Oregon Territory. That's over twenty-five hundred miles."

When she didn't respond, Asher said, "I will begin looking for a buyer for our land. That's the first step. We will need money to buy a wagon and supplies, and then to buy land in Indiana."

Emma didn't voice it out loud, but she knew he would first

need to pay his father, who'd loaned him the money for the farm.

When they reached their house, a lamp burned in the bedroom window. Emma had hoped Hansi was fast asleep, but perhaps Mamm was administering another poultice. Asher went out to the barn to check on the animals, while Emma went into the house.

Without hanging up her cloak, she went directly to the bedroom and stopped in the doorway. Isaac knelt beside the bed, while Mamm held Hansi like a baby, staring into his face. His eyes were closed, a wet cloth was draped over his forehead, and his curls were soaked in sweat.

Mamm raised her head and without greeting Emma, she said, "He's taken a turn."

"What do you mean?"

"He's hotter, and his throat is worse." She paused. "There's a gray coating covering the back."

Emma froze.

"It's diphtheria," Mamm said.

Tears instantly sprung to Emma's eyes.

"Now, now," Mamm said. "You must trust God. Have courage."

Two of Emma's cousins had died from diphtheria years ago. Finally able to move her feet, she shuffled to the bed and took Hansi from her mother, knocking the cloth to the floor as she hoisted him over her belly and to her chest. She began to cry.

"Control yourself," Mamm whispered. "Or you will scare your child."

Emma had been reprimanded her entire life about controlling her emotions and her anxiety. And she had tried. Ever since Hansi was born, she was afraid he would die. One time, she confessed her fear to Mamm, who only sighed.

Mamm had lost two babies before they'd turned three, which probably contributed to Emma's fear. There were no guarantees when it came to a child surviving. Emma knew that. God called His people to faith, to trust Him. Yet, even as others quietly seemed to accept the will of God, Emma still feared.

MAMM DID STAY the night, but then she was called away on a birth, and Emma cared for Hansi by herself, applying more poultices, including one made from turpentine and lard. She coaxed as much water and broth into him as she could. He slept fitfully, tossing and turning and calling out for her.

Asher grew quiet, and Emma feared even her optimistic husband thought their son might die.

Mamm came back from the birth, a difficult one that lasted three days. She was exhausted, and Emma insisted she go home and sleep.

The next day, when she came back, she forced Emma to sleep while she watched over the boy.

By the next Lord's Day, Hansi was delirious. Dawdi came to check on them and sat at the end of the bed, his head bent in prayer and his long white beard dipping toward the floor. His presence was a comfort to Emma.

Hansi's fever rose and fell. He lost weight, and his skin grew nearly translucent. Asher seemed to grow more and more distant. At night, when Emma had her Kapp off and her hair down, Hansi would reach up and stroke her tresses, bringing tears to her eyes. He was such a sweet boy, even when deathly ill.

Mamm came and went, as did Dat and Dawdi. On Tuesday morning, early in the morning, Emma sat beside Hansi on his little bed. His breathing slowed more and more. Emma knew what was coming, but when he didn't take another breath, she gasped, waking Asher.

He stumbled from the big bed.

Emma sobbed. "Go get Mamm."

He did as she asked, but once he left the house, she regretted not asking him to come sit first. She knew Hansi was gone, but one last memory of the three of them together was what she needed. She bent over and kissed her son's head, his curls against her lips.

Mamm, Dat, and Dawdi arrived, along with Emma's brothers. All crowded around the little bed, while Asher stood behind them. Dawdi put his hand on her shoulder, as if trying to share his strength.

Mamm washed and prepared Hansi's body for burial, while Dat and Phillip made a little coffin and Isaac rode across the county to tell Asher's parents and Abel. Asher had vanished. Emma wasn't sure where her husband went, but she guessed he went out to work on the farm. He finally returned for supper.

That night, family and neighbors came to view the body. The next day, Mamm scrubbed Emma's house and got it ready for the service. Neighbors brought food—venison and mashed potatoes, jars of beans and chow chow, fresh butter and cream.

Emma couldn't comprehend what the preacher said the next day. Jah, they all knew Jesus said, "These things I have spoken unto you, that in me ye might have peace. In the world ye shall have tribulation: but be of good cheer; I have overcome the world."

But be of good cheer. She despised those words. Hansi was gone. Her boy, gone. She would never feel good cheer again. But she didn't cry. She was trying so hard to control her emotions. But she couldn't control her feelings.

They buried him in her family plot, next to Emma's baby

sister and brother. Afterward, everyone went to Mamm and Dat's house for a meal. When Asher finally said it was time to go home, Emma, no longer able to control herself, began to cry. Mamm whisked her off to her old bedroom and sat her down.

"You have this new baby to think of, and your husband needs you." Mamm stood above Emma with her hands on her hips. "God took Hansi for a reason. You need to rest in that."

Emma buried her head in her hands and sobbed, but finally she composed herself and walked home with Asher.

They didn't talk much the next few days, except when neighbors or family stopped by. Asher busied himself with repairing the fence and then dragging the pasture.

One rainy afternoon a week later, he came into the house early, his face flushed and saying he didn't feel well. He burned with fever. Emma helped him to bed and then ran down the trail to fetch Mamm.

They both guessed it was diphtheria. Mamm assured Emma that adults didn't succumb to the disease as often as children, but Emma couldn't help but fear the worst as she applied poultice after poultice.

Asher turned and thrashed, muttering in his sleep about leaving Somerset County, about Indiana, and about the Elkhart Plain. "I'll start over," he muttered. "I'll have more sons."

Emma regretted her hesitation about going west and assured him that she would go willingly the very next spring. She'd never have more children, besides the one she carried, if Asher didn't recover.

He did get better. The fever broke, the thick gray coating on the back of his throat disappeared, and he was able to leave the bed and walk as far as the table. The neighbors, Dawdi, Dat, and the boys had been doing the chores and seeing to the farm. Asher tried to go out and help, but he would come in early, exhausted. Even so, October had turned into November, and Emma grew more hopeful. Asher was alive. Surely he would grow stronger with time.

At the end of November, she went into labor. Thankfully, Isaac was staying with them, because Asher wouldn't have been strong enough to get Mamm. When Isaac returned with their mother, Emma already had the urge to push. Perhaps the Lord was showing her mercy in her time of need, considering everything she'd gone through in the last month.

She had only pushed three times when a perfect little girl slid from her. The cord was wrapped around her neck, and she had a grayish tint to her skin, but Emma didn't react. It happened from time to time. Mamm would get her breathing.

But then Emma's mind began to race. How long had it been since she'd felt the baby move? Hours? A day? Why couldn't she remember?

No cry came. It felt as if hours passed, but it was probably only a few minutes until Mamm placed the stillborn baby next to Emma and said, "Naked came I out of my mother's womb, and naked shall I return thither: the Lord gave, and the Lord hath taken away; blessed be the name of the Lord."

Emma closed her eyes and cried.

ASHER STILL TALKED of going west with the group in the spring, but it was obvious to everyone it would not happen. He couldn't even do the chores by himself; there was no way he'd be able to farm. Emma helped him now, trudging through the snow to feed the livestock and hauling water to the trough. Mending the fence when an animal broke through. Chopping wood for the cooker and fireplace.

Mamm feared his heart had been injured by the illness, but she had no idea what that would mean for the future. "Perhaps he will still grow stronger," she said.

Emma thought of the family cemetery, of the baby girl buried next to Hansi. They hadn't named her—Emma couldn't bear to. She also couldn't bear the thought of Asher joining his children in the next life, not yet.

Her heart changed toward him. She missed his strength and optimism, and she did all she could to help him. She feared if he didn't get better then they couldn't keep the farm. And she had no idea how they could make a living without it. Crops had to be seeded, grown, and harvested to pay Asher's father back for the loan he'd given them to buy the farm in the first place. Jah, for the first time in her life, Emma had to be the strong one. She'd lost her son and daughter, but if she could keep her husband alive, she still had hope for the future.

A few times, Abel rode across the county to check on Asher and the farm. The two had always resembled each other, but now Asher was much smaller and looked much older. Abel was kind and concerned. He clearly cared for his brother. When Emma had shifted her affection from Abel to Asher, there was some animosity between the brothers—and now it was gone.

In the spring, as the Miller brothers and two of their cousins and all of their families packed their covered wagons to head west, Asher went out to start the chores while Emma finished cleaning the fish they'd caught in the creek that afternoon. The warm weather seemed to be restoring Asher's health some, and his spirits were better too.

A half hour later, Emma slipped into the barn, calling out to him, but he didn't answer. She waited a moment for her eyes to adjust to the dim light. Asher sat on a bale of hay, his head resting against the wall. Perhaps the fishing had been too much for him.

She called out his name again, but he didn't stir.

"Asher." She took his cold hand and then put her face up to his nose, hoping to feel his breath. She waited and waited. But he was completely still. She sat down beside him, resting her head on his shoulder. She sat there and held his hand and watched the light change through the barn door, as numb as she'd ever felt in her entire life. Why had he come down with diphtheria and not her? Why did he have to die young when he'd had so much vigor and hope for the future?

Finally, she rose and shuffled up the trail to her parents' house to ask for help to move her husband back up to the house to clean and prepare his body. She was a *vidvieb* now.

After they buried Asher next to their son and daughter, Emma moved back to her parents' place, and Abel moved onto Asher's farm, although Emma took Bossie, Red, and the chickens with her. They were all she had of any value.

When she was a baby, and no one, not even her mother, thought she'd survive, her Dawdi had held her for hours, praying over her. Now he often sat beside her, patting her hand. She knew he was praying but wasn't sure he should bother. She seemed to be crying more and more, not less. She felt no will to live, and she couldn't understand why the Lord hadn't taken her too.

A few times, Abel came to visit. Mamm finally spelled it out to Emma as they both kneaded dough one morning. "He wants to court you."

Emma didn't reply.

"You need a husband," Mamm said.

It had only been ten months since Hansi died, nine since she'd lost the baby, and three since Asher had passed. Jah, Abel was the most practical choice. He wasn't Asher, though, and didn't have the zeal and spirit that had drawn Emma to her husband. However, she couldn't think about courting so soon. "I'm not ready to marry again."

"Don't be foolish." Mamm wiped the back of her floured hand across her forehead. "Widows remarry within a few months all the time." Mamm sank her hands back into the dough. "It's either that or go to Indiana with us. We're leaving next May."

"Dat decided to go?"

Mamm didn't answer her directly. Instead, she said, "It's what's best for our family."

"Can't I stay here with Dawdi? If I decide to court Abel, I'll let you know. If not, I can travel west with the next group."

Mamm shook her head. "I don't want to leave you behind, not without a husband. You're not well."

Emma felt hollow inside. "What if I go to Indiana but then decide to come back here?"

"I'm certainly not opposed to you marrying Abel—if you wanted to right now, I'd be fine with that. But if you're not ready, you should go with us. Surely, you'll have recovered by this time next year, and then you can return, if that's what you decide to do." She flipped the dough over and paused for a moment. "Our ancestors fled Switzerland, then Germany, and finally left Lancaster County. Someday, some of our descendants will leave Indiana and go even farther west. Nothing stays the same, Emma."

CHAPTER 10

Dat, a little reluctantly, bought a covered wagon for the household goods and a spring wagon for his farm and blacksmith tools, extra food, and crates of chickens and piglets. Emma longed to take the cooker Asher had given her, but there was no room in the covered wagon or the freight wagon. She had to leave it with Abel.

One afternoon in mid-April, Emma ventured down the trail, stopping at the crest. Below, her old house needed a coat of whitewash, and the weeds needed to be pulled at the back door. Her heart lurched at the thought of the last time she carried Hansi down the trail to it, atop her big belly.

She found Abel in the barn, brushing his horse. "I need to speak with you," she said.

He smiled at her shyly.

"My parents are leaving for Indiana soon and believe I should go with them," she said. "I'm not certain that I'll stay. I may come back in a year, depending on how I'm doing."

He nodded. The entire community knew about her struggles.

"I was wondering, if I do . . ." She couldn't say the rest.

"If I would wait for you?"

"Jah." The word nearly stuck in her throat.

"For a year, I will." He met her gaze. "If your family doesn't return, others will. We've seen that with those who went to Ohio over the years, haven't we?"

She nodded. "Denki." Looking at Abel was like looking at Asher before he fell ill.

"Take care of my stove," she teased.

He took her seriously. "It will be waiting for you. I promise."

Besides her clothes, she took her cow, her horse, her youngest chickens and one rooster, a lamp, a set of dishes, her salt-and-pepper boxes, her crockery and tinware, her clothes and comforter, and several woolen blankets that she'd made.

Five other families were going west too, and by the time everyone was ready to depart, it was May, a year after Asher had once hoped to leave. The trip would take a little over a month. They would arrive with plenty of time to secure land and build barns and cabins before the weather turned cold, and hopefully they could grow enough vegetables to help get them through the winter.

Emma was resigned to go as she told her grandfather good-bye. His faded blue eyes grew watery, and Emma fought back her own tears. He squeezed her hand. "I will pray for God's direction for you, for wisdom," he whispered.

"Denki," she managed to say. She guessed he hoped she would return, but he didn't say so. He had been her rock and comfort through her childhood. She mourned leaving him.

"*Mach's gut.*" Dawdi let go of her hand.

As Emma walked ahead of the covered wagon, her eyes fell to the family burial plot. Her mother had told her, in time, it would seem as if the loss of Asher and the children was part of another life. But Emma couldn't believe she'd ever feel so.

She would serve her family and hope she'd grow stronger, but she would find no joy in the journey.

The travelers were known as "movers," and instead of staying in inns, they camped under the stars at night, after covering ten to twenty miles per day, depending on the terrain and the conditions of the road.

After one day, Emma had blisters on her feet. Dat, Phillip, and Isaac took turns driving the wagons, while Emma, wearing a bonnet to keep the sun off her face, mostly walked. She rode Red some, sitting on her pillion sidesaddle. Mamm rode in the wagon most of the time.

The other families had young children who tugged at Emma's heart. If only she were with Asher and their children. *If only*. It wasn't the way she was raised, to dream of what wasn't. But she couldn't seem to stop.

The constant dust, sweat, smoke from the campfires, and smell of the animals permeated her skin, and she felt as if it seeped out of her pores. Even when she bathed in a river once a week, if she had the chance, she didn't feel clean. She missed the water she heated on her stove and the tub Asher dragged into the kitchen for their weekly baths. Jah, being a mover was hard.

When they camped at night, Emma milked her cow and then helped Mamm fix dinner, while the men chopped wood and hauled water. Each family ate by themselves, but then the group would gather and one of the men would read a scripture, and they would all pray silently for the journey ahead. Emma found it difficult to pray, but no one would have guessed it by her bowed head and humble posture.

In the mornings, Emma and Mamm made breakfast, boiling strong, bitter coffee in a pot and frying corn cakes and bacon, all over a campfire.

They stayed to the east of Pittsburgh as they journeyed north and then turned west again, toward Holmes County, Ohio, to visit members of their community. Emma didn't remember the family and friends who had left Somerset County years ago, but she had grown up hearing about them. Emma and her family stayed in Holmes County for a couple of days with a brother of Dawdi's, resting the oxen, horses, and cows—and their own feet too—while they visited. A cobbler in the community repaired their boots, while the men shoed the oxen and horses. Dawdi's brother, who was the youngest in that family and not much older than Dat, warned them about the Indians out west. "You should stay in Ohio. There were massacres in Indiana," he said.

Emma closed her eyes, not wanting to even imagine such a thing.

But Dat replied, "We don't have enough money to buy farms here. We'll continue on."

After they left Holmes County, Emma's heart grew heavier and heavier with each step that took her farther away from Somerset County. She grew quieter, but only Isaac seemed to notice. Emma mostly walked in silence, lost in her thoughts and memories, interrupted by an occasional reprimand from herself to stop obsessing about the past. She smiled a little, remembering how it had annoyed her when Asher obsessed about the future.

The weather had turned hot and humid, and even though she wore her bonnet every day and her sleeves came down over her hands, Emma's skin grew darker. They headed north to Michigan to avoid the Black Swamp in northwestern Ohio and then veered down to Indiana, traveling along the border of the two states.

A month after they left Somerset County, Pennsylvania, they arrived in Elkhart County, Indiana.

Emma was amazed by the heights of the trees. Poplar and sycamore soared to the sky, some as high as a hundred and fifty feet. Ash, birch, pine, and cottonwoods were also plentiful, along with black walnut, plum, and sweet crabapple trees that would all help feed them. Wild geraniums bloomed in the woods, along with late bluebells. There were marshes in the southwest corner of the county, and deer and other wildlife, including *Beaha* and panthers, throughout. They wouldn't starve, that was for sure. And hopefully they wouldn't be attacked by wild animals either.

But the settlements in the county were few and far between, and there were few places to trade. Compared to her hilly home, the landscape was as flat as Emma was trying to keep her emotions.

THEY SOON DISCOVERED that Joseph Miller had purchased land northeast of Goshen in Clinton Township, while his brother had purchased land in Newbury Township. Dat scouted out both areas but decided to buy land south of Goshen in Jackson Township, where the land was less expensive. With the money they saved, Dat hoped he could buy a farm for Phillip too. Emma knew Dawdi had sent money to help secure as much land as possible.

The camping didn't stop. The only difference now was that they were in one spot, hauling water and chopping wood and cooking over an established campfire, while Dat and the boys sawed down trees in the woods to strip and turn into logs to build a cabin.

Mamm and Emma hoed a plot of soil and planted a garden as best they could, planting both herbs and vegetables from seeds and starts that they'd brought from home. They also planted several apple seedlings that had survived the trip because of their babying.

Dust covered everything, from their wagon to their dishes. After it rained, usually after a thunder and lightning storm that split the sky, everything was covered in mud.

It wasn't long until word got out that Mamm was a midwife. One evening in mid-July, as the family ate corn cakes and ham steaks around their campfire, a man on horseback appeared.

He took off his straw hat that appeared Plain. When he introduced himself in Pennsylvania Dutch, it was quite clear that he was Plain. "I'm Judah Landis," he said. He didn't have a beard, which meant he wasn't married. His dark hair was pushed back from his head and needed to be cut. "My brother, Walter, sent me. His wife is having a hard time. It's her first child, and she's on her third day of laboring." He glanced from Mamm to Emma with caring brown eyes. "We were told there's a midwife here."

Mamm stood. "I'm the midwife. I'll grab my things." Mamm retrieved her bag from the wagon and then turned to Emma. "Come with me."

Emma hadn't assisted with any births in Pennsylvania after Hansi died. She couldn't leave Asher after he fell ill, and she had no desire to help with births after her baby died.

Would she even remember what to do?

Mamm told Isaac, "You come too. We need you to drive the wagon. Bring your rifle." Emma guessed she wanted him to be available to scare off a bear or panther, if needed.

Once Isaac had the horses hitched to the spring wagon, they followed Judah west to Union Township. The trail was rough and bumpy, but they made it through. The mosquitoes were out in force, the biggest Emma had ever seen. The toads began croaking just as dusk fell. She strained her eyes to keep sight of Judah in the night.

Thankfully, they soon arrived at a cabin. Judah stayed outside with Isaac as Mamm and Emma let themselves in through the front door, into the dim interior. A woman lay on the bed in the corner, moaning with her arm over her eyes. A man stood nearby, his hands trembling. Relief washed over his face as he thanked them for coming. "This is Sarah." He motioned toward the woman, who wore her hair in a long braid.

Mamm stepped to the bed, placed her hand on Sarah's shoulder, and told Walter to go on out with the men. Once he was out the door, Mamm spoke gently to Sarah, and Emma lit the lamp.

Another pain seized Sarah, and she let out a cry. Emma stepped to the bed and took her hand. "Squeeze as hard as you can." It didn't feel as if it had been two years since Emma had helped Mamm during a birth. She remembered exactly what to do.

When the pain passed, Emma began massaging Sarah's shoulders while Mamm lifted up her white muslin nightgown and then ran her hands over the woman's belly. When she finished, she said, "The baby is in position." She reached for Sarah's arm. "Let's get you up."

Sarah's legs shook as she stood.

Mamm had her lean against a chair for the next pain, while Emma stoked the fire and started water to boil. She found cornmeal and started to make a gruel from it. Sarah needed some sort of nourishment.

Between pains, Mamm tried to get Sarah to talk, to try to relax her.

"Where are your folks?" Mamm asked as she rubbed the woman's lower back.

"Back in Ohio," Sarah answered.

"Holmes County?" Mamm asked.

Sarah grimaced as another pain started. When it had passed, she muttered, "Just north of that."

"Wayne County?" Mamm asked.

"That's right." Sarah continued to shake.

Emma finished the gruel and brought a bowl to the girl, spooning bites into her mouth between her pains and also giving her drinks of water. Serving Sarah in her pain made Emma forget her own.

Mamm kept rubbing Sarah's back. The pains grew even worse, and Sarah screamed again.

"You are doing what you need to do," Mamm said to her. "Your little one will be here soon." She whispered to Emma, "Make her a cup of chamomile tea."

A flash of lightning shone through the one window in the cabin and thunder crashed a moment later. As the storm continued, Sarah's pains grew worse, even after she drank the tea. With each one, she cried out, one time calling for her mother.

"Now, now," Mamm said. "I am here instead. I am your mother tonight, and Emma is your sister."

Finally, Sarah's water broke, and then the young woman started to push. Mamm and Emma helped her back to the bed. The thunder had stopped, but the rain had started, washing the outside world away. The pains went on for another two hours until the head finally crowned. Then, with one last scream, Sarah pushed the baby out, and Mamm scooped him up into her arms.

Emma's heart stopped as she remembered her stillborn baby girl, but this baby was red and began crying immediately. Still, tears stung her eyes.

Jah, midwifing had come back to her, but so had her loss and grief.

THE NEXT MORNING, as Walter held his son and Judah and Isaac hitched the horses to the spring wagon, Emma stood outside the cabin. Raindrops still glistened on Sarah's kitchen garden and on the cornstalks in the field. To the left, a flock of swifts swooped toward the willow trees along the creek and then rose in the sky and over the seemingly endless landscape. Would Emma ever get used to how flat the land was? How far away the horizon seemed?

Mamm went home with Isaac and would return the next day to check on Sarah, but Emma would stay to cook and clean for the little family. Sarah had no one else to see to her needs, and she and Walter had set aside a sack of potatoes and some produce to give Emma in return for her help.

As Emma breathed in the morning air, trying to reconcile both how hard it was to be at a birth again after her losses but also how wonderful it had been, riders in the distance appeared. As they grew closer, it was obvious it was a man and a woman. As they neared, Emma made out a child, a little boy, riding in front of the woman sitting sidesaddle. The woman wore a blue calico dress with a pattern of forget-me-nots and a bonnet with a wide rim. Around her neck was a string of shells. The man wore leggings and a wide-brimmed hat.

"Jean-Paul!" Walter called out as they neared. "A son has been born to Sarah."

The man, who had a pipe in his mouth, waved and steered his horse toward the cabin. The woman followed. The little boy appeared to be two or so. Emma's heart lurched at the sight of him. He had a straw hat on his head, and the shadow made his skin look darker. The woman's hands were darker too, perhaps from the sun.

Judah stepped out from the barn and called out a hello to Jean-Paul too. As he neared, Judah said, "This is Emma Gingrich."

Surprised he remembered her first name, Emma corrected him. “Emma Fischer,” she said.

A confused expression passed over his face as she lifted her hand in greeting toward the man and woman.

“Jean-Paul and Mathilde Bernard,” Judah quickly said. “And their son, Baptiste.”

Walter addressed Jean-Paul. “Thank you for telling us about the midwives. I don’t know what we would have done without them.”

Emma didn’t think of herself as a midwife—she was nothing more than Mamm’s assistant—but she chose not to correct that statement.

The woman said something to Jean-Paul in French. He held his pipe in his hand as he addressed Walter. “Mathilde would like to go see Sarah.”

Walter nodded. “I think she’d like that.”

Jean-Paul jumped down and took the boy, swinging him to the ground. Then he raised his arms to his wife, giving her a tender smile. Her eyes shone as he gently eased her down. Jean-Paul was quite a bit older than the woman. There was gray in his beard and mustache, and his skin was weathered and wrinkled, probably from the sun but perhaps also from age.

As Mathilde approached, it became obvious she was Native. Emma froze for a moment, thinking of all the warnings she’d heard about raids and violent attacks, but then she remembered her manners and opened the door for her. Mathilde took her bonnet from her head. She wore her hair in a bun at the nape of her neck, and beads hung from her pierced ears. Emma had never seen a Native person before. They’d left Somerset County long before Emma was born.

Once inside the cabin, Emma turned to Mathilde. “My name is Emma.”

The woman nodded. "*Oui.*" Obviously she'd understood what Judah had said in English.

Sarah, who was in a clean nightgown with the baby swaddled and tucked in beside her, smiled up at Mathilde. "We've named him Hiram."

Mathilde took the baby and held him up to her face, putting his cheek against hers. "Hiram and Baptiste will be friends." Her English was stilted.

Sarah nodded but didn't say anything.

As Mathilde placed the baby back beside his mother and then stood up straight, the fabric of her dress caught across her middle. Emma wondered how soon she was expecting another little one. Mathilde told Sarah good-bye and slipped out of the cabin.

Later that afternoon, as Emma picked beans from the garden, Judah approached from where he'd been mending the pasture fence and asked if she needed help with anything. "I can fetch water for you," he said. "Or haul wood."

"I could use more water." She had spent much of the day caring for the baby so Sarah could rest. Now she needed to prepare something for their dinner. "And is there meat in the smokehouse? Perhaps a ham? Or some bacon?"

Judah nodded. "I know there's bacon. I'll get potatoes from the root cellar too."

Another storm was brewing, so Emma would need to cook in the house. The day had grown hot and muggy, and the small cabin was already suffocating. It would soon be unbearable. Back home, during the summer, Asher would move her stove out to the cooking shed to keep the house from getting too hot.

An hour later, Judah had filled the buckets with water, stoked the fire and filled the woodbox, and brought in a slab of bacon and four potatoes. Emma buried the potatoes in the coals and mixed up biscuits, placing them in a Dutch oven and placing it in the coals too. Then she began to fry the bacon and the beans she'd picked.

Emma served the two men at the table and Sarah in bed, holding little Hiram so his mother could eat. Once they were all finished, she dished up a plate for herself. Walter sat on the edge of the bed next to Sarah and held the baby, but Judah stayed at the table.

"Why did your family come west?" he asked.

"For land," Emma answered. "My Dat wanted my brothers to have their own farms. What about you?"

He smiled. "Walter and I grew restless in Ohio."

"How long have you been here?"

"Four years." He nodded toward the bed. "Walter went back to marry Sarah two years ago, once we had the cabin and barn finished and the first two years of crops harvested. Two other families around our age said they would come, but they haven't yet. They wrote to say they've been delayed, which means Sarah hasn't had many other women around."

"Except for Mathilde."

"Jah," he said. "She and Jean-Paul have been here for four years too, settling in Union Township right before her people were forced to leave."

"Forced?"

"Well, coerced at least."

Emma broke her biscuit in two. "Who are her people?"

"The Potawatomi Nation."

"Where did they go?"

"Kansas. Many have already been sent on to the Indian Territory west of there. Some called their journey 'the Trail of Death' because hundreds died along the way."

Emma shivered. No one had said anything about the Native

people being forced off their land. They'd made it sound as if they had chosen to go.

"It's all part of the Indian Removal Act," Judah explained. "The goal is to clear the land for white settlers."

Emma choked a little on her biscuit and quickly took a drink of water.

"Mathilde's original name is Kewanee," Judah said. "It means *prairie hen*. Mathilde is her French name. She and Jean-Paul met at the mission near South Bend."

Emma exhaled. "Why did she choose to stay?"

"Because she'd already married Jean-Paul."

So she had stayed for love. Or perhaps safety. Maybe both. But, no matter what, she'd given up her family. Emma took another drink of water. Was she willing to do the same to move back to Pennsylvania? To move back home?

CHAPTER 11

Savannah

My, I certainly went on and on with that story, didn't I?" Jane stood. "I hope everyone stayed interested."

"It was captivating," Betty said.

"Absolutely," Phyllis added.

I agreed. Why hadn't anyone told me about Emma Fischer when I was younger? She was a woman who had truly lost everything, far more than I had. My heart ached for her, even though she'd lived over a hundred and fifty years in the past.

I found it fascinating that her mother was a midwife—and Emma assisted her. That was very much like my mother and me. Besides all of Emma's losses, what was also heartbreaking was that the Potawatomi people had lived in the area before my ancestors ever arrived. I'd heard of the Indian Removal Act, but I'd always thought it had applied to North Carolina and other eastern states. Not Indiana.

"I've kept you all too long," Jane said. "Here it is, after four on a dark winter's night."

"We'll help clean up." Mammi stood too.

"Oh no." Jane started toward the refrigerator. "You, Savannah, and Wanda head over to Arleta's, just in case she could use the casserole for their supper."

I nodded. "Let's grab our things and get going."

"Here's the quilt too," she said, handing me both a pan and a parcel. "Make sure she knows it's from the Plain Patterns quilters. We made it last year, before Arleta joined us."

I assured her I would.

Once we'd climbed into the pickup, Wanda asked, "Could you drop me off at home first? I don't want Tommy to wonder where I am."

"Sure," I answered as I plugged in my phone. Of course she shouldn't go out to Arleta's with us, not with Tommy being questioned about Miriam's disappearance. That would be awkward.

When I pulled into Ervin's driveway, the first thing I noticed was Tommy's Jeep. Then I saw him carrying Mason, dressed in a puffy coat and boots, down the back steps of the farmhouse.

"Ach, I've almost missed him." Wanda opened the door of the pickup. "Denki. I'll leave a message if I can go to the next quilting circle."

As we called out good-byes, Wanda made her way toward Tommy and Mason. Tommy gave his mother a smile and then looked beyond her to the pickup. He smiled again and waved, without letting go of Mason.

Both Mammi and I waved back. As I pulled out of the driveway, Mammi sighed. "I can't believe that Tommy could be involved in Miriam's disappearance."

"I sure hope he isn't," I responded.

Mammi spoke softly. "I would only say this to you." She glanced at me, a furtive expression on her face, and dropped her voice even more. "But I can't help but wonder where Kenny Miller is."

"I'm guessing Deputy Rogers is wondering that too and looking into it."

"I certainly hope so," Mammi said. "I don't want Tommy to be held responsible for something he didn't do."

"Have you heard people talk about Kenny?" I asked.

Mammi nodded. "I don't know if the talk is true or not, but I think there's probably reason to be suspicious of Kenny."

"What about of Tommy?"

Mammi sighed. "I'm not saying Tommy is without fault—none of us are—but I don't believe he would do anything to harm Miriam."

"What if he thought he was helping her?"

Mammi pursed her lips. "I don't think he would help her by causing her to disappear. I'm sure he has more common sense than that."

I drove on in silence, my thoughts drifting back to Ryan. He'd certainly surprised me by his behavior—not only ditching me at the last minute but also not paying when he said he would. I thought about calling his mom about the credit card problem but decided not to. I didn't want her to feel responsible.

The sky darkened as we drove, and a few more snowflakes fell. It appeared another storm was on the way. Hopefully, it would wait until we were home.

As I drove, my phone rang. I glanced at it as I drove, hoping it wasn't another vendor. It wasn't. It was Uncle Seth's number. I handed it to Mammi. "Would you answer it? Just hit the green button."

She fumbled as she grabbed the phone, then recovered and took off her glove to answer it.

"It's me," she said, loudly. "Dorothy."

Uncle Seth was speaking as loudly as she was. "I'm still sick." That probably meant I could wait until Friday to get a rental. I was grateful for the use of his pickup. "Could you and Savannah stop by the store?" he asked. "I need tissues, more cough medicine, and lozenges."

"Jah, we'll do that," Mammi said. "How are you doing for food?"

"I still have some of your soup," Uncle Seth answered.

"We'll stop by in about an hour," Mammi said.

"See you then." Uncle Seth ended the call, and Mammi dropped my phone, like a hot potato, back on the seat between us.

A few minutes later, I turned down the lane to the Wenger farm. As I parked the truck, Vernon stepped out the back door in his coat and boots, clapping his gloved hands together. When he saw me, he frowned. I opened the door. "I have a casserole from Jane Berger."

"All right," he said. "Go on in the house. Arleta is resting on the couch." That was good to hear.

Mammi climbed down out of the passenger side before I could help her. I did manage to loop my arm through hers, carrying both the casserole and the parcel in my other hand. I had her go up the steps first so I could catch her if she slipped.

When she reached the door, she opened it without knocking and stepped onto the mud porch and then into the kitchen. "Arleta," she called out. "It's Dorothy and Savannah. We have a casserole that Jane sent. And a baby quilt."

"Come on in!" Arleta's voice sounded more animated than I'd ever heard it. She sounded truly happy that Mammi had come to visit.

I put the casserole on the counter and followed Mammi into the living room.

Arleta sat on the couch, nursing the baby. I stopped myself from shaking my head. Vernon believed nursing a newborn was "resting." True, at least Arleta had a chance to sit down, but it's not as if she wasn't doing anything.

"Take your coats off," Arleta said. "And how about some tea?"

"Oh, we don't want to wear you out," Mammi said.

"Vernon will be doing the chores for the next couple of hours. And since Jane sent a casserole, I don't need to make supper." Her eyes lit up a little. "Now is the perfect time."

"All right," Mammi said, slipping out of her coat, which I took. But before I left, I placed the parcel beside Arleta. "This is from Jane and the Plain Patterns quilters."

"Would you open it?"

I unwrapped the package and then unfolded the quilt, a simple nine-patch pattern made out of shades of pink and red. Arleta put her free hand to her neck, just above the baby's head. "It's so lovely." She blinked quickly, as if fighting back tears.

I placed the quilt beside her, and she stroked the fabric as she continued to nurse the baby.

Touched by her display of emotion, I took in the beauty of the scene. A mother with a new baby and a gift of love from a caring community of women. Mammi often said that good works praised the Lord, which the pink quilt certainly did.

My voice was raw as I said, "I'll put the kettle on." I headed back to the kitchen. After hanging our coats in the mudroom, filling the kettle, and starting the flame, I stepped back into the living room.

Mammi had the baby up against her shoulder and was burping her. The quilt was now spread across Arleta's lap. "My milk came in this afternoon," she said to me.

"Great. How is everything going?"

"Just fine," she answered.

"Have you heard anything about Miriam?"

She didn't answer me directly and kept her eyes on the quilt as she spoke. "Deputy Rogers said he would come out in person if he found out anything so we don't have to check the messages every hour." She folded her hands over the pink squares.

Mammi shifted the baby to her lap. The little one, with piercing dark eyes, met Mammi's gaze. "What have you named her?" Mammi asked.

"Ruthie Mae," Arleta answered. "After Vernon's grandmother. We'll just call her Ruthie, though."

"Lovely." Mammi smiled at the baby.

Relieved the baby finally had a name, I sat down on one of the hard-back chairs. Arleta seemed like a different person with Mammi than with just me. If I'd only known, I would have dragged Mammi to Ruthie's birth.

"I know this is probably hard to talk about." Mammi turned her head away from the baby and toward Arleta. "Or even think about. But do you have any idea where Miriam might have gone?"

Arleta wrinkled her nose.

"Would she have gone back to Newbury Township?"

"I don't think so," Arleta said.

"Have you contacted her relatives up there to ask?"

She nodded. "Vernon left a message for them. They called back and said she isn't up there."

"Where else do you have relatives?"

"She wouldn't have gone to my sisters. She doesn't know them."

"Any other relatives?"

"There are some around Gary, Indiana."

I hadn't heard of Amish in that area. "Isn't that close to Chicago?"

She nodded again.

I asked, "Are they Amish?"

She shook her head. "Not anymore."

"Does Miriam know them?"

"She's met them. It's Miriam's aunt, on her father's side. She is quite a bit younger than he was. She married a Mennonite man a few years ago. Vernon called them too but hasn't heard back, which isn't surprising. I'm not even sure I still have the right number, honestly. They've moved around some."

I didn't know much about Gary except that it was definitely part of the Rust Belt, with a dwindling population, few jobs, and lots of empty houses.

"Do you think she left on her own or that she was forced?" I asked.

Arleta shrugged her shoulders.

I spoke slowly, dreading the answer. "Does Deputy Rogers have evidence that there's foul play?"

She shook her head. "Not that I know of, but he seems suspicious of Tommy."

The teakettle began to whistle, and I stepped back into the kitchen. Deputy Rogers did seem suspicious. But were his concerns based on the past or the present?

As I opened the cupboard next to the sink, looking for the tea, Joshua ran down the side yard toward the barn. Had someone dropped him off on the road, and he'd run through the field?

I found the tea, placed the bags in the teapot, and filled it with water. Then I pulled three mugs from the cupboard.

Mammi and Arleta's voices continued in the other room.

"Did you see Jane's column in the paper?" Arleta asked.

"Not yet," Mammi answered.

"It's there, on the table."

There was a pause and then Arleta added, "She wrote that one for me. It means a lot."

"Jah," Mammi said. "I remember her telling the stories during our quilting circle." There was another pause and then Mammi said, "She started a new one. This one is about a woman named Emma Fischer from the 1840s."

"Ach," Arleta said. "I wish I could be there to hear it."

I stepped to the kitchen window again. Joshua hadn't gone to the barn. He was still in the side yard, out of sight of Vernon, with his back toward me, texting on a smartphone. I froze, not wanting any movement to alert him I was there. Tommy was right. Joshua did have a phone. Should I tell Deputy Rogers?

I raised to my tiptoes and squinted as I peered out the window, but I couldn't read his screen. Should I tell Arleta and Vernon? Should someone be reading his texts?

"Savannah?" Mammi called out.

I stepped away from the window, hoping Joshua couldn't hear our voices.

"How is the tea coming along?" Mammi asked from the living room.

I stepped to the doorway. "It's almost done."

Mammi still had the baby on her lap, but the paper was beside her.

"I'll help." Arleta started to stand.

"No," I said. "Please sit."

Five minutes later, I delivered tea to Arleta and put Mammi's on the table. Then I took the baby. I also scooped up the newspaper and retreated to my chair.

With Ruthie in one arm and the paper in the other, I read Jane's article. It was all about the history of Nappanee. She wrote well, with clarity and zest. It wasn't as interesting as the story she started today, but then again, it was only a column. I admired the woman even more.

The baby began to fuss, and I put the paper down and transferred her to my shoulder. "Arleta," I said, "does Miriam have a cell phone?"

"Nee," she said.

"What about Joshua?"

"He doesn't either. They don't have money to pay for those things. The deputy already asked about that."

I didn't say anything more. I wasn't sure what to do. Should I confront Joshua? Or let Deputy Rogers know that the boy had lied to him? I wasn't sure if it would do more harm than good to tell Arleta and Vernon.

We stayed for about a half hour, and then Mammi said we needed to stop by the store on the way home for Uncle Seth. "I'll start your oven and put the casserole in," she said. "It's lemon chicken and rice, with broccoli."

It sounded fairly healthy, knowing Jane.

I started toward Arleta with Ruthie, who was fast asleep.

"Put her in the bassinet," Arleta said. "She'll sleep for a while."

I did as she instructed and then followed Arleta into the kitchen. As she told Mammi good-bye, I couldn't help but notice again how much she liked my grandmother. She gave me a quick farewell.

Once we had our coats on, I went down the steps first and encouraged Mammi to take her time. The last thing we needed was a broken hip. Then I held her arm as we made our way to the pickup.

We reached the pickup, and I held the passenger door for Mammi. As I closed it, Joshua came out of the barn.

"Hey, could I talk with you?" I asked.

His eyes widened, and he looked quickly in both directions.

"I just need to start the pickup so it warms up for my grandmother."

He still looked like he wanted to flee, and I expected him to as I turned the key. "I'll be right back," I said to Mammi.

When I climbed from the cab, Joshua was still there. I motioned my head toward the side of the barn. He followed me.

"I saw you using your phone," I said. "I was in the kitchen."

Even in the darkness, I could see his face reddening.

"Your mom said you don't have a phone and neither does Miriam. But I know you do, and others have guessed you do. How else could you have arranged for a ride to pick you up on New Year's Eve?"

He gave me a blank stare.

"Everyone but your parents has figured out that Miriam has a phone too. How else would she be arranging for rides?"

He shook his head. "She doesn't have a phone. We borrowed one. We don't own it." He patted his pocket. "I have it now."

"Who did you borrow it from?"

He looked down at the snow-covered ground. "I can't say."

"Joshua, your sister is missing. You need to tell me—or someone—what's going on. You need to at least be honest with the deputy, especially if you're not going to be with your parents."

He lifted his head but didn't meet my gaze. "Miriam's fine."

"How do you know?"

He patted his pocket again. "She called me from a landline. She's with relatives. An aunt on my Dat's side."

"In Newbury Township?"

He hesitated, then shook his head. "Listen, Miriam hates it here. I don't blame her for leaving. She's eighteen. An adult. She's fine."

I exhaled, sending a plume of frost into the air.

"Would you give me your phone number?"

He shook his head.

Not sure what to do, I dug in my purse for a piece of paper and then wrote my number on it. "Call me if Miriam needs help. I'll go get her, no questions asked."

He took the paper and shoved it into his pocket.

I continued. "And call me if you need help. Or if your mom or Ruthie does."

He inhaled sharply as Vernon barked, "Joshua!"

"Gotta go," he said.

I stepped toward the pickup. "Thank you for talking."

He darted around the corner without answering me.

An hour later, after going by the store and then Uncle Seth's again, we finally reached the house just as more snow started to fall. I hoped it wouldn't be another doozy of a storm. We hurried inside and warmed up soup for our supper.

By nine o'clock, I was huddled in my bed, in my coat again, trying to get warm. Why had I come to Indiana?

During the day, when I was with Mammi, life seemed bearable. But at night, I felt overcome with sadness.

Feelings of abandonment swamped me. As stupid as it sounded, I had felt abandoned when Mom died. I needed her as much at seventeen as I ever had. Probably more. Intellectually, I knew she hadn't chosen to die. But emotionally, I blamed her for leaving me.

I felt abandoned again, this time by Ryan, and at night I couldn't hold back the tears. It was as if Mom's death had just happened. As if I was mourning her again, along with being rejected by Ryan. Waves of anger accompanied my grief. How could Ryan do this to me? Especially when he knew how vulnerable I was.

During the quiet stillness of the night, I thought about him far too much, until it felt as if he were filling my entire head. I went over our relationship, detail by detail. What had I missed? Yes, he could be moody at times. And we certainly had different financial values. He, at times, seemed influenced by other people's opinions—not when it came to work, but when it came to having the latest and the best. If he read a good review of a restaurant, he had to try it. The same with the latest piece of technology. Or the newest running shoes. Or whatever. At the time, I thought it smart how aware he was of trends, but now I wondered if it was a sign of insecurity. Did that insecurity drive him back to Amber? Into the arms of a strong, take-charge woman? Maybe that was what he needed, instead of me.

Maybe I was far from being a strong, independent woman. As I dissected our relationship, I also realized how engrossed I'd become in Ryan. I had only a few other friends, which was painfully obvious by the lack of texts I'd had from anyone checking up on me after the wedding had been canceled. A few co-workers texted to say they were sorry I wasn't coming back to work, but that was it.

Shivering, I vowed—again—to stop speculating about what had happened. I had to get on with my life before my out-of-control feelings got the best of me. The next day I would go to a coffee shop, check my banking app, and look at my credit card charges. Then I would start searching for a new job. I knew it would take some time, but hopefully not more than a couple of weeks.

As much as I loved Mammi and as much as I valued her community, I had to leave Indiana before my emotions consumed me.

CHAPTER 12

The next morning, after breakfast, I packed my computer, my phone charger, and my portable battery pack and charger into my bag and was ready to leave the house when a vehicle pulled into the driveway. I stepped to the window. It was Tommy's Jeep. Why wasn't he at work?

I opened the front door and stepped onto the porch. Tommy had the back passenger's side door open and was pulling Mason from his car seat. The little boy saw me and waved, a big grin on his face. A lime green stocking hat was pulled over his curly hair, although a few strands hung down over his forehead. I couldn't help but think of Emma's little boy, Hansi, who'd died from diphtheria. If nothing else, stories from the past made one thankful for how relatively easy life was today. Even staying in an Amish household with no electricity or heat in the bedrooms was a dream compared to camping out of a covered wagon.

For a moment, I felt ashamed of my desire to flee Indiana as soon as possible.

"Hallo," Tommy called out.

"Taking the day off?" I called out.

He shook his head. "I was going to leave today for Nevada, so I'd already given my notice. They replaced me."

"Oh."

"We were on our way to Mom's."

"Even though you're not working?"

He smiled. "You don't hesitate to ask questions, do you?"

I grimaced.

"No, it's fine," he said. "I always liked that about you." He smiled again. "I thought I'd stop by, but it looks like you're ready to leave."

If he only knew how often I wore my coat around the house—and not just to bed. "I'm headed out to a coffee shop to use my laptop. But come on in. I have all day."

He shifted Mason to his other arm as he started up the steps. "We won't stay long. I just had some things to ask you."

As they reached the porch, Mason yanked off his stocking cap and dropped it.

I stifled a laugh and bent down to pick it up. When I stood back up, the boy was reaching for me. Instinctively, I took him. The weight of his body felt good in my arms.

Tommy stepped to the door and held it open for us.

As I entered the living room, Mammi said, without saying hello to Tommy or Mason, "I'll put the hot water on. Plus, I have cranberry muffins." She headed to the kitchen and we followed, leaving our coats on.

I put Mason in the high chair, left over from when Dat was a baby, and filled a sippy cup with milk for him. Once Mammi had the muffins on the table and coffee brewing, she said, "I need to go check my phone messages. Jane might have left one."

I stood. "I'll go with you."

"You stay. I need the fresh air to clear my head."

I shook my head in concern. "It's slippery out there from

the storm last night. You shouldn't be walking to the phone shack alone."

"Humor me," she said and then smiled.

Once she'd put on her coat and boots and slipped out the back door, I asked Tommy what he wanted to talk about as I stood to pour the coffee.

"Miriam and Joshua." He thanked me as I placed a cup in front of him. "And Kenny."

I sat down with my cup of coffee.

"When I picked up Kenny's phone, he didn't have any text messages showing. He must have deleted all of them. But several have popped up lately."

"From who?"

"I have no idea," Tommy said. "All of the names are weird. One person is 'Blue' and another is 'Dragon.' Things like that."

"Yikes," I said. "What are the texts about?"

"Some are asking where he's at. Why he didn't stop by when he said he would. Others are requests . . ."

"For?"

"I can't quite tell." Tommy shrugged. "But I'm guessing it's not for anything on the up-and-up."

"So the rumors about Kenny selling drugs could be true?"

Tommy nodded.

"Why haven't you gone to the police with this information?"

"I did," Tommy said. "I'm expecting to be arrested any minute now."

I couldn't tell if he was serious and gave him a questioning look.

"Deputy Rogers was practically giddy as he documented the texts and the information. It seems he thinks I'm the prime suspect." He frowned. "In fact, I got the sense that he felt I was just trying to distract attention from myself."

His words gave me pause. Should I be suspicious of Tommy too? Did Deputy Rogers have other reasons to suspect Tommy in Miriam's disappearance? On the other hand, if he wasn't innocent, who better to lead me to where Miriam was? Or at least to where he'd taken her.

I wrapped my hands around my coffee mug, concerned. "I chatted with both Arleta and Joshua yesterday. I'm thinking from what they said, separately, that Miriam might be with relatives near Gary who are Mennonite. We could start with the Mennonite churches and see if we can track her down." I met Tommy's gaze, wondering what his reaction to what I was going to say next might be. "Want to go with me tomorrow? I think it's about an hour and a half to Gary."

"Sure," he answered. "Hopefully we can make sure Miriam's safe—and clear my name with Deputy Rogers. I'll leave Mason with my mom. What time do you want to leave?"

MAMMI MADE IT safely back from the phone shack just as Tommy was brushing the crumbs off Mason and into his other hand, trying his best not to make an even bigger mess than the little boy already had.

I grabbed the broom and told him not to worry about it.

After the two left, Mammi said, "Jane needs me to stop by this afternoon with a pattern. Can you take me?"

"Of course." I swept the crumbs into the dustpan. "I'll go to the coffee shop right now, then come back and pick you up."

Ten minutes later, as I plugged in my phone, battery pack, and then my laptop at the coffee shop, I thought of how Tommy had jumped at the chance to go with me to Gary. I couldn't see any hint of guilt in his reaction. But then again, maybe he was a sociopath.

My mind wandered to when he was fifteen, the summer he was so awful to me. But the key word was *fifteen*. His rudeness at the beginning of his teen years was no indication that he was a sociopath, Amish or not.

Once the computer powered on, the first thing I did was reload my bank app and then check my credit card statement. I gasped. Every single vendor had charged me for what should have gone on Ryan's card.

I picked up my phone and called my bank. First, I asked the representative to reverse the charges.

"I'm sorry," she said, "but it sounds like a domestic misunderstanding. Your best bet is to hire a lawyer."

How ironic that here I was in Amish country amongst people who didn't sue, and she was suggesting I hire a lawyer.

"I'm not sure what I'll do," I said. "But would you add my call to the notes on my account?"

"Of course."

After I hung up, I texted Ryan. *I now owe half my annual salary to pay for the wedding YOU canceled. If you don't remedy this immediately, I will take action against you.*

After I sent the text, still holding my phone in my hand, I stared out the coffee shop window at downtown Nappanee. An Amish buggy zipped by, but not even the rhythm of the hooves comforted me. I'd been raised not to seek revenge. But I couldn't let Ryan get away with ruining me financially.

My phone began to buzz. I glanced down. Ryan was calling. Inhaling sharply, I answered.

"Hey," he said.

"Hi."

"Look, I'm sorry. My card was stolen. I totally forgot it was the one all the vendors had on file." Ryan paused a moment as if expecting me to respond. When I didn't, he said, "I promise I'll take care of it."

"Please call all of the vendors right now and give them another credit card number."

"Of course, as soon as I can," he said. "This afternoon, I promise."

"Do you have their numbers?"

"I'm not sure . . ."

I quickly said, "I'll share them with you."

"Perfect." Again he paused, but then said, "Look, I'm really sorry for all of this." He lowered his voice. "How are you doing? I can't stop thinking about you. Can we meet in person to talk all of this through?"

The craziness I'd been trying so hard to suppress came back with a vengeance. "No, we can't meet in person. I'm at my grandmother's."

"In Indiana?"

"Just fix the card problem."

"Savannah . . ." He sounded so forlorn.

"Bye." I ended the call with a flourish. Who did he think he was, saying, *"I can't stop thinking about you"* and *"Can we meet in person?"* And saying my name like that. Did Amber leave him again already?

My stomach roiled as I shared the numbers with Ryan. Then, I took a deep breath. I was going to look for jobs, not think about Ryan.

I stared out the window again. Had he really said *"I can't stop thinking about you"*? Should I have told him I couldn't stop thinking about him either?

No. Definitely not.

I opened a new tab and began searching for jobs in health-care administration. There was a position at a large clinic in Seattle. Too bad I didn't want to be on the West Coast. And an opening at a small-town hospital in Arizona. Reading between the lines, I guessed it had sustainability problems. I pulled up a different website and kept searching.

An administration position listed at Bremen Community Hospital popped up. It was less than ten miles away from Nappanee, if I remembered right. The search engine I was using must have been tracking my location. I scanned the description. Twenty-five beds, nonprofit, critical access hospital, serving Bremen and the surrounding communities.

Rural hospitals were struggling all over the United States. It sounded like more of a challenge than I wanted. Besides, it was just as cold in Bremen as it was in Nappanee. I kept scrolling.

The next job that caught my eye was at a clinic in Lancaster, Pennsylvania. That would be ironic for me to leave Nappanee and retrace the route Emma had taken to Indiana, but go even farther to where our Amish ancestors who first landed in America had settled. Then again, maybe Emma returned to Pennsylvania and married Abel. Maybe her future children or grandchildren whom I'd descended from ended up settling in Indiana. I wouldn't know until I heard the rest of the story.

I read the rest of the Lancaster job description. I was qualified. I looked at the application. It was pretty straightforward. I opened my résumé file and updated a few things. It probably wouldn't look good that I'd quit my last job so abruptly, but I'd be honest about why if I got an interview. I went ahead and filled out the application, attached my résumé, and hit send.

Then I called the car rental office in South Bend and arranged to pick up a car tomorrow on our way back from Gary. I was sure Tommy wouldn't mind dropping me off.

An hour later, Mammi and I were at Plain Patterns. I expected it to be a quick trip, but Mammi and Jane both seemed to have other plans. First, Mammi asked some questions about the quilt she was working on, while I browsed through the fabric. If I was going to move to Lancaster County, maybe I should take up quilting again. I bet there were all sorts of classes there, and I'd enjoyed the time I'd spent with Jane and the other women.

"Savannah?"

I turned toward Mammi.

"Do you mind if I quilt for a while?"

It wasn't like I had anything else to do. "Go ahead."

"Would you like to join us?" Jane asked. "It's been a slow day as far as customers. And we still have a long way to go to finish quilting this."

"I'd like that." I sat down in the exact spot I had the day before and retrieved the needle I'd left in the fabric.

Once we were all settled and started with our stitching, Jane said, "Arleta left me a message on my answering machine this morning, thanking me for the casserole. She sounded good."

"She seemed good yesterday too." Mammi smiled at me. "Don't you think?"

I nodded. "She was definitely more animated with Mammi than she'd been with me."

"Oh, don't take that personally," Jane said. "She's more reserved than most, and she probably wasn't sure whether she could trust you or not."

I focused on the quilt again. "I'm wondering if she's feeling more settled about Miriam being gone."

"What do you mean?" Jane asked.

"I'm just thinking out loud," I said, "but maybe she knows where she is."

"Why would she keep it a secret?"

"Maybe she doesn't want someone to know." I feared I was pushing things too far with my speculating.

"Such as?" Jane asked.

I lowered my voice. "Vernon."

Neither Mammi nor Jane said anything, and I was afraid I'd disappointed them with what sounded like gossip—and very well could be.

Finally, Mammi said, "I wondered that myself."

There was another long pause, and then Jane said, "Would you like me to continue the story I was telling yesterday?"

I glanced around at all of the empty chairs. "With just me? Won't everyone else be upset?"

She laughed. "Well, I'll catch them up." She glanced at Mammi and then back at me. "But I want you to hear all of it, especially if you are going to leave soon. This story is for you."

"All right," I said, touched.

"Where did I leave off yesterday?"

"Emma had lost everything—her son, baby girl, husband, and her home," I answered. "She'd arrived in Elkhart County and even helped with a birth but still longed to return to Pennsylvania."

"That's right," Jane said. "As you can imagine, everything had changed for Emma. . . ."

CHAPTER 13

Emma

That evening, Emma helped Sarah wash and get ready for bed while the baby fussed in the cradle. Walter would sleep out in the barn with Judah while Emma stayed in the cabin with Sarah.

"He'll be fine out there," Sarah said. "There's a room in the back where Judah has his things."

"Did the three of you grow up together?" Emma asked.

Sarah nodded. "Since we were babies. Walter and I started courting when we were sixteen."

"How old are you now?" Emma asked.

"Twenty-four."

They'd waited a while to marry. Perhaps Walter and Judah had the goal to move west all along and had been working and saving money to buy land.

"I didn't want to leave Ohio," Sarah said. "But Walter didn't want to stay. If it were up to me, we'd go back home."

Emma murmured her understanding.

Sarah continued. "Judah courted a woman back home, but

he rejected her. He's always been the black sheep of his family, the prodigal son. I don't know why Walter puts so much trust in him. I expect Judah to get bored here and run off before too long. There are times when he's gone off exploring for days at a time. Who knows what he's doing." She lowered her voice. "He hasn't joined the church yet, and sometimes I wonder if he ever will. He seems to act more and more like an Englischer all the time. Traveling all over the place. Working for our neighbor, George, who cheats whomever he can. Judah has different ideas than most Plain people. I don't find him, exactly"—she paused—"trustworthy. But if anyone can make it on the frontier, it's Judah." She sighed. "If anyone can't, it's me."

Emma could relate to Sarah but didn't say so. Instead, she said, "Don't be too hard on yourself. You've just had a baby."

Sarah sighed. "It's all so hard and I know it will be even harder now with a baby, with no mother or sisters nearby. The worst part about living here is not having any other women around, although there is the Englisch family about a mile away—George Burton, the cheat, and his wife, Harriet. But we don't see them much, unless he needs help. Harriet keeps to herself. And then there's Mathilde, but she's so quiet. . . ."

Emma thought of how happy Mathilde was to see Sarah and the baby. She might be quiet, but she seemed to be kind and caring.

"Mathilde is fortunate to be here," Sarah said. "To have Jean-Paul."

Emma's heart skipped a beat. Fortunate to be in her homeland but away from her family? It seemed Mathilde had been faced with horrible circumstances and choices out of her control.

"Judah seems to know quite a bit about her and Jean-Paul and the Potawatomi people," Emma said as nonchalantly as she could, not wanting to betray how interested she was in the topic.

Sarah nodded. "When he and Walter first came here, there were more of Mathilde's people in the area. Judah became acquainted with some of them as he traveled to the different areas. Even now, he's constantly peppering Jean-Paul with questions about the Natives. It gets so tiresome."

Even though she was curious, Emma doubted she would get much information from Sarah about the Potawatomi. And she also doubted she'd be able to have many more conversations with Judah—or if she should.

Once Sarah was in bed, Emma took the baby to her, holding him against her chest. He was so tiny. So beautiful. So precious.

"I'm exhausted," Sarah said, putting her head back on the pillow. "Is he really hungry?"

Emma nodded. "And it will help your milk come in." Emma handed the baby to her. "It's the same for every woman. It will be hard for a few weeks and then it will get easier."

And then, God willing, it wouldn't get harder from a broken heart and endless grief.

Sarah opened her nightgown for the baby. "That is fine for you to say, having never actually birthed a baby."

Emma hesitated. Should she tell Sarah she was a mother too, even though her children were dead? If she didn't, would Sarah feel bad when she found out that Emma was a widow?

The baby latched on, and Sarah grimaced. "I never thought it would be painful. My Mamm never had any pain with nursing her babies."

Emma had birthed two, jah, but only nursed one. Her breasts ached at the thought. She needed to say something to Sarah. "I had babies, two of them," she whispered. "And nursed one. The second was born dead."

Sarah stared at the top of Hiram's head. "Where are your children now?"

"Buried in our family plot, back in Pennsylvania."

Sarah continued to stare at her baby. "And your husband?

"Buried there too." She was sure they were all in heaven, but it sounded prideful to say so. She hoped they were.

"How sad," Sarah said without lifting her head.

Tears stung Emma's eyes as she turned away from the bed.

"The woman Judah courted was a widow named Ida," Sarah said. "Apparently, it's not what he wanted."

Emma had heard of men who didn't want to marry a widow. Thankfully, Abel didn't seem to be one of them. Judah seemed to be a caring man, but maybe she'd misjudged him. If his own sister-in-law felt he was untrustworthy, maybe Emma should be wary of trusting him too.

The cabin grew even hotter, and Emma needed some fresh air. She stepped out the front door, leaving it open a crack. She wasn't sure what was worse, the heat or the mosquitoes. Or Sarah's lack of a caring response to Emma baring her soul.

Ribbons of pink and orange streaked across the western horizon while thunderclouds gathered in the eastern sky. She heard voices over by the barn.

"George, I told you. We don't have any idea where Jean-Paul and Mathilde were headed." It was Judah speaking.

Emma stepped to the side of the cabin. A lean Englischman wearing a black suit sat tall on a stallion, talking with Judah. Walter was nowhere in sight.

"We're in need of Mathilde's help. My wife isn't feeling well."

"Perhaps they'll be back by tomorrow," Judah said. "If they stop by, I'll tell Jean-Paul you're looking for them."

The man tipped his hat. "Tell him I'm moving cattle day after tomorrow to drive to Goshen. He must come by tomorrow afternoon and bring Mathilde with him—or sooner if they can. I could use your help too."

Judah shook his head.

George held his head high. "I'll pay. My financial problems are a thing of the past, I promise."

"I'm too busy here," Judah said. "Sarah is confined and will need Walter's help more."

"Who assisted Sarah?"

"There are two new midwives over in Jackson Township."

Emma slipped back to the front of the cabin.

George said, "Good. That makes this place a bit more civilized."

Emma stayed at the door as George Burton took off on his stallion. He didn't look like a farmer, and he didn't sound like one either.

THE NEXT MORNING, Jean-Paul and Mathilde stopped by with a basket of wild berries for Sarah. This time Mathilde stayed on her horse while Jean-Paul delivered the basket to the front door. He had his pipe lit, and the smell of tobacco filled the air.

Emma's heart skipped a beat. The little family made Emma long for Asher and Hansi. She took the berries and waved to Mathilde, calling out, "Thank you!"

The woman barely smiled, but she seemed pleased.

Emma wasn't sure if she should tell Jean-Paul about George stopping to look for him, so instead she said, "Judah may have some information for you. I think he's in the barn."

"*Merci.*" Jean-Paul turned toward Mathilde and said something in French. Then he swung Baptiste, from where he sat in front of his mother, into his arms and started toward the barn.

Emma took the berries inside, where Sarah and the baby

slept, grabbed a leftover biscuit from the table, and took it out to Mathilde.

The woman smiled again—just a little—before she bit into the biscuit as the men returned.

"I'll go talk to Burton," Jean-Paul said.

"As long as he pays," Judah said.

Jean-Paul held the pipe away from his mouth. "At least you'd have cash coming from him. He does put my wage toward our debt, but it seems the interest rate keeps going up."

Judah gave the man a sympathetic look. "George was hoping Mathilde could help Harriet too."

Jean-Paul nodded. "Merci." He put the pipe back in his mouth.

Emma wondered if what Mathilde earned went toward Jean-Paul's debt too.

Mathilde held up half the biscuit and nodded her head, as if in thanks.

Emma smiled in return. She found the woman fascinating.

When Jean-Paul swung Baptiste back on the horse, Mathilde gave her son the rest of the biscuit. Emma thought of Hansi again, and her heart felt as if it might stop altogether. In the cabin, the baby began to cry. Emma waved her hand in farewell and stepped back inside.

After Emma settled the baby down, she headed outside to weed Sarah's garden before the sun grew too hot. She wore her bonnet and pulled her sleeves down to her wrists.

Walter went into the cabin, and after a few minutes Judah stepped to the edge of the garden. "I can do the weeding," he said to Emma.

"I don't mind."

"Mathilde helped us plant our first garden three years ago, when it was just Walter and me. She gave us seeds to get started—corn, squash, and beans. And tomatoes."

Emma glanced around the garden as Judah spoke. All of the plants were high and healthy. Thyme, rosemary, mint, and parsley all grew on the inside of the garden.

"The first summer, the deer ate most of the vegetables," Judah said. "But not as many come around anymore. Mathilde showed us how to plant onions and garlic on the outside, and that's helped." Emma noticed the rows encasing the garden as she swatted at a mosquito that buzzed around her face.

"I have to haul water for the plants," Judah said. "Two buckets at a time from the creek. We're hoping to dig a well soon."

It wasn't far to the creek, just beyond the willow trees, but carrying water for the house, the livestock, and the garden surely took a lot of time.

She stepped to the row of beans. "Sarah said there were Potawatomi in this area when you first arrived."

"Some." Judah started weeding along the tomatoes. "They fished the Elkhart and Saint Joseph rivers and hunted in the woods. The women tended gardens. They had villages up by Goshen and close to South Bend, which is where Mathilde's people were from. There's a Catholic mission up there, and her family converted."

Emma tossed a handful of weeds on the other side of the onions, outside the garden. "Converted to Catholicism?"

Judah nodded. "The priests—Black Robes, as the Natives call them—served the Natives and wanted them to be able to stay here, while the Protestant missionaries thought the Potawatomi should leave the area and go west."

She thought of the violence her great-uncle in Ohio had warned them about and shivered as she asked, "Were the Potawatomi peaceful?"

"Mostly." Judah tossed weeds into the pile that Emma had started. "Although there were . . . events that I'm afraid painted them in a bad light, but the violence wasn't representative of all of them." He bent down and continued to weed as he spoke. "One happened years ago at Fort Dearborn, which is where the town of Chicago is now. Braves, alarmed by the invasion of their lands, attacked the fort and defeated the US soldiers stationed there, killing many. As a result, the US government assumed all Native groups were hostile and needed to be removed from the vicinity for the safety of settlers. They held the sins of a few against all Native people."

"So they started forcing them to leave right away?"

Judah shook his head. "The Indian Removal Act didn't become law until 1830, under President Jackson. It wasn't until 1838 that the government started leading the Potawatomi away from Indiana, and it took a couple of years until most were gone."

"Why didn't they leave sooner?"

"Well, even under the Indian Removal Act, the Natives couldn't, technically, be forced to leave. But many were coerced—some by deceit and trickery. Some signed treaties for land that didn't belong to them and accepted cash payments that the true landowners never benefited from. Some were called 'whiskey treaties.' You can guess what the circumstances of those were."

Emma nodded. "Did all of the Potawatomi go to Kansas?" She stood tall for a moment, stretching her back and then brushing the soil from her hands.

"Some fled to Canada, and there's still a group just over the Michigan border. Chief Shipshewana, who lived northeast of here, was removed in 1838 and escorted to Kansas by soldiers. A year later he returned to his old camping grounds and then died beside Lake Shipshewana soon after."

"When did Mathilde's family go?"

"They and others resisted as long as they could, until they

had no other choice," Judah answered. "They left three years ago."

Emma began pulling weeds again. "How did Mathilde come to marry Jean-Paul?"

"He worked as a trapper near South Bend, for a man who had a trading post nearby. He'd been working there for twenty years or so, since he was a young man. That's how he met her. When it was clear the Potawatomi would have to leave, Jean-Paul thought it better for his family to stay here than to become, essentially, refugees."

Emma's own ancestors had fled their homeland of Switzerland for the Palatinate region of Germany, and they then ended up fleeing again for Pennsylvania, all in search of religious freedom. They'd been refugees in a new land twice.

The Potawatomi were refugees too, but they'd been forced from their homeland strictly because of greed. The greed of the settlers. Emma felt sick to her stomach. Mathilde and her people had lost their property—while her family had gained new farms.

IT WASN'T UNTIL later that afternoon that Mamm and Isaac arrived. It turned out she'd gone on another birth in the northeast corner of Jackson Township, and Isaac had gone with her.

"It was uneventful," Mamm said. "But I'm ready to get some rest."

Mamm checked on Sarah and the baby and told Walter that his wife needed to rest. "You'll need help," she said.

"Perhaps Mathilde can come," Sarah said.

Walter answered, "I'll ask George."

Emma wasn't sure how Mathilde could help both Sarah and

Harriet, but didn't say anything. Back home, mothers, grandmothers, sisters, and cousins would care for a woman after she gave birth. And if she was new to the county, the women in the church would do all they could for her. But here, like Sarah said, there was a scarcity of women.

"I'll come check on Sarah next week," Mamm said as Isaac helped her up into the wagon. "Send Judah for me if she starts to run a fever or bleed heavily, or if her milk doesn't come in."

Walter assured her he would.

As they left the Landis farm, Emma felt more burdened than ever. Helping with the birth and caring for Sarah and the baby had been a blessing, but she'd been reminded of everything she'd lost. Still, talking with Judah had been a bright spot. She appreciated the information that he shared about Mathilde and her people. But Emma didn't belong here. She needed to return to Pennsylvania.

About a mile from the Landis farm, they passed the big house they'd passed two nights before. Several outbuildings, including a large barn, were behind the house, which was two stories and had a wraparound porch. To the west was a large pasture, where a herd of cattle grazed, fifty or more head. Clothes hung on a line, and a little boy and a girl played in the area in front of the house. Emma was sure the little boy was Baptiste.

She scanned the property. A woman wearing a blue calico dress walked toward the clothesline.

Emma guessed it was the Burtons' place. "We should stop," she said. "Harriet, the woman who lives here, may be wanting Mamm to help her soon."

Isaac stopped the horses and Emma climbed down, then helped her mother. Mathilde waved from the clothesline and started toward them. Baptiste and the girl stopped and stared.

Mathilde reached Emma. They all greeted her, and Mathilde

reached for Emma's free hand and squeezed it. She didn't smile, but her doe-like eyes were warm and kind. The gesture warmed Emma, nurturing the connection she felt with the woman.

Emma introduced her mother and said, "We were hoping to meet Harriet."

The girl, who appeared to be six or so, turned toward Emma and said, "She's not feeling up to visitors."

Mathilde whispered to Emma, "Little Minnie is correct. Harriet is not well."

Emma thanked Mathilde and started walking back to the wagon as two men on horses started toward them.

"Here comes Father!" the girl yelled. Mathilde scooped up Baptiste and headed toward the clothesline.

The other rider was Jean-Paul, who steered his horse in the direction of the barn. George Burton continued to ride toward them on his stallion. Today, he wore work clothes instead of a suit.

Emma called out a hello as George neared the wagon.

Without returning the greeting, he asked, "What do you need?"

"We just stopped to say hello, but your wife isn't feeling up to company," Emma answered.

George ignored her, turned in his saddle, and stared at Mathilde for a long moment. Her attention, however, was on Jean-Paul, as he made his way to the barn.

After a long moment, George, without replying to Emma, turned and followed Jean-Paul.

Isaac urged the horses forward as Mathilde, with Baptiste on her hip, raised her hand in farewell. Emma waved back, hoping she'd see her new friend soon.

But she doubted Mathilde would tell her why everyone seemed to fear George Burton—and why the man was so rude.

CHAPTER 14

The next Sunday, Emma and her family joined the others from Somerset County in Clinton Township for services at Joseph Miller's home. A handful of more families had just arrived, along with several from Ohio. Emma found herself looking for Judah, but he wasn't present. Why hadn't she asked if he attended services with the group in the northeast part of the county? Perhaps Sarah had been right about him being a prodigal son.

After church, during the meal, a young woman named Barbara caught Phillip's attention, and when the Youngie went off on a hike, the two walked together. A young man by the name of Eli Wagler, who had been staring at her during the service, approached Emma and asked if she would like to join the others. She declined, and as she did, she noted a wave of disappointment pass over Mamm's face.

After he left, Mamm said, "It wouldn't hurt to walk with him."

Emma shrugged. She had no intention of marrying someone in Elkhart County, not when Abel waited for her back home.

"Eli's from a good family from Holmes County. They've been

here over a year and have already bought four farms, including one for Eli."

"Does he know I'm a widow?" Emma asked.

"Jah," Mamm said. "As a matter of fact, he does. I made sure to tell his mother, Fannie." Mamm took Emma by the elbow, directed her toward a woman near the middle of the group, and then introduced her.

A few minutes later, one of the other women asked about Mamm's midwifery services. Moving and settling didn't slow babies from coming, that was for sure. Mamm was now playing a needed and respected role in their new community, one she seemed to relish.

Emma caught a few words of another conversation, one that involved Fannie. "They hate it here," the woman said. "And their husbands have agreed to return east."

"To Ohio?" another woman asked.

Fannie shook her head. "To Pennsylvania. Lancaster County, I think."

Later, Emma approached the woman Fannie had been talking to. "I overheard you talking about two families who plan to return east. Whom were you talking about?" She kept her voice low.

"The Martins and Slaybaughs," the woman said. "They live in Newbury Township. Only the Martins are here today. The children in the other family have chicken pox. It's been one thing after another since they got here. The wives are sisters, and they've convinced their husbands to leave next spring."

Emma asked, "Where are the Martins?"

The woman looked around and then said, "Over there, by the sycamore tree."

Emma thanked the woman for the information and walked toward the couple, who were surrounded by nine children, ranging from a toddler to a boy around Isaac's age. Surely they'd be happy to have a single woman to help with their children along the way.

As she approached them, they seemed to be deep in conversation, but then the woman glanced up. She didn't appear to be very friendly. Perhaps Emma had caught them at a bad time.

Still, she explained that she was thinking about returning to Pennsylvania next spring. "I was wondering if I could journey with you. It would just be me and my horse and cow, plus a few belongings." She'd leave her chickens behind.

The husband and wife exchanged glances.

"I could help with your children." She gestured toward the group of women. "My mother is Tabitha Gingrich, the midwife, and I work with her. She's taught me remedies and such. My knowledge might be beneficial."

The woman smiled a little.

"I realize you might change your mind by then—" Emma began.

"Oh, we won't," the woman said quickly. "But let us know if you are still interested when the time comes closer. We'll see you at other services, I'm sure."

"We plan to leave the first week of April," the husband said. "If we don't see you before then, be at our farm by the first Monday of the month. If you haven't arrived and we're ready to go, we'll leave without you."

Emma thanked them and returned to the group of women. The conversation had fallen to some Englisch neighbors, Yankees from Massachusetts. "They seem to think all of Indiana is their Promised Land," one of the younger women said.

"Won't they be surprised when more Plain people keep coming?" Fannie said. "We sent a post back to Holmes County.

Here all of our Youngie can have land to farm. Indiana is an answer to our prayers."

Emma imagined the Yankees felt the same way.

When they left late in the afternoon for the farm, Phillip had stars in his eyes about Barbara. Emma was happy for him and longed for those days when she had felt that way about Asher.

Two weeks later, after Dat and the boys had completed both the barn and the cabin, and Mamm and Emma had stuffed tickings with pine needles for their beds and moved the furniture into the cabin, Phillip started looking for a farm of his own. He wanted to buy before more settlers flooded into Elkhart County and the prices increased. When he found a farm in Union Township in late August, not far from the Landis place, Dat went to see it with him. When they returned, Phillip owned his own farm, thanks to money from their grandfather. The land had cost four dollars an acre, and he'd purchased one hundred acres.

Isaac would inherit Dat's farm, in time.

That night, after Isaac had gone to bed, Dat, Mamm, Emma, and Phillip all gathered around the outside fire that they were still using to cook their meals, not wanting to heat the cabin. Dat's next task was to build a cook shed.

"Emma," Dat said, "you need to go keep house for Phillip and Isaac while they build the barn and then a cabin on the new farm. And you can help your Mamm out by attending the births in that area."

Emma shook her head. "I don't want to do deliveries alone."

"Ach," Dat said. "It is understandable that you don't feel ready. But the mothers down there need help. You are more qualified than you believe."

Even though many of the midwifery fundamentals had

come back to her when helping deliver Sarah's baby, Emma was still afraid to be on her own. Would she ever stop missing her own children when she helped bring other babies into the world?

Mamm leaned toward Emma. "God often calls us to do more than we think we can—or want to do."

Emma's face grew even warmer than it had been. She knew that.

"We need to make sure we work together to create a firm foundation for our family in this new land," Mamm said. "And that means pushing ourselves and being diligent with the gifts God has given us. In turn, we'll be able to serve Him more."

By the light of the fire, Emma could see her father's eyes were full of care, just as Dawdi's had always been. "Pray, Emma," he said. "God will give you the strength you need."

As the others went inside the cabin, Emma stayed outside, staring into the flames. She didn't mind keeping house for her brothers, but how she wished she was keeping house for Asher and tending to her own two children, perhaps having another one soon. Tears pooled in her eyes.

"Emma," Mamm called from the doorway.

"I'm coming." Emma wiped her tears away.

Mamm walked back and met her. "I know this is still hard for you, but it will get better with time. We're praying for a wife for Phillip. And a husband for you."

She met her mother's gaze. "I plan to return to Somerset County."

"I thought you'd put that foolishness behind you."

Emma shook her head. "That's home."

As they reached the door, Mamm whispered, "We're your home. This is what God wants for you."

Emma didn't respond. Leaving without her mother's blessing

would be harder than she thought. But she didn't want to stay. Life was much more manageable back in Pennsylvania.

Two days later, Phillip drove the covered wagon, with his horse and Emma's cow tied to the back, while Isaac and Emma rode their horses. They plodded along, swatting at the mosquitoes.

They came upon an apple tree and stopped. Emma filled her apron with fruit, mostly from the ground, and dumped them in the back of the wagon. Back home, Emma would be making apple butter and apple crisps. She'd be putting up beans and tomatoes and making plum preserves. And cheeses.

Time would tell what she'd be able to preserve here, but if they were going to eat through the winter, she would need to put up some sort of food. They would also need to dig a root cellar on Phillip's property and build a smokehouse like they had on Dat's farm.

They turned off the main trail, and as they neared Phillip's property, they saw a small cabin at the edge of a wood. Emma smelled the pungent smoke of a campfire and the stink of a hide tanning. She shaded her eyes. There was a lush garden on the property—rows of corn, squash, beans, tomatoes, and greens, much like the one on the Landis farm but twice the size.

A woman stepped from the cabin. Mathilde. She wore a buckskin dress instead of her blue calico one.

"Hello!" Emma called out.

As Mathilde waved, Jean-Paul started toward them from the opposite direction on his horse.

As he neared, he called out, "Mathilde, Harriet needs you. It's her time." When he caught sight of Emma, he said, "I was going to go get your Mamm. But would you come instead? George fears for Harriet's life."

EMMA GRABBED THE bag of supplies that Mamm had packed for her from the wagon, including cloths to staunch bleeding, ergot fungi to speed labor, and rosemary oil for pain.

Phillip and Isaac continued on to Phillip's farm, while Jean-Paul hitched his horse to a cart and then drove the women and Baptiste to the Burton place as he smoked his pipe. Again, Emma found the scent of tobacco soothing. On the way, Emma asked him how Sarah and Hiram were doing.

"*Très bien*," he answered. "Mathilde helped her off and on for a few weeks, when she wasn't at George's. Sarah isn't strong, not like Mathilde was after Baptiste was born, but she seems to be doing all right. Walter is very happy."

Emma wanted to ask how Judah was but feared her query might be taken as interest in the man. She found him interesting to talk with, but that was all.

When they reached Harriet's house, the little girl, Minnie, was outside, sitting on the steps in the heat of the day, while George paced along the porch. As they neared, he strode down the stairs toward the cart.

Jean-Paul stopped the horse, but before he could jump down, George reached for Emma to swing her to the ground. She winced at his roughness.

"Where's the other midwife? The older one?" He helped Mathilde off the cart but had his face turned toward Emma.

"In Jackson Township." Emma grabbed her bag from the back of the cart.

"I can go get her," Jean-Paul responded.

Mathilde reached for Baptiste, but George shook his head. "Leave him with Jean-Paul."

Baptiste began to cry.

Jean-Paul put his arm around Baptiste and gave Mathilde a

nod, then snapped the reins. The horse lurched forward, and the cart rolled away. Baptiste began to yell, "*Maman*!"

Mathilde strode toward the house without looking back. From behind, with her buckskin dress and her hair in braids, she looked like a girl. But from the side and front, she looked as if she would deliver her baby soon too.

They could hear Harriet's screams by the time they reached the front door. Mathilde opened it and led the way. Emma wished Mamm was with her. What did it mean that George feared for her life?

The house had two narrow staircases, both taking off from the foyer. Emma followed Mathilde up the steep stairs to the left, and then into a bedroom. A woman, flat on her back in a big four-poster bed, kept screaming.

"Harriet," Mathilde said. "Emma is here."

The woman raised her head, just a little. Her long light brown hair fell around her shoulders, and her hazel eyes were lively. "Who is Emma?"

"My mother is a midwife, and I work with her." Emma put her bag on the bench at the end of the bed and walked to the side of the bed. "Jean-Paul has gone to find her. In the meantime, Mathilde and I will help you."

Harriet fell back against the pillow and groaned. "My other baby didn't feel like this."

Mathilde glanced at Emma and raised her eyebrows. Emma guessed her other baby was the little girl, who appeared to be six or so. Perhaps Harriet couldn't remember how much pain she'd been in the last time.

"Let's get you off the bed." Emma thought of Mamm getting Sarah to stand and how her labor progressed after that.

"No. I can't." Harriet lay still. "Last time I had a doctor, and I stayed in bed. I'll do the same this time."

Emma sat next to her. "How long have you been having pains?"

"A few hours."

"Have you had the urge to push?"

The woman shook her head.

When it took nearly five minutes until she had another pain, Emma guessed Harriet's labor hadn't progressed very far. When it passed, she said, "Never again. I'm staying on this side of the house with my mother."

Emma was baffled. Why were there two sides to the house? And what was Harriet saying? A woman's duty was to her husband.

"Harriet." An older woman, perhaps in her mid-fifties, with her gray hair piled on her head and wearing a fancy dress with a full skirt, stood in the doorway. "How are you doing?"

Harriet answered, "Mother, I'm frightened."

The woman frowned.

Emma stood and introduced herself.

She replied, "I'm Lenore Andersen. Harriet's mother." She pushed a stray strand of hair from her face. "Thank you for coming. Our maid left a few weeks ago—the last of the three who came from Philadelphia with us. It's impossible to keep anyone all the way out here."

Emma smiled at her, trying to be sympathetic.

"Come downstairs with me," Lenore said to Emma. "You can tell me what you need for the birth."

Mathilde took Emma's place at the side of the bed, and Emma followed Lenore down the steps. A moment later, they stepped into the parlor on Lenore's side of the house. All around were beautiful pieces of furniture—an upright piano, a china cabinet, two settees, and a large cherrywood table with red velvet padded chairs. Emma had never seen such fine things.

Lenore turned toward Emma. "Are you Plain?"

"Jah, I am."

"My father had a shipping company back east," Lenore said. "I'd see Plain immigrants on the docks sometimes when I was a girl, right off the boat."

Emma nodded as another of Harriet's screams drifted down the stairs.

"I don't know what we'd do without Mathilde," Lenore continued as they caught snatches of Mathilde's reassuring French words. "She needs to stay here all the time, though. They owe George money, and we keep telling him to collect it that way, but he says Jean-Paul objects." Lenore shrugged. "Hopefully we'll soon be moving on to Norwood Park in Chicago. We've indulged George with his farming experiment long enough. It's time for us to go."

Emma, surprised the woman had confided in her, said, "Right now we need to concentrate on Harriet."

"Of course." Lenore sighed. "What do you need? Hot water? Cloths?"

"Nothing right now, but we'll need cloths and heated water later."

"I'll do my best, with Mathilde's help," Lenore replied. "Send her down when needed."

Emma thanked her and headed back toward the bedroom. She was confused by all that seemed to be going on in the Andersen-Burton household. Separate sides of the house? A fancy dress on the edge of the frontier? Talk of moving to Chicago? Jah, Emma had never been around such people.

HARRIET DELIVERED A little boy two hours later after only three pushes, before Mamm arrived. It was one of the easiest births Emma had ever attended. While Emma cared for Harriet, Mathilde cradled the newborn in her arms.

"Go show the baby to George," Harriet said. "He'll be so pleased."

Mathilde obeyed, and soon they heard a loud *whoop*. And then George yelled, "I have a boy!"

Minutes later, Mathilde came back in the room.

Harriet lifted her head from the pillow. "Was I right about him being pleased?"

Mathilde nodded.

"He got his boy." Harriet lowered her head again. "George Jr., but we'll call him Georgie."

When the baby began to fuss, Harriet asked Emma, "Do you know of a wet nurse I can hire?"

"*Nee*," Emma said. She knew of several Plain women from the services she'd attended who were nursing, but none of them would leave their families to live in the Burton household.

Mamm arrived soon after, declared herself not needed, and then asked Harriet, "Do you have help for the next several days?"

"We're between maids." Harriet slunk down in the bed. "The last of the girls who came west with me went on to Chicago, but Mathilde works for us."

"I can stay if Baptiste can be with me." Mathilde still held the baby.

"Of course. Why would he not be able to?"

Mathilde didn't answer Harriet's question. Instead she said, "I'll go speak with Jean-Paul."

"Give the baby to Harriet," Mamm said. "I'll stay here. Emma, you go with Mathilde."

Although confused by Mamm's request, Emma followed

Mathilde down the stairs, stopping in the foyer on the right side of the house. George and Jean-Paul, who appeared uncomfortable, sat in the parlor on the other side of the foyer. George smoked a cigar while Jean-Paul, sitting on the edge of a chair, smoked his pipe. Baptiste sat on his father's knee and lifted his arms to Mathilde as soon as he saw her.

Mathilde took him, holding him close. She spoke in French to Jean-Paul. He glanced at George and then said something back to her. Finally, he addressed George, "Does Harriet need Mathilde's help?"

"Of course," George answered. "We can't find another maid, and Mother Andersen doesn't know what to do."

"Will you write up a contract? So we know how much will go toward our debt?" Jean-Paul asked.

"She won't do it out of kindness?"

Emma couldn't tell if George was teasing or not.

Finally, he laughed and said, "Of course I will."

Mathilde said, "Baptiste must stay too."

George frowned but then said, "All right."

Emma didn't believe Baptiste could be a problem. He reminded her of Hansi, quiet and eager to please.

Jean-Paul addressed Emma. "I'll take you to your brother's place and then take your mother home."

"All right," Emma answered, feeling uneasy about leaving Mathilde, but surely she'd be all right. She had been before.

Without saying anything, Mathilde disappeared into the foyer with Baptiste still in her arms.

Emma wasn't sure how Mamm did it, but by the time she and Mathilde returned to the bedroom, Harriet was nursing the baby.

An hour later, as Mamm and Emma walked down the stairs, Emma tried to contain her curiosity. Mamm had always made it clear that working as a midwife meant shutting one's ears. *"You'll hear things not meant for you,"* Mamm had said more than once. *"You'll be tempted to share the information, to gossip. But you can't. They aren't your secrets to reveal, unless you feel someone is at risk of being harmed."*

But to Emma's surprise, as Jean-Paul took them to Phillip's farm, it was Mamm who quizzed him about the Burtons. Perhaps she believed Harriet was at risk.

"They came west four years ago from Philadelphia, planning to go to Chicago. But George had gotten it in his head that he wanted to try his hand at farming," Jean-Paul explained. "Harriet, who I'm sure regrets this, convinced her mother to finance the endeavor. Lenore had the house split in two—one side for Harriet and George and their little girl and the other for herself."

Jean-Paul paused a moment and then said, "The original plan was that Lenore would go on to Chicago, where she had invested in real estate."

"Why hasn't she?" Emma asked.

"Harriet hasn't been well since they got here—or so she says. The maids who came with them weren't happy here and all have left." Jean-Paul frowned. "But Lenore doesn't know the first thing about cooking or cleaning." He shook his head. "Lenore and Harriet seem to relish in being miserable, while George pretends he knows how to farm, which he doesn't. But he does know how to play the role of *seigneur du manoir*."

"What do you mean?" Mamm asked.

"Let's just say he knows how to take advantage of people."

Something about Jean-Paul's tone put Emma on edge. Did the debt they owed the Burtons come from deceit? And why would Judah associate with the man?

"What about Mathilde?" Emma asked, concerned for her

friend and wondering if she should have stayed with her. "Is it hard for her to work for Harriet?"

"She does her work and ignores the rest." Jean-Paul stared straight ahead at the trail. "We do what we need to do to survive."

CHAPTER 15

Phillip and Isaac worked nonstop for two weeks, cutting trees from the woods that covered most of the property and dragging them to the barn site. Once the trees were cut, Judah, Walter, and Sarah, along with the baby, came on a Saturday morning to help strip the logs. Dat and Mamm hoped to come later, if Mamm didn't have a birth to go to.

As they worked, Sarah commented on what a hard time Harriet was having. Emma didn't respond. Harriet had summoned Emma five times in the last two weeks, even though Mathilde had been with her the entire time. Each time it was because Harriet "didn't feel well." The first time, Emma suspected milk fever, but that wasn't the case. The other times, Emma believed Harriet felt weak because she seldom left her bed.

Emma had heard that wealthy women stayed in bed for up to a month after giving birth. Harriet was still in Lenore's bed, with Mathilde seeing to her every need. Amish women took care of each other, true, but no one stayed in bed that long unless they were truly ill.

Attending Harriet frustrated Emma, but she enjoyed seeing Mathilde. Each time it felt as if Emma's connection with

Mathilde grew through a quick smile or a shared laugh. And Emma found herself caring more and more for little Baptiste too. He no longer made her long for Hansi. Baptiste was his own person, who adored his mother and was warming to Emma too.

But Baptiste seemed afraid of Lenore and Harriet. And he was also frightened by George. Whenever the man came into the room, he would hide behind Mathilde's skirts and whimper. Even Lenore had noticed it.

"If it were up to Lenore," Sarah said, "they'd all be headed to Chicago by now."

"What keeps her from going?" Emma asked. She seemed to be the source of wealth in the family.

"Harriet is Lenore's only child, and she wants to give George a chance at farming. It seems he's failed at everything else he's done—banking, shipping, and the law," Sarah said. "Lenore's stayed to be with Harriet. But now that they can't find a new maid, besides Mathilde, I think Harriet won't want to stay much longer either."

Hiram, who lay on a blanket nearby, began to fuss. Sarah sighed and scooped him up.

As the others continued working, a rider approached.

"Jean-Paul!" Judah called out.

He waved as his horse slowed to a trot. Pulling his horse to a stop, Jean-Paul locked eyes with Emma. "It's Mathilde's time. She said the baby flipped last night while she was at Harriet's, and while she was walking home today with Baptiste, she began her labor. She asked if you would come."

"I'll grab my bags." A breech baby could be tricky, but Emma had assisted Mamm with one back in Pennsylvania.

Judah started toward the barn. "I'll saddle your horse."

When Emma came out with her bag, Judah led Red out of

the barn and helped her mount it. Then he turned to Jean-Paul. "I'll come over soon to help with your chores."

As Emma followed Jean-Paul down the trail, she prayed for Mathilde and for the baby. And for herself too, that she would be wise and remember all Mamm had taught her. She didn't understand the kinship she felt with Mathilde, but out of everyone she'd met since arriving in Indiana, she felt the strongest connection to the Native woman. She prayed the Lord would help her serve Mathilde and her baby and not be reminded of her grief.

When they arrived at the cabin, Baptiste sat in the open doorway. When he spotted them, he jumped up and ran into the house. Then Mathilde appeared with him, standing sideways, with one hand pressed against her back and the other on Baptiste's shoulder.

Jean-Paul dismounted, helped Emma down, and then led the horses toward the barn, while Emma headed to the cabin with her bags.

"Merci." Mathilde stepped back into the cabin. "I wasn't sure if you would come."

Emma followed her. "Of course I would. I'd do anything I could for you." She meant it.

Mathilde tried to smile, but it was more of a grimace. She was in the middle of a pain. Judah arrived soon after, and Jean-Paul took Baptiste outside, while Emma brewed Mathilde a cup of chamomile tea from the kettle hanging over the fire. Mathilde sipped some between pains.

The cabin was one room, with a bed covered with a wool blanket in the corner and a table and four chairs near the fire. It wasn't long until Mathilde was ready to push, and she squatted on the floor near the bed.

Emma heard voices outside and wondered if she should send

Judah back to Phillip's to see if Mamm had arrived, but then a foot appeared. After the contraction ended, Mathilde stood.

Another pain overtook Mathilde, and she kneeled against the bed. Emma knelt behind her, and when the foot appeared again, Emma took hold of it and pulled. "Keep pushing," she said, breathing a silent prayer as she did. Mathilde pushed, continuing to even after the pain stopped. Emma held on to the foot, and with the next pain, the baby fell into her hands.

She cried, "You have a girl!" Startled, the little one gazed up at Emma and began to cry. Mathilde climbed onto the bed and reached for her daughter. Emma slipped her into her arms, and, for a moment, the three were connected. The baby suspended between the two women, all of them entwined. And then Mathilde clutched the little one to her chest and whispered a prayer of thanks. "Merci, Seigneur." Then she raised her head. "Merci, Emma. Merci."

"What will you name her?" Emma asked.

"Agnes," Mathilde answered. "After Jean-Paul's mother. And her Potawatomi name is Wawetseka, after my mother. It means *jolie*." Emma had heard Mathilde use the word before—*very pretty*. But it was more than that. It indicated a beauty on the inside too.

As she stared at Mathilde and Agnes, Emma suddenly realized that she hadn't thought once of the baby girl she'd lost, or of Hansi. All she had thought about these past few hours was Mathilde and her beautiful family.

By midafternoon, Mathilde insisted she didn't need help. Emma said she was happy to stay, but even Jean-Paul said it wasn't necessary.

"Come back tomorrow to check on Mathilde." He pressed a coin into Emma's hand.

Emma refused to take it, thinking of the debt the couple

owed to George. "Mathilde is my friend. It was my privilege to be with her."

"Then when you come tomorrow, we'll have produce for you to take from the garden."

"Merci," Emma said and smiled. Maybe Mamm was right—the best way to forget one's own troubles was to reach out and serve another. That was exactly what had happened to Emma in serving Mathilde.

As Emma rode beside Judah on the way back to Phillip's, he said, "I hope I'm not being too forward, but Sarah told me about your losses, about your husband and children. I wanted to let you know that I'm sorry."

"Denki," Emma whispered, but she found it odd he would be so empathetic toward her when he'd rejected the widow back home. Judah Landis was a complicated man.

"I imagine," he said, "that working as a midwife must bring you both joy and sorrow."

Emma was surprised a man would understand what no one else, including Mamm, seemed able to comprehend. She smiled at Judah and then said, "Today, it was all joy."

EMMA CHECKED ON Mathilde several times during the next week, along with being called to Harriet's as well. Without Mathilde's help, the home had fallen into disarray. Each time she visited, Emma helped with the washing, cooking, and cleaning. All Harriet could talk about was when Mathilde would return. Emma assured Harriet that Mathilde needed time to heal too, but the woman didn't seem to believe her.

On Saturday, when Mathilde, Jean-Paul, and their little ones showed up at Phillip's farm, it was obvious Mathilde didn't need as much time to heal as Harriet. It was now near the end of September. The weather had held, and Jean-Paul said sometimes the rains usually didn't begin until mid-October or later. But sometimes they began sooner.

Jean-Paul began helping Phillip and Isaac finish fitting the logs on the barn. If Emma had to, she'd keep house in a room of the barn, but she hoped they'd be in the cabin soon.

Agnes was strapped into a cradleboard with a hoop made out of hickory near the top to protect her head. A smaller willow hoop, with a weaving secured in the middle and a blue feather and a white shell hanging from the bottom, hung from the larger hoop and dangled over the baby's head.

"It protects her from bad dreams," Mathilde explained as she saw Emma glancing at it. "And catches the good ones."

Emma had never seen anything like it.

Mathilde unwound strips of deer hide on the cradleboard that secured the baby and then lifted her out to clean her bottom, using a wet rag. She pulled out a tray of soiled moss from the cradleboard, discarded it, and then filled the tray with clean moss. Emma thought that much easier than changing a cloth on a baby's bottom.

Agnes's legs and feet were wrapped in rabbit fur, and she wore a long-sleeved tunic, also made from fur. She also wore a hat and seemed as warm and cozy as could be.

Mathilde swung the cradleboard onto her back, over her buckskin dress, while Baptiste stayed close to his mother's side. She pointed to the pile of river rocks and the buckets. The rocks were for the fireplace, which Emma hoped to cook over during the cold winter instead of a campfire outside. Her stove back in Pennsylvania was a distant memory now.

"Do you need more rocks?" Mathilde asked. "I can help." She grabbed one of the buckets and started for the creek, while Baptiste bumped along beside her, determined to keep up. Emma followed, not sure Mathilde should be lifting rocks. She said so, but Mathilde simply said, “I am fine.”

When they reached the creek, Baptiste picked up a stone and hurled it into the water. He threw another and another as the women placed rocks into the buckets. When they’d finished, Mathilde picked up hers, and Baptiste, without being summoned, wrapped his tiny hand around the handle beside his mother’s to help her carry it.

Once they’d unloaded the rocks close to the cabin site, they headed back down to the creek. When they reached it again, Mathilde looked at the water and said, “*Il me fait reposer dans de verts pâturages, Il me dirige près des eaux paisibles.*” Then she looked up at Emma. “From the Psalms.”

“Ach.” Emma recited, “He maketh me to lie down in green pastures: he leadeth me beside the still waters.”

Mathilde nodded and then smiled. “The Black Robes taught us about the Bible, about Christ. My father believed because some of what they said was like our own teachings. Then all of us were baptized.”

“How old were you?” Emma asked.

“Twelve or so.”

“When did you meet Jean-Paul?”

“I saw him as a child when I went to the trading post with my father. But I was sixteen when Jean-Paul first noticed me,” Mathilde said. “Seventeen when we married.”

Emma guessed Mathilde was twenty or so now, maybe half the age of her husband. She hoped he would live a long and healthy life so he could care for his wife and children.

Once the buckets were filled again, the baby grew fussy, and Emma said, “Let’s sit and rest for a minute.”

Mathilde took the baby from her cradleboard and then placed

her in her lap. As the baby continued to fuss, Mathilde untied the front of her dress and began to feed her. Baptiste threw another stone into the creek, and Emma searched for flat stones to skip across the water. When she found several, she stepped to Baptiste's side and flung one across the water. It skipped twice. She threw the next one. It skipped three times.

He laughed.

She handed him the third rock and showed him how to hold it. She held on to his chubby hand, which felt like heaven to her, and flung it out toward the water. But he wouldn't let go of the stone. She tried again. It appeared he didn't want to release it.

Mathilde laughed and patted the ground beside her with her free hand. "*Viens là.*"

Baptiste plopped down, offering the stone to her. Then he began collecting more, placing them in a pile beside her instead of throwing them in the water. Emma thought of Jacob in the Bible making a pillar of stones to mark where God had spoken to him.

"I came here before with my family," Mathilde said. "With my parents and two sisters."

"Here?" Emma was startled. "To this creek?"

"Yes." She nodded toward the water. "There's a natural bridge, of rocks. Flat ones that are pretty easy to cross."

Mathilde pointed to the thickets on the other side of the creek. "Jean-Paul and I picked berries over there, the day Sarah's baby was born." Mathilde's English was better than it had been, perhaps from her time at Harriet's. Or perhaps she'd grown more comfortable with Emma.

"Did you spend much time in this area as a child?"

Mathilde nodded. "We'd come here in the late summer and early fall. We'd fish from the river and creeks. Pick berries. Trap rabbits and squirrels and wild turkeys. Collect turtle eggs."

Emma rubbed her brow. "Your family came here? Where my brother's farm is now?"

Mathilde nodded.

"I'm so sorry," Emma said. Mathilde must be thinking of her parents and her sisters now, of her own heartbreaking memories.

Mathilde leaned toward Emma until their shoulders touched. "Don't feel bad. It's not your fault. Besides, after we spent time here, we would go back to the land by the mission and harvest our squash and corn and learn more about God the Father and Jesus the Son and the Holy Ghost."

Emma stared out at the water. The rejection of Catholicism was behind the Reformation, responsible for the schism that led to the Anabaptists, which led to the Mennonites, which led to the Amish. Emma's people believed only adults should be baptized once they'd made the choice to follow the Lord and join the church, while Catholics believed in baptizing babies, such as Agnes. Of course there were many other differences too.

But Mathilde found comfort in the same scriptures that Emma did—or that she used to, anyway. Emma couldn't remember the last time she had read scripture or truly prayed. But not Mathilde. Both seemed to be in the forefront of her mind, along with her family and all the ways her life had changed.

THE NEXT DAY, Emma and her brothers rode the horses to Dat and Mamm's place, where the church service was being held. Phillip had invited Judah, who accompanied them.

All four of them planned to spend the night and leave early in the morning for Union Township. Walter had said he'd do Phillip and Isaac's chores while they were gone.

Emma would sleep in the cabin, and Judah would sleep in the barn with Phillip and Isaac.

Eli Wagler approached Emma before the service, happy to see her. She was thankful when everyone sat down on the log benches, divided in two groups, one for the men and one for the women. A bishop from Ohio preached from the book of Joshua, about the Israelites arriving in the Promised Land. "God has brought us to our own Promised Land," he said. Emma couldn't help but think of the Potawatomi people being forced to Kansas so white settlers could have their land.

"We must honor Him with our lives," the preacher said, "as we serve each other and the Lord. May we bless our neighbors as the Lord has blessed us."

Emma thought of her neighbors. The Landis family. The Burtons. Jean-Paul and Mathilde. One Plain. One Englisch. And one French-Potawatomi. All three families were in Union Township for very different reasons.

Before the meal, Eli approached Emma as she spoke with Mamm, telling her about Mathilde's baby girl. Mamm nudged Emma and stepped away.

Eli seemed attentive, telling Emma that he had been disheartened to find out that she'd been staying in Union Township. "It's not permanent, is it?"

"Nee." Emma explained that she was keeping house for Phillip.

Eli nodded his head toward the field, where Barbara and Phillip were deep in conversation. "Perhaps you'll be out of a job soon."

Emma smiled, deciding that it wouldn't hurt to become acquainted with Eli. She appreciated that it didn't matter to him, unlike Judah, that she was a widow. "How have you been?"

"*Gut*. Busy with harvest. I've started the corn, and then I will do another cutting of hay. I'm grateful the weather has been cooperative."

Emma nodded in agreement.

"Later this fall, I'll cut more trees and then pull out the stumps so I can plant more crops in the spring."

He was definitely ambitious. He continued talking about his plans for his farm until Emma became aware that all of the women, even Barbara, were helping put the food on the long table outside the cabin. "I need to help," she said.

"How about a walk later?" Eli asked.

She hesitated but then said, "All right."

After the meal, Emma joined the other Youngie, which felt odd to her. She was different from the others. She'd been married. She'd been a mother. But now she was a single woman again. She started out walking with Eli, but he soon became distracted by one of the other young men, asking about the best corn seed to plant in the spring.

But then, about ten minutes later, there were heated voices behind them. Eli and Judah seemed to be arguing.

Emma slowed her pace.

"They were all savages," Eli said. "Of course they had to be removed."

"Do you know any Natives?" Judah asked.

"Of course not. They were gone before we arrived."

"Not all of the Potawatomi are gone."

"Pot-a-what?" Eli asked.

"Potawatomi." Judah spoke slowly. "That's the name of the tribe who lived here."

"Savages," Eli retorted. "They fled like cowards."

"They were forced to go," Judah said. "Most of them, anyway."

"You said some are still here?"

"Jah," Judah said.

"Who might yet attack us?"

"They're peaceful," Judah answered.

"They're not," Eli said. "They're killers."

"That's not true." Judah's voice grew firmer. "Their culture is based on what they call the Seven Grandfather Teachings, which are wisdom, respect"—Emma turned her head and watched as Judah counted the topics off on his fingers as he spoke—"love, honesty, humility, bravery, and truth. They teach equality and respect for all creation—"

"Instead of for the Creator," Eli interrupted.

"*Nee*, that's not true either," Judah said. "Many have embraced Christianity. Because they were taught there was a Creator, it made sense to them."

Eli shook his head. "You're lying."

Not taking her eyes off Judah, Emma tripped on a root. In a split second, Judah was at her side, taking a hold of her arm. "Are you all right?"

"*Jah*," she answered, embarrassed.

Behind them, Eli had turned to someone else and said, "Can you believe he'd say such heresy?"

The other person laughed.

Judah lowered his voice and tilted his head toward Emma. "Did you stumble because you were eavesdropping?"

She shook her head. "You were both so loud that I was simply listening. I can tell you feel strongly."

"I do," he said. "But I'm afraid I wasted my words. And I'm sorry if I offended your friend."

Emma's face grew warm.

Judah cleared his throat, as if he wanted to say more. But he didn't.

Eli caught up with them and stepped to the other side of Emma. "Are you enjoying the walk?"

"Jah," she answered. "It's been . . . very enlightening."

"We've come to a beautiful country. We're blessed to be in a new land, with all of life ahead of us," Eli said, his arm grazing hers. "This is truly our Promised Land."

Emma stepped away from him but bumped into Judah. She quickly centered herself between the two of them. Eli started talking about the four properties his family had bought, all adjoining each other in Newbury Township. "I didn't tell you about our buildings," he said. "We finished the third barn and the big house this summer. I'm working on making furniture now. . . ." He talked on and on.

Judah stayed at her side, quiet but seemingly attentive.

"What about your farm?" Eli asked Judah. "Where is it?"

"Oh, I don't have a farm," Judah answered. "Not really. I'm helping my brother."

"Oh, a farmhand. That sounds disheartening."

"It's fine," Judah answered. "The Lord will provide."

Eli didn't answer. Instead, he started talking about how many acres of woods he planned to clear for his next field. She felt grateful toward Judah for his defense of the Natives. And she felt sympathetic toward him concerning his lack of resources. But that didn't mean he was of good character, generally speaking.

The best plan for Emma was to return to Pennsylvania and marry Abel. There was a possibility that Judah wasn't trustworthy, and Eli had definitely proven himself to be a bore.

When they returned to Mamm and Dat's cabin, Emma joined the women putting out the puddings, pies, and cobblers.

Mamm, just as she'd been back home, was in the center of the group of women. There was a confidence about her that Emma didn't see in other women. She wasn't sure if it was because Mamm was a midwife—or if Mamm had become a midwife because of her confidence.

As the women dished out the sweets, a man on a horse, with a child riding in front of him, came into the clearing. It was Jean-Paul, with Baptiste. "Tabitha," he called out. "Mathilde is ill. And I can't find Emma."

"Here I am." Emma stepped out of the group of women, her heart racing.

Jean-Paul held on to Baptiste with one hand and the reins with the other. "I need one of you to come with me, *s'il vous plait*. Mathilde is burning up with fever."

CHAPTER 16

Savannah

As I stood at the window of the farmhouse waiting for Tommy the next morning, I thought of Emma. She'd made it to Indiana and was quickly thrust into helping her mother deliver babies again. Eli Wagler offered security but seemed full of himself. Judah Landis didn't have anything to offer Emma, and he didn't want to marry a widow.

I sighed. I hoped I could hear the rest of the story before I left. Would Emma stay in Indiana? Or go back home and marry Abel? Jah, she'd have to leave her family, but life would definitely be easier than in Indiana.

A sentiment I shared.

On the phone, Ryan had said, *"I can't stop thinking about you."* Did that mean he regretted what he'd done? My heart began to race. Did he want me back?

I shook my head. How could I even entertain the idea? He'd dumped me. Heartlessly and emphatically. The sooner I forgot him and put him behind me, the better.

Tommy turned his Jeep into the driveway just as Mammi came into the room, heading toward her quilting frame.

"I'll be gone all morning," I said. "I'll let Uncle Seth know I'm picking up a rental and will return his pickup this afternoon."

"All right." Mammi peered over her reading glasses. "I'll be here when you get back."

"What do you have planned for tomorrow?"

"I thought I'd go out to Jane's."

"Perfect." I grinned at her. "I'll take you." And hopefully hear more of Emma's story. I gave Mammi a wave as I walked out the door, pulling it shut behind me.

The morning sky was blue with just a few puffs of white clouds. It was cold, but not bitterly so. The thermometer on the other side of Mammi's kitchen window had read thirty—the warmest it had been since I arrived.

I grabbed my phone charger from the pickup and then climbed into Tommy's Jeep, this time in the front seat.

He wore a San Francisco Giants hat. The black and orange looked good over his brown eyes and goatee. "*Guder mariye*," he said, with an impish grin.

"Good morning to you too." I laughed. "Nice hat."

"Thanks. I bought it at a game."

"At Oracle Park? In San Francisco?"

He nodded.

Incredulous, I asked, "You were in the city and didn't let me know?"

"I didn't know you lived there," he said. "Otherwise I would have."

What would that have been like? Would Ryan and I have taken him out to dinner? Offered him a place to stay?

"I've been to San Fran a few times over the years," he said. "But last I heard you were going to UCLA."

"And you thought I was on the ten-year plan?"

He laughed. "No, I always knew you were smart. I was pretty sure you'd do well."

I always knew he was smart too. I held up my charger. "Mind if I plug this in?"

"Go ahead." He pulled out the cigarette lighter so I could.

"I'm a little obsessive about taking advantage of every opportunity I have to charge my phone," I explained.

"Please note that I have an apartment in town." Tommy backed out of the driveway. "With electricity."

"Did you give notice on your apartment? Like you did your job?"

He shook his head as he pulled onto the highway. "Kenny took over the lease."

"But now he's not here."

Tommy nodded. "I'm not sure what to do about that. I keep expecting Kenny to show up any day now. When he does, I'll let Deputy Rogers know."

"That puts you in a difficult situation."

Tommy shrugged. "He's put me in difficult situations before. He knows how this works."

I couldn't help but be a little suspicious. Was Tommy trying to put himself in a better light by criticizing Kenny?

But he seemed so matter-of-fact about all of it. He didn't seem arrogant or self-serving. I decided to change the topic. "So what's the story with Mason's mom?"

"She was in rehab but has been out for a few months," he answered. "The court determined she can have Mason back in a halfway house kind of situation."

Dumbfounded, I asked, "And you're okay with that?"

"Why wouldn't I be?"

"Isn't he better off here, with you?" I paused and then added, "With his father?"

He raised his eyebrows and then suppressed a smile. "I can see why you would think that, with him calling me Dada and all. But he calls every man he meets Dada. I'm not his father."

"What?"

"Kenny is."

Dumbfounded again, I leaned back against the seat. "But your mom is his grandmother, right? And I'm pretty sure Mammi thinks he's your son."

Tommy wrinkled his nose. "I think a lot of people do. My mom doesn't, of course. But she tells everyone Mason is her grandson, which is somewhat true since she certainly took Kenny in. They have a mother-son relationship. Kenny has broken her heart more than any of us." Again, I wondered if by being negative about Kenny, Tommy was trying to make himself look better.

"Is Mason more attached to you than Kenny?"

"No, Mason is pretty fond of him too. I'm just more available." Tommy pulled onto Route 6, heading west. When I didn't say any more, he finally continued. "Christine is the name of Mason's mom. She grew up in Texas and met Kenny in Las Vegas, when he and I were living out there. Kenny was on the up-and-up then. Not doing—or selling—drugs. He was working construction and met Christine at an AA meeting, which is the closest he's come to any kind of therapy or rehab. He fell head over heels.

"She got pregnant and stayed clean, but then started using again after Mason was born. When she went into rehab, Kenny and I headed home so my mom could help with Mason, which turned out to be the best option." He had a sad, faraway look in his eyes. "But then Kenny started acting weird here, staying out late, sleeping all day, being evasive. Mom was taking care of Mason during the day, and I was taking care of him at night."

He sighed. "I have no idea what's best for Mason, if taking him back to Nevada is even the right thing to do."

"Why doesn't Kenny drive Mason back to Nevada?" I asked.

Tommy stared straight ahead, not taking his eyes off the road to even glance at me. "He and Christine were fighting when she went into rehab. No one thinks it's a good idea for him to go down there."

"But what about custody?" The pitch of my voice was rising. "Is Kenny just going to give Mason up?"

"I'm not sure." Tommy shrugged. "Hopefully Kenny will move back to Nevada soon or at least visit regularly—once Christine is in a better place and once he's in a better place too."

"It doesn't sound as if he's doing anything to get in a better place."

"That's true," Tommy answered.

My voice stayed high and was tense now too. "Will you stay in Nevada? And be able to see Mason?"

"I'm planning on staying, and I hope I can see Mason," he said. "If Christine will allow it."

"Does Christine have support?"

He glanced over at me, a smile twitching at the corner of his lips. "This reminds me of when we were little. Of all the questions you asked."

I grimaced. "Sorry."

"No, it's fine," he said. "It's good to talk about it." He took a deep breath. "The only support Christine has will come from the staff at the halfway house, but they say that women do better in recovery if their children are with them." He checked his side mirror and rearview mirror and then passed a semi. "Christine had a pretty rotten childhood. Lots of trauma, thus the addiction. Her parents were out of the picture, but she had a grandmother who raised her. She died right after Mason was born, which probably accounted for her relapse." He gripped the steering wheel tighter. "That and the fact that Kenny wasn't the best partner."

I exhaled as Tommy passed another semi. "Poor Christine."

Tommy nodded. "Kenny's had his own trauma. His mom died from cancer when he was fourteen, and his dad was never warm and fuzzy, certainly not supportive. Kenny was out on his own at sixteen." He sighed. "At least Kenny and Christine both have reasons for their downfalls. There are lots of things I've done for no reason that I regret."

I was impressed with how empathetic Tommy sounded when talking about Christine and Kenny. He didn't sound judgmental or unforgiving. Then again, if he had regrets, maybe his empathy was based on his own experience. I had no idea what he'd done.

Before I could ask more questions, my phone rang. I didn't recognize the number, but I answered it anyway. "Hello?"

"Hello, this is Joshua Wenger. Listen, I haven't heard from Miriam since Wednesday. I'm afraid something's happened to her."

"What do you mean, you haven't heard from her?"

He didn't answer.

"Joshua, be honest with me. Does she have a cell phone?"

After a long moment of silence, he said, "Jah. But like I said, I haven't heard from her. Maybe she hasn't been able to charge it. Or maybe something's happened."

"Would you please give me her number?"

"No," he said. "She wouldn't answer her phone if you called, even if I did."

Exasperated, I replied, "I'm on my way to Gary to try to find her." I didn't add that Tommy Miller was with me. That would be hard to explain.

"I'll text you the address of our relatives that she was staying with," he said. "If she's not there, I have no idea where she might be."

"I'll talk with them," I said. "And call you back."

"Hurry," he said. "I'm worried about her."

TOMMY MERGED ONTO the interstate, which meant we had about twenty more minutes to Gary. I was about ready to punch in the address, when I decided to check my email first. Nothing from the hospital in Lancaster. Quickly, I zipped over to my banking app. I groaned. None of the charges had been reversed.

"What's up?" Tommy asked.

"Credit card problems."

"Stolen?"

I nearly laughed. If only. "It's a long story."

He wore a concerned expression on his face. "Does it have to do with your ex?"

I exhaled. "You know?"

"I heard you had a canceled wedding is all."

"Who from?"

"A guy at work whose wife knows someone who is pregnant—"

"—and who knows my cousin Delores." I groaned again.

"That's probably the connection." He glanced at me. "Sorry."

"No worries." I knew I couldn't keep it a secret. I just hoped I wouldn't have to talk with anyone about it. "Yeah, there was a canceled wedding. Ryan, the canceler, said he'd pay for everything, but his credit card was stolen and all the vendors charged mine."

"That's horrible."

"Hopefully it will soon be remedied. He was supposed to have called everyone with his new card number." Desperate to get his attention off of me, I tried to change the subject. "How about you?" I asked. "Any heartbreaks in your past?"

"Oh yeah," he said. "I've had my share, starting with Sadie Yoder."

I smiled. "The girl you ditched me for? For a walk down the lane?"

He laughed. "Sorry about that." Then seriously, he said, "I can definitely feel your pain. I know this has to be an especially rough time for you."

I swallowed hard, willing myself not to cry.

"I won't say it will get better." He smiled shyly. "I mean, I know it will, but it doesn't help you to have me say that. Although I hope it will—and soon."

"Thank you," I said. "I appreciate your kind words."

"I hope I'm not being too nosy, but any idea what happened?" Tommy asked. "Why Ryan called it off?"

I hesitated for a moment, not sure how transparent I should be with Tommy. I decided it didn't matter. I'd soon be headed far away from Nappanee, while he would be going back to Las Vegas, if he was innocent in Miriam's disappearance.

I told him about Amber. "But obviously that wasn't the only reason. There had to be other issues too." I was feeling sad about Ryan at the moment, and I didn't paint things between us in as a harsh a light as I sometimes felt.

"I suppose the situation would be pretty complex," Tommy said.

"I just wish I could understand what happened. Ryan was the one who got me to return to church, to have hope for the future. I finally felt as if I wasn't alone anymore."

"I'm really sorry," Tommy said.

"Thanks. I've heard there are others who've gotten dumped right before their wedding. I've just never met any of them."

"Jah, I am sorry that you got dumped. But what I meant was that I'm sorry you'd felt so alone for so long."

Tears sprung into my eyes. Before I could think twice, I poured out my sorrow about Mom dying and Dad remarrying so soon. Finally, I caught myself. "I'm being insensitive to you, about your father's death."

"No, you're not," Tommy said. "He had cancer. I had years to prepare myself. I still have my mother. Losing your mom and then your family was a big loss. And now losing Ryan too."

I nodded as my throat filled with grief. Tommy really did understand.

He slowed behind a van in the left-hand lane. "I thought of you a lot when I heard about your mom's car accident and death. I know how much you loved her."

"Denki." This time I couldn't stop the tears and began wiping them from under my eyes.

He quickly patted my knee.

I couldn't speak, but I tried to smile, which didn't help as it only made me cry harder.

"You have your own trauma," he said as I rummaged through my purse for a tissue.

"Don't we all?" I managed to choke out.

Tommy smiled sympathetically and concentrated on passing the van.

I didn't recognize I was traumatized after Mom's death at first. It wasn't like Dad hauled me off to counseling or anything. It wasn't until I started at UCLA that it became clear to me I had a problem. One didn't have to be a party animal to find solace in drinking. The girls on my floor seemed to always have alcohol around, especially on weekends, and when it was offered to me, I drank.

It really did numb the pain, and it was soon obvious that I had a surplus of untreated trauma, with no one to talk to about Mom's accident and death. But then one of my roommates, after I'd sloppy-cried on her shoulder the Sunday night before, walked me to the counseling center the next day.

Therapy helped me see that grief manifested itself in many different ways, including anger, control, and denial. Counseling didn't cure me, but I believe it saved me from a much rockier path.

After I met Ryan and we started attending church, I still didn't talk to God a lot, but the music, scripture, and teaching turned my heart toward God. After a while, I found myself praying occasionally again.

I realized I'd been lost in my own thoughts when Tommy said, "I'm happy to listen if you want to talk."

"Oh," I said, "I've just been thinking about how I'd been depending on Ryan more and more—more than on God—because Ryan was what I *wanted*. But I'm finally beginning to comprehend that what I *needed* was an entirely different matter."

I'd wanted financial security. A family. A beautiful home. But I didn't feel as if I could be entirely honest with Ryan. I often felt I was hiding a part of myself. The part that grew up rural, that had spent time on an Amish farm.

"What do you need?"

"Honesty," I answered. "To be honest about my past and honest as I try to figure out my future."

"Does your future still include you becoming a midwife?" Tommy asked. "Because I remember you talking about it all the time when we were kids. You idealized your mom. And Delores too."

I smiled at the memories and then shook my head. "I don't foresee being a midwife in my future, but wanting to be one was part of my past—a part I've been hiding as of late. It's been good for me to revisit all of that. I've neglected it."

Spending time with Tommy made it obvious I'd pushed a lot of my memories and feelings away. He was showing himself to be a caring person.

Unless he had something to do with Miriam's disappearance.

Then he was the biggest fraud ever, and I was the biggest fool, an even bigger one than I'd been with Ryan.

We'd reached the outskirts of Gary already, and I quickly keyed the address into my maps app. It directed us to the east side of town, which consisted of mostly single-dwelling wood-frame houses. Many had plywood over the windows. Haphazard troughs had been made where people had walked on sidewalks that weren't shoveled.

When we reached the address, Tommy pulled over. The sage green house on the corner was small, but it appeared well kept. Smoke curled out of the chimney. The sidewalk was shoveled and the driveway cleared.

"Ready?" As I climbed out, a compact car on the side street pulled away from the curb, fishtailing a little.

Tommy led the way up the steps to the wide porch. He knocked on the front door.

We could hear the patter of feet, and then a small woman dressed in a Mennonite dress and Kapp opened the door. Behind her were two blond preschool-aged little girls who clung to her skirt. "Hello," she said with a Pennsylvania Dutch accent.

"I'm Tommy Miller." He motioned toward me. "And this is Savannah Mast. We're looking for a young woman named Miriam. Her brother thought she might be here."

"You just missed her," the woman said. "She left a minute ago."

I turned toward the street. Had she been in the compact car on the side street?

"Do you know where she's going?" Tommy asked.

"I'm not sure." The woman motioned to the inside of the house. "Come on in."

Tommy took off his baseball cap and stepped aside, letting me go in first. The room was sparsely furnished, with just a couch and one chair. A few toys, a dollhouse, and a play buggy with a horse sat on a low table against the wall. The hardwood floor shone as if it had just been polished, and a small wood stove in the corner had a fire burning in it.

The woman motioned toward the couch, and Tommy and I both sat down, while she sat in the chair, the girls still holding on to her.

"I'm Ethel King, Miriam's aunt. My brother was her father." She was the aunt Arleta had mentioned, the relative Joshua had referred to.

"Nice to meet you," Tommy said.

The woman nodded but didn't smile. "Why are you looking for Miriam?"

I answered, "I was at Arleta's, helping her birth her baby, the night Miriam disappeared."

"And I was the driver who dropped Miriam off back at home right before she disappeared," Tommy added.

Neither explanation gave us credibility to be looking for her, but it was the best we had. "Joshua told me he's worried about her. He gave us your address."

She nodded. That seemed to reassure her. "When her father passed last year, I told her that if she ever wanted to leave the Amish, my husband and I would help her. A man, probably in his late twenties, dropped her off on Sunday."

I glanced at Tommy, wondering what his reaction might be. Could it be Kenny? But Tommy continued to keep his gaze on Ethel.

"I thought she was serious about leaving the Amish—and not just because things are so miserable at home." Miriam pulled her youngest girl onto her lap while the other one draped around her legs. "But then about ten minutes ago, this same man showed up at the house again. After a short conversation, Miriam told me she was going with him. I tried to talk her out of it, but she wouldn't listen to me."

"What did the man look like?" Tommy asked.

"Like I said, late twenties. Brown hair and brown eyes. A small tattoo on the side of his neck. It looked like a cactus, maybe, I couldn't tell exactly."

By the expression on Tommy's face, he knew someone with a tattoo of a cactus on the side of his neck. I guessed it was Kenny. "Was the man driving a gray Camry?" Tommy asked.

"I don't know. He didn't park in front of the house."

The car parked on the side street when we arrived was gray. I didn't notice whether it was a Camry or not. I turned back toward Ethel and asked, "You don't know where they were going?"

Ethel shook her head. "I assumed back home, but when I asked, she wouldn't say."

"Did she have a cell phone with her?"

Ethel nodded. "She didn't have the right charger, so it was dead. But she has a phone, although she wouldn't give me her number." She looked on the verge of tears. "Miriam seems like a lost soul, as if she doesn't have any idea what she needs for her future."

I was most concerned about her immediate well-being. Was she safe with Kenny Miller? Was she safe going back home to Arleta and Vernon's? "Do you think it's a good idea for her to go back?" I asked. "Vernon might not be very happy with her."

"Oh, I think Arleta can handle Vernon."

I wasn't so sure.

Ethel said, "I have a question for you. I appreciate your concern, but why are you so worried about her? She's an adult."

I leaned forward. "She went missing under mysterious circumstances, in the dead of night during a blizzard. And from what you've told us, it sounds like she might be running again. If she's not headed back to Nappanee, do you have any guess where she might be going?"

Ethel wrinkled her nose. "Maybe to Chicago. She said she has a friend there." Ethel pulled her daughter against her chest. "I hope she's going home, but if she is, then she needs to be honest with Arleta and Vernon."

"Honest about what?" Tommy asked.

"Being pregnant."

Immediately, I feared Kenny was the father. And Tommy might have been too because he asked, "How far along?"

"Six months," Ethel answered.

I could sense Tommy's relief as I did the mental math in my head. He and Kenny had been in Nappanee since September—a total of four months. There was no way Kenny could be the father. But he did appear to be helping her.

Ethel dropped her voice, as if she thought maybe her girls wouldn't hear her, even though they were glued to her. "Miriam says the father is a young man from Newbury Township, from their old district."

"Maybe she's going there," I said.

Ethel shook her head. "I don't believe her about the father. I think she made that up."

"Why?"

"She didn't say it with much conviction. It sounded like an answer to get me to stop asking questions."

CHAPTER 17

Ten minutes later, Tommy, with his Giants cap back on his head, and I sat in his Jeep. "Yeah, Kenny got a cactus tattoo when we were in Arizona. He was drunk at the time."

"Do you have a matching one?"

Tommy laughed. "At least not where anyone can see it."

I smiled. "What should we do now?"

"There's no reason to go to Chicago without any idea where they might be." He started the engine. "Why don't you call Joshua and tell him what Ethel said?" He paused. "But maybe leave out the pregnancy."

"I agree." I pulled out my phone. "And then I'm going to call Deputy Rogers." I glanced at Tommy, looking for a reaction.

"Good idea," he said.

Maybe Deputy Rogers had his reasons to be suspicious, but the fact that Miriam had been with her aunt and had just left on her own seemed to exonerate Tommy. Unless Deputy Rogers knew something he wasn't sharing. "At least it sounds like you're free and clear to go to Nevada now."

Tommy grinned. "Trying to get rid of me?"

"Actually . . ." I couldn't come up with a clever comeback, so I decided to be honest. "I'm not. I've enjoyed spending time with you."

He gave me a sideways glance and a vague smile, but that was all. As he pulled away from the curb, I called Joshua. Just when I thought it was going to go to his voicemail, he answered with such a soft "Hello" that I could barely hear him. "Hold on a sec." A rustling followed.

Finally, he came back on the line. "Hi, Savannah."

After I got over my surprise that he called me by my name, I relayed to him that Ethel told us a man, who appeared to be Kenny Miller, had just picked up Miriam. "Ethel said Miriam has her phone, but she didn't have a charger. Hopefully she's charging it in the car. Maybe try calling her in a few minutes."

"She's coming home?"

"Ethel wasn't sure where they're going." I spoke slowly. "She said Miriam talked about going to Chicago, but hopefully they're headed home."

"All right," he said.

"Will you let me know if you speak to her?" I asked.

Before Joshua answered, Tommy called out, "And ask her to tell Kenny to call me."

"I'm with Tommy Miller," I said. "He wants Kenny to call him. It's important."

"All right," Joshua said. "I'll call Miriam, ask what her plans are, tell her to tell Kenny to call Tommy, and then call you back."

"Perfect," I said. "Denki."

He hung up without saying good-bye.

I held the phone for a minute in my hand. "What a funny kid."

"You have no idea how awkward it is to be an Amish adolescent," Tommy said. "And it's worse for boys than girls."

"You weren't awkward."

"What?" He started to go through a four-way stop and then slammed on the brakes at the last minute. If he hadn't, he would have T-boned a taxi.

After I let go of the dashboard, I laughed.

And then so did he. "Look," he said. "I'm still awkward."

"No, you're not. And you weren't back then either. You were cool."

"Cool?" He shook his head as he accelerated. "I was anything but."

"Driving around in that Thunderbird. Walking that cute Amish girl home." I laughed. "Blowing me off like you'd never seen me before."

He cringed. "I was hoping you didn't remember *everything*."

"I'm just teasing." I didn't expect him to feel badly about it all of these years later.

"No, I was horrible." Tommy stared straight ahead as he drove toward I-80. "Awkward, yes, in general, but to you—simply horrible. And after you'd been such a good friend to me all of those summers too."

"Don't worry about it," I said. "I was a little slow to realize you'd grown up, that you didn't want to hang out anymore."

Now he laughed. "But I did want to. I just didn't feel like I should. I figured I needed to start being an Amish man. I couldn't have an Englisch best friend anymore."

Best friend. That was how I'd felt about Tommy, but it was validating to hear him say he felt that way about me too.

"Maybe I shouldn't say this." Tommy stared straight ahead.

I waited and then finally asked, "Say what?"

"Funny that this is hard, even though it's been all these years, even though we're all grown up," he said, "but the summers you were in Indiana were my favorites."

I wasn't sure what to say in return, so I settled on, "Mine too."

When he didn't say anything more, I said, "I'm going to go ahead and call Deputy Rogers." He didn't pick up, so I left a message.

We were back on I-80, headed toward South Bend, when the deputy called back. I explained what we'd found out and the two possibilities where Miriam was headed. "She did leave on her own volition. So Tommy is free to go, right?" I asked.

"I'd rather he didn't."

"But there's no reason for him to stay. Not if Miriam left on her own and is all right."

Deputy Rogers cleared his throat and then in an even deeper voice than usual said, "I'd like to confirm that. Tell Tommy I'll call him later." Was there something he wasn't telling me?

TOMMY AND I rode in silence until he said, "You sounded pretty chummy with Deputy Rogers."

Was Tommy hiding something after all and my conversation with the deputy made him nervous? "I hope I didn't sound chummy. I was aiming for businesslike."

Tommy didn't respond, and I guessed he was feeling a little uncomfortable. After a few minutes, he turned on the radio, and we mostly rode in silence all the way to South Bend.

Maybe Deputy Rogers was right to be suspicious of Tommy. People did change, as it seemed Tommy had after I knew him. Ryan certainly had. Or, more likely, I'd misjudged his character all along. Maybe I had misjudged Tommy's too. Maybe the boy he was, as a teenager, was who he still was.

There wasn't a run on rentals in northern Indiana in January, so I pretty much had my pick of vehicles. I decided to get the safest one available, a Chevy Suburban, since I'd be driving Mammi around on snowy roads.

Tommy waited until I'd completed the paperwork and had keys in hand. "Thank you," I said to him as we walked outside.

"I'll follow you to Dorothy's," he said. "And then we can return the pickup to Seth. I'll follow you and give you a ride back to the farm."

"Thanks," I said. "But how about if I follow you to the farm? You know the roads around here much better than I do."

As I drove the rental with Tommy's Jeep in front of me and the back of his head in view, I thought about what he was like when I first met him. Eight years old. Tall and lanky. Big, toothy grin. Straight light brown hair. Dark eyes. It seemed there was nothing he couldn't do. Climb the tallest tree. Ride bareback. Jump out of the hayloft window and land on his feet. Chase a runaway calf. He had so much energy. Not having a brother and being two years younger, I was enthralled with Tommy's strength and agility as I did my best to keep up with him. Sometimes it seemed like he could fly if he put his mind to it.

And he was so kind to me. Showing me how to feed the chickens and gather eggs. How to milk a cow. How to bury a deceased baby robin. Tommy was always waiting for me when Uncle Seth turned into Mammi's driveway. Year after year, it had been the same.

Until it wasn't.

Yes, I'd decided to study to become Mom's assistant and not to spend any more summers in Indiana, but would I have chosen to do so at that time if Tommy had continued to welcome me? I still had a big crush on him, even when he treated me badly.

Who was Tommy Miller now? A caring man, concerned

about someone else's child? Or was he in cahoots with his cousin in exploiting a naïve young Amish woman and selling fentanyl?

When we reached the farm, I checked in with Mammi and said I'd be back after I returned Uncle Seth's pickup.

"You and Tommy need something to eat," she said. "Tell him to come in for a bowl of bean-and-ham soup and a piece of peach pie."

After the awkward way we'd ended our conversation on the ride to South Bend, I just wanted him to leave, but I couldn't explain that to Mammi. "I'll ask him," I said.

When I asked Tommy if he wanted to come in, he tugged the bill of his baseball cap. "Are you sure you want me to?"

"Yes." *No*. What mattered was that Mammi wanted him to.

He frowned. "Look, I'll go in and tell Dorothy good-bye, but then let's get Seth's truck back. I'd better go pick up Mason from my mom's."

"Do you plan to leave soon?" I asked.

"Probably." He turned off the engine and opened the door. "Unless something comes up. Like Deputy Rogers arresting me."

"You're joking, right?"

He exhaled. "I hope so."

A HALF HOUR later, with the pickup delivered to a much healthier Uncle Seth, Tommy pulled back into Mammi's driveway.

"Thank you for everything," I said.

He gave me a wry smile. "I've been more trouble than I've been worth, I'm afraid."

"No," I said. "It's been good to see you. Really."

"Same," he answered. "I've thought of you often through the years and wondered how things turned out for you."

"Well, now you know." My phone pinged, and I pulled it from my coat pocket, wondering if it was a message from Joshua. But it was an email from the hospital in Lancaster. I held up a finger to Tommy to hold on as I read it, then looked up at him. "Sorry. I applied for a job in Pennsylvania. The HR department wants to do a phone interview tomorrow morning." I was surprised they wanted to do it on a Saturday, but perhaps it was a good sign that they were serious about me.

"Great!" he said. "See, you've had a setback, but you're bouncing back already. That's wonderful."

"Thank you."

His eyes were so kind and generous with support. There were so many things I hadn't asked him, including why he'd left Indiana in the first place. And now I might not have a chance. "Well, I guess you need to go get Mason," I said.

"I'll walk you up to the porch."

"You don't need to."

He already had his door open. "I want to." He hurried around to the front of the Jeep and caught my door as I opened it, holding it for me.

As we walked up to the porch, he put his arm around me and gave me a half hug. "I really am grateful to have gotten to see you."

Surprised by the emotion I was feeling, I only managed to say, "Ditto."

When we reached the front door, he gave me another side hug. "Take care," he said. "Follow God's leading. He has a good plan for you."

My voice caught as I said, "He has a good plan for you too."

Tommy nodded and then walked down the steps. I watched him go, wishing he'd brought up God sooner. That was another thing I didn't ask him about. I guess I assumed, since he left the Amish, that he'd left God behind too. But he hadn't said that. Or even indicated such a thing. True, he seemed to know a lot about addictions and all of Kenny's vices, but he'd never implicated himself in any of that. And even if he had, it wouldn't tell me anything about his present relationship with God.

As he left, I realized I didn't have his phone number. I had Kenny's, which I'd saved in my contacts the night of Arleta's delivery, but I had no idea what Tommy's was.

He backed out of the driveway.

My heart did a lurch as he reached the lane. I watched his Jeep until it turned onto the highway and disappeared. Just like that, he was gone.

Instead of going into the house, I retreated to my rental SUV to call the HR department at the hospital and set up a phone interview for the next morning. Then I called Joshua. He didn't answer. I left a message and waited. A few minutes later, he called back.

"I've left five messages on Miriam's phone but haven't heard back from her," he said.

"So she hasn't come back home yet?"

"No."

I wondered if perhaps Kenny would have taken her to his and Tommy's apartment. "Okay. Would you let me know if she shows up or calls?"

"Jah." He hung up, again, without saying good-bye.

Should I call Deputy Rogers? Follow Tommy to his apartment? Or stay out of it? After weighing my options, I settled on calling Deputy Rogers again.

"I'm close to your grandmother's house," he said. "I'll stop by."

I hesitated a moment and then said, "All right." Why did I feel as if I were betraying Tommy?

I hurried into the house to give Mammi fair warning. "I'll talk with him in the kitchen," I said.

"Everything all right?"

I nodded. "I'm just going to fill him in on what we learned."

Five minutes later, I poured Deputy Rogers a cup of coffee, placed a piece of peach pie in front of him, and then sat down across the table.

"None of this is probably a big deal," I said. "But I thought I'd tell you just in case." I explained that Miriam hadn't gone home.

"That's not surprising," he said.

I wasn't surprised either. Miriam didn't want to be there, and it didn't sound as if her home life was very stable either.

"Why does Tommy say he's in such a hurry to leave Nappanee?" Deputy Rogers asked and then took a bite of pie.

I hesitated. The deputy narrowed his eyes.

I didn't think the fact that Tommy was caring for Mason had anything to do with Miriam going missing, but what if it did? Finally I said, "He's taking a little boy back to Vegas."

"A little boy?"

I nodded. "Kenny's son, Mason."

Deputy Rogers speared another bite of pie but left it on the plate. "What are you talking about?"

"Mason's mother got out of rehab and is in a halfway house. The program allows her son to be with her, so Tommy's returning him to Vegas."

"What about Kenny?"

"He and the mom don't get along. Tommy said it's better if he takes him."

Deputy Rogers didn't respond. He ate the last bite of pie and then, after he swallowed, said, "Sounds fishy."

It hadn't to me before, but I could see his point. "What are you thinking?"

"I'm not going to speculate," he said. "Nothing came up when I ran Tommy's name, but I'm wondering if he has an alias. Any ideas?"

I shook my head.

He drained his cup of coffee. "So is the little boy's name Mason Miller?"

"As far as I know," I said. "Although he might have the mother's last name, which I don't know. Her first name is Christine."

His voice grew gruffer. "Why didn't you tell me earlier?"

I shrugged. "It didn't seem to have anything to do with the case, and I didn't know much about it before today."

"I'll be the judge of that." He stood. "After I contact the authorities in Las Vegas."

I exhaled as I scrutinized the grizzled deputy. "What did Tommy do when he was a teenager that ticked you off so badly?"

Deputy Rogers scowled. "That's none of your business." He strode to the front door, put his hat back on, and tipped it. "Thank you for the information." However, he didn't sound thankful—he sounded angry. And aggressive. He let himself out, pulling the door shut with a thud.

"Goodness," Mammi said, stepping into the kitchen. "I hope everything's all right."

I muttered, "So do I" and headed up to my room, feeling all sorts of conflicting emotions. Had I just betrayed Tommy?

Hopefully I'd be on my way to Pennsylvania soon and none of this would matter. I cringed. Not matter? It was Tommy's life.

The next morning, still feeling ill over my conversation with Deputy Rogers, I sat in the rental car with the engine running and the heat on for the phone interview. It seemed to go well, in spite of how unsettled I felt, and the HR person told me she'd let me know if they wanted to do a second interview.

After the call ended, I second-guessed not getting Tommy's number. But if I did have it, what would I ask him? If he'd been arrested?

Mammi and I left for Jane's soon after my interview concluded. "Are we picking up Wanda?" I asked as I opened the front door for Mammi.

"Nee," she answered. "She can't go today."

Perhaps she was feeling sad about Tommy and Mason leaving. Mammi and I didn't talk much on the way. She seemed intent on watching the snow-covered landscape, although it might not last for long. We'd already hit thirty-two degrees.

When we arrived at Plain Patterns, there weren't any buggies or cars parked outside. "Is there a quilting circle today?"

"Jah," Mammi said. "But several of the women have come down with the flu."

I shot Mammi a questioning look.

"I had a phone message from Jane this morning," she said. "She said quite a few women had canceled but to come out anyway."

Once again, by the time I made my way around to Mammi's side of the car, she already had both feet on the ground and was practically sprinting toward the quilt shop.

Jane greeted us warmly, and we took off our coats and settled down around the hearth and home quilt, still stretched across the frame.

After exchanging pleasantries, she turned to me. "How about more of Emma's story?"

"Yes, please." I eased my needle through a patch of forget-me-not fabric.

"Remind me where I left off. . . ."

"Eli and Judah got into a dispute about whether the Natives in the area were peaceful or not, and Jean-Paul had just arrived at Emma's parents' house, saying Mathilde was ill."

CHAPTER 18

Emma

Jean-Paul and Baptiste led the way while Emma rode Red, thankful she had her cloak with her. The evening had grown chilly. Isaac rode behind Emma and Judah followed, taking up the rear.

Mamm guessed it was milk fever and sent dried dandelions to make a poultice and said to use hot compresses too. She also sent peppermint and other herbs that might be helpful, all tucked into a small leather bag that Emma strapped across her body. Dusk fell, and the riders slowed. A few minutes later, she could see the outline of the Bernard cabin at the edge of the woods. As she slid off Red, Emma could hear the wail of a baby.

Clutching Mamm's bag, Emma bolted into the cabin, which smelled faintly of Jean-Paul's tobacco, while the men headed to the barn, taking Baptiste with them. It took a moment for her eyes to adjust to the dark.

The bed was in the far corner, away from the fireplace, where the wails were coming from. "Mathilde, I'm here."

First, she scooped up the baby, and then, balancing Agnes

in one arm, she reached down and felt Mathilde's forehead. She was burning up. Mathilde clasped Emma's hand. "Thank you for coming."

"Thank you for sending Jean-Paul to get me," Emma said. "Is it your breasts?"

Mathilde shook her head but placed her hand on her chest.

Confused, Emma asked, "Do you have pain?"

Mathilde nodded and then began to cough, the sound deep and raspy. Emma put the baby on the end of the bed and pulled Mathilde to a sitting position. She continued to cough and then reached for a cloth and spit mucus into it. At least there wasn't any blood.

The baby began to wail.

"Can you nurse her?" Emma asked.

"I keep trying, but my milk is gone."

"Is your cow fresh?"

Mathilde shook her head. "She's dry."

Cow's milk might make the baby sick anyway. Sarah would have to nurse Agnes.

Emma wasn't sure what was wrong with Mathilde. Hopefully it wasn't consumption. But it might be pneumonia, which could also be fatal and bring death much quicker than consumption would. The dandelion poultice might not do much good, but Emma would use it anyway, as well as make peppermint tea to help with the cough.

She left the baby screaming on the end of the bed and went to stoke the fire, which cast flickering light across the room. A pail of water sat on the floor. She filled the kettle and put it over the fire.

Jean-Paul entered the cabin, and Emma asked him to hold the baby. "I need onions for a poultice. And then you need to get the baby to Sarah to nurse. Mathilde doesn't have any milk."

Jean-Paul nodded.

"Go with Judah. Wrap the baby warmly, and put her in her cradleboard." Emma hoped that would help Agnes feel more secure. "Tell Isaac to stay here for the night in case I need him."

A few minutes later, Jean-Paul came back with onions and then left with the baby. Isaac came in with Baptiste, and Emma cut some bread for the two of them, sliced the onions and put them on to boil, and then made peppermint tea for Mathilde. Emma had Mathilde hold the hot cup while Emma placed a cloth over both her friend's head and the cup, forcing the steam toward her face.

"Breathe in," she said.

As Mathilde did, Emma prayed for her friend, asking God to heal her. Once the steam stopped, Emma urged Mathilde to sip the tea until it was all gone.

Next, Emma dipped the onions out of the boiling water, placed them in a cloth, and wrapped it tightly. She placed the poultice on Mathilde's chest for a few minutes, coaxing her to breathe deeply, and then had her roll to her stomach so Emma could put the poultice on her back.

When she started coughing again, Emma had her sit up. The congestion seemed to be loosening. When the poultice had cooled, she reheated the onions and repeated the process.

"I'm tired," Mathilde said, after she'd finished a second cup of tea.

"Rest then," Emma said. "Jean-Paul should be home soon."

Isaac and Baptiste had curled up to the side of the fireplace on a blanket and were fast asleep.

Jean-Paul was home soon after, with Agnes, who was still crying. He motioned for Emma to come to the door. Jean-Paul had the baby in one hand and the cradleboard in the other.

Emma stepped out of the cabin and pulled the door shut. The moon had risen, nearly full, against a cloudless sky.

Jean-Paul slipped the baby into Emma's arms.

"Sarah wouldn't feed her."

Aghast, Emma clutched the baby.

"She says she doesn't have much milk. She was afraid she couldn't feed both babies."

Emma wasn't sure what to do. She remembered Mathilde's joy when Sarah had Hiram. She believed Mathilde would do anything she could for Sarah, if she were able. Overcome with sorrow, Emma wanted to flee the four hundred and fifty miles back to Somerset County, back to a community with more women and more resources.

She held Agnes against her chest, and for a moment the baby stopped screaming and started rooting around. Emma's own breasts responded as if letting down, even though she had no milk. She ached the way she had when her hard, bound breasts felt as if they might burst after her little girl was born dead, when she had rivers of milk but no baby. If only she could nurse Agnes now for Mathilde.

For a minute, she thought the best thing was to send Isaac for her cow and see if the baby would take that milk, but then she thought of Harriet. Harriet was the next nearest nursing mother, besides Sarah, that she knew of. Surely she would feed Mathilde's baby after everything Mathilde had done for her.

"Can you take me to the Burtons' place?" Emma asked.

Jean-Paul shook his head. "Judah can. He's outside the barn with both horses, ready to go."

EMMA TUCKED THE baby inside her cloak, and Judah helped her up onto her sidesaddle, on Red. By the light of the moon, Emma trotted after him along the trail to the Burton place.

When they arrived, Judah helped her down and then led the way to the front door. He banged on it. George yelled, "Go away!"

Judah banged again.

Finally, George swung the door open. He had a cigar in one hand and a half-full glass in the other. A lamp in the foyer shone behind him. "What's going on?"

The baby began to scream, and Emma wiggled her out from under her cloak. "Mathilde is ill and can't feed the baby. We need Harriet to nurse her."

George's cloudy eyes narrowed. "Harriet?"

Emma nodded.

George threw back his head and laughed. "Harriet wouldn't nurse a savage's baby, even if she could."

Savage. The same word Eli had used.

"Harriet's not even nursing her own baby. Lenore found a wet nurse over by Bremen. Georgie is over there."

Emma stuttered, "Bre-men?"

"It's about ten miles away," Judah said quietly. "Let's leave."

"Tell Jean-Paul I expect him here in the morning, to work. Mathilde too." George slurred. "If they're not here, I'll double the interest on what they owe me."

Judah shook his head and started to speak as George slammed the door.

"Are we going to Bremen?" Emma felt near exhaustion. She felt like she couldn't ride another mile, let alone ten.

"No," Judah said. "We're going back to Sarah. You tell her she has to feed the baby." He helped Emma back onto Red and again led the way.

As they traveled, the screech of a panther startled Emma, causing the baby to cry out again. Judah pulled his rifle out and shot it into the air. The panther screeched again, but this time it was farther away.

When they arrived at the Landis place, Judah helped Emma down and then led the way to the door. He pounded on it.

"Who is it?" Walter yelled.

"Me, along with Emma and the baby."

A few minutes later, Walter unlatched the bolt, and Judah pushed the door open.

"Sarah," Emma said, stepping into the cabin and looking toward the bed, even though the room was pitch dark. "You have to feed the baby. We can't find anyone else. She'll die if you don't help."

"Her duty is to Hiram," Walter said.

"Just feed her this one time," Emma pleaded. "Until I can figure out what else to do."

Hiram began to fuss.

"I'll hold Hiram," Emma said. "But take Agnes."

Sarah looked to Walter.

He gave her a curt nod. At least he hadn't called Mathilde a savage. Emma handed Sarah the baby and then lifted Hiram from his cradle, giving him her finger to suck on.

A few minutes later, Sarah said she was done and pulled Agnes from her breast. The baby began to cry again and so did Hiram.

"Take her," Walter said, who stood near the door with his arms crossed.

Emma did as she was told, rolling Hiram onto Sarah's lap as she took the newborn. Judah held the door open for her, and as they shuffled back to the horses, he asked, "What now?"

"Let's go get Bossie," Emma said. Hopefully the baby could tolerate cow's milk.

Even though it was the middle of the night, Judah milked the cow, getting what he could from her. Emma took a cloth from her bag and soaked it in the milk and then formed it into the shape of a teat and wiggled it in the baby's mouth as she sat up against the wall of the barn. Agnes screamed, fighting against it, but then she finally latched on and started sucking. Emma repeated the process over and over. Eventually, the baby fell asleep.

"Hopefully she won't spit it all up," she said, as she handed the baby to Judah, who stood next to her. He held the baby with one hand and helped Emma up onto Red with the other. Then he handed Agnes to her.

The ride back to the Bernard place was slow, with Bossie plodding along after Judah's horse. Emma felt her eyes grow heavy and struggled to stay awake and keep hold of Agnes. Finally, they arrived at the cabin and Judah helped Emma down. "Go on in. I'll take care of the horses and cow."

Coughing greeted her as she opened the cabin door. But it wasn't Mathilde. It was Jean-Paul, who sat at the table.

"Have you fallen ill too?" Emma asked him.

He nodded.

"Get into bed, then. I'll make you some tea and a poultice."

The next few days were a blur as Emma cared for Mathilde, Jean-Paul, and Agnes. Mamm came between births, placing her hands on Mathilde and Jean-Paul's back, feeling the vibrations of their raggedy breaths and declaring both had pneumonia. She instructed Emma to continue with tea and poultices and to get them to drink as much water and eat as much soup as she could. Judah stayed at the Bernard cabin, hauling water, chopping wood, emptying the slop jar, and watching Baptiste. Isaac came when he could, but Phillip didn't want to lose work time getting the cabin done.

After three days, Mathilde turned a corner and began caring for Agnes, feeding her the cow's milk, which the baby did spit up, but also having her nurse again. Emma feared it was too late, but Mathilde kept at it.

Jean-Paul, on the other hand, didn't get better. He grew weaker as his cough grew stronger. The fifth day after he fell ill, with Mathilde's arms wrapped around him, he took his last raspy breath and died.

BACK HOME, PEOPLE called pneumonia "an old man's friend," but Jean-Paul wasn't an old man. Older, jah, but he had a young wife and two babies, who were far away from family. Emma's heart broke for Mathilde and her children.

Mathilde's eyes stayed dry, but her countenance was defeated. A priest came from South Bend, and he and Mathilde buried Jean-Paul in the simple coffin Judah made for him, in a grave on the edge of the woods that Isaac had helped Judah dig. Mathilde wore her buckskin dress and shell necklace. Emma stood close by, holding Agnes in her arms. In the distance, a loon wailed, as if in lament for Jean-Paul, as if mourning for them all.

As Judah and Isaac covered the coffin with soil, the others went back to the cabin, and the priest baptized the baby. Emma knew there were those in her community who would criticize her for even observing the baptism, but she chose to stand by her friend. Mathilde needed her, and she wouldn't leave.

Emma's heart ached for Mathilde losing Jean-Paul. She remembered all too well the pain and devastation of losing her husband. She vowed to do all she could to help the young widow and her children in the months to come, until she returned to Pennsylvania.

Emma left Bossie with Mathilde but rode over in the morning and evening to milk. Light rains fell for a few days, but then the weather turned dry and sunny again, and Phillip and Isaac continued to make good progress on the cabin.

Often, Judah was at Mathilde's when Emma arrived, hauling water and chopping wood. Together they helped Mathilde finish harvesting her garden, pulling the squash, digging up the potatoes, picking the rest of the beans, and shucking the corn. Mathilde dried the corn and then cut the kernels off the cobs. Emma knew she'd grind them into meal to make corn cakes throughout the winter.

One late afternoon, over the campfire in the yard, Mathilde made soup from corn, squash, and beans, while both Emma and Judah were at her place. When she handed Emma a bowl, she said, "We call it three sister soup." She smiled shyly.

It was delicious.

Mathilde was so knowledgeable and resourceful that it seemed she could survive on her land with two children and no husband. Of course, Emma and Judah would keep helping her. And surely, by spring, when Emma left to go back to Pennsylvania, Mathilde would be stable. Emma hoped, also, that other Plain women would befriend her. And other Englisch women too.

As they finished their soup, a rider approached.

Judah stood. "It's George."

Baptiste stepped to Mathilde's side, grabbing onto her skirt.

George wore his black suit and sat high in his saddle. Emma, her bowl still in her hands, stepped past the fire, where Agnes slept in her cradleboard.

"Judah," George called out as he neared. "Walter said I might find you here. I need your help moving cattle tomorrow."

"I have my own work."

George took his hat off and ran his hand through his thick hair. "If you have your own work, why are you here?"

Judah didn't answer.

George's eyes narrowed, and Judah met his gaze. After a

moment, George turned his attention on Mathilde. "We keep expecting you to show up at the house. And yet here you are, entertaining the neighbors."

She lowered her head.

"I'm afraid maybe your husband didn't keep you abreast on how much you owe me. I don't fault you for that, but I need to go over your account," George said. "Every day you don't show up for work, the debt grows."

When Mathilde didn't answer, he turned his horse. As he left, he said, rather loudly, "I'll never understand why the government wanted all of the savages to leave, not when labor is needed here. How are we to manage?"

None of them said anything until George's horse was trotting away.

"I'll go with you," Judah said to Mathilde, "to go over your account. George could try to swindle you."

"Jean-Paul told me, every day, what we owe George. I have our accounts in a book in the house." Mathilde lifted Baptiste into her arms. "I'll take it when I talk with him."

"Let Judah go with you," Emma said.

Mathilde shook her head. "Jean-Paul wouldn't want that."

Judah pursed his lips, as if to keep himself from saying more. Mathilde started toward the house with Baptiste, and Emma followed with the baby. Judah went to the barn to milk the cow and feed the horses, while Emma helped Mathilde clean the dishes and settle the children.

Later, as Judah and Emma rode toward their homes, she asked about the debt the Bernards owed George.

"He loaned Jean-Paul money to buy his land and then for a plow and seed." Judah slowed his horse more. "I'm afraid he's charging a high rate of interest, but Jean-Paul would never discuss it with me. I think he was embarrassed."

It sounded as if Mathilde was too. Otherwise, she might let Judah accompany her to discuss the situation with George.

By the last week of October, as Phillip and Isaac put the roof on the cabin, the rains started. Trying to cook and wash around the campfire became an even bigger chore as everything turned to mud, and a few times Emma fled to the barn to cry in frustration.

On the third day, Judah came over to help them finish the roof, bringing the cow with him. "Mathilde said she didn't need her anymore."

"Why?" Emma asked.

"She's going to work for Harriet for a while. George put one of his herds on her pasture yesterday, and one of his hands is going to stay in her cabin through the winter."

Emma gasped. "Did George take her cabin? As payment for what she owes?"

He shrugged. "It's not our business."

Emma crossed her arms. "Judah, of course it's our business. She has no one else to help her."

He shrugged again and walked toward the cabin, leaving Emma alone in the barn.

CHAPTER 19

In the middle of November, Isaac returned to Jackson Township to help Dat plow fields while Phillip finished the cabin. Fighting a horrible loneliness, Emma stopped by the Landis place to visit with Sarah.

Hiram was fussy, and Sarah was exhausted. She talked about how homesick she was. Emma listened sympathetically.

"I heard you're going home," Sarah said.

"Who told you that?"

"Phillip said something about it to Walter."

Emma sighed. In a moment of weakness, she had told Phillip she was thinking about returning home.

Sarah continued, "I wish I could go with you as far as Ohio. If only Walter would change his mind." She looked as if she might cry. "I've told him over and over to give this property to Judah, that my Dat will help him find a farm in Ohio if we return, but he won't listen to me."

Emma wondered if Judah knew she was leaving too. She considered him a friend now, after all they'd gone through in caring for Mathilde and the children.

"Where are Walter and Judah?" Emma asked.

"Hunting," Sarah answered. "Hopefully they'll come home with a buck to smoke so we don't starve this winter."

Emma didn't respond. She knew they were far from starving. She stayed a while longer and then said good-bye.

Once she was on her horse, she decided to stop by the Burton place in hopes of seeing Mathilde. She missed her friend.

It wasn't a warm day by any means, but it wasn't raining. The cloudy sky had threatened precipitation all day, but none had fallen. She knocked lightly on the door. And then a little louder when no one answered.

Finally, George opened it, a cigar dangling out of his mouth. "No one here is up to visitors," he said gruffly. "Harriet is still feeling poorly."

"Then may I say hello to Mathilde?" Emma took off her headscarf. "I didn't have a chance to speak with her before she left her place."

"She's busy." George took a step backward and staggered a little.

"It will only take a moment."

"Go along," George sneered. "We don't want your kind here."

Puzzled, Emma stepped backward. Her kind? Did he mean Plain?

There was a racket from the other side of the house and then a yell. "I'll take the baby," someone said. Perhaps Lenore. Was she speaking to Mathilde? Was Georgie back in the household?

George closed the door before Emma could say anything more. She put her headscarf back on and then undid her horse's reins from the hitching post. As she started down the road, she noticed someone walking through the pasture toward a shack at the edge of the woods, a woman and a child. Emma squinted. The woman had a cradleboard on her back.

"Mathilde!" Emma called out.

The woman kept walking. Would they not even let her stay in the house?

Emma called out again, but still Mathilde didn't respond. The wind had picked up and was blowing through the trees. Perhaps Mathilde couldn't hear.

"Wait!" she cried out. She tied her horse to the pasture fence and then climbed over it, running after Mathilde.

Baptiste turned and waved. The smile on his face warmed Emma's heart. She waved back and kept running, stumbling a few times. Baptiste pulled on Mathilde's hand, and finally she stopped, turning slowly.

Emma reached her. Out of breath, she asked, "How are you doing?"

"Fine." Mathilde held her head high.

Tears stung Emma's eyes. She doubted Mathilde was fine. "I've missed you."

Mathilde's eyes softened.

"I told you we didn't want your kind around here!"

Emma turned. George was striding toward them, holding his riding whip high.

"Go," Emma said to Mathilde while still facing George. "Quickly."

Mathilde didn't budge.

"Now." Emma couldn't bear it if George took out his anger on Mathilde.

Still, Mathilde stayed. But then Baptiste began to whimper, and Emma hissed, "Go for the sake of your children if not for yourself."

Finally, Mathilde started toward her shack while Emma stood her ground.

George flung out the whip as he continued barreling in her direction. Did he plan to attack her? Emma took a step toward him and then another. "I was simply saying hello to my friend," she said once he was within speaking distance.

He cracked the whip. "Your friend?"

"Jah," Emma answered, hoping her voice wasn't shaking as much as her knees. "My friend."

"Well, you're trespassing." He cracked the whip again.

Emma met his gaze. "I won't again. I promise." And she wouldn't. She couldn't risk putting Mathilde and the children in danger.

Someone called out for George from the back porch of the house. Emma squinted in the afternoon light. She guessed it was Lenore.

George tucked the whip into his belt and turned without saying another word, marching back across the field. Emma waited until he reached the porch before continuing on to the fence and Red. By the time she reached her horse, a curl of smoke came up from the shack's chimney. George was a mean and horrible man. If only Mathilde wasn't in debt to him.

Emma stopped to see Judah on her way home to tell him what happened, but he was still out hunting. She didn't bother to tell Sarah and Walter because she didn't expect them to be sympathetic.

Over the next few weeks, Emma met with a few women in the area who were expecting, ones who'd heard she was a midwife. Meeting them helped her loneliness, but she kept thinking about Mathilde. Judah had started working for George again, which disappointed Emma. Was that why he'd claimed George's actions toward Mathilde weren't their business?

Judah had been the one to help the most when Mathilde and Jean-Paul fell ill and then when Jean-Paul died. She'd begun to believe that Sarah had been wrong in her assessment of Judah. Emma had begun to trust him.

But why would he defend George and then go back to working for him? What had George done to entice him back?

Judah didn't say much about his work there, except that he seldom saw Mathilde.

On Christmas, Emma and Phillip rode to Mamm and Dat's farm. When they arrived, Dat met them in the barn. "You have a letter from Abel," he said, handing it to her.

It was just a few lines long, and simply said he expected her to return in the spring. She sighed, folded the letter, and slipped it under her cloak, into her apron pocket. On one hand, it was good to hear from him. On the other, he hadn't written anything of importance. Not that he missed her nor anything about his life back home.

She'd write a chatty letter full of news and of her desire to return to him as soon as possible. Hopefully his reply wouldn't be as brief.

Barbara and her family were in the cabin when Emma entered, which she'd expected, but Eli and his family were there too. Confused, Emma whispered to Mamm, "Why are the Waglers here?"

"Eli hopes to start courting you," she answered.

Emma was going to go back home in the spring. It would serve no purpose for her to court Eli, but even if she planned to stay, she wouldn't. Not after what he said about the Native people. Emma couldn't avoid Fannie, but she did her best to avoid Eli during the dinner.

She also did her best not to think of Christmas Day back in Somerset County, one in particular—Hansi's last. As always, they'd gathered at her parents' house with her grandfather, aunts, uncles, and cousins. Asher had talked about going west that day. At the time, Emma hoped it was nothing but a dream, and she'd barely listened. Instead, she'd cooked and cleaned with her aunts, laughed with her cousins, and ate until she was stuffed.

Today, there was plenty of food too. But it wouldn't fill her the way the meal on that last happy Christmas had.

Several times Eli tried to start a conversation, but each time Emma found something pressing she needed to do. Set the tables. Dish up the mashed potatoes. Heat water to clean up.

As Mamm stacked the dishes, she said, "It's time for you to move back here."

"I have three women who are ready to deliver in the next six weeks or so."

"Oh?"

Emma nodded. "One lives in Locke Township, and the other two are in Union Township."

"I see," Mamm said.

"I couldn't say no." Emma was relieved she hadn't.

"Don't commit to helping anyone else," Mamm said. "We'll have you come home after they've all delivered."

"All right." Hopefully that would give Emma enough time to see Mathilde again. Then, once Emma was back at her parents' farm, she would contact the Martins in Newbury Township and let them know she wanted to travel back to Pennsylvania with them in the spring.

A few minutes later, Fannie stepped in and said, "I'll help with the dishes. You Youngie go on and have some fun."

Emma put on her cape and joined Barbara, Phillip, Isaac, and Eli. Jah, she would miss her family when she returned to Somerset County, but she would be in a place of comfort and familiarity. She'd be safe. And she much preferred Abel to Eli.

THE DAY AFTER Christmas was cold but dry. After she wrote to Abel, saying she definitely planned to return in the spring and telling him in detail about her life in Indiana, Emma and Phillip hung the hams in the new smokehouse, along with some from the year before that were already cured. Emma made a double batch of molasses cookies and then convinced Phillip to visit both the Landis and Burton families with her. Surely George wouldn't be as rude to Phillip as he'd been to her.

Sarah and Hiram were in the cabin when they stopped by, huddled around the fire. Phillip went out to the barn, in search of Walter and Judah, while the women visited. After a while, the men came inside, greeted Emma, and pulled the crudely made kitchen chairs up to the fire, warming their hands.

"I'd like to go with you to the Burtons," Judah said. "I haven't had a glimpse of Mathilde in weeks."

"Oh, can't you leave all of that alone?" Sarah asked. "She's being cared for. Don't go making trouble. She has work, and she and her children are safe."

"We don't know they're safe," Emma pointed out.

Phillip cleared his throat. "Was checking on Mathilde your reason for going out visiting today?"

"Not entirely. I wanted to see Sarah."

Phillip said, "We're going back home."

Emma shook her head. "I'm going to the Burton place."

"I'm going back home." Phillip stood.

Emma stood too. "You said you'd take me."

Judah rose from his chair. "I'll take you."

Emma pursed her lips, not sure she wanted to go with Judah. Then again, George might be more apt to welcome her with Judah than with her brother. "Denki," she said to Judah.

Phillip shook his head. "You're unconscionable."

Emma didn't reply, but she found his lack of empathy far more unconscionable than her concern for a friend.

"I can't wait until you return to Dat's," Phillip said, "and

I won't have to worry about you meddling where you don't belong."

"Would you like to go now?" Judah asked Emma, ignoring Phillip.

"Jah." She hadn't taken her cloak off—it had been too cold in the cabin to do so.

"I'll take her home," Judah said to Phillip. "We won't be long."

Phillip grunted and sat back down. It appeared he planned to stay until Judah and Emma were on their way. Or maybe he wanted to gossip about the two of them with Sarah and Walter before he left.

No matter. Emma was headed to see Mathilde. At least Phillip was honest about his feelings and motivations. She had no idea what Judah's were.

As they rode along, heavy clouds darkened the sky.

"We're going to get snow," Judah said. "By nightfall, I'd guess."

When they arrived at the Burtons, Judah helped Emma down and then tied the horse to the hitching post. Clutching her bag of cookies, Emma followed Judah to the door. George might be more likely to let them in if he saw Judah first.

To her surprise, Lenore answered the door instead.

"Merry Christmas," Judah said, stepping to the side to reveal Emma.

Lenore frowned. "Come on in." Emma couldn't help but notice that the doors to the parlor on the right side were closed.

Lenore ushered them into the left-side parlor, where boxes were stacked around the room. Harriet sat on the settee, a shawl wrapped around her shoulders.

"Look who's here," Lenore said.

Harriet nodded in recognition but didn't speak.

"I brought cookies." Emma opened the bag and pulled out the

cookies wrapped in paper and tied with string. She'd made molasses with the hope that the softer cookies wouldn't crumble.

"Thank you. Merry Christmas to you too," Lenore said. "I'm rather surprised you celebrate Christmas."

Emma shrugged. "We do." She nodded toward the boxes. "Are you moving?"

"Yes, little Minnie and I are going ahead to Chicago. Harriet and Georgie will join us when she's feeling better."

"Hush," Harriet said. "We don't need to air everything to the neighbors."

Ignoring her, Judah asked, "What about George?"

"Well, unless he finds a buyer for this place or finds someone to run it," Lenore said, "I'm guessing he's staying here."

Harriet folded her hands in her lap and dropped her head.

Feeling alarmed, Emma asked, "What about Mathilde and her children?"

Lenore put her hands behind her back. "Well, I doubt they'll come to Chicago. . . ."

Emma fought the panic that rose in her throat. "May I see her? To ask what her plans are?"

"No. She's upstairs, feeding the baby," Lenore said. *The baby*. Emma was pretty sure she meant Harriet's baby.

"Where are Baptiste and Agnes?"

"In her house," Lenore said. "Mathilde only came for the feeding, since it's Christmastime. . . ."

Emma hated to think of the children by themselves.

"Where's George?" Judah asked.

"Gone for a few days." Lenore stared at Judah. "We haven't seen much of him lately. I believe you would know as much as we do."

Judah shrugged. "I don't know anything. George said he didn't need me this week."

At the sound of a baby fussing in the back of the house, Emma bolted through the dining room.

"Come back here," Lenore ordered.

Emma kept going, turning the corner into the kitchen. Mathilde stood at the bottom of the back staircase, holding Harriet's baby boy.

Hopefully Agnes was getting enough nourishment too. Emma touched Mathilde's arm. "How are you? How are your children?"

"Fine." As Mathilde turned her head, Emma thought she saw a bruise across her left cheek. Or perhaps it was a shadow.

Lenore reached the kitchen. "You need to go. As you can see, we're busy." She reached for the baby.

As Emma turned to leave, Mathilde reached for her hand and squeezed it.

"Merry Christmas," Emma managed to say. "God keep you."

"And you," Mathilde answered.

"Go on," Lenore said to Emma.

As Emma and Judah left, the first snowflake fell and then another and another.

"Try not to worry about her," Judah said as snow swirled all around them. "Mathilde is smart and resourceful."

"And all alone," Emma replied.

Her own loneliness wasn't anything compared to what Mathilde's likely was. She had to try to see her again. There must be something she could do to help.

THE SECOND WEEK of January, Emma was summoned early in the morning to help the Englisch woman in Locke Township deliver her baby. The delivery went well, and Phillip hadn't grumbled too much at going with her. With each delivery she did, her own grief became more manageable.

The next one was the first week of February for another Englisch woman about five miles from the farm. It was the woman's first, and she appeared to be all of fifteen years old. Phillip waited with the husband in the barn, bringing in more wood from time to time and dozing as much as he could. Emma knew he was impatient to get back to his farm, and at dawn, he came into the cabin with another load of wood and said he was going home but would come back in the afternoon.

Emma hoped the baby would be born by then. It wasn't. But just as darkness fell, after the girl had been pushing for four hours, she finally and painfully delivered a large baby boy. Emma had never felt so relieved, and the bone-tired young woman rallied to nurse her baby.

Phillip spent the night in the barn again as Emma cared for the mother, and then, exhausted, she rode Red back home, following Phillip, and slept for the rest of the day wrapped in a blanket in front of the fire.

Isaac, accompanied by Eli, came the next day as she kneaded dough to bake in the outside oven Phillip had built. How she missed her cooker back home, along with the hand pump and the solid outhouse. "Mamm says it's time for you to come home," Isaac said. "She said for you to bring Bossie too. Mamm thinks you should breed her soon."

Emma didn't want Bossie to be pregnant while walking all the way back to Pennsylvania.

"I have another birth to attend to," she said. At least she might. And, although she thought of her and prayed for her each day, Emma wanted to check on Mathilde in person. It had been almost six weeks since she'd seen her. "I can come back in two weeks."

Eli didn't looked pleased, but Isaac did. Emma knew he liked an excuse to be out and about.

They gave her the latest news from Jackson Township. Mamm had been keeping busy with a few births each month, along with caring for the sick. Several people nearby had influenza, and she'd been taking care of them.

"Services will be at our house the last Sunday of February," Eli said. "Surely you will be back by then."

Unless the last pregnant mother tarried, she and Phillip would be going to the Waglers' for the service. Phillip would want to see Barbara, and there would be no stopping him. Emma would need to tell Eli then that she was going back to Pennsylvania.

The following week, no one came to fetch her for the third birth, and Isaac didn't return either. The week after that, the middle of February, Emma fell ill with a fever, sore throat, and wheezy cough. Just as she was finally recovering, Judah came to summon her late one afternoon during a snowstorm.

The husband of the third Englisch woman who had contacted Emma about helping her had gone to the Landis farm to see if Sarah could help his wife because he didn't want to pay a midwife. His wife was having a harder time than usual, and he thought having a neighbor woman with her might help. When Sarah refused, Judah said he'd go get Emma.

Judah assured Phillip that he'd stay with Emma and bring her back, and Phillip seemed relieved, since the next day was the service at the Waglers'. Phillip would go—and Emma obviously would not.

As the snow fell all around them, she thought of the first storm of the winter on the day Judah took her to the Burton place to try to visit Mathilde. She didn't have much longer to see her again. By the end of the month, Emma would be back at her folks' place. Soon after, she would be traveling to Pennsylvania.

She put on all the petticoats she had under her dress, followed by her cloak, and then hitched up her dress and rode behind Judah. She was thankful for his warmth, but she still wasn't sure of what to think of him. Was he as untrustworthy as Sarah claimed? Was he loyal to George? She had no idea what the truth was when it came to Judah Landis.

CHAPTER 20

The snow fell harder as they journeyed on. Emma was seized by a cough, which caused Judah to slow the horse and ask if she was all right.

"Jah," she managed to say, hoping she was.

Finally, Judah stopped the horse at a barn. "The family didn't get a chance to build a cabin before winter," he explained. "I'll cut more wood for you and haul water too."

"Denki." She took his arm as he helped her off the horse and then looked up at the roof of the barn, where smoke curled into the snow. Judah knocked, and when a man's voice yelled, "Come in," he pushed the door open.

Emma's eyes adjusted to the dim light, illuminated only by a flickering campfire in the middle of the barn. Some of the smoke drafted upward, but some of it drifted across the barn. The family shared the space with a pair of oxen, a cow, and a horse. Emma anticipated that the conditions inside would be bad, but they were worse than she expected.

A pot of soup hung over the fire, and two redheaded children huddled together on one side, coughing, while a smaller blond child pressed himself against the mother, who was curled up on a blanket on the other side of the fire.

The husband stood nearby. He nodded at Judah as he stepped inside.

Judah took his hat off. "This is Emma. She's the Plain midwife."

"She looks awfully young."

"She's old enough," Judah said. "She was trained by her mother, back in Pennsylvania."

"I see," the man said. "I'm Neal O'Brien. And this is my wife, Betha."

They must be Irish, Emma thought. Back in Pennsylvania, in the cities, the Irish were mistreated. Some wouldn't hire them. Others told them to go back to where they came from. Many taunted them. Emma thought of the freedom her family had found in America and hoped it was still available to others, including the O'Brien family.

She stepped toward Betha and then bent down on the cold, hard earth. This was no place to have a baby. She wished she'd brought another blanket. The toddler sat up and rubbed his stomach. "Food?"

Emma glanced at the hungry faces across the fire and then at Neal. He shook his head. "I need to go hunting. . . ." Emma doubted Betha would be ready to push the baby out until her older children went to sleep, and they probably wouldn't be able to fall asleep until they got some food in their bellies.

Leaving her bag beside Betha, Emma stepped across the room to where Judah still stood by the door. "Would you go get some food? Tell Phillip what's going on. I cooked a venison shoulder yesterday. Bring the rest of that, the potatoes in the coals, and some of the apples in the cellar. And one of the loaves of bread I baked this morning. Oh, and I need the blankets from my bed too."

Judah nodded.

"That will be a lot to carry," Emma said, suddenly realizing how many requests she was making. "Will it be all right?"

"I'll manage." He gave her a kind smile. "I'll be praying as I ride."

"Denki."

As Judah turned to leave, Emma instructed Neal to go chop more wood and then asked the oldest child to sweep the barn floor. She took one of her cloths from her bag and changed the toddler's diaper.

Betha moaned every few minutes from her place on the floor. It took some urging, but Emma finally got her up and walking around.

Emma suppressed a cough. "Tell me about your pain."

The woman touched her lower back.

"And when did they start?"

"Yesterday morning." Betha had to be exhausted.

After Neal returned with the wood and stoked the fire, the two older children helped him feed the animals and shovel the manure out the side door. Emma put the kettle on to boil and then kept Betha walking as much as she could. After the water was hot, she made her a cup of chamomile tea.

Emma had heard older women say that the pain of childbirth made mothers love their children all the more, but she wasn't sure about it. Who couldn't love their baby, whether they'd had a hard or an easy birth? The older women also said that mothers in labor shouldn't moan, yell, or call out. Emma didn't agree with that either.

Betha's children didn't seem concerned about their mother,

at least not yet. Perhaps they would be soon, if they didn't go to sleep.

Judah returned sooner than Emma had anticipated, shaking the snow from his head and carrying a bundle of food wrapped inside her blankets, all tied together with a rope. He recruited the two older children to help set up the meal on the table, and they gathered around to eat. Emma managed to get Betha to eat a piece of meat and some bread and drink a cup of water. Then she gave her raspberry tea to hopefully speed up the pains.

Once the children were done eating, Judah tucked them all under a blanket on the other side of the fire, and then he disappeared into one of the stalls with his bedroll.

Neal sat back down at the table and turned the lamp to low. Usually, men completely left the room during a birth, but that was hard to do in a barn.

Finally, Betha had the urge to push. Emma hoped, since it was her fourth, that it would go quickly. But it didn't. After an hour, the pains had only grown worse and now Betha was flat-out paralyzed from all of it. When the next pain came, Emma ran her hands over Betha's belly, feeling the baby. The face was up.

No wonder Betha's back hurt so badly. Emma feared the baby was stuck. There wasn't time to go get Mamm, and Emma, still recovering from her illness, feared she wasn't thinking clearly.

"Judah," she called out. "I need help."

He appeared, bright eyed, looking as if he hadn't slept at all.

"There's an issue with the baby," Emma said in a low tone so Neal wouldn't overhear. "Would you go see if Mathilde will come? Don't ask George," Emma said quickly. "Go straight to her shack. Make sure she brings the children."

Judah left again. Emma was thankful he'd come instead of Phillip. She hoped she wasn't putting Mathilde at risk, but she didn't know what else to do.

Betha's pains slowed, and she dozed between them. But each time one started, she cried out. The children continued to sleep, although all of them stirred and coughed fitfully.

An hour later, Betha continued to push, ten minutes apart, but it seemed the baby would never come. Emma glanced at the door, longing for Judah and Mathilde to arrive. Finally, the door opened and Mathilde stepped through holding Agnes, wrapped in rabbit furs and tucked in her cradleboard. Judah followed, carrying Baptiste close to his chest.

Emma nearly wilted, her head dipping forward in relief, until Neal stood. "What's going on?"

"Mathilde is here to help," Emma said.

Judah nodded. "She's very knowledgeable." He placed Baptiste next to the other children and sat down at the table, motioning for Neal to do the same, but the man didn't budge.

Mathilde put Agnes next to her brother and then joined Emma and Betha on the floor. "Thank you for coming," Emma whispered.

"I knew Judah wouldn't have come and gotten me unless you needed me," Mathilde replied.

Finally, Neal moved to the table, and Judah stayed there with him, their backs to the women.

Another pain gripped Betha, and again she pushed, screaming as she did, but the baby's head still didn't crown.

As Mathilde inched closer, Emma saw another bruise on her friend's face, one that didn't change with the shadows in the dim barn. She'd ask her about it later.

Mathilde said, "She should get up."

Emma wasn't sure if Betha would agree to that, but she took her by the hands. "Let's try something else." The woman cooperated.

"You rest," Mathilde said to Emma. "I'll walk with her."

Grateful for the break, Emma wrapped herself up in her cloak and rested next to Agnes and Baptiste. Betha's cries kept coming every five minutes or so. Somehow Mathilde kept her walking between her pains.

After another hour or so, Mathilde placed her hand on Emma's shoulder. "The baby is definitely stuck. What should we do?"

Emma closed her eyes, trying to think through what her mother would advise. Back home, she'd seen Mamm put a woman in a rocking chair to shift a baby. Or rock her hips around. One time she'd seen Mamm coax a woman onto her hands and knees. That's what she hadn't tried with Betha.

She opened her eyes and reached for Mathilde's hand. Her friend pulled her up. Emma approached Betha, who was curled up on her blanket again, and put her hands on the small of the woman's back. "You need to move to your hands and knees," she said. "And rock forward and backward. We have to get this baby moving." She'd been pushing for five hours now.

Betha groaned. Mathilde slid her arms under Betha's chest, and Emma lifted her hips until they had gotten her into position. Then Emma placed her hands on Betha's hips again and pushed forward. "Move back and forth," she said. She then forced the woman's hips from side to side. "And sway as you do."

Mathilde bent down in front of Betha and made eye contact with her as another pain started.

Betha stopped moving and started to groan.

"Keep swaying." Emma felt for the baby. As the pain continued, the baby's head finally started to bulge.

"Keep moving," Emma encouraged. "The baby's shifting down."

When the pain stopped, Emma gave Betha more of the raspberry tea. Betha was shaking from exhaustion, and Emma and Mathilde both held her up. When another pain started, Emma told Betha to sway again. Again the baby's head bulged but didn't crown.

But during the next pain, it did finally crown. Emma ran her fingers around the head as much as she could, and finally the membranes broke in a rush of waters, splashing onto the dirt floor. With the next push the baby crowned again and then the head came out, face up, just as Emma had predicted. On the next push, the baby came out enough for Emma to grab the shoulders and pull it out the rest of the way. It was a boy.

And he was blue.

Emma fought back tears as she remembered her own little girl. Paralyzed, she held the baby in her hands, staring into his closed eyes. But Mathilde swept to Emma's side, took the baby from her, and started rubbing his skin. She swiped her fingers in the baby's mouth and then turned him upside down. He started to whimper faintly and then began to cry. His skin began to pinken.

Mathilde wrapped the baby in wide strips of cloth that Betha had ready, and then handed the baby back to Emma. Mathilde turned her attention to Betha, covering her with a blanket. Neal stepped over to the women, glanced at his son, stoked the fire, and then grabbed his rifle and headed out.

Emma glanced up at Judah, who faced them now.

"He's going hunting," Judah said. "To feed his family."

Relieved, Emma nodded.

Judah stood and headed to the stall. Emma continued to hold the baby while Mathilde cleaned Betha and then gave her meat and bread to eat. Then Mathilde took the baby from Emma and put her next to Betha to nurse. The woman did what she needed to do, closing her eyes and soon falling asleep.

Agnes began to fuss, and Mathilde nursed her and then rose. "We need to go," she said.

Emma felt dazed. "So soon?"

"Before George wakes. He'll expect his breakfast soon."

"Did Harriet leave for Chicago?"

Mathilde nodded.

"Is anyone else at the house with George?"

Mathilde shook her head.

Emma stood and reached to touch the bruise on her friend's face.

Mathilde turned her head. "I'm fine," she said.

Emma stepped closer. "Who hit you?"

"We need to go." Mathilde knelt and wiggled Agnes back into the cradleboard.

"You don't have to," Emma said. "You can come home with me."

Mathilde shook her head.

"I can come get you, then. After George eats his breakfast. I'll take you to my parents' place in Jackson Township."

"George would find me," Mathilde answered. "I owe him money. Jean-Paul signed a contract."

"But he can't beat and imprison you."

"Maybe he can." Mathilde shrugged. "I need to go."

Emma ventured back to the stalls. "Judah," she whispered. "Mathilde needs to go back."

Though he had likely just lain down, he was on his feet immediately.

Emma lowered her voice even more. "Mathilde has a bruise on her face."

"I asked her about it. . . ."

"Did she explain what happened?"

Judah shook his head.

"I think George hit her," Emma whispered. "But she won't come home with me."

"I'll talk with her again," Judah said. "And George too."

"Denki," Emma said, hoping he would follow through on his promise and that he wasn't protecting George.

A couple of hours later, after the children had woken up and Emma had fed them bread and apples, Neal returned with two ducks. At least they'd have some food. Emma would bring more apples and potatoes the next day, and some milk and eggs too.

THE SNOW HAD blanketed the world entirely in white, muffling the usual sounds of the countryside. If Emma hadn't been so tired, she would have marveled at the beauty. Instead, she leaned against Judah's back as she rode behind him, hoping to draw some strength from him. She'd never been so exhausted in her life, not even after her own babies were born.

What if Mathilde hadn't come to help her? What if Betha had died, leaving those children on the edge of the frontier without a mother? All alone with a father who hardly spoke. A coughing fit shook her.

Judah slowed the horse. "Are you all right?"

"Jah . . ." But she wasn't. "What did Mathilde say about George?"

"Nothing," Judah answered. "She wouldn't talk about the bruise except to beg me not to bring it up with George. She said that would just make it worse."

"He doesn't respect her," Emma said. "He's hurting her, and I'm afraid it will grow worse."

Judah's voice grew deeper. "I know. I've heard of Englischers treating Native women as slaves, and then even trading the women among themselves, taking their children from them." He sounded so honest in his concern. But was he?

She hoped so. She'd lost her children to fate—she couldn't imagine having them taken from her. She couldn't let that happen to Mathilde.

"Those men treat the Native women worse than they would their livestock." Judah stared straight ahead as he spoke. "And nothing is done, not by the law or the Englischers' communities."

"What can we do?" She bit her lower lip.

"I'm afraid Mathilde is right that confronting George might make things worse," he said. "I'll check with the sheriff in Goshen and see what he can do."

Emma thought of the verse from James, that pure religion was to visit the fatherless and widows. Surely, God wanted them to care for Mathilde as best they could.

They rode in silence for a while. Emma coughed again, and when she finally stopped, she began to cry. And then she began to shake.

"Are you all right?" Judah asked.

"I'm sorry." How immature of her, not to be able to control her emotions. What would her Mamm say to her right now?

"Don't be sorry," he said. "It's all right to cry. We'll figure out what to do about Mathilde."

Emma cried harder. "It's that and more. The baby could have died and Betha too."

"But they didn't."

"Those children could be without a mother."

"But they aren't," Judah cooed as softly as a dove.

Emma drew in a ragged breath. "I never wanted to come west, and I was right not to want to. I thought the worst of it would be living in a cabin instead of a house, cooking over a fire instead of in a stove, using a hole in the ground instead of an outhouse, and getting water from a creek instead of a pump." Another sob racked her. "But it's so much harder than that."

"You'll be back at your parents' place soon."

She bristled. "Who told you that?"

"Eli," Judah answered. "I saw him in Goshen last week."

"What were you doing in Goshen?"

"Looking at land to buy." Judah sighed. "But I couldn't afford anything. The price has gone up again with so many people moving here." Judah paused. "Eli also said you two are courting."

Emma shook her head. "That's not true."

"Well, maybe he said you will be once you return to Jackson Township."

"No." Emma's voice shook as she spoke. "In fact," she said, "I won't be staying in Indiana for much longer. I'm going to go back to Pennsylvania in the spring. I just need to make the final plans."

Judah turned his face toward her and smiled.

"You're happy I'm leaving?"

He shook his head. "Nee. Not at all, but I am happy you won't be courting Eli."

Stunned, Emma wrinkled her nose. They rode on in silence. Why would he care if she courted Eli or not? He was the one who didn't want to marry a widow.

Finally, he said, "I had an idea you might be going back. Sarah mentioned it."

Emma's face grew warm even in the freezing cold, remembering Sarah saying Phillip had told her. As the horse trotted along, someone shouted Judah's name. Across a field, a rider came toward them.

Judah pulled the reins to slow the horse. "It's George."

Emma groaned.

"Where's Mathilde?" George shouted. "What have you done with her?"

"I don't know what you're talking about," Judah called out to him.

"I saw you on my land last night."

"Jah, I fetched Mathilde to help Emma with a birth. I took her back this morning."

George was only a few feet away now. He pulled his horse to stop, and the stallion grunted and blew through his nose as George sneered. "She's gone."

CHAPTER 21

Savannah

As Jane finished, the bell on the front door rang. "Excuse me," she said.

I sat there, Emma and Judah and George fresh in my mind. And Mathilde. Where had she gone?

"Is Wanda here?" a woman asked.

Mammi stood and whispered to me, "It's Catherine."

"No," Jane said. "Why do you ask?"

"I wanted to make sure she knew what her son did."

My heart skipped a beat.

Calmly, Jane said, "You could stop by Wanda's house."

Catherine continued as if Jane hadn't said a thing. "Kenny Miller is back in town. On his testimony, Deputy Rogers arrested Tommy for dealing drugs and trafficking girls, Miriam in particular."

Stunned, I choked out, "What?"

Catherine turned toward me, probably happy to have a willing audience. "That's right. He planned to take her to Las Vegas, but she escaped. No one can figure out where she went, though. She drove away in Kenny's car last night. Tommy was arrested this morning, as part of an ongoing investigation."

Had Deputy Rogers uncovered evidence that could prove this? I couldn't believe it. But, again, I knew people weren't always what they seemed. Had Tommy played me? Had I been a fool *again*?

I managed to ask, "Where's Mason?"

"Who?"

"Kenny's little boy."

Catherine shrugged.

"Who told you all of this?"

"Vernon. He came by to speak with the bishop."

"And why did you want to talk with Wanda?" Jane asked.

"She's been enabling Tommy." Catherine's voice grew louder. "Now look what's happened."

Jane exhaled. "Is there anything else I can help you with? Fabric? Thread? A new pattern?"

Catherine's expression morphed into disgust, but then she lowered her voice and said, "Jah, I do need some thread. Black. And batting."

Mammi already had our coats in her hand. "Let's go," she whispered.

"Thank you, Jane," I said. "For the quilting and the story."

"Come back as soon as you can." Jane looked as if she'd been kicked in the stomach.

I reached out and squeezed her hand. "We will."

"*Mach's gut*," Mammi said to Catherine. "See you tomorrow."

I hadn't thought about the Sunday service. I used to go with Mammi as a girl, but should I go tomorrow? It probably depended on what we learned later today.

When we reached the rental car, Mammi asked, "Could we stop by Wanda's?"

"Of course."

As I turned down the lane to Ervin's farm, a white sedan slowed in front of me. As it parked in front of the farmhouse, the driver turned toward us. It was a middle-aged woman. I drove past the sedan and parked in front of the Dawdi Haus.

Mammi was out of the SUV before I had the engine off. I strode after her to the front door, which she opened without knocking. "Wanda!" she called out.

"I'm in the back, with Mason."

Whew! I exhaled a breath I didn't even realize I'd been holding. At least Mason was with her.

Mammi led the way down the hall, and I followed into the back bedroom. Wanda stood at a changing table, pulling a sweatshirt over Mason's head.

"Tommy's leaving tomorrow," Wanda said. "I begged him for one more day with this little guy." She gave him a hug and then turned toward us.

"Catherine stopped by Plain Patterns a few minutes ago." Mammi told her what the bishop's wife had said about Tommy as a knock fell on the front door.

Wanda put her hand to her chest as she scooped Mason to her hip with her other hand. "Are you sure Catherine knows what she's talking about?"

"She seemed to," Mammi said.

Wanda turned to me. "Have you called Tommy's cell phone?"

"I don't have his number."

She rattled it off. "Go ahead and call him now. It's an emergency."

I pulled out my phone and keyed in his number as another knock fell on the door, this time louder.

Wanda led the way back down the hall, muttering, "Who could that be?"

Tommy's phone rang. Once. Twice. Three times.

Wanda opened the door.

The woman from the white sedan stood in front of us, carrying a briefcase.

Six rings. Seven. Eight. Tommy's voicemail came on.

The woman said, "Wanda Miller?"

The voicemail beeped and started recording. Numbly, I held the phone in my hand without speaking.

"Jah, that's me."

"I'm Cheryl Johnson, a case manager with Indiana Children's Protective Services." The woman stepped into the living room and closed the door behind her as we all stared. "I have a court order to take Mason Miller into protective custody."

MAMMI HAD THE presence of mind to offer the woman a cup of tea. "And then let's all sit down so you can explain what's going on," she said.

I slipped back down the hall to the back bedroom and ended the call to Tommy. If he wasn't in jail, he'd have the weirdest message ever. I immediately called Deputy Rogers, although I didn't expect he'd answer. But he did.

I blurted out, "Did you arrest Tommy Miller this morning?"

"Affirmative," he answered.

I suspected Catherine knew what she was talking about, but it still shook me to hear it from Deputy Rogers. "Listen," I said, "I'm at Wanda Miller's house and there's a CPS case manager here trying to take Mason."

"I know," he said. "With your information about the boy, I got a court order yesterday, but it was late. Last evening, I spent quite a bit of time questioning Kenny and Miriam too. In the meantime, Tommy had already dropped the boy off at . . ." He paused. "At Wanda Miller's. We had to reroute the CPS manager."

I guessed Kenny must have facilitated the deputy's conversation with Miriam the evening before. My thoughts quickly turned to Mason.

I cleared my throat and then said, "Mason should stay here with Wanda. You're going to traumatize him by taking him away from her."

Deputy Rogers snorted. "I'm going to traumatize him? That's on Tommy," he said. "He's the one who involved an innocent child in all of this."

"No, that's on Kenny. Tommy's trying to help."

"So he says."

I exhaled and then asked, "What do you mean?"

"Do we know for sure that the child isn't Tommy's son?" Deputy Rogers voice grew louder. "Maybe he just told you the boy is Kenny's."

I flinched. I hadn't thought of that. Had Tommy lied to me?

I managed to keep my composure. "Regardless," I said, "there's no reason Mason can't stay with Wanda. She's been caring for him since September." I concentrated on lowering my frantic pitch. "He's attached to her."

"She could be a flight risk."

"*She's an Amish grandmother*," I said, exasperated. "She's not going anywhere."

When he didn't answer, I asked, "Do you have children? Grandchildren?"

There was a long pause and then he said, "Is the case worker still there? Could I speak with her?"

"Yes and yes." I quickly jogged down the hall.

As I entered the living room, I extended my phone to Cheryl, saying, "Deputy Rogers would like to speak with you."

A puzzled expression settled on her face as she took the phone. She listened for a moment and then stepped to the front door and opened it. "I'd need to take a closer look around, of course. And you would need to get the court order reversed. . . ." She stepped onto the porch and pulled the door shut behind her.

Wanda pulled Mason from her lap and into a hug while I began to pray. Hopefully God was appealing to Deputy Rogers's paternal side, if he had one. Finally, Cheryl returned, handed me my phone—the call was over—and sat back down. Mammi quickly appeared with cups of tea, and then Cheryl turned toward Wanda. "Could I ask you some questions to see if perhaps this would be the right place for Mason to stay, at least for the time being?"

Wanda nodded.

Cheryl took a clipboard with a piece of paper on it from her briefcase. "I'll also need to take a look around."

"All right," Wanda said. Mason began to squirm and then wiggled down to the floor. Mammi motioned to him, and he followed her into the kitchen.

Cheryl asked Wanda about accommodations in the house for a child.

"I've babyproofed it," Wanda answered. "All of the cleaners are on the top shelf in the kitchen. I don't take any medications, so there are none in the house. The toilet seat has a lock on it. There's a barrier around the wood stove, and I've draped all of the cords to the window coverings over the rods. Tommy did all of it for me."

"Great." Cheryl marked the sheet of paper. "How about outlets?"

Wanda grinned. "Those aren't a problem either."

"Covered?"

"No. I don't have any," Wanda said.

"Oh." Cheryl smiled and shook her head. "Forgive me. I knew that—I just forgot. What kind of lamps do you have?"

"All battery operated. Tommy insisted."

Cheryl kept asking questions, eventually landing on the topic of discipline, corporal punishment in particular.

"That's never been my style," Wanda answered.

Cheryl asked about nutrition next. "What sort of meals do you serve?"

"All home cooked." She nodded to the kitchen where Mason sat at the table with a bowl of apple slices in front of him. "Mason is a good eater."

Cheryl continued with the questions, asking if Wanda would cooperate with authorities and any permanent plan for the child. Wanda hesitated and then said, "Jah."

"Can you keep all information that may be relayed to you private?"

"Definitely."

"All right," Cheryl said. "I need to look around."

Wanda showed her the kitchen, where Mason still sat at the table, now eating peanut butter on homemade bread. Then Wanda led Cheryl down the hall to Mason's room. I didn't follow them, but when they returned, Cheryl asked, "Does anyone else live here with you?"

Wanda shook her head. "Just Mason, during the days. And sometimes he spends the night."

"Do you travel much?" Cheryl asked.

Wanda shook her head. "I don't travel at all. I haven't left Elkhart County in nearly a decade."

Cheryl jotted that answer down and then looked up at Wanda. "Thank you for your time and for providing a good home for Mason." Then she said, "Excuse me just a minute. I need to make a phone call." She pulled out her phone and stepped out onto the porch again. Mason slipped down from his chair and toddled over to Wanda. She lifted him up and he settled on her hip, patting her shoulder as he did.

Wanda gave me a questioning look. I shrugged. Mammi stepped to Wanda's side. It felt as if we were all holding our breath—except Mason, who started blowing spit bubbles. All three of us burst into laughter as Cheryl opened the front door.

Silence fell over the room. Even Mason stopped his silly behavior, seeming to comprehend the seriousness of the moment.

"I've talked with the judge and with my supervisor," Cheryl said. "We're all three okay with leaving Mason with you, at least until Monday." She handed Wanda her card. "Call me if you have any problems. Otherwise I'll be in touch on Monday."

I held my breath, expecting her to ask if Wanda had a phone, fearful she'd think the phone shack inadequate. Thankfully, she didn't and instead told all of us good-bye.

Mason shouted a hearty, "Bye-bye" and waved.

The rest of us, as soon as she closed the door, breathed a sigh of relief.

I WAITED UNTIL Cheryl had driven away and then went out to my car, leaving Mammi with Wanda and Mason. I wanted to go see Joshua. But first I needed to see Tommy at the jail, although I doubted I'd be allowed to. I decided to call Deputy Rogers again, but just as I pulled out my phone, it rang.

Ryan. I went ahead and answered it.

"Savannah, I'm working on getting my credit card stuff figured out," he said. "I don't want you to think I'm trying to cheat you."

Cheat me? That was an interesting choice of words.

He must have realized his faux pas because he said, "You know. Make you pay."

"When do you think it will be figured out?"

"I don't know," he said. "But soon." There was a long pause. "I was also wondering if we could talk."

"Aren't we doing that now?"

"I mean in person. When are you coming home?"

I couldn't breathe. He wanted to talk. Did he want me back? I forced myself to inhale—and come to my senses. "I have a lot going on out here."

"Like what?"

"Spending time with my grandmother. Job interviews."

"Interviews? But you have a job."

"I resigned."

He didn't respond.

"Look," I said. "I need to get going. I appreciate you taking care of things with the vendors. I really do. But I need to go. Bye."

I hung up before he could say anything and didn't accept the call when he immediately called back. Instead, I called Deputy Rogers.

When he answered, I said, "Savannah here."

"What do you want?"

I took a deep breath, trying to keep my voice calm. "Thank you for being flexible and allowing Mason to stay with Wanda."

"It's just until Monday."

"Any chance Kenny can take him by then?"

"Probably not. Mason's mother does want him back, and CPS in Nevada approves."

"How will he get there?"

"A caseworker from there will probably fly here and escort him back," Deputy Rogers said.

"Is there any chance I can talk with Tommy? I'm going out to Vernon and Arleta's to see Joshua, to see if he has an idea where Miriam might be, but I thought Tommy might be able to offer some insight first."

"I already talked with both Tommy and Joshua."

"Right," I said. "But maybe Tommy will open up with me a little bit more. And Joshua too. If I ask him questions in Pennsylvania Dutch, he might be more likely to answer."

"There's no chance of that."

"There might be," I replied. "Tommy too."

"Why would Tommy give you information he wouldn't give me?"

"He might," I responded. "I'll pass on what he says."

Deputy Rogers didn't respond right away but finally said, "All right. Visiting hours end at two thirty. I'll meet you at the police station."

Ten minutes later, I drove past city hall to the police station, which also housed the Nappanee jail. At least Tommy hadn't been transferred to the Elkhart County jail in Elkhart yet. Deputy Rogers met me at the door and led the way back to the jail.

"So where is Kenny now?" I asked.

"At his apartment," the deputy answered. "He doesn't have his car, so he's not going anywhere."

I didn't want to push too far, considering he was letting me see Tommy, but I did say, "That seems awfully trusting on your part."

"Everything he said has panned out. One person said Tommy sold him fentanyl, including on the night of New Year's Eve." Deputy Rogers stopped in front of a door. "That cell phone Tommy said was Kenny's is actually Tommy's."

"Where was Kenny all this time?"

"Searching for Miriam." Deputy Rogers crossed his arms. "When he found her, he brought her back here, but Tommy intervened and tried to send her away again. Kenny said it's not the first time he's done this. Kenny said Tommy was questioned in Las Vegas for the same thing, but there wasn't enough evidence to arrest him. "

Maybe, just maybe, Tommy could be involved in selling drugs. But I couldn't believe he'd traffic Miriam—or anyone else. "Could you corroborate what Kenny said?"

"I'm working on it."

I nodded toward the door to the jail. "Is Tommy in there?"

He nodded. "You need to check your purse, phone, all of your belongings and go through a metal detector. Then you can see him."

After I'd shown my license, checked my stuff, and walked through the metal detector—with my arms crossed over my chest so the wires in my bra wouldn't set it off—they led me into a supervised room with tables. Tommy was the only other person who wasn't an employee in the room. Deputy Rogers stood, with a guard, at the back of the room.

I slid into the seat across from Tommy.

He met my eyes. "You shouldn't have come."

"But I did," I said.

"Mason is with my mom, but I'm afraid they plan to take him. Could you check in on him?"

"I already did." I told him about the caseworker and that his mom could have Mason until the court decided what to do. "What happened? What did Kenny tell Rogers?"

"That I've been selling fentanyl. And that I kidnapped Miriam on New Year's Eve night and drove her to Chicago."

"Not Gary?"

He shook his head.

"I'll give them Ethel's address."

"I already did," Tommy said. "Rogers tried to contact her but couldn't reach her. And then an officer in Gary went to the house and no one was there." He shrugged. "By then, Rogers had interrogated two people who supported Kenny's testimony, including Miriam."

"So then Deputy Rogers arrested you?"

He nodded. "Kenny said that I left Miriam with a trafficker and that I had plans to kidnap more Amish girls, and Englisch ones too. That my plan was to get more kids hooked on fentanyl and then steal them too. Rogers cited an Indiana code, charging me of intentionally removing another person from one place to another by threat of force."

"Wow."

"Kenny told Rogers the phone I said was his is really mine. And he's kind of right—it's on my account, but I was trying to help him out." He put his head in his hands. "I don't blame Rogers for believing Kenny. He's pretty persuasive, and the phone thing convinced him I was lying about everything."

I lowered my head, trying to meet his eyes. "But why would Kenny say all of that?"

"He's angry with me. Mad I got involved with taking Mason back to Vegas. Mad I was going to stay there. Mad he's been such a bad father . . ." Tommy shook his head. "Kenny has refused all of these years to get help. I don't know what's going to make him change."

"Did you tell Deputy Rogers all of that?"

"I tried."

"And he still believed Kenny?"

Tommy nodded. "Like I said, he's convincing. Charming. Gregarious. Anything I said seemed to make Rogers believe Kenny even more. It was déjà vu."

I leaned toward Tommy. "What do you mean?"

"Back when we were teenagers, something similar happened." He sighed. "Deputy Rogers is even questioning who Mason's father is. He's sure it's me—and Kenny didn't correct him. But I shouldn't go on about Kenny anymore, not now."

I exhaled, grateful he'd brought it up. Instinctively, I didn't think Tommy would lie about that. It didn't make any sense. And Wanda seemed sure that Mason was Kenny's son. I couldn't think of any reason that Tommy would deceive his own mother.

"Deputy Rogers said Kenny's at your apartment," I whispered. "Should I go by?"

Tommy shook his head.

My voice was barely audible now. "What should I do?"

"Find Miriam." I could barely hear Tommy. "She took off in Kenny's car—and it doesn't sound as if she went back to Gary."

I leaned even closer to him. "Did she really steal Kenny's car?"

"No, he said he gave her permission to take it." He touched my wrist, sending a shiver down my spine. "See if you can find her."

"All right," I said. "I was going to go out to Vernon and Arleta's and talk to Joshua. Hopefully he has an idea where she is. Or maybe she'll contact him."

"Yes, go. But if you find out where she is, take someone with you. We don't know what Kenny's really been up to or who he's been dealing with."

"Like?"

He glanced toward the back of the room. This time he didn't whisper. "How about Deputy Rogers? Maybe he'd go with you."

CHAPTER 22

As Deputy Rogers escorted me from the jail, he asked if I'd found out anything more. "No," I answered. "But could I speak with you in private?"

He stopped in the hallway and crossed his arms over his broad chest. "You can speak to me here."

I squared my shoulders, wishing I could match his in-charge attitude, but I knew I couldn't. "I was wondering," I said, "if you would go with me to Chicago to look for Miriam."

"When?"

"Tomorrow."

He raised his brows and then said, "I have too much to do here—another lead to follow concerning Tommy."

Without thinking it through, I blurted out, "Do you think your bias toward him is affecting the investigation?"

His hands dropped to his side, hovering over his gun and baton. "What did Tommy tell you?"

"Nothing," I said. "Absolutely nothing. You just seem determined to 'get' him."

He shook his head, a look of disgust on his face. "You have

no idea what kind of person Tommy really is. He's not the boy you remember and hasn't been for the last decade."

"Decade? I have no idea what he did that made you so mad, but the span of a person's life from nineteen to twenty-nine involves a lot of brain development and maturity. Have you taken that into consideration?"

His expression went flat, and his eyes narrowed. "Leave this investigation to me. Do not go to Chicago. Do not go looking for Miriam. I have this under control." Without saying goodbye, he turned on his heels and strode back toward the jail.

I cringed. Would he take out our conversation on Tommy? Perhaps Deputy Rogers was afraid I would find Miriam, that she'd contradict all of his theories.

That's what I hoped, at least. There was still a part of me that feared Deputy Rogers might be right and Tommy was lying. But I was more determined than ever to go to Chicago and see what I could find.

But first I needed to speak with Joshua again. I went straight to Vernon's farm, arriving just before three thirty. After I parked, I checked in the barn, hoping Joshua was there and I could speak to him privately. No such luck. It was empty except for the calves in their pens and a kitten that darted away from me.

After I knocked on the door, I waited and waited and waited. Finally, Arleta answered, with Ruthie Mae tucked in one arm.

"Hi," I said. "I'm looking for Joshua. I have some questions to ask him about Miriam."

"He's out in the pasture with Vernon. A cow broke through the fence."

"I'll go find them," I said. "How are you and Ruthie doing?"

"Just fine."

"Have you heard from Miriam?"

She shook her head. "The deputy was out here asking about all of that. We didn't have anything new to tell him."

"All right," I said. "I just need to double-check with Joshua."

"Miriam's an adult. She has a right to leave."

"But Deputy Rogers arrested Tommy Miller for kidnapping Miriam."

"Jah, but this time she left on her own, in Kenny's car."

"Did you know she could drive?"

Arleta shook her head.

I had a million questions racing through my head. Why wasn't Arleta more concerned about Miriam? And why was she being so passive?

Arleta finally exhaled. "She needs to find her own way. I've tried with her, over and over, but I'm out of ideas."

Ruthie began to fuss.

"Go talk with Joshua," Arleta said. "He's been sneaking around here like he doesn't think I know he has a cell phone. It's become obvious the last few days. You're probably right about him knowing more than what he's told us or the deputy."

The baby was crying now.

"Thank you." I turned to go, wishing I knew what else to say. Maybe Arleta was doing the best she could. I had no idea what all was going on in their family, but I did know what it was like to be a teenager whose parent had died and whose remaining parent seemed to move on effortlessly. My heart ached for Miriam.

Once I reached the pasture, I climbed the fence. In the distance, I could see Joshua and Vernon.

As I neared them, I called out, "Hallo."

Vernon turned his head and obviously saw me, but he turned back to his work without an acknowledgment. Joshua didn't even turn his head.

When I reached them, out of breath, I said, "Joshua, may I speak with you?"

"What about?" Vernon, asked, his eyes still on the fence.

"Miriam."

Vernon grunted. "Joshua, you finish this up while I get started on the milking. Come in as soon as you're done." Vernon handed Joshua the wire cutters and then started toward the barn, sticking along the fence line.

Joshua knelt down.

I stepped closer to him and kept my voice low. "Have you heard from Miriam?"

When he didn't answer, I said, "I'm concerned about her. She could end up in a dangerous situation." Not to mention her baby. She needed prenatal care, as stress-free a living situation as possible, and good nutrition. "I'd like to help her, if I can."

When he didn't answer, I asked again, "Have you heard from her?"

Finally, he nodded.

"Is she in Chicago?"

He nodded again.

"Do you know where?"

He stood and took his phone from his pocket. Then he opened his Find My Friends app and held it up for me. The orange dot was in Chicago, on the east side.

"Do you have an address?" I asked.

He clicked on the dot and it pulled up the address, which I knew might or might not be exact.

I asked, "Could you send me her phone number?"

He shook his head.

"Look, Joshua," I said. "I know she's your big sister and she's probably asked you to keep secrets. But that's wrong because she might be in danger. Whatever she's told you, you need to share with an adult. If you won't tell me, give it to someone else who will help Miriam. Like Deputy Rogers."

I paused, reconsidering. Deputy Rogers seemed so blinded by his desire to convict Tommy that I wasn't sure if he could be trusted to do what was right for Miriam.

Joshua raised his head, his expression furtive. "She's pregnant," he said. "She doesn't want anyone to know."

I exhaled. "That's all the more reason for me to help her." He looked down at his phone again, but I couldn't see what he was doing. But then my phone pinged. I glanced at my screen. He'd texted me a screenshot of Miriam's location.

"It a convenience store on Port Street, in East Chicago," Joshua said. "I looked it up. I took a screenshot of the address before she turned her phone off—or maybe it died."

It wasn't much, but maybe a clerk would remember her. "Thank you," I said, relief spilling through me. "I'll let you know when I find her."

AFTER I LEFT Vernon's farm, I returned to Wanda's to pick up Mammi. Both wanted to know if I'd seen Tommy. I told them about my afternoon, what Tommy had said, and that Joshua had given me Miriam's location, or at least her proximity. Vaguely I remembered that I'd also talked to Ryan, but I didn't tell them about that.

I didn't need to. He called again while we were telling Wanda good-bye. I sent the call to voicemail, but when Mammi asked who was calling, I said it was Ryan.

"Are you going to call him back?"

"Not now." I stuffed my phone into my purse and zipped it.

I figured Sunday morning would be the best time to leave for Chicago and show up at the convenience store—and maybe knock on doors around it. I needed to do that in the light of day, not the dark of night.

I told Mammi I was sorry I wouldn't be able to go to church with her the next morning.

"I'll see how much it snows," she said. "If I can't take the buggy, I'll stay home."

The next morning there was only a few inches of snow, but Mammi was still undecided if she'd take the buggy or not. I told her I didn't think she should, but she was still mulling it over when Uncle Seth arrived in his pickup.

A few minutes later, he opened the front door with a hearty hello. "Need a ride to church, Dorothy?"

Mammi laughed. "I believe I do."

That was my cue to leave. I called out a good-bye to Uncle Seth as I sailed through the open door and said, "Mammi can fill you in on where I'm going and why."

As I drove, I thought of Emma the night of Betha's birth. Of the snow and bitter cold. Then I thought of Mathilde. Where was she hiding? And why? She owed George money, but why was he so cruel to her? Was he going to try to sell her to recoup some of the money she owed him? He certainly felt entitled to her, as if he owned her. He certainly believed he was above the law in his treatment of her. Mathilde and Miriam's circumstances weren't the same, but both were vulnerable young women with few resources at the hands of powerful men.

Jah, an Amish young woman was at risk, and in modern times, Native women continued to be at risk too, just as they had in the past. From what I'd remembered when I took health-care sociology during college, Native women in both the United States and Canada continued to be abused at much higher rates than any other group, and nine times out of ten the perpetrators were non-tribal members.

The roads were completely cleared once I reached the highway, and I expected to arrive in Chicago by 10:30 a.m. But because of an accident as I crossed into Illinois, it was closer to eleven by the time I reached the address Joshua had texted me. There were bungalows mixed in with businesses and apartment buildings. A few blocks away was the Calumet River to the west and Lake Michigan to the east. Lenore, along with Harriet, Minnie, and Georgie, had all moved to Chicago, but to Norwood Park, in the northwest corner of the city. That had always been a wealthy neighborhood. The East Side, with its industry and shipping, had always been a working-class neighborhood with, I guessed, more crime. Certainly more than Norwood Park.

I parked in front of the convenience store. Perhaps Miriam had just stopped in there on her way to somewhere else. Maybe she wasn't staying in the area at all. But hopefully someone would remember her.

I had no photo of her, only a description—the most defining one being that she might be dressed in Amish clothing. I walked into the store. A middle-aged woman stood behind the counter, her hands wrapped around a travel mug. Her name tag read *Pam*.

"Good morning," I said. "How are you today?"

Pam shrugged.

"I'm looking for a young woman," I said. "Eighteen years old, five foot five or so, brown hair and brown eyes."

The woman raised her eyebrows slowly. "A dime a dozen," she said.

"But this one may have been dressed Plain, wearing a dress and a Kapp."

"Amish?"

"Exactly," I said.

"Why didn't you start with that?" She put her mug down on the counter. "There was a girl dressed that way in here yesterday. She was with a man who's in here almost every day. I think he lives in the neighborhood."

"Any idea where?"

"No."

I reached into my wallet, pulled out an old business card of mine, and crossed out everything except my cell phone number. "Would you call me if she comes in again?"

The woman took the card and read it. "You're not with the police or anything, right?"

"That's correct," I said. "But she could be in danger."

"The guy she was with doesn't seem dangerous. In fact, he has a bit of an accent. Similar to hers."

"Is the man dressed Plain?"

"No. Jeans. Boots. Leather coat. Normal, I guess. He's a bit older than she is."

"Thank you," I said. "You've been really helpful." Was the guy she was with ex-Amish? If so, I felt a little better about her safety. But perhaps I shouldn't. Kenny—and Tommy too—were ex-Amish.

When I exited the store, I scanned the street for a Toyota Camry and then drove around the neighborhood. I spotted three Camrys, one even gray, but it had an Illinois license plate, not Indiana. I pulled over to try to decide what to do next—go back to Indiana or knock on doors—when a man wearing jeans, boots, and a leather coat walked past my SUV.

I watched him go by and counted the houses he walked by. When he went up the steps of the seventh house down, I started the engine, pulled onto the street, and drove by slowly. When

I reached the house, I fixed my eyes on the address—486 East Port. I knocked on the door, but no one answered. As I turned to walk down the steps, I noticed the man's face in the window, frowning at me before disappearing behind the curtains.

I found a coffee shop to get some caffeine, warm up, and collect my thoughts. A half hour later, as I nursed my latte, a text came in from Joshua. *I have another address for her, from this morning. She had her phone on again for a while.*

I held my breath as I waited for my phone to chime.

486 East Port.

I had to try again.

RETURNING TO THE area, I scanned the street up and down. There wasn't a Camry in sight. I walked over to 486, up the steps, and to the front door. I knocked.

And knocked.

No one came to the door, so I walked down to the convenience store. Before I could even ask, Pam said, "She stopped by a little while ago. Bought some chips, stuff like that, and then left. She was by herself. I was going to give you a call, but I had other customers."

"Thank you," I said. "Please call when you see her again."

She fished my card out of her smock pocket, held it up, and said, "I will."

Defeated, I decided to go back to Mammi's. What else could I do? Except pray that Miriam would stop by the convenience store again and the clerk would call me, or that the ex-Amish man would do the right thing. My hope that she was safe with him didn't seem very realistic.

As I left Chicago, I decided to drive through Gary and stop by

Ethel's house again. Hopefully she was home. There were lights on in the windows, which I found encouraging. As I walked up to her porch, a few snowflakes began to fall.

I knocked on the front door and again heard the pitter-patter of tiny feet. Then the door swung open, and this time a man stood in front of me. Early thirties, with a trimmed beard, and wearing black pants and a forest green shirt. He invited me in but didn't ask me to sit down.

After telling him who I was, as the little girls waved at me on either side of his legs, he said, "I'm Daniel, Ethel's husband."

"Is she home?"

"She's up at the hospital," he answered. "One of the women in the neighborhood is ill."

"Do you know if she's seen Miriam recently? Or have you?"

He shook his head.

I told him about my trip to Chicago. "There was a man, probably ten years older than she is, who she might be with. Do you have any idea who it might be?"

Daniel shook his head. "From what I understand, her boyfriend back in Newbury Township already joined the church and doesn't plan to leave, so it wouldn't be him." Then he sighed. "But I can't keep track of all of the details. You'll have to ask Ethel what all is going on."

I pulled a card out of my purse. "Would you ask her to call me, please?"

He took it and sighed. "I'll give her the card, but I'm not sure if we can help anymore. I don't think Miriam wants us to."

I doubted she wanted me to either, but I wasn't going to stop. I'd keep looking until I found her.

CHAPTER 23

In the few minutes that I'd been in Daniel and Ethel's house, the snow had started to come down with gusto. It was a good thing I was headed back to Mammi's. It appeared the storm might turn into a full-fledged blizzard before long.

When Ryan and I became engaged, I had this idea that we would be the perfect couple, have perfect kids, and be perfect parents. I knew my parents loved me beyond reason, but they were young when I was born.

Now I knew there would have been nothing "perfect" about Ryan and me as a couple or as parents. When I'd told Deputy Rogers there was no such thing as a fully functional family, I meant it.

Tommy's family seemed close-knit, but I could see all sorts of fissures in it too. As good as a mother as Wanda was, I'm sure Tommy, like most Amish kids, was never encouraged to show his emotions. And then the family went through financial difficulties, enough so that they lost their farm before their father died. Perhaps Tommy left because he didn't feel as if there was a place for him to stay.

In the end, I guessed the most parents could do was hope

their best would be adequate—and then somehow make up for what they didn't know by admitting it as soon as they realized it, even if their children were grown. Surely it was never too late to learn and grow and become more functional.

But what did I know? I wasn't a parent. And I wouldn't be, at least not anytime soon.

I merged onto the interstate. The snow was blowing straight at my windshield now, in a mesmerizing, hypnotic pattern. I blinked my bleary eyes, deciding I'd stop and get another coffee.

When Mom died, Dad wouldn't—or couldn't—say how he felt. I could see that he was hurting, but he wouldn't talk about it. So I didn't feel I could talk about how I felt either. I didn't want to make it worse for him than it already was. After I shut down Mom's business, I didn't have a job and had no real marketable skills, so I took a job in town at a café, first as a dishwasher and then as a waitress. Several of the other girls worked at the café during the summer but went to college the rest of the year, one at UCLA. Another two, who worked all year round at the café, took classes at the local community college. One was studying business. Another nursing. I began asking questions about things that hadn't been included in my home-school education. What did I need to do to apply to college? What should I consider as far as deciding on a major? What scholarships were available?

By then, it was pretty clear that Dad and Joy would soon marry, and I wanted to have an escape plan. I signed up for classes at the local community college and met with an academic counselor. After one year of classes, I transferred to UCLA and settled on a health administration major. And I never returned home for more than a night or two at a time, now and then.

I was so sure I was doing the right thing. And at the time, I probably was. But leaving so abruptly left a hole in my heart.

Miriam might think she could escape her new family and make her own way, but she still needed her remaining parent. She still needed her mother's wisdom and care.

The lights of a semi in my rearview mirror grew brighter. I tapped on my brakes a couple of times. Did he see me? I sped up a little, but visibility was bad, and I didn't feel comfortable going any faster than fifty.

The truck slowed, and the distance between us increased.

But a minute later, the truck was too close again. And growing even closer. Another semi was beside me on the left, so I couldn't change lanes. I was as close as I felt comfortable to the car in front of me, a large sedan that was going forty-five. As the semi came even closer, I put my hazard lights on, trying to get the truck driver's attention. I glanced in my rearview mirror one last time—just as the semi plowed into the back of my SUV.

THE NEXT HOURS were a blur. A kind soul held my hand through the broken window until the firefighters arrived and pulled me from the wreckage. No one had to tell me the SUV had saved my life.

I had bloody cuts on my forehead and hands. Something was wrong with my left ankle. My chest, arms, and knees all ached from the deployed airbags. But as the ambulance took off for the hospital, I knew how fortunate I'd been. It could have been so much worse.

They took me to the Porter Regional Hospital emergency room. At some point, a nurse asked me about my insurance, and I asked her to get the card out of my purse. The next time she came by, she said she'd contacted my emergency number but wanted to know if I needed to contact anyone else.

"My uncle," I said. "His number is in my phone." Which, thankfully, had survived the crash. I left a message for Uncle Seth, giving him the short version of what had happened, and asked him to go talk with Mammi.

"What did my dad say?" I asked the nurse when I finished the call.

"Your dad?"

"My emergency contact."

"Hmm." She glanced at the computer screen. "Is Ryan Woodward your father?"

I groaned. "That's my ex. I forgot he was listed as my emergency contact." I grabbed my phone again and quickly sent him a text. *The hospital calling you was a mistake. Ignore it. I'm fine*. He didn't reply right away, but maybe he was busy.

Then I decided to let the nurse call Dad, since I was afraid I might start crying and alarm him. I didn't want that. She went to the nursing station to make the call, while I put my phone in my purse and tried to psyche myself up for stitches, X-rays, and a CT scan, because I had a huge goose egg on my head from the airbag and steering wheel, plus the symptoms of a concussion. They wanted to make sure I didn't have any other head injuries.

They stitched up a gash on my hairline and one on my wrist and hand from the broken glass. My coat had done a good job protecting the rest of my body. After that, they rolled me off to radiology, taking X-rays of my ribs and ankle. From there, they moved me to a room. When I checked my phone, it was blowing up with calls from Dad and texts from Joy. Both asked me to call them back ASAP. I wished Dad would come, but I couldn't expect that. He'd never flown in his life, and he hadn't been back to Indiana in the thirty years since he'd left. I couldn't expect him to come back for me.

A text from Ryan popped up before I could stash my phone again. *I'm on my way.* I groaned again. That was the last thing I needed. I texted him back immediately but didn't get a reply. Surely he hadn't purchased a ticket without speaking with me. Surely he wasn't literally "on his way."

I retrieved the card the police officer had slipped into my purse and called to get details about the driver of the semi, so I could let the rental company know. After a couple of rounds of phone tag, the officer called me back.

He had the information that I needed and also added that the truck driver had a few minor injuries, as did the driver in the sedan in front of me, which I'd plowed into, but both were going to be okay. He said I'd need to fill out an accident report as soon as possible and, of course, report it to the rental car company too. I was thankful to have had the foresight to buy the additional insurance.

A doctor came in and told me I had two cracked ribs and a fractured fibula. "It'll take about six weeks for it to heal," she said. "We'll splint it in the morning and then you'll need to get fitted for a boot."

"What about the CT scan?"

"It hasn't been read yet." She lifted her eyes from my chart and met my gaze. "We'll know by the morning. In the meantime, stay off your phone and no TV."

After she left, I finally gave in to the pain meds and the low lights and fell asleep.

The next morning, after a restless drug-induced and dream-filled sleep, I literally felt as if I'd been hit by a truck. The nurse gave me more pain meds around six in the morning, and I dozed again, waking on and off. Ryan hadn't shown up, and I didn't have a text from him. I figured he probably wasn't coming after all.

But then, just after the nurse brought in my lunch tray, he appeared, sporting dark bags under his gray eyes. He had a backpack slung over one shoulder, and he wore his Patagonia jacket. He took off the hood, revealing his dark hair, which was the messiest I'd ever seen it.

"Hi." He stepped to the edge of my bed.

"You didn't need to come."

"I wanted to," he said. "Sorry it took so long. I got stuck in Denver—fog and then mechanical problems."

"You must be exhausted."

He nodded, not quite looking at me. "How are you?"

"All right. But I'm sorry you came all this way. You really didn't need to. I forgot to update my emergency contact person after . . . well . . ." I swallowed hard. "I didn't give it a thought until the nurse said she'd called you."

"I was really glad she did. I'm so sorry you were in an accident."

It felt both so normal and so awkward to have him show up. "I'm going to be fine, though. I'm afraid you wasted the trip." Not to mention the money that could go toward the wedding bills.

"I had some frequent flier miles." He lowered his backpack to the floor and pulled up a chair. Then he finally met my eyes. "And I needed to apologize to you. What I did was absolutely horrid. I . . . I lost my mind for a few days."

Tears stung my eyes.

"I've felt so out of sorts. Clearly I have some stuff I need to figure out."

"With you and Amber?"

He looked as if he was going to cry as he shook his head.

"Amber hung around for a week, but then it hit me what I did to you, what a fool I was." His voice grew quieter. "Then I got the call about the accident and your text telling me not to come, that it was a mistake. I ignored it because I wanted to apologize in person and realized I might not have another chance if you . . . if you don't come back to California."

I stared at the blank TV in the corner and concentrated on not bawling.

"I didn't come to win you back. Obviously, I had second thoughts about getting married, ones I should have talked with you about months ago. I just . . . I hope you can forgive me."

I gave a small nod, not trusting myself to form any words.

"And I wanted to let you know that I got the credit card disaster figured out. While I was stuck in Denver, I called all of the vendors and had them credit your card and charge my new one. It should be all straightened out. If not, let me know."

"Thanks," I whispered.

He exhaled. This was a hard conversation for him to initiate, but I really appreciated his honesty. "Do you have a ride back to Nappanee?"

"Yes." I wasn't sure who it would be, but I'd find a ride. It was good of Ryan to come, for us to clear the air, but I didn't want him here.

"I don't expect you to ever trust me again," he said. "But I want to thank you for your friendship, for the time we had together."

I swallowed hard and nodded again.

"I won't stick around. I have a friend from college who lives in Chicago, who I'm going to hang out with for the week. Then I'll head home and try to figure out just how messed up I am." He stood. "It's good to see that you're okay, though, to know you're going to be all right."

"Thank you." Traveling all this way to apologize was decent of him. There was still good in Ryan Woodward, after all.

I whispered, "Good-bye," and he left the room with a last glance over his shoulder.

After he was gone, I realized, even though I was stuck in a hospital bed, that I felt a freedom I hadn't for months. Coming back to Indiana and spending time with Mammi, even helping Arleta birth her baby, had reminded me of who I'd been, of that girl who had wanted to be a midwife, of that girl who had loved farm life and her family.

I'd lost myself trying to mold into who I thought Ryan wanted, trying to hide my insecurities and forget my past pain. As much as it hurt—and as untimely as it was—Ryan had done me a favor by calling off the wedding. On Christmas Eve, he'd said breaking up was best for both of us. He'd been right.

Now, hopefully, I could find a new path where I could be true to myself and to who God had created me to be.

Just as I'd nestled into the pillows to try to take a nap, I heard a man's voice outside of my door and feared Ryan had returned. I was too emotionally spent to see him again. But to my surprise, it was Uncle Seth, with Mammi and Jane flanking either side of him.

"Look who I brought to see you," he boomed.

Jane stood back while Uncle Seth and Mammi rushed toward me. Both gave me hugs, and Mammi kept patting the top of my head as she stared at the stitches along my hairline. "Oh, Savannah," she said over and over.

"Mammi, I'm fine. Really."

Her eyes filled with tears. "And to think I worried about you flying."

Uncle Seth laughed. "I've told you the statistics on that a hundred times, Dorothy."

"Take off your coats," I said. "Stay a while. I'm still waiting for a doctor to come in and give me the results of my CT scan."

As Mammi and Jane took off their coats and bonnets, Uncle Seth said he was going to go find a cup of coffee. "That drive almost put me to sleep."

I winced, thinking of three people I cared dearly about traveling together in that old pickup on icy roads. They shouldn't have.

Mammi held up a bag. She'd brought me clothes and one of her warm coats—her nicest one, I was sure.

"Jane, who's watching the shop?" I asked.

"No one," she said. "I put a sign in the window that it's closed for the day. Coming here was much more important."

"Denki," I whispered.

Mammi and Jane pulled up chairs, and then after I'd given all the details about the accident, I finally said, "Enough about me." I smiled at Jane. "How about more about Emma? I've been wanting to hear the rest of her story."

"Oh, I don't know if this is the right place," she said.

"What could be a better place? It's winter and snowy here, and I'm unwell. When you stopped last time, it was wintery and snowy there, and Emma was ill. And Mathilde was missing."

Just as Miriam still was.

Jane gave Mammi a questioning look, and she nodded.

"All right," Jane said. "Jah, Mathilde was missing. . . ."

CHAPTER 24

Emma

Judah assured George he'd help him search. "Go back to your house," Judah said. "I'll meet you there as soon as I take Emma home. She needs to rest."

George didn't answer Judah, but he rode away toward his farm.

Before George was out of hearing distance, Emma snarled, "Why would you offer to help him?"

"Because I don't want him to find her," Judah whispered. "And I certainly don't want him to be alone with her if he does."

Emma wasn't sure whether to believe him or not.

By the time they reached Phillip's cabin, Emma was shaking again, but this time from the cold. Judah helped her down and then to the door.

It swung open, and Isaac stood before them. "When you didn't come to the service, Mamm sent me to get you," he said.

"I can't go." She fell into another coughing fit.

"She's ill," Judah said.

Emma headed for her bed, pulled off her boots, and climbed under her remaining blankets, still in her cloak.

In the background, Judah told Isaac what had happened. "I'm going to go meet George at his place. I'll check back later. Take care of your sister. . . ."

After Judah left, Isaac said he'd brought a letter from Abel.

"Would you read it to me?"

Again, it was only a few lines. He was happy to receive her letter. He was doing well. He'd expect her return in the spring.

It seemed such an odd way to phrase it. Did he look forward to seeing her? Or just to her return? He'd written absolutely nothing of any importance. The long letter she'd sent hadn't inspired him to reciprocate in kind. What sort of life did he envison for them?

As Isaac folded Abel's letter, Emma fell asleep and didn't awake until several hours later, coughing again. Isaac bent over the fire, stirring something in the big pot, while Phillip, back from Jackson Township, sat at the table, eating a piece of bread. She lifted her head.

"Are you awake?" Phillip asked.

She nodded as she coughed some more. Once she stopped, with a raspy voice, she asked, "Has Judah returned?"

Isaac shook his head.

"No word about Mathilde?"

"That's right," Isaac answered.

Phillip shook his head. "You shouldn't be involved in any of that."

Emma fell into another coughing fit. When she recovered, she said, "Mathilde's a widow. We're told that pure religion is to care for widows and orphans."

"You're a widow," Phillip said. "Look after yourself."

"I am," Emma answered. "And so are all of you. Mathilde has no one but herself."

Phillip just shook his head. "She has George." He pushed back his chair and walked to the door. "I'm going out to do the chores. I expect supper to be ready when I return."

IT WAS AFTER dark by the time Isaac, Emma, and Phillip sat down at the table. Emma had rallied enough to fix the meal. When a knock fell on the door, Phillip opened it to reveal Judah.

As he walked into the cabin, Emma said, "I'll get another bowl of soup."

"Denki," Judah said. "I'm famished."

"We're having three sister soup, with a little ham added."

"What?" Phillip asked.

As she stood, Emma felt light-headed and steadied herself with a hand to the back of the chair. "That's what Mathilde calls it. Corn, squash, and beans."

Phillip frowned. "You've been influenced too much by that woman."

Emma ignored her brother and filled a bowl of soup for Judah. After Phillip led all of them in a silent prayer, Judah said, "We looked everywhere but didn't find Mathilde. We tracked her horse through the snow to the creek, but then we had no idea if she went northwest or southeast. We rode both ways but never saw where she came out. Of course she could have back-tracked anywhere along the way and brushed over her tracks." He shrugged. "As long as she's all right, I hope she's far away from the Burton place."

"Why?" Phillip asked. "She had a place to sleep and a job."

"It appears that George Burton beat her." Emma passed the

bread to Judah, fearing George might do worse, in time, with Harriet gone. If only George would move to Chicago too.

"I'm going to ride to South Bend tomorrow." Judah passed the bread on to Isaac. "And talk with the priest there, the one who buried Jean-Paul. Perhaps Mathilde spoke with him about leaving this area."

Phillip's irritation seemed to be growing as he said, "You seem awfully interested in the woman. Do you have some ulterior motive?"

"Of course not." Judah dipped his bread in the soup. "Her husband was a good friend to me. I know he'd do the same if our roles were reversed."

Phillip chortled. "But you're not even married."

"True."

"Why aren't you?"

Judah put down his spoon and sighed. "I don't have much to offer a wife. The farm is in Walter's name. We'd hoped to have saved enough to buy another property by now, but with the price of land going up, it doesn't seem likely." He shrugged. "The farm we have isn't enough to support two families."

"Other men figure it out," Phillip said. "I'm sure you could too."

Emma cleared her throat.

Phillip turned toward her. "What?"

Had Phillip forgotten that his land was paid for by their grandfather? Not everyone had help. Was he that unaware of his blessings?

"It's all right," Judah said. "I know God will take care of me. Perhaps I'll continue to work for Walter. Or come across another situation."

"Shouldn't you and Walter split his farm? Or sell it and go farther west and buy something cheaper?" Isaac asked.

"Walter has a family," Judah said. "All I have is myself. I'd rather he have the farm."

Was Judah really so generous? Or was he simply trying to make himself look good?

He thanked Emma for the meal and then said, "I'm hoping the priest can tell me places Mathilde's family used to frequent. Perhaps if she's not heading to the mission, she's gone to one of them."

Emma pursed her lips together as a memory of gathering rocks with Mathilde and Batiste by the creek came to mind. But she wouldn't say anything out loud, not now. Not when Phillip might overhear her, not when she wasn't sure if she could trust Judah. Sarah had said he wasn't trustworthy. Emma couldn't take a chance, not with Mathilde and the children's lives.

After Judah left, Phillip said, "He seems humble enough, but maybe it's all for show. What if George offered to pay him to find Mathilde, to force her to return to the Burton farm and keep working there?" He shook his head. "Emma, you don't have any proof that Judah's concern is for Mathilde. It's most likely only for himself."

Phillip was right. She didn't have any proof. All she had were her own doubts about Judah too.

THE NEXT MORNING, once Phillip and Isaac went to check on the cattle, Emma bundled up and hurried down to the creek, stopping to weather a coughing spell just as she reached it.

Although it would run high once the snow melted, the creek wasn't much higher than it had been in the fall, when she and Mathilde had sat along the banks with Baptiste and Agnes. Emma looked for the natural bridge, for the stones Mathilde had mentioned. She grabbed a small branch that had fallen from a willow tree and stripped the switches from it. Then she poked it into the water a few times, finally finding a stone close to the bank. Lifting her skirts with her free hand, she stepped onto it. Then she found the next one. And the next. Quickly, she made her way across. Her boots were wet but not soaked.

On the other side, a coughing spasm slowed her again, but then she continued on to the bushes. The outline of a fire pit showed through the snow, but she didn't see any recent signs of people. She made her way through the bushes and then looked to the right and to the left. There was a thicket big enough for someone to hide in. But there was no sign of a horse.

Emma walked around the thicket until she came to the far side. Both footprints and hoofprints led into the thicket, which towered over Emma's head. After walking a few more feet, she realized the inside had been hollowed out. Ahead was Mathilde's horse, and behind it a wigwam. Emma stepped closer and whispered hoarsely, "Mathilde!"

No one answered.

But then she heard Baptiste's voice. "Maman. Maman."

"It's me, Emma." She bent down at the entrance of the wigwam and pulled back the hide. Inside, Mathilde was flat on the ground, with several hides on top of her. She had a fresh bruise on the side of her face. Agnes was at her side, and Baptiste sat up, rubbing his eyes as he said, "Maman" again.

"Mathilde," Emma said. "Are you all right?"

Her friend opened her eyes and then whispered, "I prayed you would come."

"You didn't tell me there was a wigwam back here."

"Jean-Paul and I made it last summer. We wanted a place to hide if we ever needed to. We left furs and dried food. Some hay for the horse."

"Why did you plan ahead like that?"

"Jean-Paul didn't trust George. He felt he might turn on us."

"Why didn't you leave then?"

"We had nowhere to go. . . ." She paused, as if looking for the right word. "Permanently. Nowhere that George wouldn't find us."

Heartbroken that George had caused the family so much trouble, Emma asked what Mathilde planned to do next.

She shook her head as tears filled her eyes.

"What do you want to do?" Emma asked.

"Find my family. But how can I go a thousand miles with two little ones? I'll never make it."

"What about your land?"

"George owns the deed now."

Tears stung Emma's eyes. George had taken her land, and yet he still wanted Mathilde's servitude too. Still expected it. She placed her hand on Mathilde's arm. "Being with your family would be best, but I agree that going on your own is too risky." She pointed toward the fire, which had gone cold. "I'll get it going."

Mathilde shook her head. "I don't want any smoke to show. I only burn it at night."

Emma nodded. That made sense.

"How did you get here so quickly?"

"I'd been planning to come for a few days, since Harriet left. I was ready to go when Judah came and said you needed help. When I returned the next morning, George was angry I'd been gone and hit me again. When he passed out, I grabbed a few things from the shack and then we rode down the creek so he couldn't track us." Mathilde raised herself to one elbow. "Don't tell your brother."

"I won't," Emma said. George hadn't mentioned he'd seen

Mathilde that morning Judah and Emma saw him. The man couldn't be trusted about anything. "Should I tell Judah you're here? He's been looking for you."

Mathilde shook her head. "He might be following George's instructions. He seemed strangely friendly with George when he was working with him."

Emma's heart sunk. She remembered Judah saying he hardly saw Mathilde when he was working for George. If Mathilde didn't trust Judah, she shouldn't either. "What do you need?" she asked. "Food?"

Mathilde nodded. "Anything you can bring."

"I need to go check on Betha and her baby and take them some food," Emma said. "I'll come here afterward and bring you some too."

"But you're ill," Mathilde said. "You shouldn't be out in the cold."

"I'm all right." At least Emma hoped she was. "I'll see you this afternoon."

NEAL WAS OUT hunting, and Betha was frying corn cakes for her children when Emma arrived with venison, more apples and potatoes, and a loaf of bread. Emma woke up the baby. He was alert and seemed to be doing well.

She took over the cooking so Betha could nurse the little one. After the children ate, Emma told them to rest so their mother could rest too. Then she left and rode her horse to the creek and forded it quickly.

She dismounted, grabbed the full saddlebag, and slipped into the thicket. "Mathilde," she said. "I'm back."

When she opened the hide across the doorway, Baptiste smiled at her. Mathilde slipped Agnes, wrapped in furs, back into her cradleboard. Emma took the food out of the saddlebag and placed it next to Mathilde.

"Merci," Mathilde said, locking eyes with Emma. "*Mon amie.*"

Tears stung Emma's eyes. "You are welcome, my friend."

As Emma left the thicket, another coughing fit stopped her. By the time she reached Phillip's cabin and dismounted, she felt feverish and was coughing harder. Isaac took the mare to brush her down and unsaddle her while Emma headed straight to her bed.

When Isaac woke her up at dusk, she couldn't manage to leave the bed, not even when Phillip came in for supper. During the night, she coughed and coughed, eventually leaving her bed to stir the fire and heat water. She took the kettle off the fire, put it on the table on a stone, then put a scarf over her head and breathed in the steam.

She planned to make an onion poultice in the morning, but she couldn't drag herself from her bed. Phillip ordered Isaac to help him pull more stumps out of the field, but Isaac said he needed to stay inside and care for Emma. Phillip wasn't happy, but Isaac stood his ground.

Emma thanked the Lord for her little brother, for his sympathy and care. He was growing into a good, reliable man.

Isaac made the poultice and then later boiled water for peppermint tea. He also fixed some broth for her and sliced some bread, but she could hardly eat any of it. She slept in fits and dreamed of Mathilde and the children in the thicket. She had to get better so she could take them more food. And check on Betha and her family too. She couldn't abandon the two women.

Isaac brought Emma water to drink, and then she slept again, this time dreaming of Asher and Hansi and her daughter. But the baby girl was alive. And they were all with her, in Indiana.

She woke as her fever broke to find Isaac sitting on the edge of her bed. "You were speaking of Mathilde," he said quietly. "Of helping her. Do you know where she is?"

Emma drifted off again. She burned with fever for the next two days.

On the third day, Judah arrived and sat beside her bed. "Please tell me where Mathilde is."

"She doesn't want George to know."

"I won't tell him."

She searched his eyes. Was he telling the truth? Emma drifted back to sleep.

When she awoke again, Isaac said more snow had fallen. "Judah's frantic about Mathilde and her children. There's a storm coming."

Emma threw back her covers. "I'll go."

"No," Isaac said. "You're too weak. I'll go with Judah. I promise you he won't tell George."

Emma fell back in bed, exhausted. Should she trust Judah? Did she have a choice? What if Mathilde and the children were freezing? Or starving? She didn't know how much dried food they had.

No matter what, she could trust Isaac.

She exhaled, trying to trust the Lord too. Finally, she said, "They're across the creek, in a wigwam in a thicket."

"Which creek?"

"Phillip's creek."

"Where?"

"The creek where I got the rocks for the fireplace."

"They're that close?"

Emma nodded. "There's a natural bridge there to cross the water."

Isaac whistled. "We'll take them food. If the storm is too bad, we'll bring them here."

"Phillip won't like it."

"He's not here. I sent him to get Mamm to come look after you."

"I'm fine."

Isaac shook his head. "I hope you're getting better, but you aren't fine."

She closed her eyes. "Go check on Betha too, please. Judah knows where they live. But don't bring Mathilde here. I'm afraid Phillip will tell George."

"All right," Isaac said. "Judah will be back soon, and then we'll leave. We won't be gone long."

A while later, Emma heard Judah's and Isaac's voices, and then Isaac telling her good-bye. She nodded, too tired to open her eyes.

"Thank you," Judah said before he slipped out the door. "I won't betray Mathilde. Nor you."

CHAPTER 25

The next time Emma opened her eyes, Mamm was pushing Emma's hair away from her face. "You're burning up."

"No." Emma wanted to cry. "I'm freezing."

As Mamm tended to Emma, Judah and Isaac came into the cabin. Phillip asked where Isaac had been, chiding him for leaving Emma.

"She asked us to go check on the O'Brien family and take them food," Judah said. "We weren't gone long." Then he said to Emma, "Everyone is fine. They were cold and hungry but doing better now."

"Denki," Emma said sincerely, knowing he was talking about Mathilde and her children.

Phillip scowled at her. "We won't have enough food for ourselves if you keep giving it all away."

"Hush," Mamm said. "The Lord will provide."

Later that night, after Mamm had fallen asleep, Isaac brought Emma a cup with an inch of liquid in the bottom. "It's from Mathilde," he said. "A dogwood decoction. She said to give you a quarter cup every night."

Emma drank it, swallowing hard to get it down. It burned, but she coughed less during the night.

Over the next two days, Mamm cared for Emma, bringing her back to health. Isaac was around—bringing water and wood in, tending the fire, helping with the cooking, and secretly giving her Mathilde's decoction at night.

Judah didn't come by at all.

On the third afternoon, as Mamm prepared a poultice, Emma whispered to Isaac, "Where is Judah? Did he go to George?"

Isaac shook his head. "First, he checked with the sheriff in Goshen, who said no one would protect a Native woman in debt to George Burton from being mistreated. So now he's riding his horse south, down to see the bishop of Vincennes, at the cathedral there. He's hoping to find out if anyone is going to Kansas this spring and can take Mathilde and the children."

Emma hesitated and then asked, "Do you think Judah is telling the truth?" Mathilde was valuable to George. She was sure George would reward Judah for turning her in. Perhaps the story of going to Vincennes was to deter Isaac and Emma from suspecting him of helping George.

"Jah, I know he's telling the truth. He's a good man, Emma. It's not like you to be so suspicious."

"His own sister-in-law doesn't find him trustworthy. He hasn't joined the church." Emma stopped to cough. Then, in an even raspier voice, she added, "And he started working for George again."

Isaac shook his head. "He told me it was so he could keep an eye on Mathilde."

"He might have been lying."

Isaac shook his head. "I don't think he was."

"But we can't know for sure." Emma put her hand to her face. "How far is it to Vincennes?"

"Two hundred and fifty miles or so."

"And he's going in this weather?"

"He's had experience traveling in the cold, and his horse is reliable."

Emma thought it awfully bold of him to seek the help of a Catholic bishop. She didn't know much about the religion, but she knew their bishops were different from the Amish ones. There were far fewer Catholic ones, and they seemed to hold a lot of power.

Mamm cared for Emma for a few more days and then said she needed to go home. She had a mother in Newbury Township about to deliver, and she hoped she hadn't missed it already. "I need to speak with you about something first," she said to Emma, who sat on the edge of her bunk. "Eli is anxious to court you. He's waited long enough."

Emma shook her head. "I'm returning to Pennsylvania."

Mamm's thick eyebrows arched. "With whom?"

Emma had been waiting to tell her mother until it was closer to April, wanting to avoid a discussion with her. "Two families from Newbury Township are returning to Lancaster County. They said I can ride with them."

"Don't be ridiculous," Mamm said.

"But you agreed to it before we left," Emma responded. "That's the reason I came—because you said I could return."

Mamm crossed her arms. "I didn't think you would actually go back."

"Please honor the promise you made to me. I'm a grown woman."

Mamm leaned toward Emma. "You're not acting like a grown woman. You're acting like a child. You haven't changed."

The words stung Emma, but she bit her tongue from responding. Mamm was still her mother. She needed to honor her.

"Come back to our place and court Eli Wagler," Mamm said. "You'll soon have a husband again and more children. That's what will make you content."

"I have no desire to marry Eli," Emma said. "I'm going back to marry Abel."

"You'll be bored by the second week."

"Mamm!"

"Abel has no vision. No ambition." Mamm shook her head. "He's nothing like Asher."

"And you think Eli is?"

"Compared to Abel?" Mamm sighed. "Jah, he is."

"I'm not interested in Eli. He's arrogant."

Mamm shook her head again. "He's confident. He'll make a fine husband."

"No. He said horrible things about the Native people."

"They killed people around here," Mamm said, "soldiers and settlers alike."

"A handful of Potawatomi did those things." Emma exhaled, trying to calm herself. "And then others asked for forgiveness for the entire tribe, just as they forgave the settlers for their violence. Should an entire group be judged for the sins of a few?"

Mamm crossed her arms. "I'm only suggesting that you consider how Eli sees things is all. He's being pragmatic."

Emma shook her head. "I think he's trying to justify the land we've taken."

"We paid for the land," Mamm said. "All of us have."

"Ten years ago, Mathilde's family picked berries on this land." Emma pointed south, toward the creek. "It was stolen from them by the government and then sold to settlers."

"That might be so, but remember *we* didn't steal anything. Everything we've done has been legal. We bought our farms, paid for with our money. Lots of it."

"But can't you see?" Emma kept her mother's gaze. "If Asher and Dat and so many like them hadn't yearned to go west, hadn't coveted land for new farms, this never would have happened."

Mamm shook her head. "We simply heard there was land available, and we needed more for your brothers. You can't blame us for the Natives being forced out. It happened before we arrived."

"What happens when settlers set their eyes on Kansas? Where will the Potawatomi go then?"

"Nowhere," Mamm said. "That's their new land. Their new home, as this is ours."

"That's not true." Emma struggled not to cry. "Judah said some have already been forced farther west, to the Indian Territory."

Mamm gave her an exasperated look.

Emma decided to return to the topic of Eli. "Regardless of whether Eli is arrogant or pragmatic, I'm not cut out for life here. I'd much rather be bored back home than despondent here. I need to be at the Martins' place in Newbury Township on the first Monday of April to start the journey."

"You shouldn't have gone behind my back to make those arrangements." Mamm's eyes sparked.

Emma didn't say any more. She didn't believe she'd gone behind Mamm's back. Mamm knew her intentions.

Unfortunately, Mamm wasn't done with the conversation. "Reconsider Eli."

Emma laid back down on her pine-bough ticking. "I can't."

Mamm waited a moment and then said, "Goodness, child, no husband is going to please you all of the time or hold your exact beliefs. And even though I agreed when we left Somerset County that you could return, I don't want you to go. You're my only daughter. I want you to stay in Indiana so that you will be close. But maybe, as much as it grieves me, you *should* go back to Pennsylvania. Maybe it *is* too much for you to be in this new land."

Emma closed her eyes. She knew Mamm was trying to get her to change her mind, but she wouldn't. Her mind was made up. She just hoped she could help Mathilde before she left.

MAMM LEFT FOR home a few hours later. Day by day, Emma recovered her strength, and winter finally retreated, causing the snow to melt and the creek to flood. Isaac assured her Mathilde and the children were fine.

A week later, as Emma cooked breakfast while Phillip and Isaac did the chores, a knock fell on the door.

Drying her hands on her apron, she went to answer it. Judah stood there, with a scruffy growth of beard and a much thinner face. "Guder mariye," he said, and then quickly added, "I know Phillip is out doing chores. I wanted to speak with you before he returned. First of all, how is your health?"

"Much better." Emma suppressed the cough that had lingered now for weeks.

Judah, with an expression of compassion on his face, smiled slightly. "I spoke with a priest at the mission in Vincennes. He agrees Kansas would be the best place for Mathilde. There, or Indian Territory, if her family was sent farther west. Two priests and several nuns are leaving in the next few weeks. If Mathilde and the children can get to Vincennes by April first, she can travel with them."

"Is there anyone who can help you get them there?" Emma's heart raced. Come April, she would be headed home.

"No. And I don't think I should go alone, not with her and the children."

Emma agreed. It wouldn't be appropriate.

"Could you go with me?" he asked.

Her heart skipped a beat.

"I'll ask Isaac to go too," Judah quickly added. "I've thought it through, as far as decorum. If just you go along, the two of us cannot come back unaccompanied. With Isaac, we'll be well chaperoned. Plus, I think a larger party would be safer."

"Safer? What are the dangers?"

"Marauders." He paused. "And other people."

"George?"

He nodded. "He came by several times while I was gone, asking Walter about Mathilde, if I'd found her."

"So what good would two Amish men and an Amish woman, all nonresistant, be against marauders and George?"

Judah's face reddened. "I understand your concern, but I don't think George understands we're nonresistant—and others we meet on the road most likely wouldn't either. Not that we would engage in any violence, but they wouldn't know that, and perhaps they would be deterred by a group. I believe there's strength in numbers."

"But you were fine traveling alone?"

"I joined other groups of men," Judah said. "But I wouldn't want to risk that, traveling with women."

"Could we leave sooner that you planned?" Emma asked. That way she could be back in time to go to Pennsylvania.

Judah shook his head. "I don't think so. The roads and trails that weren't blocked by snow were covered with water or mud as I traveled. It was rough going and would be hard with the children. I had to ford flooded creeks several times. We need to let the roads dry out more."

Emma crossed her arms. "You should speak with Isaac about it."

Judah nodded. "I'll do that, but can you go see Mathilde today and ask her what she thinks of my plan?"

Emma nodded. "I'll take them some food later."

The door swung open, and a voice barked, "Judah. What are you doing here?"

"I came to speak with you," he said, turning toward Phillip. "About spring planting. Walter and I wondered if you need any help."

"Is that really why you're here?" Phillip harrumphed. "I'm guessing you're up to something."

Judah ignored him. "Do you need our help?"

"No, I don't believe I do. Isaac will be around, and then we'll both go up and help Dat."

Judah stepped outside. "Let us know if you change your mind. Mach's gut."

Isaac hadn't come inside, so Emma did her best to keep Phillip engaged in conversation so Judah would have enough time to broach traveling to Vincennes with Isaac.

"Ready for your coffee?" she asked, pouring him a cup that was strong and bitter, just as he liked it. "Do you think we're done with winter?"

"I hope so. We need to get the planting done as soon as possible." Phillip stood. "What's taking Isaac so long? I'm starved."

"I'll go check on him," Emma said. "Drink your coffee."

She headed out the front door into the chilly morning. The sun was rising over the eastern horizon in a vibrant splash of purple and pink. Judah and Isaac stood in the barn doorway with their backs toward the cabin, deep in conversation.

Emma walked halfway to the barn and said, "Isaac." She motioned toward the cabin.

"Just a minute."

She waited for him, facing the cabin in case Phillip came out. After another minute, Judah waved good-bye to Emma, climbed on his horse, and rode away.

"We need to talk," Isaac whispered as they walked briskly toward the cabin. "How about if I go with you to see Mathilde today?"

"Only if we can sneak away without Phillip getting suspicious," Emma answered, her heart sinking. How was she going to tell him she couldn't go to Vincennes?

How was she going to tell Mathilde?

AFTER THEIR NOON meal, Phillip announced that he was taking the wagon to buy seed. "I'll be back by supper time."

Emma said that she planned to check on the O'Brien family.

"Don't overdo it," Phillip said. "It won't do any of us any good for you to be ill again."

"I won't," Emma said.

"And don't take them any food."

"I'll only take some of the bread I baked this morning."

Once Phillip and the wagon were out of sight, Emma sent Isaac out to saddle the horses and then gathered up a loaf of bread, a couple of leftover baked potatoes, some venison jerky, and a few apples from the cellar for Mathilde and the children. She also grabbed a loaf of bread for the O'Briens.

She met Isaac outside. "Let's go see Mathilde first. But I need to tell you something."

"What is it?"

"Mamm knows this and so does Phillip, although he doesn't know the details. I plan to return to Pennsylvania at the beginning of April—"

"No," Isaac said. "You can't."

A wave of sadness swept through her. Isaac was so dear to her. Not seeing Mamm and Dat and Phillip was one thing, but never seeing Isaac? In the moment, it felt nearly unbearable. She spoke slowly. "There are two families in Newbury Township who are returning. They said I could go with them."

"Are you going to marry Abel?"

Emma nodded as she put the food in her saddlebag.

"Why would you do that?"

"Why?" She spread her arms wide. "I want to go back home."

"But it won't be home—your family won't be there."

She didn't say it *was* there, buried in the cemetery plot. Instead she said, "Maybe you'll all come back too, within a few years."

Isaac shook his head. "I'm never going back. I like it here. And if you go, you'll never see me again."

Tears threatened her eyes. "Don't say that."

"What's so bad about Indiana? Why don't you want to stay?"

"What's so bad? The dirt and dust and mud. These cabins that aren't homes. The hard winter. How far apart everyone is. The bears and panthers sneaking through the forests. The way Mathilde has been treated. The things Eli said about her and other Native people."

"Ignore Eli. You don't need to have anything to do with him," Isaac said. "Come with Judah and me to take Mathilde to Vincennes. She wouldn't feel comfortable with anyone else."

"And miss my chance to go home?"

Isaac sighed. "I'll take you, if you still want to go, after we get back."

"You said you'd never go back."

"I will for you."

"Dat won't let you," Emma said. "He'll need you to help farm, both places."

"Then I'll find someone else to take you. Maybe someone will be going in May or June. Or next spring."

"Abel said he'd wait a year for me." Emma didn't want to delay her trip any longer.

"Write to him," Isaac said.

She owed him a letter, but that wouldn't be what he expected to hear, not after she'd written previously about returning in April. "Let's go see Mathilde and then decide."

Isaac helped Emma mount Red, and then he climbed on his horse and led the way to the creek and then across it.

A few minutes later, they crawled through the thicket to the wigwam. Mathilde and the children both sat at the entrance, in the sunshine.

As Emma approached, Mathilde reached for her hand.

"I'm here," Emma said.

"Are you better?" Mathilde asked.

"Much."

Mathilde shifted her eyes to Isaac. "Is Judah back?"

"Jah." Isaac kneeled down beside her, and Baptiste inched closer to him. "A priest at the mission in Vincennes said you should go there. That there's a group going to Kansas in a few weeks."

Mathilde's eyes grew wide. "Merci, Seigneur," she whispered. Then she turned to Emma. "You'll go with me to Vincennes, oui?" Emma glanced at Isaac.

He said, "Judah and I will go."

"Do you trust Judah?" Emma turned toward Mathilde.

Mathilde shrugged. "At this point, do I have a choice?" She turned to Emma. "I will go, but only if you'll come too. I can't make the trip on my own, with the children. I need your help."

CHAPTER 26

Savannah

I'd listened with my eyes closed, trying to ease my headache. When Jane finished, Mammi whispered, "She may have slept through the whole thing."

"No." I opened my eyes. "Emma has to decide whether to go back to Pennsylvania or go to Vincennes with Mathilde."

Jane smiled. "You were listening."

"Absolutely."

Uncle Seth's voice boomed from the chair by the door. "So was I. Fascinating." He stood up and glanced at his watch. "But we'd better get going, ladies. More snow is on the way."

"Yes, you should go," I said. "ASAP. I don't want the three of you out in this weather."

Jane and Mammi slipped into their coats and tied their bonnets over their *Kappa*. Then Mammi stepped to the side of my bed. "We have some good news."

"Oh?"

"Tommy is out on bail."

"Wow. Who paid it?"

"He'd put Wanda on his bank account years ago, for when she needed a little extra money now and then," Mammi said, "so she was able to access the money for him."

I was surprised at that. "Any news on the charges?"

Mammi nodded. "The kidnapping one has been dropped."

"That's great."

She nodded. "The county sheriff took a look at the evidence and believed the deputy jumped to conclusions, which is why bail was granted. However, the drug charges still stand."

"Well, that's better than nothing. Are there restrictions?" I wondered if he might be able to drive Mason to Las Vegas instead of having a caseworker escort the little boy there.

"Because Wanda paid cash, he can travel within a one-hundred-mile radius of Nappanee but no farther—as long as he shows up at his next court date," Jane said.

"His lawyer made those arrangements because he works in construction and it's winter," Mammi explained. "Obviously he won't be going back to Las Vegas anytime soon and will need to find another job here. The court makes those sorts of allowances, depending on the situation."

That sounded better than it could have.

"Even though the kidnapping charges have been dropped," Jane continued, "we still think Miriam might be in danger."

"I agree," I said. "We need to find her. If anything, Emma and Mathilde's story makes me want to search for her even more."

Jane patted my arm. "Bless you," she said, "but you're in no shape to go looking for her. I'll get in touch with Tommy and see if there's anything I can do to help find Miriam."

I sighed. I wasn't sure what she could do, but still I said, "That's good of you. Hopefully I'll get out soon, perhaps this afternoon, and then I can help too."

"Should we wait to take you home?" Uncle Seth asked.

I shook my head. "There's no guarantee I'll get out today. I want the three of you to get home as soon as possible."

"But who will take you home?" he asked.

For a moment, I panicked. But then a sense of peace came over me. God had been with me through every step of the accident. I needed to trust Him to see to this detail as well.

There was another rustling at the curtain. For a moment, I hoped it was Tommy. He was out on bail. He could have come to see me.

"Baby." It wasn't Tommy—it was Dad.

Tears flooded my eyes. After not returning to Indiana for thirty years, he was here. For me.

He made a beeline to the bed, as if he hadn't seen the others in the room at all, and wrapped his strong arms around me as I began to cry.

I CONTINUED TO weep as he held me, as I buried my head in the fleece collar of his suede coat, breathing in its leathery scent. "It's okay, baby," he said over and over. "It's okay."

Finally, after several raggedy breaths, I was able to talk. "You came."

He nodded, his brown eyes filled with compassion. "I couldn't bear not to," he said. "I was so worried about you. Joy and Karlie are here too." He released me and then said, "Hold on a minute. There's another lady I need to hug."

As he stood, Mammi stepped to his side. In a very non-Amish way, he wrapped her up in a hug and lifted her off her feet. She burst into tears, which alarmed me. I'd never seen Mammi cry before.

"Jimmy," she said. "You finally came home."

Now he was crying too. "I should have come home years ago and brought Savannah's mother with me."

"And I should have gone out to California," Mammi said.

"Well." Jane stepped forward. "Jimmy is here now. That's what counts."

"And Joy and Karlie are in the waiting room," he said. "Hold on. I'll go get them."

A minute later, I watched as Dad introduced his wife and daughter to Mammi, Uncle Seth, and Jane. Joy greeted all of them, then found her way to my bedside. "We've been so worried about you."

Karlie stayed back, but I motioned to her. "I'm okay, really. I know all of these machines and sounds are unsettling, but if you want to come closer, you may."

She stepped to her mother's side and gave me a shy smile and then said, "Hi, Savannah" in her sweet six-year-old voice. She was my baby sister. All those years I longed for a sibling, and then, when I finally had one, I hadn't embraced her as I should have.

I reached for her hand and squeezed it. "Thank you for coming all this way to see me."

Karlie looked up at her mother and then back at me. She smiled broadly, showing the gap in her mouth where she'd lost both of her front teeth. And then she hugged me gently.

A few minutes later, Uncle Seth interrupted the chatter and said, "We really should get going." He looked at Mammi. "Dorothy, do you want to ride with Jimmy?" He turned toward Dad. "I'm assuming they're staying at the farm."

"We don't want to impose," Joy said.

"Of course you're staying with me," Mammi said. "But, Seth, I'll ride with you and give Jimmy and Savannah a little more time together. Could we stop at the grocery store once we get to town?"

Uncle Seth rattled his keys. "Of course."

"No, Mamm," Dad said. "I don't want you to go to any trouble."

"Listen." She put her hand on her hip. "I've waited thirty years for you to come home. I'll go to whatever trouble I want."

Dad laughed. "You're as spunky as ever."

"She's worse," Uncle Seth whispered loudly.

Once they left, Dad sat down in the chair beside my bed. "What did the doctors say?"

"I have a broken bone in my ankle. And a concussion. I'm still waiting for the results of the CT scan."

"When will you get out?"

"I'm not sure. Maybe this afternoon, but maybe not until tomorrow. I can let you know."

Karlie tugged a few times on Joy's sweater, whispering in Joy's ear once she bent down to her level. Standing back up, Joy cleared her throat and then said, "Karlie and I are going to go find a restroom."

After they left, Dad blinked his eyes rapidly, as if he was fighting back tears. When he spoke, his voice was deep and raw. "I meant what I said to your Mammi. I should have come back to visit. With you, along with your mom. It's one of my many regrets."

"It's okay," I said. "We all have regrets."

"And I should have been more of a father to you after your mom died." He leaned closer to me. "I was on my own by the time I was seventeen, but that didn't mean you should have been forced to take care of yourself like you did."

"I left on my own accord," I said.

"But I was emotionally distant with you." I guessed he'd learned that term from Joy. "Like I was with your mom at times." He met my eyes. "Can you forgive me?"

"Jah," I said. "I know you were grieving. I know you were hurting."

"We both were," he said. "But I'm going to try to do better, I promise. I hope it's not too late."

"It's not." I knew we'd have to work to move forward. But if we were both willing, I was sure we could.

I thought of Emma and her relationship with her mother. They were two very different people. So were Dad and I, but that didn't mean we couldn't mend our relationship and, with some understanding, grow closer.

It was never too late.

As wonderful as it was to have my dad with me, I felt anxious thinking about all of them driving back to Nappanee. The sooner they left, the better. "You should go get Joy and Karlie and get on the road," I said. "More snow is predicted."

An hour after they'd left, the doctor finally came in. First, she apologized for taking so long to make her rounds. "It's been a crazy day," she said. "We've had quite a few emergencies. Your CT scan looks good, but I want to keep you under observation one more night. I'll check in tomorrow morning, and then we'll get you a boot and pain meds from the pharmacy before you're discharged. Limit your screen time as much as possible for the next week. Spend as much time in a dark room as possible, and make a follow-up appointment with your GP."

I nodded. Part of me was disappointed to have to spend another night, but on the other hand, I felt exhausted.

I slept restlessly and awoke groggy and in horrible pain. After my morning pain meds, I felt as though I could rally and go back to Mammi's. But it wasn't until midmorning that the doctor finally came in, checked me one more time, and then said I could be released. Of course, the discharge process would take a while. They weren't ready to wheel me to the front door yet.

I needed a ride back to Nappanee. I thought about texting Joy and asking her to send Dad back, but the thought of him with Mammi stopped me. I wanted them to have as much time as possible.

I'd been willing to trust God the day before for a ride. Was I still? I decided to wait until I was closer to actually being discharged to figure out what to do.

An hour later, as I started to compose a text to Joy, a text came through from Tommy. *Hey, are you up for a visit? We want to see you.*

I texted back. *Who's we?*

Jane and me.

I turned my head toward the ceiling and smiled as a shiver shot down my spine. Then I texted, *Where are you?*

Near the hospital. Getting coffee.

May I call you?

Sure.

When he answered, I said hello and then asked, "What are you doing up this way?"

"Jane convinced me to go to Chicago to try to find Miriam."

"Any luck?"

"No," he said. "Jane's not ready to give up, though."

I appreciated her taking up the cause while I was out of commission.

"We're probably about ten minutes away," Tommy said.

"Great!" I answered. "I need a ride home. Do you know of any ride-shares in the area that will pick me up from the hospital?"

"Lucky for you I know a great driver," he teased back. "But it will cost you."

I was smiling as we ended the call, but I wondered how Tommy knew where to look in Chicago for Miriam. Had he been in contact with Kenny or Joshua?

A half hour later, I was climbing into the back seat of Tommy's Jeep once again. This time he reached over and fastened my seat belt for me, then tucked a blanket around me. I guessed it was Mason's.

Jane reached through the front seats and patted my leg. "So good to have you out of there."

I nodded in agreement. "It sounds like you and Tommy have been on an adventure."

"Well, not a very productive one, I'm afraid," she said. "I couldn't bear another day of worrying about Miriam, but none of our searching has led to her."

As Tommy climbed into the driver's seat, I asked him, "Where have you been looking?"

"The East Side. Turns out Kenny had two cell phones. The one on my account that he used to pick up ride-shares and local clients, and another one that he used to communicate with a guy living in Chicago." Tommy shook his head. "He's disappeared again, but he left his second cell phone behind. I don't know if he forgot it or didn't want it. But I saw a text that read, *She's not cooperating + car broke down. Make things right today or I'm done.*"

"Yikes," I said. "So how did you know to go to the East Side?"

"Joshua," Tommy answered. "He's starting to freak out. He thought Kenny was trying to help Miriam, but she texted him that the place she's at is scary. Joshua gave us the address. He said it's the same one he gave you."

My heart started to race. "The bungalow down the street from a convenience store on East Port?"

Tommy nodded.

I shuddered, thinking of that man peering out of the curtains at me. I opened my mouth to ask another question, but my phone rang before I could.

"Hey, I'm trying to get a hold of Savannah Mast," a woman said. "This is Pam at the East Side convenience store."

"Oh, hi," I answered. "This is Savannah."

"She's here."

"Miriam is there?"

"Yep," the woman said. "Crying in the back room. I don't know how long she'll stay. . . ."

"We're on our way! Thank you!" I ended the call. "We need to go back to Chicago, to the convenience store. Miriam's there now."

Without a word, Tommy turned toward the interstate, heading west. When we reached it, however, it was essentially a parking lot. I craned my neck to try to look around the sea of cars. Flashing lights up in the distance indicated that there was a wreck ahead.

Perhaps Jane sensed my discomfort because she said, "How about if I finish our story while we wait?"

"Sure," I answered somewhat distractedly. "As long as Tommy doesn't mind coming in on the end."

He glanced in the rearview mirror. "Not at all."

I wasn't sure exactly what he meant, but my face grew warm anyway.

"All right, then," Jane said. "If I remember correctly, Mathilde said she would go with Judah to Vincennes but only if Emma would go with her. . . ."

CHAPTER 27

Emma

Mamm had been busy with births in the northern part of the county. Emma doubted that her mother had given up on her staying in Indiana, but at least she hadn't had time to come back down to tell Emma that she needed to stay.

George had stopped by the Landis place several times and asked Judah if he'd found Mathilde, and Judah had managed to distract George without actually lying. Emma couldn't get Mathilde's words out of her head. *"I'll go, but only if you'll come too. I can't make the trip on my own, with the children. I need your help."*

The soil remained too wet to plant, so Judah made a plan. They would leave the last week of March, sometime during the night, after Phillip had fallen asleep. That way, hopefully, George wouldn't find out they'd left. Emma listened to Judah's plan without commenting. She couldn't go with Mathilde *and* go back to Pennsylvania. She had to choose one or the other.

George had a new farmhand named Frank Lawrence working for him and seemed set on staying on his farm instead of going to Chicago, hoping Harriet would return to him. Judah didn't think the new hand was a good influence, though, and said he seemed to be a heavy drinker too, from his limited interactions with the man.

As the date to leave approached, Isaac asked Emma what she planned to do. "We can't take her without you," he said. "Are you going to put your desire for an easier life before Mathilde's chance at having any life at all?"

Her little brother's words put her to shame. He was right. Emma knew, if their circumstances were in reverse, Mathilde would do anything to help her. She'd come out in the middle of the night with Judah, whom she didn't fully trust, when Betha was giving birth. She'd told Emma not to feel badly that Phillip's farm was on land Mathilde's family used to gather food on. Mathilde had sent the dogwood decoction with Isaac that had helped heal Emma of her illness.

Emma had to go with Mathilde. It was what the Lord would want her to do. She would write to Abel and explain about the delay and that she would return to Somerset County as soon as she could. She would post the letter immediately, once they returned from Vincennes.

Emma put away dried fruit, jerky, cheese, and the walnuts that she'd collected from the tree on Phillip's property and stored it all in the cellar he and Isaac had dug. She tucked their provisions into a bag. They would need them while they were on the trail. Hopefully Isaac and Judah would be able to shoot small game they could cook over the fire at night. She also packed a small bag of bandages and herbs, as well as a needle and thread, just in case anyone was injured. Isaac had his bedroll, and Emma could roll up one of her blankets. She prayed it wouldn't rain and that the road—and ground—wouldn't be muddy.

Emma wrote a note to Phillip, explaining she and Isaac were taking Mathilde to a safe place, without saying where, and that they'd be home in less than two weeks. *Isaac will help you with the planting and then go on to Dat's to help him after that, if Dat doesn't get started before we return. We don't entertain any ideas that you will agree with or support what we're doing, but both Isaac and I feel led by the Lord to assist Mathilde, who is a widow in need of our help.* She signed it, *Your sister, Emma.*

On the last Monday of March, after Phillip fell asleep, Isaac slipped out of the cabin first, and then Emma followed ten minutes later. The moon was just rising, casting light over the barnyard. She hurried through it and kept going to the creek, where she met Isaac, who had both of their horses and full saddlebags. He helped her onto Red, and then the horses sloshed across the creek and then around the thicket to the entryway.

Emma's heart raced. Judah stood there, holding the reins of his horse, waiting for them. She was going to Vincennes. It would be the most daring thing she'd ever done in her entire life. Asher would never have believed it. The thought caused a lump to grow in her throat. If only she'd been more willing to seek out adventure with him.

Judah greeted them and nodded toward the thicket. "Emma, would you go in?"

"Jah." She walked through the tunnel, which was illuminated by the rising moon. "Mathilde," she called out softly. "We're here."

"Oui," Mathilde said. "I heard you." She wore her buckskin dress and had the horse saddled and packed. Agnes was asleep in her cradleboard, strapped to Mathilde's back, with her dreamcatcher dangling above her head. Baptiste, with a bleary look in his eyes, sat at the entrance of the wigwam. Emma scooped him up into her arms and patted his back until he rested his head on her shoulder.

Mathilde grabbed the reins of her horse and led the way out of the thicket. When they reached the men, Judah first helped Mathilde onto her horse and then took Baptiste from Emma, holding him with one arm while he mounted his horse. He then continued to hold Baptiste, whose eyes were heavy with sleep, as he led the way. Mathilde followed, then Emma, while Isaac positioned himself in the back.

The group rode at a comfortable pace. Emma's eyes grew heavy too, and she began to recite scripture in her head to keep awake. The Twenty-third Psalm. Then the Beatitudes. Judah turned his head slightly, his finger to his lips. Ahead was a campfire with a group sleeping around it.

Someone called out.

"We're friends," Judah answered. "Close to our cabin." It was true; they weren't far from the Landis farm.

"All right," the man responded. "Move along."

SEVERAL TIMES, UNDER the light of the moon, Emma felt herself nodding off and woke up with a start as her head bobbed. When the sun began to rise, they passed a farm with a white clapboard house that reminded Emma of her home in Somerset County. By the time the world had grown light, it was obvious the horses were exhausted. Judah pointed to a grove up ahead. He turned into the trees, and when the others followed, he stopped and said, "We'll eat and then rest for a few hours before we go on."

It was early afternoon by the time they were on the road

again, and by midafternoon they arrived at the Erie-Wabash Canal. It wouldn't open for a few more months, but Judah said they would travel the path alongside it to Lafayette. Then they would continue on along the Wabash River the rest of the way.

"If George is coming after us, he's either going through Indianapolis and then heading southwest or else going along the canal too," Judah said. "There's no way to know."

She hoped Judah was being honest, but she couldn't help but question if he did know—and if he'd told George exactly what route they were taking. He would be able to travel faster than they could.

"The canal will be over four hundred miles long when it's completed," Judah said as he led the way. "Going all the way from near Toledo, Ohio, to Evansville, Indiana."

The path was lined with evergreens and lots of maples, cedars, and larch trees, with brush growing between them. Ducks bobbed along the water, and a hawk soared overhead.

A slight drizzle began to fall, and Emma pulled the hood of her cloak over her head. Baptiste babbled from his place in front of Judah. Raindrops danced along the water, casting circles across the surface. Emma tried to suppress her yawns, but she couldn't seem to stop. Toward early evening, Judah veered off into the woods and said they'd set up camp for the night.

They traveled on, day after day, remaining on the east side of the canal, through rain, sunshine, and moonlight. From his trip the month before, Judah remembered the best places to camp, the spots where the fishing was good, and the farms where they could buy eggs. Emma coughed some but mostly felt better each day. Baptiste grew restless at times but mostly enjoyed sitting in front of Judah. Agnes continued to be a happy baby, smiling more and more each day.

Isaac behaved as if he were on a grand adventure, hunting

for squirrels and rabbits when they stopped and catching fish from the canal. From Lafayette they continued along the east side of the Wabash, although the pathway for the canal had ended. Yet there was still a trail, probably first established by Native people. Emma began to believe that George hadn't followed them after all. Hopefully that meant that Judah was as trustworthy as she hoped.

When they neared Terre Haute, Judah said they had a little over fifty miles remaining. They passed lush meadows and orchards along the river, and once they reached the town, where the junction with the road from Indianapolis was, the group continued west along the Wabash River to the Illinois border and then continued to follow the river south.

As they neared their destination, Emma had stopped thinking of George entirely—almost. The sun was shining, and Emma turned her head toward it, soaking in its warmth. In another week, she would be back in Elkhart County, looking for a different group to travel home with. Or perhaps the Martin and Slaybaugh families had postponed their trip and she could go with them after all. She'd have Isaac ride up to Newbury Township and check as soon as they returned.

God had guided them on this journey and, at the moment, she truly believed she could trust Him to get her home, to give her a good marriage with Abel and a home full of children.

Just as the houses on the edge of Vincennes came into view, the beat of horses' hooves startled Emma, and she shifted in her saddle. Isaac had stopped his horse and turned it around. Two men galloped toward them.

"It's George!" Isaac called out.

Judah turned his horse toward Mathilde, sliding Baptiste into her arms. "Hurry!" He slapped the rump of her horse. "Go with her," he said to Emma, his eyes alarmed.

He started off on his horse toward George, yelling at Isaac to follow the women as Emma dug her heels into Red. Her heart raced. The cradleboard bounced on Mathilde's back, and Baptiste's little legs flailed up and down.

A shot rang out.

"Don't look back!" Isaac shouted. "Keep riding!"

Was George shooting at Judah? Or was Judah shooting at George? Perhaps Sarah was right about Judah adopting the Englisch ways.

Another shot rang out. She ignored Isaac's command and turned her head anyway. She had to know what was going on.

Judah was on his knees on the trail, still holding his horse's reins, and George was thundering toward him.

She turned Red around. "Keep going," she said to Isaac. "Save Mathilde. I can't leave Judah behind."

CHAPTER 28

George shot his rifle at Judah again. But this time he missed. His stallion reeled, and the man with him, most likely his hired hand, Frank Lawrence, appeared alarmed. Once he had his horse back under control, George yelled, "You had no right to take Mathilde away. She's obligated to work for me. I want her back."

"She doesn't belong to you," Judah yelled, clutching his arm.

George pointed the rifle at him again. "Her labor does."

"You've mistreated her."

"You coerced her to leave. You probably have plans to sell her."

Judah shook his head. "You know that's not true."

Emma stopped Red beside Judah's horse and slid from the saddle. Then she grabbed Judah's rifle, which was on the ground. She swung around toward George, pointing the rifle at him and stepping in front of Judah. George didn't flinch, but Frank did.

"Go on home," she yelled.

George laughed. "Emma Gingrich."

"Fischer," she yelled back.

"You're just a little lady."

"With a gun," she shouted. "You'll have to shoot me before you harm Judah anymore. Do you want to be charged with murdering a woman?"

"Your brother came to me after you left and showed me the note."

Emma stifled a gasp. Why would Phillip do such a thing? He'd betrayed them.

"Together we determined you would probably head south," George said.

"Come on, boss," Frank pleaded. "This isn't worth it." He appeared frightened.

Emma didn't blame him. She was too. She bent her knees to keep them from shaking.

"You're right, Frank." Judah's nostrils flared. "You don't want to be implicated in George's violence."

George shook his head at his hired hand and then pulled a flask from the pocket of his coat and took a drink. As he did, a group of riders came around the bend of the trail.

"What's going on here?" an older man in a suit called out.

"Nothing," Frank said. "We were just finishing up some business."

George stared Emma down and took another swig. Then he held up his rifle and shot it into the air. As he turned, he shouted, "I'm not done. I'll see you in town."

As he turned north and took off at a trot, past the other party, Emma kneeled down to examine Judah. He let go of his left bicep, where a bullet had torn through his flesh. She pulled away his shirt to reveal the torn, bloody muscle. The bullet had most likely hit his bone too, although it had passed on through.

He looked into her eyes. "I don't think I'll bleed to death."

"That appears to be true." She tore a strip from the hem of

her dress and wrapped it around his arm. "We'd better hurry and catch up to Mathilde and Isaac. And warn those at the mission to expect trouble."

"That's if he comes back," Judah said. "We may have seen the last of George Burton."

Emma doubted it but didn't say so.

The other party reached them, and the man in the suit asked if they needed help.

"Thank you," Judah said. "But I don't think we'll have any more trouble." He helped Emma onto her horse with his good arm and then managed to swing up onto his. He motioned for her to ride in front of him. Soon the steeple of the church loomed ahead.

The church was positioned on a piece of property that bordered the river. There was a cross atop the steeple and statues above the doors. There were also several outbuildings on the property, both houses and stables, as well as a few cows and a large garden.

In the center of the property, Baptiste clung to Isaac's leg, while Mathilde held her horse's reins. A smile slowly spread across her face when she saw Emma and Judah, but immediately an expression of horror followed. She grabbed Baptiste as she yelled, "George!" and began running toward the church. Isaac rushed after her.

Emma pulled back on Red's reins. Judah slid from his horse and grabbed Emma around the waist with his good arm, pulling her down.

A boy called out, "I'll take care of the horses. *Allez!*"

With his arm still around Emma's waist, Judah began to run, sweeping her along with him. As they reached the front door of the church, George jumped down from his saddle, his rifle still in his hand. The front door swung open, and a man in a black robe ushered them in. Then he stepped outside and slammed the door.

Mathilde stood toward the front of the church, Baptiste still in her arms. Behind her was a painting of Christ on the cross and then statues on both sides. Emma shivered in the unfamiliar structure. The Anabaptists had left the Catholic Church over three hundred years before, choosing simplicity of worship, nonresistance, and adult baptism.

But here she was in a cathedral, doing what she believed God wanted her to do.

There was shouting outside, yet Emma felt oddly safe. She passed by Isaac and continued on to Mathilde, putting her arm around her. Isaac stepped to Mathilde's other side. And then Judah joined them. They huddled together, with Baptiste in the middle.

"Peace be with you," the priest called out, speaking in a thick French accent from the other side of the closed door. "This is a place of safety, not of violence."

"Someone will summon the sheriff," Judah said.

"Is the priest going to be all right?" Emma asked.

"The bishop," Judah corrected. "He's Father Célestine de la Hailandière, from France."

"Oh." Emma was surprised he was the one who met them.

"He's been expecting us. I told him we might have trouble—although I expected George would have found us earlier."

There was a long stretch of silence and then the firing of a gun, again.

Emma flinched. There was more shouting and someone yelled, "Drop the rifle. You're under arrest!"

Another voice called out, "George, give it up!" Probably Frank Lawrence.

Mathilde sighed in relief.

But then there was more shooting and then another yell. As an eerie silence settled, Emma could hear someone say, "Is he dead?"

Tears stung Emma's eyes. She didn't want George to be dead. Just locked up in jail.

She couldn't hear what the answer was, but a few minutes later, the bishop opened the door. "It is now safe."

"George?" Emma squeaked.

"Wounded," the bishop answered. "They are taking him to the jail. A physician will attend to him."

The bishop came toward them and extended his hand to Mathilde. "*Bonjour*."

Before he reached her, she bowed slightly.

The bishop took her hand and lifted it. "God has answered my prayer. Now I pray he will reunite you with your family."

EARLY THE NEXT morning as the sun rose, Isaac and Judah, who did the best he could with his injured arm, saddled the horses while Emma told Mathilde good-bye. "Please send a letter and let me know you and the children are safe in Kansas."

"Oui," Mathilde answered. "I'll ask one of the nuns to write it for me."

Emma's eyes filled with tears.

"When you get back to Union Township, go to my wigwam. I've left something there for you."

Emma gave her a questioning look.

Mathilde smiled. "You'll see."

"Denki." Emma smiled back. "For whatever it is." Then she said, "I wish I had a good-bye gift for you."

Mathilde shook her head. "You brought me here, and hopefully I'll be with my family soon. It's the greatest gift you could give me." Mathilde squeezed her hand. "Judah is a good man after all."

Emma nodded and wiped away a tear. "God be with you."

Mathilde replied, "And with you."

As they mounted their horses, the sheriff rode up. "Glad I caught you before you left. I wanted to tell you that George Burton succumbed to his wounds during the night."

Emma gasped. She despised George, but she didn't want him dead. Judah sagged a little in his saddle. She guessed he felt the same way.

The sheriff asked, "Do you know his next of kin?"

Judah sat up straight again. "George was living on their farm in Elkhart County, Union Township, but his mother-in-law, wife, and children are all living in Chicago now." He listed all of their names. "Lenore owns property there. I believe her home is in Norwood Park."

"All right," the sheriff said. "I'll write a letter to his wife there."

"What about Frank Lawrence?" Judah asked.

"I let him go last night," the sheriff said. "The boy said his folks live in Missouri, and he was going to return there." The man tipped his hat.

After the sheriff rode off, Isaac led the way out of town and Emma followed, with Judah taking up the rear this time. But after a few miles, he caught up with her and rode beside her.

"I have a confession to make," she said. "I wasn't certain until George took the second shot at you, that you were being honest about not working for him, about truly trying to save Mathilde."

"I wondered about that," he answered.

"Isaac told me that the reason you went back to work for George was so you could keep an eye on Mathilde, but she told me she hardly saw you and that you seemed friendly with George."

"Jah, I didn't want it to be obvious what I was doing. George wouldn't have trusted me then." Judah glanced toward Emma. "I know Mathilde wasn't the only one suspicious of me. Others were, long before she became so."

Emma thought of Sarah and her harsh words. And Phillip and his suspicions. She'd let what others thought sour her own opinion of Judah.

"I regret not trusting you," Emma said.

"You couldn't know for sure," Judah said. "It's not bad to be cautious. I'm glad you weren't too trusting."

The trip home was mostly uneventful. The weather had started to turn warmer and wildflowers were blooming—Virginia bluebells, poppies, and skunk cabbage. The leaves of the trees filled out, and the wind rustling through the branches serenaded them as they rode.

One night just before they reached Lafayette, Isaac fell asleep while Judah and Emma remained around the fire.

"Isaac told me you wanted to be on your way to Pennsylvania by now," Judah said.

She nodded.

"You gave that up for Mathilde?"

Emma waved the shifting smoke away from her face. "For the time being, anyway."

Judah leaned toward her. "Are you that unhappy living in Elkhart County?"

He wouldn't understand. He seemed to relish the frontier life. He didn't care about the dirt and mud. About cooking over a campfire or a fireplace. Clearly he'd left Ohio behind for good, without a second thought.

Jah, Judah had turned out to be a good man with good

intentions, but living on the frontier was a grand adventure for him, as it would have been for Asher before he lost his health. Judah wouldn't understand why she wanted to leave.

"Does it have to do with your husband and children passing away, with them being buried back in Pennsylvania?"

Emma wasn't sure how to answer him. Finally, she shook her head. "It's more than that. I'm not a strong person. I'm not cut out for this."

"This?" Judah appeared confused.

"How hard everything is. I could barely handle life in Pennsylvania, when things were going well. In Somerset County, I have others to rely on. Here I have to be stronger than I am—even more so now, with Mathilde gone."

Judah placed his hands on his knees, leaning even closer to her. "Look at everything you've done. How you helped Betha. What you did for Mathilde. What you did for me. You risked your life for mine. George could have murdered me."

"That was impulsive. You and Mathilde would have done the same for me, but ten times better. And the only reason Betha survived was because of Mathilde." Emma sighed. "My husband was so excited to move west, but I didn't want to go, and I let him know it. Then I fell apart when our children died." She shook her head as the memories threatened to swamp her. "The truth is, I wasn't a very good wife or mother."

"You might feel that way," Judah said. "But that doesn't mean it's true. Isaac said you loved your husband and son very much and served them well. That you were heartbroken when they, and your baby girl, died. Isaac said you were a wonderful wife and mother."

Tears stung Emma's eyes, and she stared into the fire. "Well, Isaac is young. There's a lot he doesn't understand."

"I've never experienced death as you have, but I know it takes time to recover. The Lord works, jah, but oftentimes mysteriously. And sometimes, from our perspective, slowly."

She met his gaze through the smoke. "Do you know this from experience?"

He nodded. "Not as deeply as you do, but I thought I'd marry a woman in Ohio. But after I left, she decided she didn't want to marry me."

"Sarah said you didn't want to marry her."

"Really?"

Emma nodded. "Because she was a widow."

Judah shook his head. "I'm sorry she said that, especially to you. Sarah's made several assumptions about me—I didn't realize that was one of them." He rubbed the back of his neck. "I would have returned to Ohio if I'd known how badly Ida didn't want to move west, but by the time she wrote to me, she was already being courted by someone else."

"So you really cared about her?"

"I thought I did."

The smoke shifted away from the two of them, and Judah looked determinedly at Emma.

"Listen," he said. "I'll go with Isaac to take you back to Pennsylvania."

"Why would you do that? Because you haven't traveled enough this year?" she joked. "Because you want to go an additional eight hundred miles?"

He grinned. "Something like that."

She wrinkled her nose. "But seriously, why would you do that for me?"

"There's not really enough work for both Walter and me on his farm." He shrugged. "I'll probably join the church when I go through Ohio, and then perhaps I'll find a place to settle down on the return trip. Or just keep going west. I've heard of some Amish settling in Illinois and thought I might go there. Helping you get back to Pennsylvania wouldn't be that much of a hardship for me before I settle down."

"Well, denki, but perhaps I can find another family going in the summer or fall." She stood. "*Gut nacht.*"

Emma left the fire and curled up in her blanket. But she couldn't sleep, not even after she heard Judah leave the fire too.

WHEN THEY CROSSED the border into Elkhart County, Judah said quietly, "I'd like to go with you to Phillip's cabin and speak with him, if you don't mind."

"All right." Emma wasn't sure if it was a good idea or not. She feared Phillip would deny sending George after them or confront them for leaving in the first place, which he had every right to do.

It was early evening when they arrived at the cabin. At the sound of the horses, Phillip stepped out of the front door. But the expression on his face was one of relief rather than anger. "You're back." He folded his hands together. "Is everyone all right?"

"We are," Isaac answered. "But George is dead."

Phillip exhaled. "He caught up with you?"

Emma nodded.

"He shot at us," Isaac said. "And hit Judah."

"Got my arm is all," Judah said. "I'm fine."

Phillip ran his hand through his hair. "It wasn't until I guessed, out loud, that you'd gone to Vincennes that I realized George's plan was to take Mathilde back by force. At first, when he stopped by, he pretended to be concerned about her. He'd found her wigwam down by the creek and assumed I knew about it." Phillip exhaled. "He said he couldn't figure out why you hadn't told him what you were planning to do and assured me he wouldn't hurt anyone, but the more I thought about the way he acted, the less I believed him."

"All is forgiven," Judah said. "I'm sorry we left you in a bad situation with the planting."

Phillip shrugged. "It rained the first week you were gone, and it's only now drying out. I'll plant in the next couple of days." He turned to Isaac. "And then we can go help Dat plant his field."

Isaac nodded.

"By mid-May, Barbara and I plan to marry." Phillip gestured toward Emma. "So you'll be free to return to Mamm and Dat's, or Pennsylvania."

Emma didn't respond right away. Finally, she said, "I'm happy for you and Barbara."

"Denki," Phillip answered. "I have a pot of beans on in the house, although they're not very tasty."

Isaac started toward the barn, but before Emma could follow him, Judah said, "Could I speak with you for a moment?"

"Jah."

"On the last night in Vincennes, Mathilde said she'd left you something here. She wanted me to tell you when we arrived, and she also sent a note for me to give you. Could we go to her wigwam? For just a moment?"

Curious, Emma answered, "Jah." Hopefully George hadn't damaged Mathilde's wigwam too badly.

She led the way. The creek was high, but Red crossed it quickly. Judah followed on his horse.

After they'd both dismounted, Judah said, "I need to say something before we go into the thicket."

Emma turned toward him.

"I understand you want to return home, and, like I said, I

will take you if you want." Judah leaned toward her. "And I'm guessing there's someone—a man—back there for you."

"Did Isaac tell you that?"

"He started to, but I said I shouldn't know all of your secrets."

Emma shook her head. "Believe me, I don't have many. Abel is my husband's brother—Asher's twin. At one time it seemed like a natural choice for me. But . . ." She wasn't sure what to say. It was becoming more and more clear to her that she didn't want to marry Abel. His letters had been terse, with no emotion or even any details of his life, even when she'd tried to connect with him through her own letters. Maybe her Mamm was right in her assessment of him too, that he lacked vision and ambition.

She'd planned to return to Pennsylvania and marry him because that was what was easiest, but that wasn't right for her or fair to him. She couldn't go through with marrying him just because it was convenient.

"All right." Judah cleared his throat. "I still need to tell you . . ."

Emma met his gaze.

"I've come to care about you." He put his hand on her shoulder. "If I go back with you to Pennsylvania and you don't marry Abel, I would like to stay—as your husband. I'll take the money I've saved to set up a household, start a business. I know I won't be able to afford a farm, but I'll do whatever I can to support you."

So many thoughts rushed through Emma's mind. Asher and their children. Her grandfather. Her house in Pennsylvania. Her feeble commitment to Abel.

But what fully filled her heart was Judah. She could love again. Jah, Judah was a dreamer, like Asher was, but she felt better equipped this time to join in on the adventure. Still, as she reached for his hand, she said, "Give me some time."

He nodded.

She led him through the thicket to the wigwam. The hide that had covered the doorway was now hanging lopsided, but as Emma crawled inside, it didn't seem that George had disturbed anything, not the way she'd feared he had.

"Look." Judah pointed to the pile of furs. A cradleboard sat in the middle, not Agnes's, but one that Emma had never seen.

"It was Baptiste's," Judah said. "But the dreamcatcher is new."

Emma reached for the cradleboard. It had a hickory hoop over the top like Agnes's, but the strips of deer hide were twisted with blue ribbon, from Mathilde's calico dress with the forget-me-not pattern. The dreamcatcher was the pattern of a cross with the feather of a loon hanging from it. A piece of paper fell from the top. On it was written, in charcoal, *pour Emma*.

Judah pulled a piece of paper from his pocket. "This is the note Mathilde wanted you to have."

The paper was folded and sealed. Emma opened it. In the same script as the first, but written in ink, were the words *pour Emma et Judah*.

Wordlessly, she handed it to Judah.

He smiled. "That last night, in her quiet way, she suggested I pursue you. Of course, she didn't need to give me any encouragement. . . ."

Emma touched the dreamcatcher, causing it to swing on the hoop. She would recover. So would Mathilde. And Baptiste and Agnes too. They would embrace their new lives, thanks to the grace of God. That didn't mean they would forget those they had lost, those they mourned, but they could hold all of it in their hearts. And then step forward in faith.

Emma turned toward Judah. "You don't need to go to Pennsylvania with me."

"Nee? Why not?"

She took his hand. "Because I'm staying here. With you."

CHAPTER 29

Savannah

As Tommy's Jeep inched toward the Chicago city limits, Jane said, "That's all."

"It can't be," I gasped. "What about their wedding?"

"Well, there is that. They married the next August on Emma's parents' farm as the blue daisies bloomed in the pasture. By that second summer, Emma had come to love Indiana, and, in time, she became an important member of the Plain community."

"What about Mathilde?"

"In September, Emma received a letter from her, written by one of the nuns. Her family had been sent on to the Indian Territory, which later became the state of Oklahoma. Sadly, her mother had died on the trail. But Mathilde was reunited with her father and sisters. "

I blinked my eyes to stop the tears. "Did Emma hear from Mathilde again?"

"I'm afraid not. That was the one and only time."

My chest ached, and not just from my injuries.

"But," Jane said, "Emma never forgot Mathilde and her family. In fact, she named her oldest daughter after her. Emma passed the story of her friend and the Potawatomi people down to her children and grandchildren and even great-grandchildren. The story has lived on through the generations."

"What did Judah do to support Emma?" Tommy asked.

"Well, that was really something." Jane shifted in her seat and glanced from Tommy to me. "Lenore wrote to Judah and asked him if he'd farm her land. When Lenore died, she left a stipulation in her will that Judah could buy the farm outright for a good price, which he did. By then, he and Emma had nine children and filled both sides of the house. Unfortunately, that original house was torn down in the early 1900s. My brother's house, down the lane from my shop, was built on the property in 1904."

Tommy glanced in the rearview mirror again, smiling at me. I asked Jane, "Did Emma continue to work as a midwife?"

"Jah, she did. Even though she thought of her two children she lost every day for the rest of her life, she grew in confidence and ability as a midwife, all the more determined to care for others and bring babies safely into the world. She ended up exceeding her mother in her midwifery skills," Jane said. "She also made it a special point to minister to the women who didn't have a built-in community—the newcomers, the Irish women, such as Betha, and also the few Native women still in the area. In fact, she traveled to Michigan frequently to see women in the Potawatomi tribe up there, both to see to their health needs and also to learn from them about midwifery, medicine, and crops."

That warmed my heart. "What happened to Eli?"

"Well," Jane said, "he continued to prosper and became a leader in the community, but whenever she could, Emma stood up to him and others who were critical of the Native population. And, of course, Judah did too."

"And to think we're both descendants of Emma," I said. "What an honor."

"It is, isn't it?" Jane turned around and smiled.

Here we were, both descendants of Emma, a woman who had done everything she could to help another woman in need. "Wait," I said. "Is Tommy related to Emma too?"

Jane shook her head. "Not that I know of. But remember Joseph Miller from the beginning of the story? The man who first traveled to Indiana with the other three men from Somerset County?"

I nodded. "Vaguely."

"That's Tommy's story. So there are parallels as far as the early settlements here," Jane explained. "From 1840 to 1850, the population of European descendants in Elkhart County increased from 935 to 12,690."

Yes, but preceding that period, thousands of Native Americans had been forcibly removed, I reminded myself. Those two realities would always exist side by side.

As far as Tommy and I went, our roots went deep, but neither of us was Plain. However, our lives had certainly been shaped by the actions of our ancestors, creating patterns that lived on in each of our lives, much like the quilt we'd been working on at Plain Patterns.

My thoughts went from those patterns to Emma and Mathilde. "You know what would have made the story even sweeter?" I said. "If Emma had given Mathilde a quilt as a good-bye gift."

"Jah," Jane said. "I agree. But she couldn't have. Amish women learned quilting from the English and Irish. Our ancestors didn't start quilting, as far as I can tell, until around the late 1860s."

"Really?"

"That's right." Jane's eyes twinkled. "And, as you can imagine, I do have more stories from the past, ones that include quilting."

"I wish I could be around to hear them," I said. "Have you decided whom to give the hearth and home quilt at Plain Patterns to?"

"I have an idea."

"I think you should give it to Miriam, once she's back."

"I hadn't thought of her." Jane smiled. "But I appreciate the idea."

It wasn't long until we were in the East Side neighborhood. I'd had a few texts from Pam, saying Miriam was still in the back room. Pam hadn't told her we were on our way, but she had encouraged Miriam to stay, even saying she'd help her when she got off work.

When we reached the convenience store, Tommy turned into the parking lot. "I should go in," I said. "Pam will recognize me."

Tommy walked around to help me out of the Jeep, and then I led the way, limping along in my boot. Tommy and Jane followed.

Pam met me at the door. "She just left. The same guy I saw her with before came and got her."

"Any idea where they went?" I asked.

"No, but they didn't climb into a car or anything. They walked up the street." She pointed toward the direction of the bungalow.

I thanked Pam for her kindness, and then Jane, Tommy, and I piled back into the Jeep and drove straight to the house. Although the porch light was off and the front of the house was dark, there was a light on in the back.

Carefully, I toddled up the steps, with Tommy holding on to my arm. He knocked, but no one answered. After a few more bouts of knocking, I tried the doorknob. It was locked.

"Let's see if anyone's around back," I said. We walked around the side of the house, using the light of the flashlight app on Tommy's phone. In the back was a deck. We made our way up the steps to a door. We knocked and, again, no one answered. I tried the door.

This time it opened.

There was Miriam, wearing her coat and sitting at a table, staring at us. She stood.

"Who's there?" someone yelled from the basement.

"Please come with us," I whispered.

Jane darted around me and wrapped Miriam up in her arms. "Child," she cooed. "Come along." With one arm still around her, Jane started toward the back door.

Miriam glanced back at the basement door as someone shouted, "Kenny! Is that you?"

"Hurry," I hissed to Jane as she reached the door and a thundering of footsteps started up the stairs.

The man I'd seen on the street appeared.

Tommy stepped in front of me. I held my phone up above Tommy's head and announced falsely, in hopes of gaining more time, "I've called the police. They're on the way."

The man stopped. "Where's Kenny?"

"I have no idea," Tommy said. "But I'm his cousin, and I'm guessing he'll do you as dirty as he did me."

"Tommy?" the guy asked.

"Yep."

He frowned. "I've heard about you. I'm calling Kenny."

"All right." Tommy wrapped an arm around my waist. "Let me know what he says."

As the man pulled out his phone and stepped into the dining room, Tommy swept me up and lifted me out the back door and down the steps. A phone in Tommy's pocket was buzzing. With his free hand, he was clicking his Jeep's key fob as he helped me hobble along the side of the house. By the time we reached the Jeep, Jane and Miriam had already climbed into the back seat, so Tommy practically shoved me in the front.

"Here comes Ivan!" Miriam yelled.

Sure enough, he was running out the front door, yelling.

"What's he saying?" Jane asked.

"'Wait.' He's saying 'wait.'"

"Who is he?"

Miriam leaned her head against Jane's shoulder. "My baby's father."

As Tommy drove out of the neighborhood, Miriam revealed that Ivan was close to thirty and had left the Amish over a decade ago. She believed he and Kenny knew each other from when they were teenagers and had been working together since Kenny returned to the area in September.

I did the math again and said, "But you knew Ivan before September, right?"

She nodded. "He spends time in Newbury Township. I've known him for a while."

"What do you mean 'spends time'?"

"Shows up at parties. Sells drugs."

And preys on girls. Miriam had been seventeen when she got pregnant.

"How did you get to Ethel's house the night you disappeared?" I asked.

"Kenny picked me up in his car that night, right after Tommy dropped me off, and drove me there. He knew I was miserable at Vernon's and thought my aunt's house would be a better place for me."

I glanced at Tommy and then back at Miriam. "Did your mother know Kenny took you to Ethel's?"

Miriam wrinkled her nose. "No, but Joshua told her I was in a safe place so she wouldn't worry."

"Why didn't she tell Deputy Rogers? Or Vernon?"

Miriam leaned her head back against the seat. "This has been really hard for her, I know. Vernon blames her for my behavior, which isn't her fault. And she didn't know where I was, just that I was safe, so it wasn't as if she had any particular information to give them. And I am eighteen."

That made sense, from Arleta's point of view, although certainly not from mine. Miriam might be eighteen, but she could have been in danger. "Who taught you how to drive?"

"Ivan," Miriam answered. "Two years ago, when we still lived in Newbury Township."

"Why did you come to Chicago? After you left Nappanee the second time?"

"Besides Ivan being the father of my baby?"

I waited for her to say more.

Finally, she said, "I figured out he's not safe. He told me he'd stopped selling drugs, but he lied. He's working with Kenny, which I'm pretty sure Deputy Rogers knows. But all of Rogers's questions for me were about you, Tommy, not about Kenny." She sighed. "I'm sorry I misled him. I tried not to lie, but there were a few times I agreed with Kenny when I shouldn't have."

"Apology accepted," Tommy said, which I thought was awfully kind considering he'd spent time in jail because of what she'd gone along with.

"I did get the sense," Miriam continued, "that Deputy Rogers doesn't really want to get to the bottom of what Kenny and Ivan have been doing."

I shot a glance at Tommy. Deputy Rogers's grudge against Tommy, whatever it was for, seemed to have blinded him.

"We need to let the Elkhart County sheriff know what's going on," Tommy said.

"All right," Miriam said wearily.

I sent a quick text to Joy, telling her I'd been discharged and was on my way home with Tommy, Jane, and Miriam, although it might take a while because of traffic. *I'll explain everything later. Please tell Mammi we're all fine.*

A few minutes later, Tommy pulled over at a diner, off the interstate. We were a ragtag group as we made our way through the front door.

"Are you doing all right?" Tommy asked me as I hobbled along.

I nodded. There was no need to mention that my ankle was throbbing because of all the activity. I'd take my meds once I had something to eat.

We got a table in the very back, away from any other patrons. Tommy dialed the sheriff. He explained what was going on and that Deputy Rogers had been working the case but now it had grown larger. Tommy put Miriam on the phone. She corroborated Tommy's story, and then Tommy spoke with the sheriff again.

After Tommy ended the call, he said, "He's going to call the Chicago Police Department, but he wants us to meet him at his office in Elkhart. Deputy Rogers will be there too. And hopefully Kenny, if Rogers can find him." He focused on me. "It will be late."

"That's all right," I said. "Let's get this taken care of."

Once we were back on the road after eating, Miriam and Jane fell asleep in the back seat. I couldn't help but wonder if it would be a good idea for Miriam to live at home through the rest of her pregnancy and then after the baby was born. I glanced over my shoulder. Miriam had her head against Jane's shoulder. Maybe there was another option for her, at least until she could figure out where else she could go.

"I'm so sorry," Tommy said quietly. "For everything."

"What do you mean?"

"That I didn't figure out what Kenny was up to. That you got dragged into this. That you were in that accident."

"None of this is your fault," I said. "I'm just relieved Miriam is okay."

He nodded. "You know what else I regret?"

"You need to stop beating yourself up."

"No, I need to say this." He shot me a quick glance and then returned his eyes to the road. "I regret being so mean to you that last summer you were out here when I was still around, and I need to tell you why I did it."

I sat forward, my curiosity getting the better of me.

"I did it because I still cared about you. I was young, true. And you were even younger, and not Amish, but I'm pretty sure I loved you."

"Tommy."

"I tried so hard to shift those feelings toward Sadie Yoder." He sighed. "But it didn't work. And then she rejected me anyway. Somewhere in there I decided to leave and live the Englisch life. And, jah, I was never wild like Kenny, but I wasn't exactly innocent either." His voice grew quieter. "Lame, huh?"

I reached for his hand. "No," I said. "Not at all. Honest and transparent, yes, but not lame."

We rode that way for a while, silently holding hands. God

had answered my prayers as far as Miriam. She had challenges ahead of her, but she was safe. Dad, Joy, and Karlie were at Mammi's house. That was an answer to a prayer I hadn't even thought to pray. I'd survived a horrible accident. Ryan had given me the closure I needed.

Little by little, I could see God at work. And through that, my faith was growing.

But something niggled at the back of my mind.

"Tommy?" I said, breaking the silence.

"Mm?"

"Why does Deputy Rogers have a grudge against you?"

I needed to know what Tommy had done a decade ago that made Deputy Rogers so angry. Jah, a person could change immensely in ten years, but I needed to know if his actions were indicative of a larger character flaw.

Tommy sighed. "It's a long story, but we've got the time." He explained Deputy Rogers was known as being a no-nonsense officer to some—and a hard-nosed, unforgiving lawman to others.

He had a pattern of targeting young men in the community. He started tailing Tommy when he drove his Thunderbird. Then he started pulling him over. For not signaling. For having a broken taillight. Even for going too slow.

A few times, Tommy ditched him while driving, taking back roads Rogers wasn't familiar with, which angered the deputy and caused him to target Tommy all the more. During that time, Kenny had been arrested for possession of drugs and had spent six months in jail. Deputy Rogers was convinced, perhaps by something Kenny said, that Tommy was selling drugs too, but he couldn't pin anything on him.

"Eventually," Tommy said, "I wrote a letter to the editor of the newspaper about police harassment. After that, several other young men complained about him, including a couple of Hispanic men. That kind of negative press made Rogers all the more determined to arrest me for something big."

He continued with the story, saying his Dat had been diagnosed with cancer in early October 2008. They all felt optimistic that he could beat it. Tommy was working swing shift at the RV plant, making good money. He was doing as much of the farming as he could before work and on Saturdays.

His parents decided to travel to a niece's wedding in Michigan on the last weekend in October, thinking they might not have a chance to travel for a while, with the cancer treatments just getting started.

That Friday, Tommy was let go at work. The recession had just started, but the writing was on the wall. On his way back to the farm, Tommy noticed Deputy Rogers following him. When Tommy arrived, the shed was lit up like a pumpkin and probably a hundred Youngie were on the property. Kenny had decided to throw a party.

Tommy got out of his car and shouted at everyone to go home, that a police officer was right behind him. People took off running across the pasture to where they'd parked their cars. By the time Rogers got out of his vehicle, there were only a few stragglers left.

Rogers barged toward the shed door, ready to barrel in, but Tommy blocked his way, saying he needed a search warrant. They argued until Kenny came staggering around the side of the shed with a kerosene lantern in hand. He'd pulled hay bales up around the shed for people to sit on and he tripped over one.

"He managed to right himself," Tommy said, "and I reached for the lantern. But he swung it out of my way and started taunting Rogers, who gave him a shove.

"Again, Kenny and the lantern started to fall." Tommy

paused for a moment, as if the memory pained him. "I grabbed him by the arm, but he shoved at me. He went down, the lantern broke, and one of the bales caught fire. I grabbed Kenny and dragged him away, but he kept trying to go back to put the fire out. I held him down as I yelled, 'Fire! Everybody out!' and then begged Rogers to call for help. He just watched the fire spread, like he hoped it would all burn down. Finally he called it in. By the time the firefighters arrived, the shed was a complete loss."

He stopped.

After a long pause, I asked, "What happened next?"

"Kenny and Rogers both blamed me. Said I'd knocked the lantern on the hay and started the fire. Kenny was wasted and only remembered parts of what happened, but Rogers out and out lied. My parents believed me but asked that I leave. They were afraid what might happen if I didn't. So I left and Kenny followed later. We ended up in Arizona, where I went to community college and then university. I didn't come back until Dat's funeral in 2013. In the three days I was home, Rogers gave me two tickets."

I winced. "Wow. Even after all that time he couldn't let it go?"

Tommy shook his head. "I forgot to mention that I mailed a second letter to the editor as I left town the first time. It sparked an internal investigation and Rogers got demoted."

"So why isn't anyone suspicious of Rogers investigating you now?"

"Everyone retired. New sheriff. New supervisors. And he's getting ready to retire in a few months himself, which is the reason I finally came back. But I should have just waited until it actually happened."

"Someone needs to tell the new sheriff all of this."

"Probably, but now I'm afraid if I say it, I'll sound as if I'm making excuses."

"I'll say it, then," I said, "when we meet with him—and Deputy Rogers." I hesitated a minute and then asked, "Why did he take it all out on you? Instead of Kenny?"

"Because I wrote the letters. He's far more concerned about his image than about the truth or justice or any of that. Kenny was a pain, but he never made Rogers look bad."

Again, we rode in silence, but then, just as we reached the Elkhart County line, Tommy said, "Once I get these bogus charges dismissed, I'll take Mason back to Las Vegas. But I've changed my mind about staying there. I've decided to return here instead."

"What will you do?"

"I have a lead on a social work position."

"Social work?"

He nodded. "I have a degree in sociology. I had a position with the state as a social worker in Las Vegas."

"Huh." That explained a lot. His empathy. His knowledge about addiction. His determination to reunite Mason with his mother.

"What about you?" Tommy asked. "What are your plans?"

"Well, I'll see if I'm offered the job in Lancaster or not. But maybe I'll apply for the job at the community hospital in Bremen and see what happens."

He squeezed my hand. "That sounds like a good plan to me."

EPILOGUE

Jane

January 23, 2017

Jane scooted her chair up to the desk and placed her fingers on the keys of her typewriter. Plain Patterns was ready to open. The fire was roaring in the wood stove. The coffee was started. The new quilt, a checkered garden pattern, was stretched across the frame. And the last quilt they'd made, the hearth and home pattern, was folded and ready to give away.

Now she had a half hour to put the finishing touches on her column for the *Nappanee News*. She'd chosen Emma—Emma Gingrich Fischer Landis—as her subject for the month. Of course, it wasn't anything close to the length of the story she'd told Savannah. She'd had a word count, after all.

Jane was pleased that Emma's story had touched Savannah, and she believed it played a role in her giving Tommy a chance.

Of course, it helped that he was innocent. The Elkhart

County sheriff cleared Tommy of any wrongdoing that night they all met. And after Savannah brought up Deputy Rogers's history of targeting Tommy, the sheriff chastised Deputy Rogers for jumping to conclusions without the proper evidence. The Chicago police also arrested Ivan that night, around the same time Kenny was arrested by the sheriff. And Deputy Rogers was forced to retire three months early.

Tommy left to take Mason to Las Vegas and returned within the week. And Savannah, even though she was offered the job in Lancaster, turned it down and applied for the one in Bremen. Hopefully she'd get it and stay in the area. If she did, Savannah said perhaps she'd see about assisting Delores part-time with her midwifery business. Only time would tell.

Jah, nothing ever stayed the same.

Things had changed for Jane too. She spoke with the bishop about Miriam living with her, and everyone, including Arleta and Vernon, thought it was a good idea. And it had been. It had been less than two weeks, but Jane was grateful she was able to help Miriam. Jah, sharing a home with a teenager was providing plenty of learning opportunities for both of them.

Jane focused on the last paragraph of Emma's story. *Today, Emma Gingrich Fischer Landis has over three hundred descendants in Elkhart County and hundreds more throughout the United States. Her example of persevering in the face of fear is a tribute to her faith in God and her love for others.*

Jane rolled the last page out of the typewriter, addressed and stuffed the envelope, put a stamp on it, and placed it beside her typewriter, ready to be put in the mailbox at the end of the day.

"Jane? Where are you?"

She hadn't heard the front door. "Back here!" she called out.

Arleta appeared first, carrying the baby. Next, Dorothy and Wanda rounded the corner, followed by Savannah.

"Did you all ride together?"

"Jah," Arleta said. "Savannah was our ride-share."

Savannah laughed. "That's me." She grinned. "I have good news. I got the job in Bremen."

Jane clapped her hands together. "How about a place to live?"

"I'm looking at an apartment in town this afternoon."

"In Tommy's complex?" Jane asked.

Savannah shook her head as she blushed, just a little. "A few blocks away."

Lois and Phyllis arrived next, followed by Betty, Jenna, and Catherine.

The only one missing was Miriam. Jane wasn't sure what to do. She'd intended to give the hearth and home quilt to Savannah, although at one time she thought it would be nice to give to Arleta. But Arleta had a home, and Savannah, with plenty of resources, would soon have a home again too. On the other hand, although Miriam had a place with Jane, she didn't have a home of her own and might not for quite some time. Jane prayed every day that the girl would find her way and find her future, through her faith in the Lord.

"Where's Miriam?" Savannah asked.

"I'm not sure," Jane answered. "She said she'd come over. . . ."

Savannah glanced toward the front of the shop. "I'll go get her."

The other women hung their coats and then made their way over to the baby as Savannah pulled the front door shut behind her. Arleta passed Ruthie to Wanda, who, Jane could tell, was missing Mason.

Catherine asked Dorothy about her visit with her son, daughter-in-law, and granddaughter. "It was a dream come true," she answered. "They plan to come back in the summer to help me make some decisions about the farm and spend time with Savannah. And, of course, she'll be going back out to California to stay with them from time to time."

After a while, Jane left the women and stepped to the front of the store, wondering if she should go speak with Miriam too. But just as she reached for her coat, the door opened. Savannah stepped in first and then Miriam. The girl's eyes were red and puffy, and she wore a scarf over her head instead of a Kapp.

"Come in," Jane said. "I have something for you."

Miriam followed Jane into the quilting room, with Savannah at her side. When Miriam saw her mother, her eyes clouded with tears. But then she took a deep, raggedy breath and said, "Hallo, Mamm."

Arleta patted the girl's shoulder and smiled gently. Betty and Jenna introduced themselves to Miriam, and then Lois and Phyllis said hello. Catherine pursed her lips together and simply nodded. They didn't need Catherine's judgment today, but Jane didn't say anything. She'd leave it to the Lord.

Jane reached for the folded quilt, patting a square of forget-me-not fabric. Emma couldn't give a quilt to Mathilde, but she and Savannah could give one to Miriam. She cleared her throat. "As you know, it's time to give away the hearth and home quilt that we made." She turned to Savannah. "I'd like you to say this next part."

Savannah took the quilt and turned toward Miriam. "By giving this to you, we want you to know that we're committed to loving and helping you and your baby."

Miriam took the quilt with one hand, pressing it against her body, and wiped at the tears rolling down her cheeks with her other hand. "Denki," she whispered.

Savannah put an arm around Miriam, and the others gathered around.

Jane prayed the quilt would comfort Miriam in the months to come. She would need the love of others to move forward, into the future the Lord had for her. Piece by piece. And so would Savannah.

The truth was, no matter how old, they all needed each other. That was one thing that would never change.

Acknowledgments

When I first visited Elkhart County, Indiana, in 2011, it immediately captured my heart. From the numerous towns to the Joseph River to the beautiful farms and wooded areas, I found the area full of history and intrigue. Of course, the heart of all of it for me was the large Amish community. Several of the farms I visited had been established in the 1800s. I couldn't help but speculate about those early settlers—and about who had lived on the land before them.

Through the years, I poured through information about the Potawatomi Native Americans who inhabited Elkhart County until the 1830s, along with other nearby areas, and the first white settlers, who came in the late 1830s and 1840s, including members of Plain communities. Four books that were particularly helpful to me were *The Last Blackrobe of Indiana and the Potawatomi Trail of Death* by John William McMullen; *Amish and Mennonites in Eastern Elkhart and Legrange Counties, Indiana, 1841–1991*; *From Sigriswil to Nappanee: 300 Years of Stähli History* by Bruce W. Stahly; and *They Call it Nappanee: A History, 1874–1974*.

As I thought more and more about the first Plain families who came to the area, I discussed my ideas with my good friend Marietta Couch, who shared some of her Amish family's stories, all of which took place in northern Indiana. (A big thank-you to Marietta for brainstorming with me, reading my manuscripts, and encouraging me! Any mistakes are my own.)

All of the characters in this story are fictitious, except for four historical characters who make a very brief appearance in the novel—Joseph Miller, Daniel Miller, Joseph Speicher, and Nathan Smeily, who traveled from Pennsylvania to "western" states, including Indiana, to search for a location where Amish families could settle.

I couldn't write my stories without the help of my husband, Peter. I'm very grateful for his visionary ideas, his support on my research trips, and his care when I'm on deadline. I'm also thankful for the support of my four adult children—Kaleb, Taylor, Hana, and Lily Thao—and for all the ways they've made me a more empathetic person.

I'm also grateful for my agent, Natasha Kern, and her confidence in me and my writing, and to the entire team at Bethany House Publishers. This is my eleventh book with this amazing group of people. I continue to learn and grow as a writer because of their investment in me.

Lastly, I'm thankful for you, my readers! God cares for me through you—through your encouraging words, your reviews, and your word-of-mouth sharing. You are the best!

Leslie Gould is the #1 bestselling and award-winning author of over thirty-five novels, including the SISTERS OF LANCASTER COUNTY series. She holds an MFA in creative writing, teaches at Warner Pacific University, and enjoys research trips and traveling. She and her husband, Peter, are the parents of four adult children.

Sign Up for Leslie's Newsletter

Keep up to date with Leslie's news, book releases, and events by signing up for her email list at lesliegould.com.

More from Leslie Gould

In this captivating dual-time series, three young Amish women find inspiration and encouragement for their uncertain futures in the stories of their brave ancestors who lived during the Revolutionary War, Civil War, and World War II.

THE SISTERS OF LANCASTER COUNTY: *A Plain Leaving, A Simple Singing, A Faithful Gathering*

BETHANYHOUSE

Stay up to date on your favorite books and authors with our free e-newsletters. Sign up today at bethanyhouse.com.

facebook.com/bethanyhousepublishers

@bethanyhousefiction

Free exclusive resources for your book group at bethanyhouseopenbook.com

You May Also Like . . .

Desperate for help on the farm, widow Sylvie Schrock King hires her bitter neighbor's son, Jimmy Fischer, who understands horses like no one else. While Jimmy's lazy smile and teasing ways steal Sylvie's heart, her neighbor is working on a way to claim her land. Has Sylvie made another terrible mistake?

Two Steps Forward by Suzanne Woods Fisher
THE DEACON'S FAMILY #3
suzannewoodsfisher.com

In this continuation of *The Tinderbox*, young Amish woman Sylvia Miller's world is upended by the arrival of Englisher Adeline Pelham—whose existence is a reminder of a painful family secret. Sylvia must learn to come to terms with the past while grappling with issues of her own. Is it possible that God can make something good out of the mistakes of days gone by?

The Timepiece by Beverly Lewis
beverlylewis.com